Your Friday, My Sunday

Your Friday, My Sunday

Claude Pemberton

AuthorHouse™ UK
1663 Liberty Drive
Bloomington, IN 47403 USA
www.authorhouse.co.uk
Phone: 0800.197.4150

© 2015 Claude Pemberton. All rights reserved.

No part of this book may be reproduced, stored in a retrieval system, or transmitted by any means without the written permission of the author.

Published by AuthorHouse 02/19/2015

ISBN: 978-1-5049-3720-7 (sc)
ISBN: 978-1-5049-3719-1 (hc)
ISBN: 978-1-5049-3738-2 (e)

Contact the author at:
Facebook = www.facebook.com/Claude Pemberton
LinkedIn = www.Linkedin.com/Claude Pemberton

Print information available on the last page.

Any people depicted in stock imagery provided by Thinkstock are models, and such images are being used for illustrative purposes only.
Certain stock imagery © Thinkstock.

Because of the dynamic nature of the Internet, any web addresses or links contained in this book may have changed since publication and may no longer be valid. The views expressed in this work are solely those of the author and do not necessarily reflect the views of the publisher, and the publisher hereby disclaims any responsibility for them.

Contents

Monday
Chapter 1 3
Chapter 2 19

Tuesday
Chapter 3 45
Chapter 4 70
Chapter 5 94

Wednesday
Chapter 6 125
Chapter 7 155

Thursday
Chapter 8 187
Chapter 9 231

Your Friday, My Sunday
Chapter 10 265
Chapter 11 292

Monday

Chapter 1

By night the atmosphere might have been better: a cool moon, just something to take the heat from this turgid boat, a breath of breeze. Instead, a hot sun bore down on the straw roof of the old tramp boat, moored upon a milky residue from the docks. The wind did not blow. The air was still. The heat penetrating, focused, and all enveloping.

At least the air would have remained still but for the excited movement, the sways and sounds of travellers on the broken quayside carefully picking their way around the rusted iron rods that poked out of the dilapidated concrete walkway and skywards, and with the carelessness of the holiday traveller, one arm waving, the other grabbing at anything to hold in the jump across the gap to the plank and then into the darkness of the lower deck. Some laughing, some clutching things, some still smeared along the arms with sun cream poorly and hurriedly applied. And most of them were women. Old women in a second, more committed phase of youth.

As his turn came to pitch across the void, one of them in front of Ellis stumbled slightly, and playing with characteristic gallantry, he grasped a sweaty arm and steadied his fellow traveller as she looked up in grateful thanks. Although laughing nervously and thanking Ellis, there was no way that she would see into his face, for to do so meant staring directly upwards at him as he towered over her, and directly behind his head was the sun, more or less directly overhead.

So more or less noontime.

Ellis smiled down graciously into the screwed-up eyes, and it was at that moment he noticed what people meant about hair gel. The top of the woman's head and her hair was perfectly moulded in what was probably a sea-blue rinse; but it held in place. And beneath the blue rinse, beneath the thinning hair, on the skin surface itself Ellis saw the telltale signs of sweat.

On one so elegant, however, it may have been a glow; it was hard to say. But sweat or glow, she luckily had some hair still in place. It seemed to Ellis that the hair and the scalp, though biologically linked, had an extraordinary detachedness about them.

The splendour of the coiffeur versus the depredations of sweat.

The sweat was losing.

It had to be gel.

The woman had this shiny scalp and a well-treated head of hair, though if it were extremely thin, such as his own, Ellis reasoned, he should have persevered with his own experiment with the gel. A thinning pate, a shiny scalp – that's what these women had, yet, hardly in their first youth, they still looked half decent. Ellis thought about these women and he thought about his own hair and he thought about the burgeoning stomach and oversized clothing and he remembered the manner of his furtive dash to the pharmacy to scour the shelves for information and perhaps a sample pack of something to make him, well, less worn.

When he had got home and torn open the pack, he discovered he'd bought conditioner, and by now it was nearly six at night and the pharmacy nearly closed. Back with the product and a tetchy assistant. What had she said?

'This is conditioner, yer know.'

'Yes, I know,' Ellis replied sheepishly.

'What do you want to exchange it for?'

'Hair gel.'

'Pardon me?' The assistant pursued her interrogation.

'I bought the conditioner by mistake. Now I want to change it for hair gel. If that's all right by you.' Ellis quietened as he mumbled the words *hair gel*.

The assistant noticed the rather furtive manner of his approach and wondered whether in fact he might have preferred condoms. But a big, grown-up man of around forty-five-ish, she reckoned, why would he want hair gel? He was very thin here and there; surely gel would make more trouble than sir realised?

But the customer wanted hair gel.

'Oh, right, you want hair gel!' she chimed noisily.

'That's what I said,' replied Ellis, becoming convinced that, as he seemed to be hearing only an echo of his own voice, her head was running on empty.

'Right.'

Thank God, he thought. But then she reeled off a list of tubs, tubes, tins, vials, and pots with any number of variations of exotic ingredient, capacity, colour, and smell. As the queue of late shoppers became audibly more annoyed, some tutting and sighing and shuffling feet around impatiently, by means of escape he'd plumped for a simple tub of green gel with a screw cap and a holiday offer.

It had all been a disaster.

The simple screw-top pot, made of cheap and flexible transparent plastic, had developed a crack and spilled just enough gel to lightly oil the inside of the carrier bag and the front page of the evening paper. When he got home, he unusually followed the instructions, almost, but still applied about four times the maximum recommended single application. And with hair gel running down the back of his neck and hating the chill as his hair began to mat, everything beyond his control, he took a shower and washed the whole silly idea from his head.

Which was why the stumbling lady, or rather her blue rinse, had caught Ellis's attention. If it was gel, it had clearly worked for her. Maybe he would give it another try. Sometime. Perhaps when he got home.

At least he had got a half-price holiday in the Gambia on the strength of his purchase.

As Ellis left the admiring gaze of the lady, his way was drawn along the walkway, picking over some uneven, sun-baked planks of wood that had splintered from the once elegant polished surface, further along and into the darkness of the midship.

The midship comprised a dark area of flooring spotted by shards of light leaking through the worn straw thatch that may once have offered the traveller total protection against the sun. Against the far side lay the bar, but between that and the entrance coming from the walkway lay what would be a good-sized dance floor for a party of this size. Except that nobody felt brave enough to walk across the space. All huddled closer by the door, smiling and nodding to each other, chatting nervously, their faces and scalps glimmering variously in the light and in the shade, depending upon where they stood in relation to the holes in the thatch.

As more guests joined the throng, those already on the dance floor reluctantly, and to a great extent in spite of themselves, edged a little further away from the doorway. There appeared to be nobody there who would be able to serve some drinks. All on the far side of the dance floor appeared empty.

All except for that chap in the corner.

Slumped onto his stool and supported only by a tattered sleeve, that chap would soon have fallen to the floor. A heavily bearded man, he stared into his beer, tracing his fingers thoughtfully around the rim of his glass, reflecting, perhaps, on glorious times, thinking of a girlfriend, a scowl across a wrinkled forehead, eyes gripped against the light, for it was bright out there, the sun pouring in through the slats in an unforgiving onslaught.

Ellis pushed a way past the fire-exit stragglers into the empty space and, approaching the bar, plunged some fingers into a very large and unseemly generous glass bowl of peanuts.

'Give me a beer, my man,' called Ellis.

'Heineken, sir?' The cheery barman appeared from a task at the rear of the bar.

'If it's all you have.'

The barman made to pull a pint, enquiring on the size and configuration of the glass that would satisfy sir, and without moving his lips, he seemed to say, 'He'll be 16.'

'I beg your pardon?' Glaring at the barman, whose demeanour and smile were unaffected by the heat, the glare, or the clientele.

'Nothin', sir. Didn't say nothin'.'

'I did, bumhead,' growled the drunk in a voice as gravelled as his scrawny face.

Ellis drank quickly, a lunchtime thirst developed and enveloping. He looked around, through a small, rectangular slat open to his right and above the greasy head of the drunk. The drunk belched once and summoned up sufficient abdominal pressure to force him to straighten his spine. He joined Ellis's gaze through the slat across the narrow confines of the waterway and its jungle location. Together they viewed silently all the vegetation and the animals and the oily deposits and the rubbish that Banjul harbour floated upstream.

The drunk put out a hesitant arm and tentatively touched Ellis's forearm, the beer-laden forearm. On failing to connect, the drunk's hand fell to the dish of peanuts, and, grabbing a handful and spilling a similar quantity onto the floor, the bar, and his lap, he munched noisily, pausing only to wash some more cocktail into his throat. He dashed the glass onto the bar, spilling some, and looking at Ellis through half-closed eyes, he said, 'I told you. He'll be 16. Not just yet. Few months maybe.' Ellis's reaction was to dodge the small fragments that sprayed freely from the drunk's mouth.

Ellis caught sight of some more fellow travellers joining, the fire-exit hoarders edging inwards, reluctantly, looking this way and that to avoid having to accommodate others who would seek to take over their space. The bartender was now in full cry – all types of drinks and beers and cocktails and soft drinks and 'not too much lemon in mine' and 'this one I didn't want any ice'; the barman hated all of them. Still, though, he smiled.

He knew how to mix a mean cocktail, so mean that much of its content was spilled on the floor so that a large portion of lemonade was required to make up the short measures.

'If you don't listen to me, how'd it be if I was to be sick on that yukky jacket you're wearing?' The drunk had cranked himself up with sufficient energy to make another attempt at impolite conversation.

An engine started up, and an excited rise in the tenor of conversation accompanied nervous giggles of expectation.

Then silence.

A starter motor, clearly unused to any level of service, struggled to bring the boat engine to life. With a scream, a crunch, and a few other expensive mechanical noises, the engine finally fired up, a sudden flurry of slimy black diesel exhaust edging irresistibly along the deck, along the brows of those brave enough to sit on deck.

As there was nothing else for the drunk to concentrate on now that the engine was running, he turned back afresh to Ellis, whose eyes were determinedly fixed elsewhere.

'I said, he'll be 16 … sooner or later.'

'What are you on about, you drunken old prat?' demanded Ellis, now impatient with the abdominal rumblings and utterances which, to his ear, were broadly indistinguishable.

The drunk twisted himself around, almost as far as the bar stool would allow, and looked up. And looked at Ellis straight in the eye, belying any drunkenness; he seemed to have a fixed and iron gaze that Ellis had seen somewhere before.

Perhaps it was Anderson.

It was Anderson. Was it?

It had to be Anderson.

'I'll tell ya what I'm on about.' A very small piece of peanut landed on Ellis's lapel, for he was dressed as an Englishman abroad, wearing a light jacket to absorb the sun.

'I'm on about the boy. He's 16, goddammit. If he gets to 16 and he says yes, then …' The drunk picked up his drink, discovered it nearly empty, and called eternal evil upon the bartender, who produced a further drink with the speed of a man possessed.

'Then what?' asked Ellis impatiently.

'You ask then what?' The drunk became almost lucid.

'I'll tell ya what. If the little shit says yes, then off comes Clitty's head.'

Clitty.

Ellis remembered Clitty. He hated to think it was the Clitty he had spent some months with, for he thought that Clitty had been taken care of years ago. But what had this drunken sot got to do with the past?

Before replying, he looked at this creature. Was there anything familiar about him?

No.

Except the eyes did seem to be familiar, eyes looking two ways at once.

Was there any chance he might have known him somewhere before?

No.

Except for his ring. There was something familiar about the ring, worn on his middle finger, silly place for a man to wear a ring. Something about the design of the signet ring, a crest on a golden ring, worn in the same way as that American idiot Anderson.

Anderson.

What, here? What was he doing here?

He had made so much money as an expatriate that he was going home into real estate. That was if they'd paid his leaving bonus, which they probably didn't because they'd all been shipped out in disgrace and penniless, leaving Clitty to face the music.

But here was, ostensibly, the one and the same Anderson. Ellis pretended not to remember.

Oh God, it was him.

'What are you on about?' Ellis's question was emphatic.

The bar stool took on some surprising capabilities as the man who might be called Anderson pulled himself up to Ellis's eye level and bellowed, 'Cast off. Take the bloody buggers to the crocodiles.'

Somebody below and beyond acknowledged the command; the bartender replenished the glasses, particularly Ellis's. Few people engaged the American in any form of conversation.

This one must be special, thought the barman, placing a double portion for his British guest to enjoy. The engine note changed; some shouts, some trembling from the soul of the boat; the deck shuddered; the trees moved; the shadows through the slat lengthened, then rotated; the sun poured in through the other quarter.

The man Anderson smiled at his drink and, while addressing the froth, set about Ellis again.

'Listen, you stupid punk …' and while turning to face Ellis was surprised to find his throat in a vice-like grip as the strength long forgotten returned.

His eyes bulged, his brow frowning in some series of regrets, but it was the left eye that caught Ellis's attention.

Anderson had had an eye problem, an astigmatism, some sort of problem that made the left eye look away while the right eye did all the focusing. And as the left eye was looking at the optics, the right eye had Ellis in its sights.

'Remember me, Ellis?' The *Ellis* was spat out. A cry went out as a crocodile or maybe an alligator came into sight. The camera shutters whirred. The alligator seemed to know what it was, and Ellis was quite sure it was Anderson, yet the man had been only 26 when last they met. Some more drinks were ordered, the engine note changed, died and was restored to full chat by an unseen hand.

A riverside boy waved.

Somebody threw him a biro. Two more followed. They fell in the water; the boy looked crestfallen. One was better than none. He waved again and disappeared behind the vegetation.

What the hell do jungle bunnies want with biros? Ellis asked himself, a question soon answered by Anderson.

'I know what ya thinking. The little sods want biros, or goddamn ballpoints as the civilised world calls them, and while we give them hydro-electric schemes, power stations, and industrial plants – true, they come from reject European stock – all the bloody buggers want is bloody biros.' Anderson calmed himself with a palmful of peanuts and a resounding belch.

Ellis had a problem with a piece of peanut stuck firmly in Anderson's moustache.

If it was Anderson.

Every time he spoke, the piece moved, tantalisingly close to his tongue, and if he didn't mind, easily accessible to a deft finger … sweep it away, smarten up his face, yet Anderson always had been a slouch.

The slouch turned to Ellis and said again 'He'll be 16, you bloody shitbag.'

At that moment, during a holiday designed to place the cares of his world in another orbit for two weeks, Ellis had finally discovered his nemesis and found that wherever he went, he had no control over events. He had reopened the wounds of long ago, and worst of all, he had found a drunk, barely able to stand, but remembering his own face from incidents taken place in a far-off land fifteen years ago, their paths long since uncrossed. And yet this drunk, incapable as he was, could still remember a face.

And some navigational commands.

'Bring the fuckin' ship around to the fuckin' port side, or the fuckin' starboard side, I don't really fuckin' care which,' he bellowed, at which point someone stalled the engine and all fell quiet. Some muffled voices below were calling prayers and heaping insults on the engine, in roughly equal measure.

As the passengers murmured in concern, faces furrowed against the light, heads shaking in exasperation, the rabid sounds of spanner against sump announced the probable and final demise of the engine.

The silence was broken by Anderson mishandling his glass, then dropping it squarely onto the bar top, swearing all demons and menace on the glass. He swayed, laughed a little, and vomited neatly and squarely into the centre of the dish of peanuts.

Then somebody restarted the engine, a noisy clunk, some diesel smoke drifting angrily in through the slats, and the wind blew a little. Another boy on the shore appeared from the bush, waved, but when nobody threw him a biro, he bent down and exposed his buttocks and may have farted. The drunk finally slid from his seat in a vapour of vomit to the floor.

The sum total of Ellis's holiday to date was a tenuous skirmish with hair gel, a slight level of contact with a little old lady, and the drunk now quietly slumbering on the deck amongst an array of dishevelled clothing, and fragments of food in his beard. Somebody, God bless them, had put a biro in his mouth. The boat meandered on its way, as if on autopilot, the engine throbbing uneasily, while the man to whom the travel company had entrusted its lot on this excursion lay unconscious among the products of his own overindulgence.

The barman, a small man, coloured, but whose colour deepened as his stress level rose, noted Ellis's revulsion of his gaze and became quite dark as he approached with a wet rag, wiped the vomit from the peanuts, wondered if there were any he could save, cleared the mats and the glasses, and with one peremptory wipe cleared the bar top of all evidence of malefaction.

'You know Mr Anderson, sir?' he asked of Ellis.

'Maybe.'

Ellis's gaze explored the fellow travellers who still cooed and aahed at the monkeys and at the anthills and then at the mess of Banjul harbour and the tankers and all the tank washing going on and the rainbow stains dancing on the surface of what had been originally pure seawater. People took pictures and videos of each other in this posture and that, and somebody spotted a dead rat floating by and wouldn't that make a good photo?

'Give me another beer.'

'Yessir.' The barman drew a special, a glint in his black eyes, a special for a friend of Mr Anderson.

As the barman carefully laid out a new bar mat, put new peanuts in a smeared glass bowl, and lovingly put a full tankard of beer under Ellis's nose, Ellis himself looked back at what also might have been a familiar face.

'What's your name? Oh, thanks for the beer.'

'On the house. sir ….' Pausing a little, 'My name is Edgardo. Edgardo Largamson.'

'Is that all? You don't have a nickname?'

'Pardon me, sir?'

'Edgardo Largamson. It seems like a long name. Isn't there a shorter version?'

'I don't know, sir, but in here they know me as Toots.'

'Then Toots it is. Tell me, Toots,' lowering his voice and sharing a conspiratorial pose, 'what do you know about Mr Anderson?'

Toots didn't seem to know how to react to such a question. He picked up his cloth and wiped furiously at anything close to hand. Ashtrays were emptied, drinks served, bar top cleaned again and again, and only the sight of a fifty-dollar bill clutched tightly in Ellis's hand regained his attention.

'Sir? Mr Anderson, he is a very kind man,' glancing nervously over the edge of the bar towards his boss to make sure he had not awakened. 'I am not known him for very long time.' The fury of his glass-wiping threatened to shatter the very substance of a recently returned carafe.

'Since how long?'

'Since … ooh …' His eyes wandered to heaven, looking for a sign to improve his problems with mathematics. 'Two years.'

The glass-wiping became even more vigorous.

'That's more like ten years!' Ellis exploded.

'Yessir.'

Ellis noted the Americanised way of saying yessir and also noted the defensive nature of Toots's replies. It seemed likely that this was Anderson, the Anderson whose recollection of events nearly fifteen years ago had driven him to be the master of some clapped-out boat on the Banjul River – probably in an effort to run away from what had happened – get very drunk over the years, and now lie on the floor close to the feet of a balding man in wire-framed spectacles expounding his theories on the history of English local government management since the local authorities were reorganized in 1986, and how Labour always overspent, and how political correctness now extended to changing the colour of disabled stickers to green to avoid offending ethnic minorities. Everyone laughed sycophantically at all these utterances while Anderson moved an arm, uttered an obscenity, scratched his groin, ignored the assembled group, and went back to sleep.

Ellis called for another cooler to overcome the excitement of the Banjul River and somehow to cut off the noises of the camera shutters. Toots smiled and produced an overlarge measure. The little lady bumped Ellis's elbow as she thought a better view of something could be had from the window nearest to Ellis. All she did was smile sheepishly. Putting the eyepiece of her camera somewhere on the side of her head, she took a photo of something, apologised, smiled nervously, and ran back to her own fellow travellers.

Her hair remained perfectly formed, a perfect azure sheen.

Toots thought some music would break the tension of this day and ripped through all the under-the-counter cassette tapes to find a tape he thought would be appropriate to a boatload of Brits, or mostly Brits. He put on a cover tape of Abba songs. Those now well lubricated by Toots's generous portions swayed, hummed, and tottered to the oompah of Abba. Others clutched their drinks. The boat swayed. Anderson didn't move. Others just stared at the ripples on the water. Others aligned the far horizon and the chimneys of industrial downtown Banjul with one eye and the banks of the river with the other to work out in a crude fashion how fast they were travelling. In truth, the boys on the bank could run faster and smile wider.

That face, Anderson's face, the dodgy eye: it was all there, those memories, the thoughts of that self-assured pseudo-American who knew everything and could give plausible explanations for everything scientific, artistic, cultural, and military, and what's more, he was loathed for all his swagger. Ellis marshalled thoughts long hidden and winced at the arrogance of a man now splayed across the floor, a man so driven that he could offer up his colleague to some foreign authority for the ultimate penalty.

The Abba soundalikes droned on and on, and even when Toots couldn't be prevailed upon to put on anything else because he had glasses to polish and a white-toothed grin to offer to his customers, just then Ellis called for one more drink and asked as if by the way; he asked Toots what was what. How was Anderson, if this was he, linked to Toots?

It just seemed that Anderson had taken a shine to Toots way back in Saudi Arabia, and he had given a business card with a UK number for Toots to call just in case he was ever over in London.

Just about everybody did that with their business cards.

Toots came over some months later, took a job as a bell hop in an Earls Court hotel, then called Anderson's number. He got redirected to somewhere abroad, where he was offered a lucrative contract serving on a … wreck, and he left his family in Manila for two years to wash glasses, to fix drinks, and to smile.

'All good for the business, Mr Anderson he say, so I come here, and maybe after one year more I go home to my family, maybe not. I don't know.'

Ellis wondered if any of this paid for itself, let alone Toots's salary but then his pay before tips was probably ten pounds a month with tips doubling that, a fair old income for a boy from the murk of the Philippine capital. Anything metal on the boat seemed rusty and unkempt, everything rather malodorous, nothing really cared for. But now as Anderson rolled over to pretend-bite the ankle of a particularly unimpressed female passenger, clearly already overwrought by her latest experience, Ellis thought again about the state of his hair, a bead of something forming and tickling his forehead. He wiped a hand-broad brush to clean himself up. He thought about the gel. The little old lady caught his eye and gave him a gin-laden smile.

She was by now looking less serene than earlier.

But then so was Anderson, and nobody seemed capable or willing to do anything useful to throw him over the side, where he obviously belonged.

Your Friday, My Sunday

Ellis thought of getting even with the slob, but had a bit of pity, just enough to stop him taking four paces, picking up the wretch, and depositing him among the detritus of an underdeveloped sewerage system.

Temptations all, but best resisted, particularly Anderson's reference to the boy. He would now be getting pretty close to being 16, and if so, the authorities would be driving round to his house any day now to ask permission to do the needful.

Toots laughed as he heard Ellis say his words aloud, as 'doing the needful' was an expression particular to his own part of the world.

Then the penny dropped. Toots had not seen Ellis for a good few years and was only being friendly because that was his way.

Toots.

Yes.

Anderson's houseboy at the start.

Could make some very fine tuna cutlets, could Toots. Ellis had initially lived the other side of town but remembered some visits which began with one drink, soon a second, and then the large measures and tuna cutlets were served. Again with a white-toothed smile. Then more drinks, and maybe a woman, and if anybody was still upright, they'd go home by taxi. Otherwise they slept on the floor, or they'd sleep in the spare room, or they'd sleep with a woman on the floor, or they'd sleep with a woman in the spare room. If nothing else was available, the more extreme would sleep with a man, either on the floor or in the spare room.

Either way or which way, they would wake up with some sense of regret about five hours later.

Anderson on the floor of the boat stirred and spat. Perhaps he felt some sense of regret. Whatever, the folks now were more inclined to be anywhere but on this hulk and had moved to leave him a clear space. All tried to look to the shore for any other, more alluring sights. Toots called kindly to the group of young women, offering more drinks – on the house, naturally. A grey coiffeur was idly studying Toots as he wiped the top of the bar and made to walk the few paces to clear the couple of tables laden with empties and peanut shells; she watched his hips and she watched his movements, and Toots smiled, and she watched his teeth and his lips.

Nice young local boy, she smiled at him.

She spoke few words to him, preferring to look at the front of his jeans; he didn't say much, just smiled and gazed curiously at the cut of her dress and her cleavage, just smiled and cleaned the tables before treading carefully over the body on the floor and retreating to the relative solace of the bar area.

A voice called from somewhere on board, requesting sailing instructions. The engine changed its tone, shuddered, and continued, the boat heaving a little as it began some unauthorised manoeuvre. The voice called again, this time with some impatience; still nobody, particularly the one on the floor, made any suggestions.

Toots put down his towel and pulled himself through the slat far enough to obtain improved verbal contact with the helmsman outside, give some emergency return-to-port instructions, and elicit a gasp of admiration from the blue-rinse ladies, whose view of the profile of such an uncomplicated and strong nether region was a treat not mentioned by the holiday courier.

Another round of drinks, more smiles, and pictures taken of Toots with his arms round the ladies, Toots smiling, Toots giving them pecks on the cheeks, ladies blushing with desire, hands almost too close to Toots.

Suddenly Toots was the star.

A young girl, a pretty young girl, in the gloom of the furthest deck space, had a view of all this and hated it. Hated all the old women, but reckoned on being that age one day, so grimaced, then locked eyes on Ellis as the boat swung again and shards of sunlight were drawn across his face. The boat swung further, apparently in a complete circle, it appeared to Ellis, but the light nevertheless blotted out his sight, then hers. The pretty young girl's face was all that Ellis needed to be in love.

Anderson farted.

The girl seemed to change her mind but still had to push past Ellis to get to the toilet, which she did with some style: long legs, long arms, tan, breasts. Ellis shuddered and smiled, and she smiled and then was gone.

Anderson groaned, and even above the music he retained the menace. He pushed himself onto all fours as the guests ceased chattering and watched the kraken awake. He stretched, knelt, pushed himself onto one knee, belched, and looked long and hard at those within his myopic gaze. He rubbed his tousled beard, glared towards Ellis or the optics or both, then remembered where he was.

'Thank you so very fuckin' much for this happy journey today,' Anderson started, much to Toots's dismay, realising that a tirade was the most likely forthcoming event. He smiled sheepishly and perhaps wantonly at some of the ladies, and put a biro and a pad of paper on the bar top for calculating any takings and what he needed to order for the next group of travellers. 'And we all hope that …' he paused to wipe some spit from his mouth, the act of kneeling on one knee too much, '… an' we all hope that …' The boat lurched a little, voices muttered dark words; the boat stopped, everyone rocked. 'Stop the fuckin' engine, you goddamn pillock!' he shouted at whoever, or whatever was training in the art of negotiating the Banjul River. 'And don't come back. Not you, you silly sods … that idiot driving the bloody boat!'

Anderson realised that he had lost much empathy with his guests and drew a greasy hand through equally greasy hair and, shaking his head in exasperation, pushed himself to stand up. For once, just once in the last two hours, he became relatively friendly and began to explain the sights and sounds of the river; only the guests were, like lemmings, going over the side to escape him, in no mind to have any more to do with 'such an, an, animal', one guest was heard to say.

'That's right!' he shouted once more. 'Get off the bloody boat before it sinks. With buttocks like yours, madam, we were bound to sink. Thank God you're getting off.'

Anderson saw that Ellis was the only guest left. He also saw Ellis watching that ring on his middle finger. That awful ring with the crest.

'As for you, shithead …' Anderson started, ignoring the staring at his middle finger, and began to scribble some numbers furiously onto the pad from which Toots had lovingly removed some pages and folded them for later reference, '… just call me on this number.' Anderson creased the paper and threw it at Ellis, then walked through the boat towards the stern. He looked at the rubbish, kicking at some wrappers, then leapt unexpectedly over the rail, landed in a foot of water, trod carefully to the top of the bank, entered the bush, and was gone.

Ellis shook his head. That wasn't Anderson. Looking at the note, it wasn't Anderson's writing. But then the last time he'd seen Anderson, they were both sober and the pair of them were a lot cleaner.

The tour bus horn sounded intermittently and urgently, jolting Ellis from the scrawl on the paper – a telephone number, surely this would give Ellis the chance he needed … The girl with the breasts looked away as Ellis got on the bus and sat some rows back.

The engine started with as much smell and smoke as the boat had; the windows were open, and the girl's hair waved gently and sensuously in the breeze. Some of the group were already thinking of consulting solicitors. Others were going to get the courier by the tits and throw her to the crocodiles. Ellis knew his luck was out with all the women, cursed himself for ever getting involved in buying hair gel, and decided to make the call just as soon as a reliable estimate might make this Anderson sober enough to talk sense.

Within an hour of a shower and some recuperative hair treatment, Ellis did just that.

Chapter 2

The Kombo Beach Hotel had all the features one normally associated with quality European hotels: four stars, good food, good rooms, good drink, nice beach location, fifty feet to the water. What it was unable to provide was a working external telephone system – hardly the hotel's fault, and the manager probably wouldn't have cared if it was not possible to make contact with the outside world anyway. Anything to focus the traveller's mind on the hotel's myriad appointments, facilities, and activities to consume his interest and money.

On return to the hotel, the day trippers' minds were focused on only one thing: the travel representative. A pretty girl, she seemed powerless to stop the upsurge of threats, all relating to that disreputable character lying on the floor of the boat, covered in vomit – his swearing, his navigation, and the total lack of any commentary on the stark beauty of the black heron and the stunning elegance of the red-bellied paradise flycatcher, with its eighteen-inch tail feathers playing games with the sun and the camera lenses. Everybody had seen this bird, all took photos of it, but nobody was conscious enough to give any indication of whether it was a migrating bird, male or female, or even that any sign of life beyond the bar merited any sort of comment.

With a plastic bag of local coins weighing heavy in his trouser pocket, Ellis approached the one external phone on the edge of the mêlée. Hanging at an angle, apparently nailed to the wall, it offered all the expectation of a gruelling exercise in telegraphic malfunction. An old Ericsson telephone, it had a redundant credit card slot jammed with chewing gum. As Ellis raised the receiver, a wavering, if soft and distant tone could not be silenced by pressing any of the standard buttons. In desperation he hit the star button, which connected him to an irate voice; in the background some anxious shouting, shouting that seemed remarkably similar in nature and tone to the upset occurring in the foyer just over Ellis's shoulder.

The operator intoned in an interrogative style, demanding his room number, while Ellis looked for somewhere to put his money.

'I want to dial a number,' Ellis demanded. 'Just give me a line!'

'What is your room number?' demanded the operator.

'What price a call using my room number?' asked Ellis.

'Two hundred *dallara*. Sir,' intoned the operator. 'But maybe for you, sir, this is negotiable.'

'One hundred.'

In the background the operator spat, connected another line. Things whirred and clicked.

'Two hundred, sir; this is set by the government for all internal calls.'

'One hundred, the last price,' Ellis interjected angrily.

'But only ten *dallara* if you wanna call Serekunda, some nice lady there?'

Ellis thought about some woman, wondering about a Serekunda woman. He wondered whether the operator could fix him up. Perhaps later.

'Sir?'

Ellis wondered about a woman amongst all the sounds and the music and the smells and the memories and reckoned he was only fit for a night with Anderson.

Life had become that bad.

'OK. Let's do one hundred.' Ellis gave the number and the operator duly dialled and got a busy line, cursed, dialled again, and got a ringing tone with the hallmark of being placed in an empty bucket. The operator coughed, enjoying the shared anticipation of the call with Ellis, while Ellis told the operator to get off the line. The operator cursed some more in Mandinka and left Ellis to enjoy his forthcoming conversation.

The telephone continued to ring as Ellis gazed through the lobby to explore the developments in the life expectancy of the travel courier, past the cobwebs hanging from the edges of the phone booth, both decked in a pseudo-Spanish hacienda: lots of brown paint and some plastic flowers, some very dusty plastic flowers. Still the phone rang.

'No reply,' called the operator.

Your Friday, My Sunday

'Sod off!' Ellis cried impatiently. The bloody man had to be there.

Ellis bent down to look at the credit card slot, just to examine the antiquity in some detail, rubbing a finger along the edges and ledges; in looking, he was suddenly brought up with a jolt by two things.

One, the hotel management, in an attempt to soothe harried nerves in the lobby, had turned on the taped music at maximum volume, drowning out momentarily the sound of anger. Two, Ellis realised that the music playing, though a cover version, had been a favourite with him and his lovely Cheryl all those years ago. To compound it, he remembered that all their problems had begun with an illicit telephone call.

The pattern of their married life had been a strain to Ellis. A loveless coexistence followed years of child rearing and playing with the ducks in the park; what's more, Ellis had become bored. They argued, they shouted, the smell of his breath drove her to insults beyond imagining, his thinning hair an indication of how the man had fallen.

And he was next to useless in bed.

So she said.

In order to prove that she was wrong, he started to look around, to look for a young woman in need of some solace and companionship, those old soubriquets that gave a glamorous gloss to illicit sexual activity. Still believing himself to be attractive, he went to young bars, stayed out late, and came home drunk, the grimaces of the young women he'd propositioned still horridly fresh in his memory. Then he'd tried singles bars; they weren't much better. It appeared one had to get to know somebody well before getting down to the real business.

The dating game all over again.

Then one day, glancing through the local free paper, he saw a telephone dateline filled with lots of people offering all sorts of discreet dalliances. Women non-smokers seeking non-smoking men with lots of money and no responsibilities. Men looking for just about anybody. All their descriptions and desires and more agreeable habits, the whole thing, all of it there to see.

All you were invited to do was dial a prime-time number, then dial a few more numbers, and there was the voice of your potential bedmate.

With some nervous hesitation, Ellis cut the details from the newspaper, left the house, walked to a call box, and dialled the number, hoping to hear the voice of somebody who would reassure him and prove that his wife was quite wrong.

The description offered the caller a fortyish, Virgo, sensual, and undemanding woman giving comfort and understanding to a similarly challenged male who could provide a discreet relationship and maybe more.

The voice of the woman was subtle, sweet, and inviting.

It was also the recorded voice of his own wife.

Ellis's thoughts of that unfortunate encounter and the eruption that followed were interrupted by the tones of a woman speaking little English and incapable of much understanding.

What she did understand was Ellis's demand to speak to Anderson.

'Let me talk to Anderson!' Ellis charmed.

There seemed a lot of noise wherever Anderson was staying.

'Hold on, pliss.' In the background, compounded by electrostatic sounds, the sounds of a male voice, grumbling and muttering and swearing.

The sound on the line was at least as interesting as the sounds of the foyer, where the travel courier seemed to be getting the better of the most vociferous of the complainants of the boat journey: something on the lines of free meals or cash refunds or another boat trip organised with somebody who apparently knew the area intimately and would not vomit into the bar snacks.

It was hard to hear Anderson at first, with the noise here, the noise there, and the echo of the telephone system, but it was clearly the voice of the man on the boat.

'Yeh …' the voice started, '… that you? Shithead?' The epithet was hissed with some venom. In the background, the sound of music and somebody, could have been a woman, tunelessly singing along, a dog barking somewhere nearby, static on the line.

'I see you're still as crass as you ever were,' Ellis hit back. 'And presumably you've still got problems with your piles and problems with your contact lenses and problems with your top spin—'

'Go on ... shithead.' Anderson burst open a new can of something toxic.

'—and your phoney bloody American accent.'

That did it.

'Listen. Ellis. Goddammit, you sonofabitch, still stupid after all these years.'

Anderson paused, belched, made some utterance to his companion, and carried on. 'And you come in here on some crusade. What d'ya want here anyway? A blow job? I can fix that. You wanna boy? I can fix that too. Ha bloody ha. Or would you like a dose of the pox, some touch of syphilis? I got that, and you ain't fuckin' me.' Anderson paused. 'Where you phonin' from anyway, shithead? A fuckin' hotel? Sounds like all the girls are strutting fanny from where I'm sittin'.'

'Yup,' replied Ellis. 'I've got twenty of them. All sitting on my face. All at once.'

'No wonder you ain't makin' no sodding sense.'

'You want three more minutes? Sir?' interrupted the operator.

'Course he fuckin' well does!' Anderson shouted.

'Very good, sir.'

'OK. Ellis. Here's the fuckin' juice. Get on down here and see Dulcie and me and we'll give you a ball.'

'I don't need a ball.'

'You never had none in Saudi, you shithead, so if at least ya got one now, one's better than none.'

'For one without brains enough, or sober enough to operate a pair of balls, that sounds pretty empty advice.'

'Yup, sureizz.' Anderson hesitated, now a little more relaxed. 'When you comin'?'

'I don't need to see you, Anderson.'

'Oh yes, you do.'

'Why?'

'Three, thirty thousand dollars each. That's why.'

That's quite a bit towards maintenance payments, Ellis reflected, muddling the decimal point in a mental conversion to sterling. Plus Anderson must know about the money.

'OK. So what do I have to do?'

'Come down here, 28, *A* for alpha, Albert Street. Eight. Tonight.'
The line went dead.
The operator hung up too.

The travel representative, in a state of exhaustion, was supping from a beer glass something that had all the hallmarks of a very large gin and tonic but was presumably being paraded as a wholesome mineral water. She walked slowly through the now-empty foyer, sighing, reddened, chastened, and maddened.

Shaking her head, she walked in authoritative circles, clipboard under one arm, drink in the other hand, still also somehow clutching the embers of a long cigarette, her battle-stained face, well, pretty, Ellis thought.

Ellis walked from the telephone area towards the bar and saw her.

He was walking this way and she was walking that.

Then they met.

Ellis wondered what he might say but had little time for rehearsal, so smiled some compliment as she came near, he en-route to his room, she on a route of escape from these ghastly people, but it was a compliment readily ignored with a look of 'don't patronise me, you bastard'.

Ellis thought his approach was somehow short of measure, the courier wishing bad luck upon anybody within her sights.

It was therefore safe for Ellis to presume that the courier would have gone to bed with him but for her bad demeanour.

That's what he thought as he went to his room on the first floor, unlocked the door, and wondered on the state of his hair. The shuttered windows excluded most light, the bedside light sufficient to show the hair less smart, more streaked, but just about as smart as it had been when this whole wretched day began.

With money in pocket, glasses in hand, a final comb of the hair, Ellis went to the foyer to hail a taxi.

The last thing he expected was a queue.

There was reportedly very little for the average holidaymaker to do or see outside the confines of a Gambian holiday complex, yet there was a queue for taxis. Ellis watched with some wonder on realising the queue comprised many of the ladies with the blue rinses who had been on the ill-fated boat trip. Now preened and ready with handbags, they waited in line, chatting and laughing with each other, calling goodbye and good luck to the first in the line as another taxi rolled under the hotel canopy, beeped its horn, words uttered, a deal done. Then another taxi, then another. Soon it was Ellis's turn.

He waved at the stationary taxi and got into the front seat; the driver, apparently a little annoyed at this informality, grunted disapprovingly and brushed the seat absently to make it more presentable for his guest. The engine was running roughly, and what appeared to be a first generation Skoda, judging by the upholstery and the crude Eastern Bloc design, dejectedly joined the tail of the taxi cortege all turning right from the hotel.

'You British?' asked the driver, now a little more cheerful.

'Yup. Through and through.'

'Whatdat?'

'Yes, I am. British.'

'Just as I thought.' And leaning across to the glove box, the driver almost touched Ellis's knee. He wrestled with the catch of the glove box. The door fell off and spewed a hoard of unboxed cassettes onto the floor around Ellis's feet.

'Damn and shit,' cursed the driver, weaving an uncertain track onto the main road. 'Thought you'd like to hear some Britisher music. What you'd like. Some Beatles or some Rolling Stones maybe? They're Britisher, OK?'

With a lunge of one hand, he grasped a cassette from the floor, held it up to the soft orange of the street lights, and declared it to be a Britisher band. Sir would like it very much. Without waiting for Ellis's response, he ejected a tape of what Ellis considered a poor example of neoclassical Turkish love songs and hurled it disparagingly over his shoulder into the darkness of the back seat somewhere behind them.

Apparently content with his choice, he inserted the new tape, turned up the volume, and asked Ellis where he wanted to go.

'Banjul. Albert Street.'

'Whatjer wanna go Banjul?' the driver asked menacingly. 'No one goes Banjul at night.'

'Where's all the other cabs going then?'

'Serekunda. That's the place. That's where they'll be goin'.'

Suddenly the sound of the Beach Boys split the only working speaker of the Skoda.

'Beach Boys are American,' Ellis shouted kindly.

'Buncha shit anyhow. They screwed the sound system … bah.'

In an instant the sound system cancelled itself as the driver hit the fascia with a clenched fist. Silence. Except from the engine, where a worn valve gear tapped exhaustedly and a loud, rhythmic tapping emanated from somewhere near the front wheels.

'So like I said. Whatjer want in Banjul? I said Serekunda's the place,' the driver asked rhetorically.

'I need to get to the address I gave you.' Ellis paused. 'So what's so special about Serekunda that all the taxis are heading that way?'

Certainly all the taxis were following the same crocodile, and nobody seemed to be turning off.

'Mister. Let me tell you.' Conspiratorially, the driver picked up a pack of cigarettes from the dashboard and offered Ellis one after taking one for himself. Ellis declined with a disapproving wave of the hand. 'Back there, at the hotel. Did ya see all them old women all lined up, all mopping their heads an' all tarted up an' all them handbags? D'ya see it?'

Ellis nodded. And yes, he had wondered.

'You wanna know where they're a goin'?'

In the absence of any response from Ellis, the driver pressed on with his monologue.

'Them old girls. Them's a goin' shaggin'.'

'What?' Ellis was incredulous.

'Yessir. Them's a goin' shaggin'.'

The silence seemed heavy in the driver's victory, the heat closing right in.

The only sound came from the unserviced engine and the gentle drub of the worn tyres on the potholes and the laterite surface, the steering also seeming to be fairly unambitious as the car swayed from one part of the road to another, but keeping a broadly straight-ahead aspect.

'Not shaggin' in the immediate sense, yer understand. They go a lookin' for nice boys. Nice Gambian boys. An' yer know what?' The driver did not wait for a reply. 'The Gambian boys are a lookin' for old bags to do a bitta shaggin' with, rob the old faggots, marry them if they have to, and then ...' The driver's voice trailed off in his own thoughts of shaggin'.

Shaggin' anything. Absolutely anything.

They drove in silence for the best part of a mile, past single-tier buildings, some brick, some corrugated iron, all eerily shaded in the orange light of the street.

'And then what?' Ellis asked solicitously.

'You ask, and then what? I'll tell ya. If they get married, usually in the church in Serekunda, they go all happy and live in England or the US of A, depends where Mama comes from, and then these sweet Gambian boys live off these, these,' the driver in his excitement angrily waved one arm, the other loosely controlling the direction of travel, 'sugar mamas.'

There.

It was out.

Untrammelled resentment.

'Let me get this straight,' Ellis began gently. 'You're saying the old faggots come to the Gambia, ostensibly for a holiday, look for young local boys, promise them a good time, then take them home for a good servicing every night?'

'Yessir. Shitty, ain't it? And the bloody old farts are loaded with money. All they want to complete their widowship is a nigger's prick. Tell ya another thing. They may be all done up on top, all the blue hair an' the tits hanging out of dresses an' 'at, but boy, they smell down below. The smell in my car some nights. At least it ain't the drains, lousy as they are hereabouts.'

Ellis thought and remembered the ladies of the boat and the lascivious glances towards Toots's nether regions, and understood.

Pity it didn't work in reverse. Gambian girls on the make with a white male. But then Ellis didn't have an index-linked pension to squander on this dubious purpose.

'Don't think about it. The hookers here, they all got the pox. If they ain't got the pox, they at home with Daddy. All nice an' clean, you see.'

The driver may just have read Ellis's thoughts.

The driver's words put paid to the stirring in Ellis's loins when thinking of an evening, maybe a life, of carnal pleasure with a black girl with big tits, smooth skin, and that special smell of untapped and unstoppable sensual energy.

Instead all he had to look forward to tonight was an evening with Anderson.

Maybe tomorrow night. Maybe the driver knew where to go.

Maybe he had some phone numbers. Maybe. Maybe. But then, maybe not.

All the taxis were travelling in the same loose convoy, but as the number of houses, shops, and offices increased on the approach to the city, it became pretty clear that, despite all the pitching and weaving, most of them were headed towards the lane taking them over the bridge to Serekunda.

'Ya see, sir,' started the driver, 'Banjul night-time is just too damn disgustin', even for the Gambian folks. Me? I'm Mandinka. Tha's Gambian. Me, I tell you some useful Mandinka. You like?'

'Not at the moment,' Ellis replied absently.

The irony of a white man going to Banjul at night was not lost on the driver, who banged the wheel and began to chuckle, then cough, then wheeze, then wheeze, cough, and chuckle simultaneously. He wound down his window a little using the broken operating lever, spat deftly through the gap, coughed some more, flicked his cigarette butt in hot pursuit of the phlegm, pulled another cigarette from the pack, did a one-handed strike light with a match, and lit it with the practice of a committed smoker. But he'd been so busy with all his bodily requirements and functions, he had quite forgotten what he had been saying.

The taxi approached a road junction where the traffic signals were operating on an intermittent basis: occasionally red, sometimes green, but often red and green at the same time, then again sometimes just orange.

The taxis ahead swept to the right, towards Serekunda, the lights equally for them and against them. It didn't really seem to matter if anyone obeyed the lights. It all depended on the tightness of the connections made by the traffic engineers, and all of them were at home in Serekunda.

'See?' the driver started shouting, the spare arm waving angrily, 'they're all off to Serekunda. But this bloody English, he goes to bloody Banjul ... Ah, Serekunda, over the bridge to Serekunda.' The driver sighed impatiently.

'If I had business in Serekunda, I'd go to Serekunda,' Ellis reminded the driver sharply.

'You got no business in Serekunda. You wanna go Banjul. Shit, no one got no business in Banjul,' the driver insisted. "Cept maybe in daytime. Offices you see. Government offices. And hospitals. Well, one. The old Queen Vic where you see when we go past, you'll see the patients in their beds, bloody funny really.' The driver smiled at his own recollections and let fly a long, long cough. 'The way the ministers and the bankers and the clerks and all the folks go to Banjul to the office; then at five o'clock, or sooner if they fiddle it proper, they get on the bus, across the bridge ... and home.' He paused, coughed, hopefully manipulated the sickened sound system, wound the window control the wrong way, spat into the glass, wished he hadn't done that, shook his head, and sighed. 'Ah ... Serekunda.'

Must go there when I've finished with this dog Anderson, mused Ellis, as the road, formerly well-lit for the tourists, meandered into the outskirts of Banjul, where only an occasional street lamp flashed and flickered, its power overwhelmed by the neon light of advertising hoardings proclaiming a drink with the promise of perpetual relief from thirst and perpetual youth with equal certainty.

The buildings on either side of the highway appeared to have been built in a 'laid waste' scenario. Difficult to see in the darkness any suggestion of planning or coordination or thought or foresight, just waste ground with the occasional guest appearance of concrete slabs, steel beams, and rejected, solidified bags of cement. Dogs ran for cover from the sound of the taxi while a man squatting on a nearby footpath absently swatted something from near his face.

Then the real buildings of Banjul began. Originally painted white and built in the grandeur appropriate to British Empire opulence, the houses, palaces, and offices were now redolent of their past: cracked or absent panes of glass, driveways long neglected, grass and vegetation overwhelming neatly laid pavé, once elegant flowerbeds unable to resist the return to endemic flora.

The taxi driver pressed on, swerving to avoid drain covers made proud of the road surface by the onslaught of the July rains. Then for no apparent reason the driver dived on the brakes, pulled up, and stopped.

'You gotta map?' he demanded.

'No. I thought you, being a taxi driver and all, might know where to go.'

'Serekunda, yes. Day or night, yes, yes, yes. Banjul. And at night. Not a chance, mister.'

'So?'

'So. I ain't goin' no further.' The driver correctly wound the window to the open position, spat, and, in a final act of defiance, crossed his arms, uncrossed them, switched off the engine, then recrossed them for emphasis.

'If you ain't goin' no further,' mimicked Ellis, 'I ain't gonna pay you nothin'.' Ellis put a hand on the door lever.

'Listen here, mister,' the driver snapped back angrily, all the earlier bonhomie now evaporated, 'I said I ain't goin' no further, so you owe me 135 *dallara*. Or else.'

The final words were laced with a generous portion of menace. Ellis leaned across and pulled the driver and the driver's shirt to within an inch of his face.

'Listen to me very carefully, birdbrain. You'll get nothing for nothing. If you don't take me to where I want to be, I don't pay you. OK?'

The driver's eyes were wide in his rage and probably in his fear of a lost fare. But he said nothing, simply shivered and breathed shallowly and quickly, hoping for an early release from this client.

'By the way,' Ellis started as he released his grip and part opened the door, 'your breath smells.' And leaping into the road, he slammed the door and called a cheery goodnight. As the driver cursed the engine back into life, he cursed evil upon most living things, then performed an untidy U-turn over the central reservation, whereupon something on the underside of the car caught the kerbing, some sparks showering from beneath, and a piece of metalwork clattered noisily to the ground.

Undeterred, the driver completed his wild manoeuvre and drove back in the direction of relative civilisation in search of a more compliant fare.

As the noise of the valve bounce and neglected engine dissolved into the distance, there was only a dense silence. That sort of black silence where no sound is possible and any sound that is made is immediately neutralised and absorbed.

A ringing in his ears reminded Ellis of the nothingness of this part of town. Only some crazed crickets sounded company for him. But in which part of town was he? And was it anywhere near where he should have been nearly an hour ago? The only chance was towards the fluorescent port lights, the lights of Banjul harbour. Those lights, mounted high on shiny aluminium poles, dispersed a bright light on high, becoming more dilute and weakened as it descended uncertainly into the dust and airborne detritus still stirring close to the grey, sandy ground.

As Ellis pounded breathlessly along the uneven pavement, he had to agree with the driver. It was true: there was nothing in Banjul. There was the far-off sound of a car being abused in episodes of high acceleration and instant braking, a whirring from something mechanical in the dockyard, some laughter nearby quickly suppressed. The only other sound was Ellis's quickening breath and the thudding sound of his own footfalls.

The only thing in its favour was that all the ground in all directions was perfectly flat and without feature. Continuing along what was signposted as Independence Drive, Ellis noticed a building of some austerity, with opened windows and some dulled lights struggling to illuminate the outside world.

The silhouette suggested a hospital.

The Queen Victoria.

Thoughts of the standards of care, health of the Gambian people, and Ellis's sore feet filled his mind and dulled his awareness of the throaty thrub of a car slowly approaching from behind. Step by step, it gradually drew alongside Ellis. A uniformed figure, hand held open on the end of an arm draped from the window as the car squeakily drew to a halt, asked him for some form of identity.

The problem lay in the fact that Ellis's only identification, his passport, lay reluctantly in the safe of the hotel. He carried the bare minimum: some *dallaras*, enough for a taxi if he ever bothered to pay for one, enough for some drinks, and enough to bribe willing policemen such as these.

'ID. Back at hotel,' Ellis shouted slowly.

The hand still lay open. Then the fingers snapped impatiently, inviting Ellis to enjoy an eye-to-eye encounter with the arm of the law. The heat and the oppression and the noise of the crickets all closed in on Ellis as he lowered his head by way of submission to face the officer.

'Passport,' the policeman uttered menacingly. 'Passport.' And he snapped his fingers even more aggressively to emphasise his impatience.

So Ellis repeated his loud English-for-beginners sentence, complete with absent verb. 'Passport,' he bellowed. 'Hotel!'

The policeman rocked away from the volume. Perhaps he smiled a little. He pushed open the car door, leaving Ellis no alternative but to jump smartly out of its way. The policeman grunted a little as he heaved himself from the car and stood, by Ellis's reckoning a good six foot two, towering over him. Ellis made a mental note that he only came up to the policeman's shoulder. Just.

'Where are you going?' the policeman asked in a deep, cultured voice.

'I have an appointment with an old friend in Albert Street. I suppose you don't know where that is from here?'

The cop smiled. 'Come on. Get in. We'll give you a lift.'

Ellis kissed goodbye to his freedom as he entered the rear area of the car, fetid from the sweat and fear of felons.

'What number do you need?' the driver asked, equally clearly in perfect English.

'Twenty-eight a.'

The driver and his colleague conferred excitedly. They seemed to know the whereabouts of Albert Street; the numbering seemed less clear. The car turned right, and the officers confirmed that this was Albert Street. As the numbers went in singles from the port, up Albert Street to the far end and then back in singles to the port, he really should be able to work it out for himself. So they pulled up, dropped Ellis off, and acted as if the tip Ellis gave them was, somehow, rather short of their expectations. Wide eyes looked at the money proffered. They held up the notes with grubby hands to examine them in the weak street lighting. It seemed that Ellis's payment for the good turn was short by some considerable margin.

'Better than a kick in the pants,' the driver muttered as he engaged gear and waved perfunctorily. In a moment the car was gone. All its rattles and its radio and the smell. All of it gone into the distance and the heat and the unfathomable depth of the putrid Banjul night air.

The houses carried the occasional number, some jaded by exposure to the sun, others lost by neglect. One mansion with peeled paint pronounced itself as number 11. The house immediately adjacent and with no space to fit an anaconda was number 17. The policeman's explanation of the town numbering plan seemed already in tatters.

Ellis moved on, up Albert Street away from the docks, into an uncertain darkness. A breath of wind began and then cancelled itself, Ellis's breath and the gentle sound of his sandals the only real sounds to disturb the otherwise heavy sound of silence. Ellis moved on, looking all ways to find the damned Anderson in his number 28 A.

There really was no obvious sign of anything approaching anything in the twenties. Ellis started to feel tired, a fatigue driven by his unwillingness to encounter Anderson for anything longer than was absolutely necessary.

From the deep shadows on the opposite side of the road, Ellis thought he saw a figure move. Just the wind playing tricks with the leaves of the trees in the dim light. He moved on. There were no taxis around here to take him back to the hotel even if he did abandon this trek, so, suitably buoyed by his desperation, he decided do one pass all the way one way, then down the other side all the way, then home. No Anderson.

A sound behind, perhaps a slippered footfall announced a companion.

'Shithead! You're about a fuckin' hour late for slam off.'

Anderson!

Still dressed in the stained cotton shirt and jeans worn on the voyage of adventure, Anderson remained the epitome of dishevelment. Ellis caught the strains of Anderson's breath and knew and understood.

'What the fuck keptya?'

'Your lousy instructions, a shitbag of a taxi driver who only wanted to go to Serekunda, police who needed a bribe, and this damned stifling heat. Banjul. What a shithole!'

'Yup. It's a shithole, OK,' Anderson concurred amiably. 'And it don't get no betta, no way. Not till the summer. The Yankee summer, that is. Don't recall when you get your summer – same time as ours, I guess?'

'Listen, you bloody creep,' Ellis began impatiently. 'It probably has escaped your small brain that you are actually British. With pretensions of being a bloody Yank. Have you ever considered pretending that you are actually a human being? If you do that, you may then remember you were born Brit, you have a Brit passport, and all your bloody talk and drawl about slam dunks and sidewalks and can't remember the date of the British summer is all a load of bollocks.'

'Touchy, ain't we, sweetheart?' Anderson smiled in his darkness.

'Anyhow,' Ellis said, 'where's your shack?' Avoiding the incoming hatred from an old associate.

They shuffled along for a few yards. Ellis noticed that Anderson seemed to have developed a slight limp, perhaps as a result of his overindulgence in most illicit materials, but more likely to be another of his less endearing affectations. One thing that was not an affectation was the astigmatism of the eye, no better illustrated as he pointed out that his shack lay behind the once splendid colonial mansion, its windows smashed and shattered; only the dust seemed undisturbed.

Anderson nodded awkwardly to Ellis to follow him down a pathway to one side of the mansion, a pathway with uneven and broken paving slabs, dust, discarded plastic bags, withering clumps of couch grass, and industrial plastic packaging hugging the base of what appeared to be an imported sycamore tree. Perhaps it was something Gambian.

In the total darkness at the side of the house, Anderson muttered something about being careful as he picked an uneasy path around dustbins and metal containers strewn easily around. As Anderson tripped and caught his foot against one bin with no lid, a dark, rat-shaped object equalled Anderson's curses, jettisoned itself noisily, and fled to someone else's rubbish along the path and out of sight.

As the cursing and the smell subsided, the two men walked a few paces further, and there was chez Anderson.

A single storey, prefabricated building, once painted a glorious white, now lay in a heap, apparently characteristic of most of Banjul. While the building broadly stood on its own foundations, the windows offered the seepage of light on all sides, the curtains torn, the mosquito nets ripped and lacerated. Flies buzzed and worried at the light; moths simply went round and round until too dizzy to do much else except try next door. The mansion once had an elegant garden.

Now Anderson lived here. Someone, at some time, had planted this structure into the centre of such artistry. Ellis looked and thought about the irony of the building and Anderson living on such hallowed ground.

'I know whatcher thinkin', how's an asshole like me livin' in a shithole like this with the smarty-pants mansion an' all just nearby,' Anderson wanted to explain.

'Just seems like a pity that an arsehole like you has to live at all, let alone live here,' Ellis concluded with an impatient intake of breath.

Anderson muttered something dismissive as he walked towards the shack, kicking over empties. Ellis looked upwards to see cables and telephone wires, apparently abandoned and left to dry, suspended on ceramic supports that offered a zero useful lifespan. The supports, once bolted securely, hung at angles from the face of the building, as if trying to escape.

Anderson approached the entrance and held out a hand to pull open the fly door. Its hinges had expired long ago, as had the netting as a useful means of fly deterrence. The door moved away from the shack in arbitrary directions. Anderson cursed as he opened the inner hardwood front door and flakes of paint drifted into his face. He paused and trod, tentatively, in Ellis's direction.

'How come these fly doors open outwards and then the front door opens inwards? Doesn't folks think these things out first? I mean to say, if you had a fly door opening inwards and the front door opened inwards, then all of this fartin' about with goin' this way an' that, well, it just wouldn't be necessary, would it?'

It all seemed quite logical to Ellis, who watched this man swaying uneasily on the inner door handle, angrily swiping at imaginary insects and addressing nobody but himself.

'You better come in,' Anderson said as the dim light from inside shed some explanation of the unpleasant feelings emanating from ground level. Things like broken glass pressing into the soles of shoes, the crunching of the bodies of king ants underfoot, the contact of leather against planned neglect.

Ellis could feel the smell before his nose detected it. The floor space, perhaps designed with partitions providing some privacy, had given way to an open plan room. All of it dimly lit: a double bed in one corner, a table cluttered with used plates and beakers along the far wall. A standard light without shade stood with no bulb either. The paint peeled from the wall. A faded picture of la Sagrada Familia stapled to the wall was inevitably adorned with stains of food thrown amidst some furious interchange of thought with someone else willing to stand their ground. Other detail was lost on Ellis as he smelt the content of the place. Smoke, thick smoke, distorting and absorbing the weak light hanging from the centre of the ceiling; illicit smoke; bedding, unwashed bedding; stale booze; sweat; underwear; and that characteristic smell of failure to wash person or object or place or anything at all.

Something moved on the bed.

From among the crumpled sheets a young woman, a young black woman, sleepily drew herself upwards, stretched, yawned, and looked Ellis in the eye. A challenge, no doubt, for she was quite naked. Breasts of a Gambian beauty, not too large, well shaped, nipples erect, smiles, smells, dreams. Ellis was lost in his own yearning as the girl jumped from the bed, grasped a towel lying on the floor, and swayed – particularly her hips – gracefully to the bathroom, the only room with any privacy here.

'Nice bitta stuff, eh, Ellis, you old shitbag?' Anderson hit Ellis's arm playfully as he absorbed what could be available to him on his holiday.

Then Ellis remembered the taxi driver and all he'd said about the whole thing working in reverse and how he'd need to come here with loadsa money and live and pick up some girlie and then shag the daylights out of her and promise her ultimate deliverance from local poverty and a life of luxury in London. And then shag her again and again, until …

Ellis wondered if Anderson could cope with that rate of attrition and then thought about his own ability to do the same. Ellis suddenly felt a little tired, a thought banished by the appearance of the girl from the bathroom, wearing a purple silk robe and some Estée Lauder and smiling, a beautiful, white-formed smile, and just beautiful as she stooped to welcome

Ellis. Her breasts fell forward and Ellis fell in love for the second time on the same day.

'Get us some fuckin' beers, woman,' Anderson commanded as he slapped her arse playfully.

'Sure.' The girl complied with a complete smile and a bit of an American-style military salute.

The girl ran off somewhere to complete her duties.

'See, Ellis, what these fuckin' birds need is a bitta slappin' and some good shaggin'. That way they know who's who, who's in fuckin' charge, and who's got all the fuckin' baloobas.'

Ellis nodded, not because he agreed with Anderson's dogma but with a recognition of that old expression they'd all once shared to explain wealth: If ya got baloobas, ya got wealth.

'So what has brought you to our lovely land?' Anderson became lucid.

'Holiday. Nothing else. Just a chance to get away.'

'Away from what? Cheryl given you the push? God, she was an old bitch, ringin' ya up, bloody shoutin', the bloody kids this an' that, I got my period, remember all them bloody phone calls? All the moanin' an' the bleatin' an' you six thousand mile from home an' still the old cow's shoutin' and a hollerin' an' a bawlin'. Got pissed off, did yer?' And without waiting for an answer: 'Knew ya would. Cow.'

'No. Just trying to get away from England in winter. That's all. Just to get some sun, some warmth.'

'Bullshit.'

Anderson pulled a tin from under his settee, opened it, rolled something, offered Ellis some. Ellis took some, he rolled some, and both lit up, some common purpose. The sweet smoke rose and curled upwards. Each with his own thoughts. The girl shimmered across the room, lay double cans by their places, smiled gently into Ellis's eyes, and quietly took her place on Anderson's bed.

The sweet feeling of relaxation overpowered Ellis's desire to answer Anderson back. He lay back, just as Anderson did, enjoying the smoke, watching the smoke swirl and dive, rising towards the dim lamp. The air was still. Anderson opened his beer with some grunting and heaving. Ellis did likewise. The girl smiled. She rubbed a breast carelessly, winked at Ellis, sighed longingly, and lay back. Her gently caressing her leg took

Ellis's mind off all his cares and frustrations. Only he would have liked to push those legs apart and go to heaven, but Anderson had other thoughts and tapped his glass impatiently to remind him of them.

Anderson inhaled his smoke deeply. Perhaps he smiled, but then he returned to the agenda.

'Remember what I said today?'

'As far as I remember, all you did was to puke in the peanuts.'

'Pretzels, actually. I spewed in the pretzels. It's an old trick.'

'Great. So what did you say today that had any importance?'

'I told ya about the boy.' Anderson inhaled deeply, tucked his legs beneath him on the sofa, made himself comfortable, made an obscene gesture at the girl, and continued talking. 'An' how he's a gonna be 16 not too far from now. You in or aintcha?'

'In or out. What's the deal?' Ellis could only wonder at the direction of the conversation.

'The fuckin' beer in the UK must be pretty strong if ya don't remember.' Anderson leaned forward to within an ace of Ellis's face, wriggling his hips to get more comfortable. 'Listen, you remember Saudi Arabia?' Anderson spelled out the Saudi Arabia phonetically.

'Can't say I'll ever forget it, really,' Ellis replied emphatically in an exhalation of grass smoke.

'Then you'll remember the accident, and you'll recall that our old mucker Klitowski, well, old Clitoris is due for the chop.'

Anderson sat back in the finality of his message.

'For Christ's sake, that would have been four years ago. More, possibly!'

'I agree,' Anderson concurred amiably, 'but the eldest son died of leukaemia or somethin' terminal, so the bloody authorities had to wait another three years until the remaining eldest son reached 16. And that won't be for another six months. Like I said, are you in or aintcha?'

'OK, Anderson. What's the deal?'

And while the girl rubbed her thighs and moaned, Anderson explained the plan to Ellis, and both smoked and both drank. The girl refined herself, filling the glasses upon Anderson's command, as the smoke curled and a nearby police siren came and went. The girl smiled and suggested her heaven and the whole bloody memory of life in an absolute monarchy, and suddenly the whole plan made sense, even though conceived by a drunkard and a cad, a philanderer, a useless river pilot and a pseudo-American arsehole … it still made sense.

Anderson smiled at the thought of Ellis's probable thoughts, blew smoke at the flickering light, a mosquito chasing the beams as drunken as some river pilots, coughed a little. 'What ya been doin' with yourself, Ellis, you old shitbag, since our last meeting? Since those happy, happy days of working together?'

The thought of working with Anderson now seemed an awesome prospect. But it had seemed better back then. Ellis drew his finger round and round the top of the glass, thinking of all the things he'd been doin', to quote the pseud opposite, watching the foam of the drink dancing around the inside of the rim of his stained glass. He sighed, forced a smile, and said, 'I've been saving myself.'

Anderson laughed a friendly, scornful laugh. 'You dun' what?'

'I've been saving myself. Just in case I got any interest.'

'How much d'ya get? Not a lot, I'll bet.'

'No. None at all. Everybody's too young, or if they're not young, they're married, and if they're old and not married … God, they're hideous.'

'You see the mamas?'

'Pardon?'

'The mamas. You musta seen 'em on the way here. The old bitches smellin' all farty an' sweet. All of 'em after the boys with the big dicks. They all get the cab, hundreds of 'em, and sweet ass their way down Serekunda. Bonkin', lookin' for the boys. Young, cheap boys, and them boys is lookin' for some rich old bag, shag the daylights outta her, then take the money an' run.' Anderson paused, leaned forward to light his smoke from an old tabletop lighter, the sort with an elegant marble base, lots of sparks, and a lingering smell of jet fuel. He drew deeply from his smoke, inhaled, then continued, 'An' if they ain't lucky, they have to marry the old cow, but they get to keep the money. Downside is they have to sniff mama's undies first thing every day. Preferred route, as I'm told, is to shag, get the Britisher passport, then run with the dosh. Anywhere, at least anywhere where the courts can't reach …'

The two men drank and smoked in silence.

'Best thing is if the old bag dies during a heavy session.'

'Heart failure, stroke, or something pretty fatal?' Ellis sought clarification.

'You goddit.' Anderson was pleased with his former colleague. 'But if the old bag does overstrain her greens, the boy makes off like a hot snot, takes all the money, then waves his dick at the next mama. She's probably up the road somewheres, and he pretending he don't know nothing, 'cept he smiles at her tits and her varicose veins and all she's doin' is looking not a million miles from his waist, or his knees, and she's a turnin' red and gettin' all flushed and excited, and then. Wham.' Anderson flicked some ash to the floor.

'Wham?' Ellis enquired.

'Then the little sod gives her one,' Anderson blew some smoke at the light, 'and so it goes on.'

'Ever thought of going for the mamas yourself?'

'Bullshit. I got little Lizzie here.' Anderson looked and pointed admiringly over his shoulder to the bed in the corner, where the black beauty preened herself. 'Anyhow, you wanna try for some? You ain't really pretty enough for the mamas.'

'Na.' Ellis almost mimicked the drawl he detested. 'Too smelly, plus I keep thinking I was the same shape as I was at 18, 25 – I dunno, but I don't feel like I'm 46. And the bloody crumpet look on me kindly. If they want to dance, they do so with a view to initiating resuscitation, and they smile and dance and duck and weave, all the while watching for the death hue of the eyes of a fallen soldier, and their tits hanging out … oh God, those tits …' Ellis thought of the girl on the boat, the girl to whom he had silently sworn eternal devotion, the girl with those tits …

'See what you get out here, Ellis? Crumpet.' Anderson glanced swiftly and conspiratorially over his shoulder, his voice dropping. 'See, Lizzie is the best shag you ever had, an' she don't cost me no more than some soap powder, a bitta rice, and some lamb on Fridays.'

'She's a Muslim then?'

'Yup. Sure is.'

'Shit.' Ellis reached for another smoke, the drink and the grass moving his mood.

'So you in or ain't ya?'

Ellis knew of Anderson, of his moods, of his capabilities, of his awesome abilities when sober, of his hatefulness when drunk or when crossed, of his sneer, of his awful pretences, and all of his eye troubles and his bowels and the back pains. The type of person who equally generates hatred and admiration; they have most points covered. They're vulnerable but have the ability to cope. Ellis hated to admit the plan was feasible.

Anderson smiled, rolled a new joint, commanded Lizzie to bring more drink. His right eye was having additional difficulty in locating Ellis in the enveloping smoky gloom; his left eye had more luck. He settled himself into the worn upholstery, threw the can of smoking appurtenances at Ellis, sighed, stared somewhere over the wall beyond Ellis's shoulders, and began to recollect with some relish, resentment, and reflection what had thrown such unlikely companions into the same pot.

Tuesday

Chapter 3

Anderson glanced out of the window, impatiently fanning himself with a crumpled copy of yesterday's *Arab News*, an English language newspaper of no consequence and containing nothing but plagiarised sections of the London *Guardian* of some months before. For that reason alone, reasoned Anderson, it was only useful for swatting flies and for fanning a troubled face. He snapped open a new pack of gum, withdrew a cigarette from another pack, and sipped some coffee in one long, complicated, but largely coordinated manoeuvre. Then he stared out of the window again. Based in a single-storey building, Anderson was the key biomedical engineer charged with purchasing equipment, according to Ministry of Health Specifications, to make this new one thousand bed hospital, the jewel in the crown of the Saudi Ministry of Health. The prefabricated building was in the centre of the site and subject to some movement – not of the geophysical type, just that it was now time to build the microbiology building, and the site engineers' office was in the way. So the Korean contractors would knock it down and put it up elsewhere, all in the span of a day or two. Anderson would settle to a new view from his window, and within two weeks the pathology department would be ready to be built, so down would come the site engineers' offices again and be located somewhere afresh.

Anderson disliked this particular position, for it allowed the early morning sun to drown his desk in harsh light. And by staring through the window, he simply developed headaches.

To avoid the glare, he picked up the papers on his desk, the CVs of his two new assistants. He read them again, frustrated that the system only allowed him to welcome, not select his new recruits. God knew what would be turning up this morning. It was seven thirty. And it was already hot.

'Edgardo!' Anderson yelled.

A Filipino boy nearby dropped his pencil and hurried to the master. 'Yes, sir?'

'Ed. What would you make of some guy with an ODA cert from the UK?'

Ed shrugged his shoulder in total ignorance of the question.

'I don't know either, Ed. But get me a fuckin' coffee anyway.'

'Yes, sir.'

Ed hurried off to the machine to make the exact requirements from a machine designed only to produce cocoa. Back he returned with a black coffee, one sugar. One sugar only.

Anderson sipped and was satisfied.

He lit another cigarette, picked up the papers and sighed.

'Ellis. Robert Bartholomew. Date of birth, seventeen stroke seven stroke nineteen fifty. Jesus, don't these damn Brits know there's only twelve months in a damn year? Shit, they should say seventeen July, nineteen fifty, or at least seven stroke seventeen stroke nineteen fifty. Fuck me,' he added thoughtfully, 'the man's at least two years younger than me.'

The phone bell jarred. Anderson answered with polished dismissiveness, then picked up the other crop of papers, either to wave at his face or to read. Ed was not sure.

'Jan Klitowski. Born Warsaw, 1957, educated at the College of St. Ignatius, Rome, ODA at Royal Free London, 1970 to 1974, ODA cert, City and Guilds 1972, procurement manager, G500 Dammam, 1976 to 1980, uh-huh.' Anderson read on, flicking over the third sheet of the loquacious CV, jobs listed here and there, sales rep for a couple of years, then, 1985 to date, project coordinator, MODA 700-bed hospital, Al Abqaiq, Eastern Province.

'So he has form,' Anderson said aloud and worried. Ed thought Anderson needed something and came to minister but was sent away sharply. The problem I got, thought Anderson, is if he's got form, he'll know my game.

Never mind, we'll just have to wait and see.

Your Friday, My Sunday

The chances were that this Pole had made up most of his CV anyway, had done his work in Dammam, got caught, got deported from the Kingdom, done a bit of this and that in the meantime. Then, when the dust settled, he'd applied for a new passport, and come back to do what most of them knew best … stealing.

Anderson laughed at this invention, but it was not far from the truth. His own experience had been as an operating department assistant in the cash-starved health service of the UK, with total responsibility for the correct working of all his operating theatres, equipment, instruments, and procedures. The surgeons relied on him. They valued his judgement. The nurses were condescending but still valued the contribution he could make.

Which was why he was able to fall prey to a scam that offered him payments, good payments to make recommendations that the operating theatre equipment, in particular the anaesthetic machines, were tired and in need of replacement. The practice was called scabbing: you peeled off the old and the new came through. The manufacturers of the newest and the best equipment had sales teams who focused on the ODAs to get them to pick scabs, and they paid them well. But being not from the educated elite, ODAs sometimes failed to hide their greed sufficiently from official scrutiny. Anderson had once found himself without a job, ejected without a reference from Cleveland District General Hospital in the latter part of 1979, when he was just 27.

An episode of unemployment, followed by a whirlwind tour of the US of A, thankfully arranged by a concerned though distant relative. Then, through a process of persistence and arrogance, he landed a plumb job on a turnkey project in Jeddah. For Anderson this was the turning point. With his expertise in the requirements and procedures of operating theatres, he felt he was well placed, as did the Saudis, to decide upon the merits of all items that comprise a modern hospital.

'Ed!' Anderson yelled again. 'Get down the Marriott Hotel, see where those damn fuckers have gotten to. Here,' Anderson tossed his keys at Ed's cocoa maker, 'take my motor. Make a fuckin' impression!'

'Yes, sir,' Ed responded, delighted to be free of the site for an hour and, if he was clever, go visit some friends, impress them, but anyway glad to be away from making the coffee, which was Sam's job anyway, and delighted to be driving sir's Lexus.

'An' if you're away more 'an twenty minutes, I kick ass. Ya hear?'

Ed giggled nervously and fled from the building, leaving the door swinging lazily, and stumbled into the path of a concrete mixer wading through the rubble and dust of the new building's site. Hurled words of insult were exchanged between the Korean driver and the Filipino, each seeming to ignore the other's point of view among the waved arms and the pointed fingers of accusation.

Anderson's laughter at the simple behaviour of Third Worlders overlooked the approaching footfall of Mr Choi, the Korean supremo. A man of diminutive stature, Mr Choi could squeeze untold concessions out of manufacturers proposing equipment for his site. He said once he had built about three hydroelectric power stations, two football stadiums, and a shopping mall, all in South Korea, so building a hospital was small beer, but a necessary one.

'You having drinks tonight, Mr Anderson? To welcome our new guests?'

'Guests, my bollocks. They come here to work, Mr Choi, and work they will to get this bloody project back on track.' Anderson impatiently grasped the daily paper to swat at a flying something hovering close to the top of his coffee.

'Mr Anderson, these people are our guests. I do not believe you go home in the evening and work. I think, perhaps, you become rat-bagged? You should offer them the hospitality appropriate to a warm welcome. When I was in Chis-Wick, West London, we offered all guests the same hospitality – drinks, snacks, the warmth of welcome.'

'What'ya serve them, Mr Choi? Snacks, I mean. D'ya give 'em dog cutlets, or was it dead dog scratchings? Listen here, mister, I run this outfit, and I treat the bastards the way I choose, an' if they need a welcome, I'll give 'em one. Tomorrow morning at six thirty, the bloody motherfuckers can be here with their silky-soft white skin, and oh isn't it hot here, and oh isn't this all rather quaint?' Anderson lapsed into an English accent, rather by accident. Then he crushed a fly balancing on the edge of his desktop.

'Mr Anderson. You are quite appalling.' Mr Choi suppressed a twinkle of his eye.

'Why, goddammit?'

'You know quite well that all personnel report at seven o'clock.' And with that Mr Choi retired to his desk, located no more than three feet in front of the colourful tropical fish tank.

'Bloody dog eaters,' Anderson cursed loudly. 'And they don't even breed the bloody things for eating, they just pick up any old scrawn from the street, offer it some food, get it fat, slit its throat, and then into the oven. Bastards.'

He paused to start another cigarette.

'Makes ya wonder how they manage to build bloody power stations when they're full of dead dog. Perhaps that's why the bloody shopping centres keep collapsing. Full of dog, or rather shopping centres full of people full of dog.'

Anderson had completed his rant, and seeing that nobody was taking any notice of him, he picked up the drawings of the X-ray department and sighed and fidgeted. Where was the bloody fax? The boys in London had promised some sort of special. God, this bloody X-ray department was a waste of time. Who cared anyway if the whole of the Arabic nation dropped dead with tuberculosis or cancer or if they got a starting handle wedged up inside their assholes – did anyone really care?

Anderson decided it was time to read the *Arab News*, rather than use it as an offensive weapon. The news of Thatcher's re-election in UK was the headline, but that had been about three weeks ago, according to the Voice of America. In his sense of isolation and boredom, Anderson decided to do the crossword.

None of the clues required an answer with more than four letters. As an intellectual exercise, he tried to see how many times he could use words depicting genitalia without getting misplaced words. After ten minutes of this cerebral challenge, he gave up, walked to the fax machine, cursed at it, then returned to his chair, in time to hear his Lexus being driven at high speed across the rough ground that was the current approach road to the site office.

The fans and air conditioners whirred and hummed as the sound of voices, laughter, and slamming doors entered the dusty window.

The door swayed open, and Ed proudly led a Britisher into the tabernacle. Anderson was seated at his table, furiously operating his calculator, an eye fixed on the drawings, mind fixed on the fax machine. Ed walked humbly towards Anderson as the new worker followed in tow, weighed down by a suitcase and an overnight bag.

'Mr Anderson, sir,' Ed began hesitatingly. 'Mr Ellis, may I please to introduce to you, Mr Ellis, from UK.'

Anderson remained absorbed by his calculations, fingers hitting calculator buttons at random.

Ellis stood at ease and waited. He put his bags down on the floor by his side.

'The fuckin' bags belong over there,' Anderson flared. 'What d'ya think this fuckin' place is? Eh?' Anderson leaped from his sedentary position, scattering some of the papers from his desk. 'Some sort of fuckin' camp?'

Ellis muttered something about how he hadn't understood and meekly positioned his cases, in fact all his worldly possessions, beneath a wall-mounted air conditioner dribbling coolant down the unpainted walls and onto the luggage labels announcing who he was.

Anderson's anger was immediately assuaged by the discovery of the existence of the fax, unearthed by his explosion at Ellis.

'Ed!' Anderson bellowed. 'Ed, two things.'

'Yes, sir?'

'This fuckin' fax. How long's it been here? Second, where's the other Brit? You were supposed to pick up two. You only brought one. Where's the other one?'

'Sir …'

'Sir what?' Anderson bellowed. 'Where's the other fuckin' Brit?'

'Sir, there was only Mr Ellis.'

'Mr fuckin' Ellis ain't no good. Where's Mr Clitoris?'

'Sir?'

'Mr Klitowski. Where the fuck is he? What ya do with him?'

'Not there, sir. Only Mr Ellis. And the fax, sir. It arrived two days ago. I gave it to you.' He added defensively, 'And neither did I write it in the incoming-faxes log, just as you told me. Sir.'

'Shitbags ... Ellis!'

Ellis swept a contemptuous look at Anderson and stepped from his baggage. Just one step.

'Ellis, you'll have to do. Come 'ere. You just spent an entire fuckin' night on an aircraft; now you can do some bloody work. Come 'ere and let me show you about your duties.' Ellis stepped cautiously towards Anderson. 'If you don't mind.' Anderson added as he tried to look at the fax message and Ellis at the same time.

With eyes like that, mused Ellis, anything should be possible. There was one pointing at the left and the other straight ahead, and there was some jingo sitting in front of a fish tank. There were machines outside – cranes, mixers, movers, and manipulators – all building this magnificent edifice. All a great tribute, the agency's blurb had claimed, to the wisdom of King Fahd, the Custodian of the Two Holy Mosques.

Anderson waved Ellis to a chair in front of his desk, then pulled something from his drawer, unscrewed a small stopper from a small bottle, tipped his head, and applied something to his eyes.

'Conjunctivitis?' Ellis enquired gently.

'No. I got VD in my bowels. Why the fuck d'ya think I'm stickin' in these fuckin' eye drops in ma fuckin' eyes? To convert my diverticulum into a precious metal? Course I got conjunctivitis. This sand and all the shit and all the bloody Brits who can't turn up on time and all the fuckin' crap, yeh, it gets to you, Ellis, mark my words. Six months from now you'll get operated on for something wrong with your bowels or your bollocks, and when they send you out of hospital with a leg injury, they'll give you eye drops. It's pretty scientific. Shit and Christ, we're supposed to be building a bloody hospital here, but there's so much religion tied up with the whole thing, you'd think we were buildin' a fuckin' cathedral. All the fuckin' hocus-pocus, the holy Roman church would be fuckin' proud.' Anderson paused from his tirade, slightly ashamed to have let go. 'Ellis? You believe in anything?'

'I grew up Catholic.'

'Jesus,' Anderson hissed as he lit another smoke. 'Still Catholic?'

'Nope.'

'When d'ya stop all that?'

'About age four,' Ellis calculated easily.

'Good.'

Anderson relaxed visibly, inhaled deeply, and seemed to Ellis to be focusing on Mr Choi's desk, tucked away discreetly in the far corner of the dusty shack, close to the fish tank. Anderson brought himself quickly up to date and insisted Ellis meet Mr Choi. the two men rose as one, walking over to the dog eater, as Anderson described the bossman under his breath.

'Mr Choi,' Anderson started as Mr Choi looked up, startled and a little surprised at the intrusion without advance notice, 'Mr Choi, I have the pleasure to introduce to you Mr Ellis. He's just come from UK.'

Mr Choi stood correctly, bowed, and held out his right hand.

Both men shook hands warmly.

'Mr Ellis,' Choi said, signalling Ellis to take a seat, 'you are most welcome to our project, to help us to develop and put in place the most exciting health-care project in the Kingdom. Ever.'

'I'm glad to be here, Mr Choi.' Ellis was on best behaviour.

Choi dismissed Anderson with a peremptory wave of the hand.

Anderson belched and shouting something at Ed walked back to his desk.

'Mr Anderson tells me you have extensive experience in the operating departments of English hospitals.'

Ellis's chest rose proudly. 'Yes, I have considerable experience of the state of the art requirements of any advanced hospital and health-care system.'

'Good.' Mr Choi looked up from the papers and smiled. 'Very good indeed. You see, I lived in Chis-Wick, West London, for many years with my wife and my two sons. They both went to very good nursery school, you may know it? The Peace Garden School in Putney?'

Ellis could not recall the place, nor care.

'Garden place very good for my children, they learn all about England and all your customs.'

'Really?' Ellis was too tired to be particularly polite, but perhaps he was preoccupied with the exotic colours of a tropical fish tank precariously perched on top of a rusted iron frame and located along the wall behind

Mr Choi's desk. A wildly coloured male king fighter was cruising the tank, its rubbery mouth issuing threats, other, smaller fry offering due deference and staying low and otherwise busy doing what smaller fry do in such a small space.

The problem for Ellis was that the tank was exactly at Mr Choi's head level when he sat at his desk. When he was standing, the whole thing looked right, but when Mr Choi adopted his sitting, power position, the tank was exactly at his head level. To any seated visitor, there was the desk right ahead, then Mr Choi, then the tank behind him at head level. As a result, the king fighter, cruising for a meal, seemed to be swimming into Mr Choi's left ear, reappearing a few seconds later emerging from his right ear, mouth still pouting, still posing.

Then the blasted fish did the whole thing in reverse. There seemed no real opportunity for Ellis to seriously comment on the status of primary education for Korean children in Putney.

Mr Choi, realising Ellis's interest in the tank, smiled and turned to watch the aquatic activity, smiled again, and looked back at Ellis.

'You like fish, Mr Ellis?' Choi offered Ellis a cigarette. 'Maybe you like Korean cigarettes too?'

Ellis took one of the cheroots from the proffered crinkled pack, Choi taking one for himself, and both lit up.

Ellis thought his head was about to explode. Having become a lapsed ex-smoker in the last week, his throat could handle most concoctions that mankind would consider rolling into a piece of paper and then igniting. Korean cigarettes were, Ellis concluded while still suppressing all the acid and gagging in his throat, yes, they were interesting – if Mr Choi should ask.

If he didn't, then they were like smoking dog shit.

Mr Choi was enjoying his smoke, but it didn't seem to last long. Four very committed inhalations took care of the entire cigarette. Mr Choi coughed the cough of a lifelong smoker and tossed the butt at the ashtray and returned to the topic of the fish tank.

'Fish, Mr Ellis. You like fish?'

'I like fish,' Ellis declared during his recovery from the cigarette, 'fried, and in lots of batter.'

'The British,' Mr Choi said earnestly, leaning forward and folding his hands neatly on the empty desktop, 'they really like their fish cooked in butter? This is a surprise. In Chis-Wick, West London, there was no such custom to my knowledge.'

'Batter, Mr Choi,' Ellis said impatiently, 'we cook the bloody things in batter.'

'This batter. My knowledge of English indicates that *batter* is a verb denoting violence, visited on one thing or person by another.'

The king fighter performed another pass, seeming to reserve a special look for Mr Choi.

'True, it's a verb,' Ellis explained patiently, 'but in the cooking sense, batter comes from beating eggs together for about two minutes. Then you add the flour, maybe some milk, not too much, then you dip the fish in the mixture and drop the whole lot into a fry pan.'

'An' ya cook the fuckin' thing for two minutes, no more,' yelled Anderson from the far side, apparently not out of earshot.

'Is that true, Mr Ellis? Only two minutes?' Mr Choi cast an impatient look at Anderson.

'I'm sure it doesn't really matter. Depends on how you like it. I do mine for about three to four minutes. That's the British way. Maybe the Yanks do it different. Dunno.' Ellis nodded at Anderson, suggestive of an American competitor.

'Mr Anderson. He is also British. Even English, I think; you'll need to ask. He likes to tell me about America. I know about America. I was once in Louisiana. You know it?'

'No.'

A short silence descended. Ellis gazed at the tank, aching for some sleep.

'These fish you like, behind me? You like to eat? Cook first, perhaps?'

'Sorry, Mr Choi.' Ellis hesitated. 'I'd like to hit the fuckers with a hammer and eat them raw.'

'No butter?'

'Nope. No batter, no butter, no nothing. Just raw.'

'Dear me,' interjected Mr Choi with maternal concern, 'then just how would you eat them, as a British man … I mean, no cooking?'

Ellis rose from his chair. Mr Choi looked on in some surprise as Ellis walked round behind the Korean to the rear of the power table and removed the lid from the tank. Mr Choi looked alarmed at the intrusion by a subordinate on his side of the table and the developing swathe of condensation falling from the cover and nearly splashing onto the polished surface of the tabletop. He grasped a tissue from the embroidered box nearby and mopped the desktop and floor fussily. When Ellis placed the tank lid on the desktop, Mr Choi became uncharacteristically concerned and worried, his face a sea of anxiety, one elbow on the table, the other feverishly cleaning his space.

'Watch this, Mr Choi,' Ellis called cheerfully as he plunged a hand into the warm water of the tank and stirred the water, forcing the king fighter into a declared position of defeat. Ellis splashed his hands happily, Anderson shouting encouragement, then lunged a hand in the direction of a silver-tailed guppy, withdrew quickly. With the hand covered in splashes and deflected light, he mimicked the consumption of a raw fish by opening his mouth wide and possibly dropping the fish straight into his throat.

'Mr Ellis!' Choi exploded. 'These fish are not expendable, they should not be eaten. Company rules.' Choi making up the rules on the hoof. 'I absolutely forbid you to demonstrate your English customs in such a way.'

Choi pulled himself to his feet and indicated to Ellis that he should return to the other side of the table.

'Sorry, chief,' mimed Ellis as he returned to the chair on the other side, still chewing and enjoying the joke. Laughter from Anderson suggested the initiation ceremony was complete.

Mr Choi restored his composure and his smile by taking his seat with no one but the fish behind him. But even Mr Choi was beginning to wonder about the fish following this outrage.

But then he had a hospital to build, so Korean customs regarding consumption of fish or alternatives suggested by British revisionists were irrelevant. The project was the thing; that was what paid the bills at home, paid the salaries, kept Madame happy with all the remittances home. Those kept the children happy, and all the family was happy. Not quite the same as in Chis-Wick, West London, but near enough. They were all back home in Seoul. Why not here? The separation made Mr Choi more anxious, more depressed, but it paid him more money. Someday he would go home and retire somewhere, early, hopefully, lots of money. Mr Choi leaned back in his chair, arms folded behind his head, and sighed some sort of fond remembrance of home.

They probably don't swear in Chis-Wick, Ellis concluded as he nodded to Mr Choi and returned across the shack where Anderson sat, twiddling his thumbs and offering some admiring glances in the direction of his new recruit.

'You'll do, matey.' Anderson chuckled as Ellis walked back towards his empty desk. 'Showed that yellow motherfucker just what's what.' Anderson paused. 'Dog eatin' fuck pigs … ha-ha, ya jumped him, that Mr Fuckin' Choi. We gotta drink to that.'

Anderson's mood suddenly changed. 'Ed!'

'Yes, sir.' Ed appeared from among a pile of papers.

'Ed, go get that other creep from UK.' With that, Anderson tossed the keys at his assistant. 'He might be at the hotel by now. Otherwise he's fired.'

'Yes, sir,' Ed agreed, failing the catch. He retrieved the keys from the floor with a suitable gesture of humility, stupidity, or grace; it was hard to tell. Ed saluted the guv'nor, performed a brief, complicated ritual around his wrist with the key ring, and fled back into the glare of the reality of the day.

'Ellis!' Anderson yelled at his new subordinate, seated no more than twenty feet away. 'Ellis, come 'ere. You're due for ya first tutorial.' Ellis fussed with his suitcases. 'An' don't bother unpacking all the gear now.'

Anderson laughed, looking around for someone to share his crumb of humour, but nobody heard nor cared. 'You can share out ya condoms tonight. Gonna need 'em, ya know, cuz tonight's party night. Thursday night. Always party night.'

Ellis smiled weakly and, collecting a pen and a file of papers from his briefcase, joined Anderson at the opposite side of his dust-encrusted desk.

Anderson pushed the piles of papers on the desktop, creasing them, some falling to the floor, waving to Ellis not to pick them up. That was Ed's job. Anderson ripped open a new pack of gum, put his cigarettes in front of him, pulled out two, lit one for each of them, passed one to Ellis. Both inhaled deeply and in silence. Only the whirr of the ailing bearings of the wall-mounted air conditioner broke the silence. Ellis watched the smoke curdle and weave as it danced through the sunlight above his head.

'One day God invented the world,' Anderson broke the silence with this unexpected revelation, 'and in general he made a mighty fine job. Then, like the rest of us, he once had a real heavy night, which left him feelin' shitty the followin' day. Bit like you feel now.'

Ellis nodded agreement, thankful that his unease had been recognised.

'Yeh, so God gets outta bed, he does a coupla dumps, takes some salts, still feels shitty, pukes, then invents this fuckin' place.'

'Which place?' Ellis asked innocently.

'This fuckin' place,' Anderson trilled, 'Saudi A-r-a-bia, that's where!'

'Oh.'

'Is that all you can say? Oh?' Anderson shook his head angrily.

'What do you expect me to say? "Oh yes, Mr Anderson, you're quite correct. God did hit the schnapps a bit heavy and felt shitty and invented this place"?'

'Come 'ere.' Anderson leaped from his chair, walked around his desk, pulled Ellis to his feet, and dragged him across the dusty floor to the doorway of their workplace. He yanked the door open and held it as a Korean worker urinated over the wing of Mr Choi's car. Ignoring the indiscretion, Anderson pressed on, 'Don't look at the project or the site. Look over there. What d'yer see?'

Ellis's eyes looked towards high buildings, low buildings, gilded buildings, mosques, houses, banks, and places of commerce, all of them tightly knit together, at least tight by Saudi standards. Plenty of space by central London standards, probably by Chis-Wick standards too.

Anderson followed both of Ellis's eyes one at a time as they studied the vista in detail. Not detecting any sense of response, he continued to speak. 'I know what ya thinkin', smart buildings, nice street lights, all with lotsa space around about. Let me tell you, Ellis.' Anderson turned and planted a vicious stare into one of Ellis's eyes. 'When God woke up and felt shitty, he invented the asshole of the world. All of it built on sand. First he put in the sand, and then he put in the fuckin' Bedouins, and then the bastard gave them all the oil they'd need until about the fuckin' year two thousand

and seventy-five or somethin'. And then he gave them minerals to keep them goin' for another five hundred years, so the bastards started buildin' smart-ass buildings with lifts and Pepsi machines, and idiots like us come out here and flog ourselves to death in a place built of sand, and all of it invented when God had an off day.'

Anderson sighed, shook his head, and seemed calmed at the end of his monologue.

His calm lasted until Ellis nodded and simply said, 'How interesting.'

'Is that all you can say? How interestin'?' Anderson exploded, chewing more maniacally at the gum, flicking the cigarette butt angrily towards the drying pool of urine alongside Mr Choi's car. 'Mate, these fuckin' bastards don't do nothin'. They sit on their asses doin' nothin', and then they invent residents' visas so the likes of you an' me come 'ere an' flog our asses off, six days a week, and then we go back home and die of yellow fever or somethin' equally bloody infectious.'

'Bitter, aren't we, Mr Anderson?'

Anderson turned smartly, pulled the front of Ellis's shirt, and swung his face to within an inch of his own. 'Listen, motherfucker, you come here with your cleaner than clean, I'm so fuckin' pretty and perfect, you come in here with your missionary zeal, like to tell me that God didn't have a shitty day and that all A-rabs are really quite decent, and you're quite happy to be here, this is the fuckin' zenith of your life.' Anderson pushed Ellis away. Ellis stumbled as the combination of Anderson letting the door slip and pushing him away propelled him towards the Korean's car.

Ellis wondered momentarily about home. He straightened himself, then hit Anderson with an equally meaningful stare.

'Perhaps,' Ellis suggested sweetly, 'when God had his shitty day, probably on the day he invented diarrhoea, he also invented America. Trouble is, he forgot which was which.'

Ellis turned dismissively and walked round Anderson and returned to the fetid heat, smell, and darkness of the bear cage.

Anderson followed, lighting another cigarette as angrily as it is possible to light a cigarette, chewed gum with more venom than ever, then shouted at Ellis, 'Dontcha give me no shit, Ellis. You need me.' The Ellis was sneered.

'I'm sure I do,' Ellis concurred sarcastically.

The two men went their separate ways as Mr Choi watched them with a sense of desperation that these white faces never seem to get along, then turned and looked at the king fighter cruising, pouting, and posing. Self-assured bastard. If only he knew.

Choi went back to his papers. Anderson returned to his. Ellis had little to do until Anderson defined his job. Anderson was in no mood, apparently, to teach anyone anything. So what to do?

It was a good start for day one. Thankfully and without warning, the door opened, and Ed, the Filipino upon whom all things seemed to depend, cheerily informed nobody in particular that the new guest had arrived. After some delay at the airport, that was.

'Mr Anderson, sir?' Ed ventured close to the Presence.

'Yeh, what is it Ed?' said Anderson.

'Mr Clitle, sir.' Ed giggled by way of introduction, obviously having screwed up his well-practised pronunciation of a name never encountered. Shit, he'd gone over it again and again with Mr Er, all the way in the forty-five minutes it took from the airport to the site.

Mr Er, Mr Clitle, whoever, stood at six foot six, a wild ginger beard and piercing blue eyes. A man of action, Anderson anticipated. A very big man indeed. A man to watch. Not like that creep Ellis.

What do I do with a man like this, mused Anderson as the giant strode meaningfully towards the moment of introduction. Yeh, that's it. Rubbish him.

The giant pushed Ed to one side. And held out a large hand. In the last second before contact, Anderson recognised a fellow being. The way he pushed Ed aside. He had been here before. He knew the routine, the treatment of the scumbags. First you rejected Koreans absolutely, Thais definitely, Filipinos less so. Then you spat on Syrians, Egyptians, and Sudanese if you could get away with it. Yemenis, by common consent, could be spat on by anybody. Even by one of their own considerable number. In the middle of papers on Anderson's desk, he had lost his practice notes on the pronunciation of the second recruit's surname. The hand loomed, then made contact.

'Mr Anderson.' The giant smiled and crushed Anderson's hand. 'I'm Klitowski.' Then he beamed more so.

Crush the bastard, thought Anderson, running for some form of defence.

'Any relation to Clitt-oris?' Anderson spat at the man.

'Very imaginative, I'm sure.' The giant sighed. 'No, my name has no association with the female clitoris, although my tongue does.' The giant laughed loudly, his boom seeming to shake the walls.

'So what do we call you?' Anderson asked in his moment of defeat.

'Clitty.'

'Not Bruce, or Digger, or Shitface. No? Just Clitty?'

'You got it.'

The giant fixed Anderson with an uneasy stare, the gesture reciprocated, and for good reason. Clitty had considerable experience of turnkey projects in the eastern province of Saudi Arabia and had some reputation. Anderson remembered his own life spent in the western province, on the make. Perhaps Clitty had done the same. Anderson thought and worried, my God do I know this man! I'd be sure to remember his height, his presence and hair colouring, so what's his form? I only have his CV. Yet Saudi Arabia was the size of Western Europe. Would a person working, say, in Portugal be expected to know somebody working in Germany?

Never mind all that. Sit down for coffee and have another stab at levelling the giant. Yes. He's late for duty. That's enough.

We'll have him for that.

With some strained suggestion of relaxation, Anderson indicated to Clitty that he should sit. Coffee was ordered, cigarettes passed around.

Ellis pushed pieces of paper around his desktop, awaiting the summons from his new guv'nor.

Interesting, Ellis thought. This new guy was on last night's flight. Wonder what happened at the airport?

Anderson yelled for Ed. Ed obeyed and received some form of instruction. Anderson's eyes looked towards Ellis – at least one eye was looking at Ellis – while Ed's eyes were following anywhere he felt they should go.

Ed approached Ellis. 'Sorry, sir. Mr Anderson say you are at the wrong table. This is for Mister – um, the new mister, sir.'

'Fair enough, Ed.' Ellis sighed, receiving a glower from Anderson but a friendly wink from the giant. 'Where should I sit? Where do you suggest? Saint Peter's Basilica? Or maybe at the Wailing Wall of Jerusalem?'

'That's enough fuckin' shit from you, Ellis,' Anderson bellowed. 'Any mention of alternative religions, 'specially the fuckin' Jews, is a hangin' offence. Islam rules here, goddit?'

'Bollocks,' the giant intoned easily. He removed another cigarette from Anderson's pack, lighting only one for himself, then sighed and rubbed away last night's flight from his tired eyes and mind.

'Pardon me?' Anderson questioned fiercely.

'You heard me, Anderson. Bollocks. That old religious stuff is for the kids. Here we survive on our own, no religion, no nothing – just building a hospital, pay, and then home. *Inshallah*.' The giant smiled, the words used by all Muslims afflicted by uncertainty. You have a plan, it will all come right if God pleases: *inshallah*. You didn't even need to try to make the plan come right. You said *inshallah*; then, if it came right, you said 'thanks be to God'. If it didn't, you forgot you'd made the plan in the first place.

'So don't pick up my friend over here because he makes a joke that a Filipino can't begin to understand.' The giant finished the cigarette and threw the butt at Anderson's ashtray, the butt skimming the edge and then twirling across the table to land by Anderson's coffee cup.

'He ain't your friend.' Anderson cursed, picked up the butt, and tossed it to the floor, where his boots spread it across the shadows of the desk.

'Mr Clitoris,' Anderson snarled, 'you may wish to defend your pitiful English friend over there, but I gotta tell you who's in charge here, the line of command.'

The giant laughed such that all the Egyptian draughtsmen, the Korean supervisors, the Filipino tea-boys and bearers, the Indian boys whose jobs seemed ill defined, and the British equipment procurement officials stopped their work, stunned into silence, and stood stock-still.

'Anderson,' the giant bellowed, drawing himself from his chair to his full, formidable height, 'Anderson, I know you, and if you pull all that fuckin' old crap about "I'm in charge" and all your pseudo-fuckin' American twang and all your problems with your bowels and your contact lenses and your dry eyes and your top spin …' The giant paused. 'If I hear any of that shit, I'm going to rip you apart. And if you try to deny you are a British citizen, here and now, I'm going to rip your head off. Then I'll get on the plane and go home.'

Anderson froze, wondering if rage had the upper hand over the fear of a hammering from this man. The man had his face within an inch of Anderson's. Anderson noted the aftershave. One of his eyes seemed focused on the clock on the wall, the other on the face, but in truth the giant's face filled both aberrant eyes. He was that close.

Anderson began to tremble. Everyone believed him to be American. He spoke like one if he remembered, a habit he could hardly break; he even thought like one. He couldn't deny this. But to admit it to all the Third World boys who held Anderson in some awe, it represented a major insult.

And a victory for the giant.

Ellis remembered the words of Choi: 'He's British, maybe English.' Then, realising he had an ally in the giant, he stood up, walked slowly towards the confrontation, and bravely took up station beside but a little behind the newest and strongest recruit.

'So what d'ya say?' The giant mimicked an American accent, 'you admit you're British after all and that all your goddamn this and slam dunk and cookies and gee and how 'bout that and all of that fuckin' old cobblers is a load of cobblers?' The giant put both hands on Anderson's desk. 'How about it, you goddamned freak?'

Anderson could stand it no more. He leaped to his feet and grabbed the giant by his shirt and tried to pull him across the table, at which point Mr Choi, tiring of the interruptions to his thoughts of Seoul, called gently to Anderson to let go.

'I ain't gonna let go of this shit,' Anderson bellowed feverishly, sweat pouring down his face, one eye on Choi, the other on the giant's chest. 'Choi, you gotta get rid of this sonofabitch.'

'So nice to see the First World at war with itself,' Mr Choi commented drily as he walked to the site of the conflict.

The giant released his grip, and Anderson slumped into the safety of his chair.

The giant was smiling.

'Mr Klitowski?' Mr Choi began, and at not a great deal more than half the giant's height, it was a brave beginning. 'We conduct our endeavours on the grounds of harmony. If you would be good enough to come to my desk, we may begin to describe the job laid out for you?'

'Sure.' The giant had a smile for Choi, a friendly wink for Ellis, and a dismissive glance at Anderson. He walked to Choi's table for a meaningful discussion on the project's programme, objectives, and timetable.

Mr Choi settled himself at his table, called for coffee, and offered Klitowski a Korean cigarette, Choi taking one for himself. Both smoked them in a few seconds. Choi picked up some official-looking documents, glanced at them, and began to speak just as coffee was served.

'Your surname, for a British, it's very unusual,' Mr Choi began easily.

'It's a Polish name. Parents came over in World War Two. The name's Klitowski. There had been an umlaut on a U, something to do with a family connection with Germany, but at some point some a typist thought it was an I and the Klitowski has stuck ever since.'

The Korean, with no knowledge of Polish, nodded knowledgeably, read the papers some more, and then, seeing the giant's interest in the fish tank, changed the subject and asked about fish.

The giant explained he couldn't give a shit about fish and what about the job? He was only looking at the king fighter on the rampage, and anyway it was something to look at.

Mr Choi smiled and changed the subject.

'Mr Klitowski,' Mr Choi corrected the official transcript, 'what are we to call you?'

'Mr Klitowski will do.'

'Mr Klitowski, this is a friendly place …'

'Could have fooled me.'

'Is there some sort of name we could use to address you, a name that conveys a friendship? After all, we call Mr Anderson, Anderson. Is there nothing we could use?'

'Clitty. I suppose.'

'You only suppose?'

'Yes.'

'Mr Clitty, when I was in Chis-Wick in London, I met many British people—'

'I suppose you would.'

Mr Choi pressed on undeterred. 'These people had what you call a nickname? Is that your very own nickname?'

'Yup.'

'OK.' Mr Choi smiled. 'Clitty it is.' Choi rejoiced at having placated the giant, but the outright hatred between Anderson and Clitty worried him. 'One more thing. I cannot allow you to abuse Anderson in such a way as just now.' Choi lit another cigarette and pondered the face. 'What is it that harbours such loathing?'

Clitty sat in stony silence, just looking around, but avoiding Choi's direct stare.

'It could help us all if you were to tell me,' Choi added, not unreasonably.

Clitty's silence was not to be broken. Not just yet.

'Very well,' Choi said. 'I will ask Mr Anderson to show you to your desk.'

A whirring and banging from an excavator close to the building drowned Clitty's reply. The building shuddered and the dust rose, thickening the rays of the sun as they penetrated the filth of the unwashed windows.

Clitty avoided Anderson's poisonous gaze and walked directly to the only available table in sight, sat down, pulled open each drawer in turn, looking, checking, picked up the receiver of the telephone, dialled some numbers, and discovered his extension only allowed local, not international calls.

Anderson smiled as he watched the blasted man checking his territory. Only Choi and Anderson had international telephone lines. Thank God. How else could one do the real business? Clitty could go to hell and make local calls.

Anderson caught sight of Clitty approaching his table, so busied himself in papers describing the exact specifications for a mortuary. Just to read anything was a relief. Clitty's footfall shook the flooring as he approached.

'Anderson?' Clitty began. 'I owe you an apology.'

'Oh?' Anderson looked up, relieved to be spared another mauling.

'Yeh. I had thought you were the project engineer.'

'Go on,' Anderson insisted.

'Then when I just saw you reading the drawings for the mortuary, which any old stiff knows is about the last part of the hospital to be equipped so no reason to be looking at that department yet, I realised,' Clitty sighed, 'you really are what everyone said you are. A complete arsehole.'

'OK, Klitowski. You've had your say.' Anderson was hard pushed to retain his composure. 'But tell me one thing. What is it that makes you so, so angry, so bloody agitated? I'm ya boss, ya know, an' I can have ya thrown out,' Anderson clicked his fingers loudly, 'just – like – that.'

'You can't, you know.' Clitty smiled back certainly.

'Why not? We have your passport, we get the tickets, we get a limo to take you to the airport, and then, *marsalaama*, goodbye dipstick.'

'Maybe, but before I get thrown out, I mention to the ministry, maybe even the police, that they might like to look at your bank account.'

The words hung in the air.

So that was the giant's game. He may have known of the Jeddah scam; more likely he knew the rumours of the Jeddah scam …. the Jeddah scam … oh, what a scam …

The Jeddah scam had come about when the Saudi Ministry of Health decided it needed a five-hundred-bed hospital in a hurry. It set up a turnkey operation, an operation which would take a deserted piece of land and build all over it, in this case a hospital. Equipment was purchased, installed, inspected, and passed off by the authorities, everybody got paid, everybody got happy. Then everyone went home, still happy.

Saudis very happy to have a hospital they thought might be necessary.

To get the operation started, the usual crooked process of tendering took place. A Swedish construction outfit won the contract to build and equip the place, and all the necessary materials and personnel were assembled for the task. One of those personnel was Anderson.

What the Saudis suspected but did not know for sure was that nearly all the biomedical engineers charged with the procurement of all equipment, from operating theatres to CAT scanners to rubbish bins – all of them were on the take. Then, when the hospital was completed, the Saudis made a cursory inspection, blissfully unaware that little of the equipment actually worked, paid the contractors, who paid their staff, and everyone went home richer and happier. Only when a management company was brought in to operate the hospital for a two-year term did the level of duplicity come to light. Doors that didn't fit, operating theatres that had no anaesthetic gases piped through the conduits, bedside monitors incapable of operating on the hospital's own 110 volt 50Hz electricity supply because they were 220 volt only, ceiling mounted lamps in the dentistry department that were incapable of swivelling to focus on a patient's mouth. The Saudis were not amused. Eyes were on individuals, but no law had been broken. The Saudis had (to most people's surprise) signed off the project, so no blame was attached anywhere but on the home front.

Anderson had been put in charge of procurement of equipment in the theatres and in the intensive care unit. After many lunches and inappropriate hospitality provided by some manufacturers anxious for additional quick business – tricks involving women, drinks, holidays, more women, and cash – Anderson went for the highest bidder, signed the orders after some cursory discussions with ministry officials, took the cash. But didn't run.

Which was why Anderson was able to face down Clitty in the dust of another project site. None of the money was ever paid to him in the Kingdom. First rule: have it paid into Jersey, some account somewhere where prying eyes never rested.

Clitty caught Anderson's look of relaxation. His stomach turned into a knot. If only Anderson knew why Clitty was back. No altruistic sense of helping to advance health care in a Third World country with lotsa money. He needed the money. Not salary.

Money from the same sort of source as Anderson's, but still lodged in a Saudi bank account. Nine hundred thousand pounds, all of it lodged in a bank no more than a mile from this site. And he still had the passbook, the plastic card for the hole in the wall. All he needed was the time to send it home in dribs and drabs to avoid suspicions that an account gone quiet

Your Friday, My Sunday

for eight months was suddenly being reactivated with massive telexes out to UK or Jersey.

'OK, sucker, maybe you an' me, we talk tonight.' Anderson had seen through the giant's smile, the suggestion of innocence and simplicity, perhaps covering some secrets.

'What's tonight?' Clitty asked innocently.

'Tonight, my man, is Thursday. Party night, some drinks, some women, some good food, good conversation … if you want.'

Clitty wanted to be back home. This American creep sent shudders through most people; Clitty seemed particularly vulnerable to them at that moment.

Anderson picked up the long-lost fax, gazed at it, realised Clitty was still there, and told him to join Ellis for a while. Then he realised the fax told him good news, lots of good news, good news for the savings account. The downside was they wanted the order now. The order, for full scanner and X-ray equipment, was worth four million pounds sterling; 5 per cent for Anderson was a cosy two hundred thousand pounds, tax free, all of it paid offshore.

But the order would not come now, nor in three months, nor within the next year. Any payments made were based upon the conclusion that the order would ultimately be placed with that one supplier. Manufacturers would place quotations. Prices had to be valid for five years. A 5 per cent performance bond had to be placed with the Riyadh bank. The order would be adjudicated within a five-year span, depending on the pace of the project and the stability of the Saudi economy, currently under some stress. Anyway, all being well, a substantial order would be placed.

At least, that was the local thinking.

Elsewhere, nobody used a five-year term on their quotations; nobody quoted to anybody for anything more than one year hence. Currency fluctuations, freight costs, insurrections, political instability – all these things added to the reluctance of companies to quote further ahead than existing economic forecasts could predict. Yet this was Saudi Arabia. A prime market for selling seconds into. Get rid of the crap, argued the executives.

They got the money. We got the crap, Anderson thought.

We need the money. We got crap to get rid of.

First-generation crap for the Saudis. They bought all seconds. Look at the stuff their shops are crammed with, chortled European sales executives: prime market for stuff loaded with CFCs, prime market for stuff with expiry dates long passed but relabelled. Didn't cost much to re-label. Freed the warehouses of stuff the Europeans wouldn't buy any more. Yet some manufacturers paid lots to do business in the Gulf. They listened to people who knew; they listened to high-placed officials like Anderson; they listened to the gloss put on a market reliant on imports, state of the art, and excellence. And they paid. Oh yes. They paid very well.

Anderson made some immediate calculations on the impact of such a payment, then made some darker calculations based upon playing the same trick on another player in this particular part of the procurement exercise, then reflected that neither of them was likely to get the order in the end, the decision being made by the minister of health, who would be paid the most by yet another manufacturer. So everybody on this side won, Anderson got two tranches of two hundred thousand, the minister got who knew what, and the hospital was equipped according to specifications.

Nice. Eh?

Anderson looked up to see the giant perched on the edge of Ellis's table, chatting, smiling, laughing – a touching sight, worthy of breaking up.

'Ellis!' he bellowed, chewing madly, 'Get over here, goddammit. Quick!'

Anderson shuffled more paper, able to think of nothing else as Ellis approached. Then Anderson thought of the soft approach, an unaccustomed approach. 'Ellis, I'm kinda sorry for starting off just now, things here 'ave been a bit rough just lately …'

Ellis stood off in silence. Waiting.

Silence. Anderson moved the papers a little more, not wishing to engage Ellis's eyes. For a start, that was physically impossible, with his eyes pointing two ways. Second, he didn't really know what he wanted to say, tense from months without leave, the last two engineers dismissed for being caught by the father trying to make love to two young Saudi women, in their own home, the project dropping behind schedule, the police visits, the Saudi father making an unannounced visit to the site to claim compensation for his daughters' loss of virginity, more police, more drinking at night, more smoking, more hassle from the Koreans, oh shit … Anderson rubbed his eyes, seeming to Ellis a very vulnerable man. Perhaps a holiday would help; perhaps a good woman would do. The lure of tonight, Thursday night, weekend – there was always the promise of a good woman.

Usually it ended up in bed with a woman with a past, hiding perhaps, running probably, and just as she hit orgasm, she started crying and calling for a lost love. Then she was gone, just like the Koreans were when the project went wrong or got delayed.

Ellis stood patiently as Anderson apparently struggled through some sort of proposal.

'Ellis.'

'Yeh?'

Anderson yawned, stretched his arms, stood, smiled, and, with a look of genuine warmth, held out his right hand.

'Sorry. Welcome to the Third World.'

And shook Ellis's hand warmly.

Chapter 4

Anderson awoke with a start from a troubled sleep.

The endless cranking of a worn air conditioner competed with the sound of the call to prayer from the mosque, no more than thirty feet from his window, and competed with the grunting and snoring from the remaining members of the Thursday night party, too drunk to stand and now scattered throughout the apartment. Initially the imam's call to the faithful won. 'Allah Akbar!' he yelled from an amplified sound system. 'God is great.' Then he did the whole thing again, this time the Allahu Akbar sung almost as a hymn. Almost a serene invitation. But at ten minutes past four in the morning, the moment of sunrise, few people would stir; few really cared. Most would turn over and return to their rest. Except that Anderson could not. Still tasting the home-made wine at the back of his throat, the taste of yeasts, the gritty taste of hooch, Anderson thought to go to the bathroom for some form of refreshment. Then he tried what so many do after a night of indulgence. He tried to remember.

He remembered the nurses arriving by limousine. Some were all right, some good for laying, some pretty awful, some bearing clear evidence of exposure to the cold draught of loneliness. They all arrived made up, some pretty, some average. Anderson admired his own tastes in women; they generally turned heads and made love to Anderson generously. He had a list of them, all captivated by his charm, his wit, his bizarre eyes, and his American way of expressing himself. He could call on most of them, most of the time. An unending stream of women, if he wanted.

Last night's bedmate lay next to him, sighing gently in sleep, murmuring softly, reaching for Anderson for some loving, some more loving, some more of last night's drunken coupling, stroking Anderson's hair in the darkness, rubbing his chest, caressing his thigh with a soft hand almost reaching there, almost. The hand stopped, waiting for a response. Anderson felt a stirring, a desire. Really he should have some mouthwash, make love properly, say the right things without the early morning bad breath putting things in jeopardy. The bathroom seemed a long way off; maybe he could cry out without breathing toxic fumes, keep his mouth shut. That seemed like the only way.

He reached out, desire now firmly requiring attention. He groaned expectantly and held his partner, who sighed softly, turned, and presented into Anderson's hand a fully blown, early day erection.

'Ya filthy shit!' Anderson bellowed, jumping from the bed and tearing the duvet from it, exposed a sleepy Filipino driver with an erection, doing nothing to hide his vanity. 'Get outta this fuckin' bed, you ravin' queen!'

The Filipino leaned across and turned on the bedside light with some deliberation, looked at Anderson in his nakedness, and smiled.

Anderson tightened his buttocks in his fury, then felt the wet. Then he remembered. Then he exploded. Pulling on a pair of discarded pants from the floor, he picked up the queen. Shouting and screaming obscenities at him, he staggered to the door of the apartment, struggled to open the door with the queen on his shoulder, then threw him across the landing. He slammed the door tight shut and left him to make his way home. Naked.

Anderson slammed the door, hoping no one had seen or heard.

As Anderson stepped quietly back to his bed, he looked around to see people – girls, women, men – lying on settees, some on the floor, some cuddling in their sleep ... Thank God, all of them seemed to be asleep.

All except Clitty, who cheerfully sat up, smiled, complimented Anderson on his choice of woman, asked if Anderson would like tea, got a withering look, turned over on the floor, and went back to rubbing his companion's ample breasts.

Quite a party.

If only Anderson could remember. Remember the when and the how.

Nothing much else mattered. How to explain to subordinates with whom he lived the exact truth about last night. They would nod knowingly, smile, and tell anyone who would listen that the guv'nor was queer, and then that would get out to all the ladies. They weren't going to drop them for a man more interested in boys' bums.

Anderson lay down on the bed, wishing he could disinfect the whole place, expunge all traces. It was obviously a mistake. I'm a ladies' man, he thought as he lowered his head to the pillow and smelled that man's Estée Lauder. But he did like that perfume. Some of his best loves had worn it. One in particular, he couldn't remember the name. Yvonne, yes, that was her name. Seattle. Yes. That was her. Smart piece of kit that was.

Anderson rubbed his eyes, yawned, rubbed his crutch for good measure, thrusting his pelvis rhythmically into the mattress as he remembered Yvonne. He remembered her smile, those perfect white teeth, her body, her breasts, that silk scarf she wore around her neck even when they made love, she on top, calling to him. Now in the twilight morn he could only return to a sea of memories, a world of dreams, a world where Anderson won, and a world that would, when he awoke, now probably crucify him for just one peccadillo. The confusion of dreams and reality altered by drink drowned Anderson as he slept. All he did was sleep. And regret, and think up excuses about the queen. And then, too tired to think, he slept all day.

Which was a pity because all the guests recovered, took showers, laughed at Anderson as he slept, had breakfast, sat around waiting for limousines to take them home for a decent sleep. They would have good baths first, wash away the stains of drunken and hurried coupling. The sun took on its characteristic Saudi glare: few shadows, nowhere to hide. And then somebody started to clear the glasses, empty ashtrays, people getting busy, nobody wanting to do anything but sleep quietly in their own beds, and for as long as they needed. The social requirements to be happy and loud now expired. Nobody cared who smelt like what. Nobody was interested in who worked where or what they liked to doing in their free time, nor where they went for their holidays. Everybody needed some sleep. Women had no qualities at this time of day; the men were simply other people, equally incapable of any coupling. If dates had not been arranged in the whirl and fever of Thursday night, then they never would be. It was as simple as that.

Anderson snored loudly as the last guests left. They paid him the compliment of a dismissive sneer. Ellis and Clitty finished the clearing up, then went back to bed, where all three of them slept soundly until Isha prayer, about five minutes to eight in the evening. Half an hour later they would eat in silence, none of them wanting to talk about the main event that Anderson had created. They would eat some concoction from a multi freezer, drink some more wine, and then sleep again. Sleep until get-up time at six on Saturday morning, the start of another week.

Then a shower, a snatch to eat, and eleven hours on site. Such was life to an expatriate worker in the Kingdom of Saudi Arabia.

'Ed!' Anderson yelled with a typically savage assault for Saturday, first day back and early.

'Yes, sir.' Ed rose brightly from his small table and walked towards Anderson. When he saw the Filipino approach, he winced and wondered if he'd defiled Ed or whoever it was.

Without question the news would be out in the vast male Filipino community in Riyadh. If the man Anderson had called a queen cared to badmouth the 'American', then Anderson was in trouble. All sorts would happen.

First. Anderson would command Ed to do something. Ed might feign failure to understand the command. Then Anderson might want to go to the bank to get some money. The Filipino in charge of the electronic teller might be tipped off to block Anderson's PIN number. 'Refer to main branch', the message adding to Anderson's frustration, just to make life difficult.

If only he'd been nice to the faggot. Because the Filipino wide boy, gay boy, lady boy, worked on the electronic teller at the Riyadh Bank, Malaz branch, where Anderson banked, and from where he sent all his moneys home, wherever. If anyone could block transactions of this type, it was the man who had slept with and made love to Anderson at that party.

'Ed,' Anderson began quietly as the boy stood close by, eyes twinkling, Ellis and Clitty watching from a distance. 'Ed …'

Anderson creased and worried his hands, eyes watching Choi and the clock and the shadows and Ellis. 'Ed … any faxes in?'

'No, sir.'

'Shit.'

'Nothing for the tray. One, though, for sir's attention.' Ed returned to his desk, opened the top drawer, furtively walked around Anderson's back, and laid a fax from London on top of the pile of quotations and begging letters.

'Medmark.' Anderson groaned as he saw the London-based company's eagle crest, the letter signed by the director. This meant only one thing. Calling in the favour.

'Dear Mr Anderson,' the fax began, 'following extensive consultations and a review of the project's technical and clinical specifications, we are pleased to advise that, following your positive indication of ministry approval, our XS1900 system is fully modified and ready for final testing prior to shipment. We would respectfully request that you may care to inspect the tests on site, at the same time making any final financial adjustments to the overall package. Yours, etc. ...'

'Offer a bigger bribe,' Anderson muttered under his breath. Anyway, Medmark's offer was way in excess of Siemens' offer, and Siemens could offer full cat-scanning facilities in the satellite hospitals, via data linking, at no additional cost. But no bribe, no baksheesh.

The trouble was, Anderson had promised Medmark the order in return for some favours.

So had the Ministry of Health, via the office of Mr Walid, who had committed to approving a Japanese proposal in return for flying his family to America, at a time when his wife was about to give birth. The baby would be born in the USA, would then get an American passport, and in time the whole family would get to leave this dusty place and settle in comfortable retirement in a civilised place.

So the Japanese company and Medmark both felt they had the order. The local distributor for Philips, the other X-ray manufacturer of note, had been in, made their bid, and offered no money. Anderson himself had assured them of a favourable response.

Anderson dismissed Ed, rubbed weary eyes, watched Ed sway back across the room, saw the shit was about to hit the fan, and wondered how he might fill this Saturday with anything other than the thought of three X-ray companies all thinking they had the business. Two of them had paid good money based upon certain understandings, and both of them likely to call at any time. At least it was Saturday; nobody worked in Europe on Saturdays. That gave him, Anderson, two days of peace. But suppose Medmark called today? Some keen sales manager? Oh shit.

Your Friday, My Sunday

'Ellis! Clitoris! Get over here.'

Ellis put down the paper, glanced at Clitty, nodded. Both men walked slowly to Anderson's place.

'Yes?' Clitty sneered.

'I'm talkin' ta Ellis, Mr Klitowski.'

'Please yourself.' Clitty shrugged his shoulders but added, not quite inaudibly enough, 'Ducky.'

Ellis nodded agreeably but was ill prepared for what followed.

Anderson's temples seemed to swell and pulsate, eyes almost rotating. He changed colour, then leaped full force over the top of his table at Clitty who easily rocked back on his heels and caught his flying supervisor. 'Clitoris, you're a dead man, ya hear me?' Anderson trembled in his rage, engaging one of Clitty's eyes with a look of loathing, Clitty holding his boss by the shirt. Clitty smiled, held Anderson a little higher so that he could be sure that both Anderson's eyes could focus on his face. Still he smiled, Anderson struggling for breath, anger rising further, Clitty almost holding the man clear of the table. He looked around him for witnesses, then hurled Anderson across the table to come to rest a few paces wide of his power chair.

Anderson landed on the floor and, drawing a sweaty hand across a fearful face, he began thinking through an appropriate response.

Clitty beat him to it.

'Mr Anderson, why don't you suck my dick?'

Anderson was capable of no more rage. Choi watched his new arrivals with an evident sense of inevitability. Obviously the British behaved like this.

Choi walked towards Anderson's table, just to check on things, and when Anderson saw Choi's eyes on the Medmark fax still splayed across the desktop, he regained his composure, put the place in order, and explained there was some sort of misunderstanding which he would sort out immediately, Mr Choi, sir.

'Get back to your places, Mr Ellis and Mr Klitowski, please. This is a place of honour and of peace.'

Clitty turned and muttered to anyone who might hear, 'Bollocks. The only peace we're going to get here is the peace after Anderson's orgasm with a boy. And that's on Thursdays. Rest of the time it's more of this.'

Choi heard and smiled. 'Back to work, Mr Klitowski, please.'

Anderson wondered why God had selected him for this, then decided he would need to show the new boys, especially that bloody Clitoris, how hospitals should be built and how they should be equipped. Learn the lessons of experience.

With some sense of missionary zeal, he approached the rookies and told them to get in the car and get to learn something from an expert.

Ellis joined in quietly. Clitty thought twice but reckoned it was better than a day in this chicken coop.

So into sir's Lexus, Ed given shouted instructions. Then the three of them headed up the Dammam highway to the National Guard Hospital, a five-hundred-bed edifice, fifteen miles from the city centre. Built in the dust and sand of another desolate site, the National Guard Hospital had been completed in 1985, at great expense, and completed contemporaneously with an identical facility close to the Jeddah coastline, a site some six hundred miles to the west. The identical layout of both hospitals was to prove a source of confusion to visiting trade representatives, who, on exiting the hospital, were none the wiser as to where they were, Jeddah or Riyadh. Everything looked the same; everything felt the same; everything was all hot, steamy, and very Saudi.

Both of them sucked, Anderson concluded as they approached the gates of the Riyadh hospital. Triggering his electric-winding window, he drew up at the entry barrier and began to berate the security personnel. They didn't understand. He didn't have an appointment, and sorry, the hospital was not open to sightseers. Anderson shouted louder in the vain hope of driving home some understanding.

The security men nodded, shook their heads, looked at all the three men's papers. Problem. Oh yes, problem.

'Listen, shitbag,' Anderson yelled above the sound of his own engine. 'We need to come in. *Comprendo?*'

'No speak Inglish, mister. You no come in.' The gatekeeper threw back all the papers and closed his windows against the heat. Anderson remembered there was a biomed engineer here once, a guy he'd served with in Jeddah. Was he here?

Your Friday, My Sunday

Anderson engaged gear and once again engaged the security man. Sliding open the glass window indulgently, the man awaited the next excuse.

'Mr Michael Moore,' Anderson yelled through all the heat and dust. 'Let me see him.'

The car engine purred. The air conditioner cut in, then out, decisions to be made. No. No Michael Moore. Then the security guard was reminded by a colleague behind the smoked glass that *BBC World Service News* was about to begin.

Turning a blind eye to the twisted eyes of the driver, the security man nodded, again passed back the papers, and pressed the button to raise the barrier and allow all three into the site that Anderson referred to when raising procurement standards for his own project.

The Lexus slowly prowled to the generously sized parking area, reached by following the contours of the single-storey, red-brick building, quite ordinary really, no great effort made to reflect any Arabic architecture or culture. A gentle building.

'Let's start where most patients end up,' Anderson began cheerfully, 'in the morgue.

'OK, you two, see this,' Anderson shouted as he pulled open the doors of the mortuary fridges. 'Six slots but only space for five corpses. The door's too low. See, they put the body on this metal tray here, transfer it onto this mechanical hoist here, but the hoist only reaches to the fifth slot, cuz the bloody door gets in the way. So, Mr Clitoris, s'pose you never made such a fuck-up at Dammam, everythin' just fine and dandy. Eh?'

'Some of us have standards, Anderson, though I doubt you'd understand anything about that.' Clitty smiled the smile of an experienced operator, though frustrated at being treated as a novice by this Yank. Ellis was a novice, decent guy though, plenty of clinical experience, good man, good to work with, but this cretin with weird eyes and piles and headaches and fancy boys …

Anderson slammed the fridge door tight as he realised he would exert no impact upon this damn giant, Mr Polish Vagina, desperately thinking of some corruption of the Polish surname that nobody would have thought of before … clitoris was already done, vagina didn't rhyme. Maybe something infectious? Maybe Mr Syphilis. Anus perhaps. None of it would do; the whole psychological challenge defeated Anderson as he tried to think of somewhere else to go to show up the bloody man.

Plus, the bloody man had huge hands, was built like a bear. Not a man to throw around like those bloody faggots. And thinking of faggots, Anderson remembered Thursday night. The effort of slamming the fridge door had loosened something in Anderson's abdomen, and excusing himself with some hurried anxiety, he disappeared from the mortuary to leave Ellis and Clitty to talk the sort of sense absent from their leader.

'Ellis?' Clitty broke the silence. 'How long d'you reckon you can put up with that prick?'

''Bout the same length of time as you, I suppose,' Ellis declared inconclusively with a shrug of the shoulders.

'Got kids? Got missus?'

'Did have.'

'Thought so.'

'What makes you say that?' Ellis enquired, anxious that some sort of badge may be nailed to his forehead.

'Oh, not a lot really. It's just a sense, a sense of longing. You go off with some stares lasting some time, you're thinking, you're going through a mill of thought. All that ends up is you get spat out in small pieces, no questions answered. Still the turmoil, still you remember – bet you thought you'd get away from all that regret coming here?'

Ellis thought and agreed. The pain never resolved; the regrets remained. He'd hoped that all the shouting and all the discord from a disaffected ex-wife would subside. But it didn't and never would. Even at Thursday night's party, he'd danced through songs with another woman, songs he'd danced through with his wife when they saw eye to eye on most things, and love overcame the ups and downs. The normal turbulence of marriage. But the marriage collapsed and the songs went on, the memories of the songs returning to times of loving recollection but no relationship within which to share loving feelings.

Just like a cold box. Dark and cold. Just like this bloody mortuary. Rather dark, foreboding, no spirit, just very cold.

'Yeh. Did that,' Ellis responded quietly, 'How 'bout you? You come here to run away?'

'No. I came back to come back. I meant to come back. I've got some unfinished business at the bank. I'll stay six months, if I have to. Trouble is that arsehole has as much idea how to build a hospital as I do of how to split the atom. It's a two-year contract; can't say I'll do much of it.'

'What will you do instead?' Ellis asked innocently.

Clitty did not wish to spoil the naivety of the new recruit so made up some story of a family business in Bradford and how they needed him. He just needed a few months to put some things right.

What things, Ellis wondered. Things at the bank, a Riyadh bank? Some unfinished business? That project in Dammam, did he really screw that up or was Anderson jealous of his success there?

Seemed like Anderson was just rather envious of everybody and particularly envious of somebody whose record may exceed his own.

Anderson returned from the toilet with the tail of his shirt hanging over the rear of his trousers. Obviously a heavy session.

'Air raid. Sorry, fellas,' Anderson apologised, half smiling as he tucked himself in, struggling breathlessly to persuade his shirt behind the fastened waistband, abandoned all decorum and concluded the ablutions normally performed en suite.

'Right.' Anderson picked up his clipboard from the post mortem slab, and without attempting to catch either of his charges' eyes, he pushed past Ellis and made for the mortuary exit. 'Let's go see an ICU.'

The hospital was single storey, comprising one long corridor that performed a square. Within the square there were water gardens, tropical plants and birds, and waterfalls to relax those who knew what they were. Around the perimeter of the gardens was the corridor which fed patients and visitors into the ward areas on the outer edge.

'See, Ellis.' Anderson waved his clipboards. 'These corridors, wide, yeh?'

Ellis made a visual calculation of the width of the corridors, in his mind's eye calculating how many hospital beds, at six foot long, could be laid end to end across the widest point. He reckoned five, maybe six.

'An' ya wanna know why?' Anderson continued to address his novice student whilst studiously ignoring Clitty who followed sullenly some paces behind.

Claude Pemberton

Tell us why, smart arse, thought Clitty as he observed some sparrows washing and fighting in the outer garden, the sun throwing shards of coloured light through the splashes and across his path. Then one sparrow seemed to get the better of the other, and with some accented screeches the two of them got down to what Thursday nights were all about to the humans of this world. Thoughts of Thursdays were certainly better than this.

Clitty was absorbed in his own thoughts as Anderson droned on to Ellis about the architectural characteristics of this building; and how the hospital had wide corridors to allow beds to be put on both sides, should any act of war attract large numbers of casualties; and how the hospital was designed to set the benchmark by which future hospital projects would be completed; and how the designs were adulterated by the procurement managers, who purchased anything that met specification alongside the receipt of gratuities, substantial gratuities; and how our project – Anderson stressed the 'our' – would be the ultimate and would not fall into the ways of previous projects. This one would be squeaky clean.

'Bollocks!' Clitty yelled, bringing down hushes from some Filipino nurses taking a patient to theatre. 'Anderson, you talk such crap.'

Anderson turned quickly and found Clitty within a pace, the challenge issued but not returned. 'What's the matter with you?' he growled.

Ellis watched the standoff. He could not be sure if Anderson was more disturbed to have been interrupted in his monologue than by the insults offered.

Still the two men glowered at each other, Clitty clenching his fists, hands still by his side. 'I said, Anderson, you talk such crap. You just said how squeaky clean we have to be.' Clitty paused to chuckle, an impatient shake of his head. 'So tell me. How squeaky clean are you?'

The words hung in the air; only the sound of the sparrows broke the silence.

The question had hit home.

'Mr Clitoris,' Anderson began, his composure restored, 'your experience in this particular area of health care, and in particular in this part of the world, is perhaps flawed. To ask such a question is like saying to a hooker, just after you've shagged the daylights out of ya crutch and put her off limits for the rest of the night, that she should live a life of chastity.'

'You would know about hookers, Anderson, comin' as you do from Yorkshire. What do the girls say to you as you pull up in some hire car when you're home spending all your bribes? "Hey, come on, you honeys, give ma' man here a dose of action, I'll give ya a five buck"? I bet I know what they say as you cruise the block in a hired limo, twangin' away in your American speak, I bloody bet I know …'

Anderson was, by Ellis's judgement, holding this well. He seemed to be holding back a smile, one eye, perhaps both, twinkling. Clitty's breathing seemed, however, laboured.

Anderson was also dying for a smoke.

'Bribes, mister. The pot, as you English say, seems to be calling the kettle black.' Anderson's English was classic high-class English, pronunciation perfect, inflections measured and exquisite. That silenced Clitty. Not that Anderson had said anything of note.

Anderson, refreshed in the victory of this skirmish, laughed, turned on his heel, and declared a change of plan to allow a smoke break in the theatre staff's restroom.

For a five-hundred-bed hospital, the place was eerily quiet.

Patients seemed to be a rarity. Just hurried comings and goings of the occasional members of staff along interminable corridors, Saudi nationals with coffee flasks clasped in worried hands, making their visits with an air of suspicion about all this white man's medicine.

The staff room was heaving with Westerners.

'Anderson, you old bastard, come in. Bring your troops for some typically New Zealand hospitality.' The white-coated male jumped happily from his easy chair to wring Anderson warmly by the hand.

Typical colonials, mused Clitty, still smarting from his put-down, particularly New Zealanders. White faces, fair complexions, happy souls, just like us, but inexplicably incapable of pronouncing agreement other than saying yis, or referring to another man as a blark.

Must be the aborigines. Oh no, Clitty corrected himself, that's the Aussies. Suppose they're just as bad.

A good deal of smoking and consumption of coffee followed as the list for the day had inexplicably shrunk.

'Yis, we had two cystoscopies,' began the anaesthetist cheerfully, 'a couple of resections, and an appendectomy, all of 'em cancelled.' He passed round tea around the fug of exhaled smoke. 'So we spend the rest of the day poncing around till home time.'

'Ya whole list cancelled?' Anderson enquired diligently.

'Ah, na, we had a few others that the buggers turned up for. How the hell someone with a shrieking appendix can discharge himself is beyond me. Bloody bedu, ya see. They spend their lives in a tent; then they get bellyache. The king has told them on the tee vee that free hospital care is available for everyone, so they reckon to give it a try. Then when they do need a procedure, they shit themselves and disappear back to the desert.'

'But this hospital, Mac,' Anderson began earnestly, 'this hospital was built for serving armed forces personnel and their families. Presumably they've achieved some way of understandin' what hospitals do? What you guys do?'

'Maybe, but remember, the parents are bedus. Somehow,' Mac raised his eyes in some prayer, 'somehow they produce male children who can make a pretty good effort at flying F-15 or can carry out a full ordnance output on a multiple missile launcher. Makes ya flesh creep.'

Mac paused to light another cigarette, inhaled, and thought of home. 'What's more, the bloody parents come in here with all sorts of complaints we ain't seen before: hearts on the wrong side, atria missing. We had a woman in here last week comin' in for an ectopic pregnancy. Her husband flies with the AWACs, and she was all blue and weird and hypotensive.' He paused to cough, sip some more coffee. 'Turned out she had an undetected left-to-right shunt, what you call hole in the heart, and the bloody woman already had five children, her cardiovascular system was so shagged out …'

Mac crushed out one and lit another cigarette. 'Sometimes I wonder why we have advanced health-care systems when people like that can carry on as normal with something we normally give the thumbs down to. Then these people who are living normally, breathing, eating, crapping, and reproducing, they get tarnished by health care, they get diagnoses, they get pushed from microbiology to X-ray to labs to stress labs. Who gives a shit? Ever tried, Anderson, to explain to a bedu, who normally craps in a hole he's just dug in the ground, then spends the day doing nothing else but gaze up the fanny of a camel, that he needs an angiogram? Perhaps gazing up a camel's fanny gives you angina, all that bloody excitement, dunno …'

Your Friday, My Sunday

The anaesthetist shrugged his shoulders, then stopped to excuse himself to make a telephone call. The assembled drank more coffee and smoked with due reverence. He hung up.

'One thing's clear, you guys.' Mac engaged Ellis's and Clitty's eyes with particular attention. 'You got a situation where the government wants to impose health care on an non-understanding populace who don't know what healthcare is, where at home you got ranged against governments a populace who know what health care they think they deserve. And the governments don't give a damn.'

'You cynical shit.' Anderson laughed, flicking ash on the floor and crossing and recrossing his legs on the chaise longue in one corner of the room.

'True or not so?' Mac challenged the disinterested gathering of those empowered to control the dangers of general anaesthesia. One of them was reading a three-year-old copy of a *Hello* magazine, nodding that the astrology column was correct, had it been this week.

Anderson lit one more for the road. Clitty sat with hands in his lap, clapping his palms gently, eyes and mind some way from this place.

Ellis thought about picking his nose. Wrinkled his nose, then reckoned it could wait.

'So, your new bloody project, Anderson. You and your guys,' Mac nodded towards Ellis and Clitty, 'suppose you're gonna have all the departmental names all screwed up and fucked up in the best traditions of Korean translation of American dialect?'

'What you on about now, Mac?'

'You know damn well.' Mac laughed derisively. 'You call casualty the ER, the operating theatre the OR, the ITU you call the ICU, and the only common nomenclature is CCU, coronary care unit.'

'Actually, we gonna have the King Fahd Operating Suite, or the OR or the theatre. Then we'll have the Prince Salman Emergency Suite, or the ER or casualty. Then we'll have the King Faisal Diagnostic Imaging Suite, or the scanner. Nothing and nowhere will make any sense, and the only way we can build this project is having the rooms numbered.' Anderson drew avidly on his extinguished cigarette. 'Then some motherfucker will get the room numbers fucked up, and we fit out the mortuary as the ICU.'

'Not much difference really. Not hereabouts anyway.' Mac yawned and stretched in his easy chair, his greens heavily creased from sitting, his face mask draped loosely around the back of his neck. 'Where you off to now?'

Anderson wished he could summon up some enthusiasm for showing his charges something that would not lead to a hideous argument with the giant, but the task defeated him.

He yawned, and through his gasps answered as best he could, 'Thought we might see the burns unit, then neurology, then the ER, then home.'

'See yer then.' Mac jumped to his feet and, holding out a hand to Ellis and Clitty, smiled, shook hands warmly, and made for the door. 'Sorry, fellas. This guy needs a crap.'

The three men stood, Anderson, Clitty, and Ellis. They gave cheerful goodbyes to the remaining theatre staff, who seemed preoccupied with the magazines strewn on the occasional tables. It seemed as if they read them with as much relish as if the magazines were new, even though they must have already read each one many times over, as the soiled covers suggested.

Some of them mumbled as the three hospital designers left quietly and walked in silence back to the car parked in the blazing sun, in the centre of the more or less empty car park, or parking lot, as Anderson referred to it as he hit the remote button and released the central locking. A small, insipid squeak from the alarm system advised that the car was now unarmed and ready for action.

On arrival at the site, Anderson waved at the security man, who employed his best Pakistani salute and with an extravagant gesture jumped upon the counterweights of the security barrier. The hinge groaned as he raised the barrier over the Lexus as it sped through the dust to the men's office.

Anderson leaped from the car and eyed a rental car parked in his space. He eyed it with suspicion. Rental Lexus. Not usual for rental cars of this status to come unannounced. Who the hell was it? Anderson cursed, and totally ignoring Ellis and Clitty, he walked to the car to see through the window some sheets of headed notepaper on the front seat. Left tidily with no attempt at concealment, the papers announced the unexpected arrival of Medmark.

'Jesus H.,' Anderson cursed, thinking through what he had told them, what he had told Walid at the ministry, what he had told Choi, what he had done with the money. Oh shit.

Clitty relished Anderson's obvious discomfort as they walked to the cool of their office, a shrieking earth mover nearby suggesting the imminent burial of all their cars.

'Mr Anderson,' Choi called threateningly, even before Anderson's eyes had adjusted to the darker light. 'Mr Anderson, one moment please.' It was an order, gently made, an unequivocal demand to get his ass over there quick.

Choi stood. So did his two visitors, two very large Western gentlemen, both towering above Choi. The fighter cruised the tank in eager anticipation, pouting. Anderson approached and forced a smile of welcome. Beads of sweat ran down the back of his neck as his fear of exposure tightened his guts. Oh shit, Thursday night. No, not that. Must be something else. The money – did they sign the L/C? Did he take the money?

Anderson ran out of time to think anymore, and, shaking the dry hand of one of the Medmark men, who noted the sweat of the man Anderson, Choi suggested they sit for some tea. Anderson wanted a crap, but settled for tea and a smoke. And all he could do then was watch the fish perform its usual tricks.

'Mr Anderson,' Choi began, sipping some tea and offering Korean cigarettes to all of them. With some hesitation, they each took a cigarette, as the ceremony of lighting, inhaling, and reflecting momentarily delayed the cross-examination that was bound to follow.

Whatever.

The cross-examination came. And with unexpected viciousness.

Choi made to begin gently, but his emollience was defeated by the larger of the two men, who turned to Anderson and let fly a broadside.

'Anderson, how long you want to live?'

'What?'

'OK. Here's the juice. We pay you a consultancy fee for you to evaluate our kit for the project. You say the kit's up to spec. Then we pay a five per cent for submission to MOH, and …'

'Then what?' Anderson challenged the big man with one eye, perhaps two.

'Then, we wanna know why.'

'Why what?'

The big man pulled the cup of tea from Anderson's face as Anderson tried to hide his facial expression. The tea spilled, and Anderson thought of thumping the big man as both leaped to their feet.

The big man was close to six foot five or six, Clitty estimated from a distance. Anderson was overshadowed by about a foot by the bigger man. Should be fun, this.

Upfront payments were always dodgy; no collateral, you see. No certainty of anything but a fucked-up arrangement and a whole heap of duplicity.

'Anderson,' the large man said generously, 'I'd like to give you the chance to make one or two explanations about where our money has gone. The money, you remember?'

Anderson worked hard to smile and sat down, eyeing Choi anxiously, hoping the Korean hadn't done the usual trick of assuring everybody that everything was above board and honest and how he had lived in Chis-Wick and how the British were so honest and how he had enjoyed visiting Eel Pie Island and how they should reroute the South Circular and how this must all be some ghastly misunderstanding.

'And now, Anderson. Where's the bloody order?'

The big man was done.

Choi had a problem. He could admit that his senior advisor had taken bribes on a big scale, that he was a naughty boy, and that he would have him deported immediately, or he could tell them that Siemens had made a better offer and that they had offered an after-sale service backup second to none. Trouble was, who had paid Walid? Had he also taken anything from these Medmark characters? Unlikely. They would not know how to do it. To come in like this and threaten Anderson, loathsome as he was, was not helpful. Choi thought about it. Then he interrupted the big man.

'Mr Medmark,' Choi began pleasantly.

'The name's Dyer. Mark Dyer.'

'Really? Interesting name. Is it Engerlish?'

Choi paused to light another cheroot.

'Mr Dyer, Mr Mark Dyer, have you been to London?'

'I live there, for Chrissake.'

'Good. Then you will know Chis-Wick?'

'What's this to do with our X-ray submission?'

'The way, in here, in the Kingdom, is to talk about ourselves to establish common bonds, bonds of friendship. Then we can talk the business. This is good?'

'No, it fuckin' well isn't. I paid this fuckin' creep a consultancy fee, and now I want the fuckin' order.'

The big man gestured excitedly at Anderson, who was becoming grateful to Choi for his intervention.

Choi shuffled some papers and focused on one.

'Your letter of offer ...'

'What about it?' Dyer was almost incandescent with rage at the lack of urgency applied to his offer.

'It has a five-year validity.'

'So?'

'It has a further four and a half years to run before we make a decision.'

Dyer hadn't thought that one would ever be used. Offers were made with prices valid for five years just in case a war broke out and the whole project was put on hold. But the ministry, Choi, the Koreans, and especially that bloody Anderson all said that although five-year validity was standard, the order would always come within six months, and the six months were now up, so where was the bloody order?

'Mr Mark Dyer.'

'Yes?'

'Go home to London. Go and visit Chis-Wick. As soon as we have a decision, we shall come back to you.'

Dyer leaped to his feet. 'Choi,' he shouted, waving an angry finger at the fish, 'I'm going to see Walid. I'm going to get you buried, you and this bloody Anderson, the lotta you – you'll be hearing about this!'

'I look forward to that.' Choi smiled, stood, and offered a hand of friendship, ignored by Dyer as he clasped his papers and threw himself and his driver through the door and into the heat of the day.

'Mr Anderson.' Choi looked menacingly at Anderson. 'Never again must you take any money. That was a close call. Our submissions to the ministry must be based on truth and specifications. Nothing else.'

'Bollocks.'

'Oh?'

'I said bollocks. Walid, the whole of the ministry, and that Saudi in the liaison office, the lotta them, they're all on the take. Where does truth come into it?'

'Be assured, Mr Anderson. Our job is to present the truth in the most truthful way. If we were not to do so, the whole project could collapse.'

'Just like your bloody department stores in Korea then, Mr Choi, where everybody is on the take, everybody cuts corners, then the whole thing collapses some lunchtime and kills lotsa lotsa people? That what ya got in mind?'

'My purpose here, Mr Anderson, is to ensure that specifications are met, that equipment is good for the job. If any deviation by means of financial adjustments is made, you may be assured I shall inform Mr Walid at the ministry, and I shall ask him to revoke your contract and have you deported from here as a common criminal.'

Anderson laughed loud and full. 'Oh, that's really great. You're gonna tell Walid that there's somebody here who's on the take when Mr Bloody Walid is the biggest taker invented. He's a Saudi or Egyptian, he's a bloody dentist, and he's got more free stuff in his surgery than the best dental schools in the USA, UK, and the whole of bloody Europe combined. We know he's got a ranch in Texas, USA passports for his kids, and we gotta do the whole thing to specification. Bah!'

Choi sat down to the level of the fish.

'Mr Walid, whatever he does, is still the governor, Mr Anderson. I know nothing of this alternative lifestyle that you accuse him of. Leave well alone, Mr Anderson. Leave him be. He has all the power he needs to throw us all in jail if he so chooses.'

Shit, bollocks, and shit, Anderson cursed to himself as he discharged himself from Choi's glare and straight into a challenge from Clitty.

'Gotcha self in the shit there?' Clitty asked with mimicked concern.

Anderson threw himself at his desk and clasped the edges of the table, looking for some return of his authority. 'Clitoris, get ovah here!'

Clitty challenged Anderson from a distance but came nevertheless, and sat down in mock dedication to hear the sounds of advice from his boss's chair.

None came, initially.

'Mr Klitowski, I'm movin' ya to X-ray.'

'Oh?'

'Yeh. Seems like we got behind schedule. Choi's screwed up. Wants progress.'

'Didn't sound like it to me.'

'Pardon me?'

'It sounded like you been caught with your hands in the till.'

'Till? What's 'at?'

'You've been caught by Medmark not delivering promises. Kind of hands in the till. Hands in the cash register.'

'Oh.' Anderson reflected that 'cash teller' was the normal name. 'Anyhow, I'd like you to take X-ray and complete submissions to the ministry. Complete them in three weeks. That should do.'

Anderson made some calculations on how long it would take the Medmark men to go back to London, raise another visit visa at the Saudi embassy, and return to make some real trouble.

Clitty made some mental notes that the Medmark distributor in Saudi Arabia was AIG, the AIG director was one of the princes, and the prince was the son of the king. Allegedly.

And Anderson had upset Medmark, so it could all end up at the royal palace.

Poison chalice.

'Perhaps I should stick with the laboratories. They're coming on well,' Clitty insisted.

'Ellis is better suited to that,' Anderson replied, thinking on his feet. 'Anyway, we need X-ray in quick.'

'To avoid a visit to Malaz Jail?' Clitty enquired innocently.

'Fuck off, mister.' Anderson glared hatefully as Clitty edged back towards his own table. 'You got X-ray. OK?'

'What an utter professional,' Clitty muttered to himself and winked to Ellis as Ellis worked on the intricacies of the intensive care unit, or the

ITU. As Clitty decided upon as much of a withdrawal of labour as was possible in such a place, suddenly the power went down and all went quiet.

The air conditioners wound down, the lights went out, and Choi's fish tank stopped bubbling.

Silence. Only the shouts from outside and the evidence of a pall of smoke from the wreck of a digger having successfully ruptured a 440 volt supply cable stung everyone inside the building into action.

Choi led the exodus to a point thirty feet from the building. The digger lay blackened at the edge of the trench. The driver, with a blackened red-and-white *guttrah* wrapped around his face to protect against the dust, slumped across the steering wheel, twitching in his dying moments many, many miles away from his home and his family.

'Gentlemen,' Choi commanded. 'There is nothing to be done. Let us return to our work.'

Choi, Anderson, Ellis, Clitty, the Egyptian draughtsmen, the Filipino helpers, and Sam the tea boy silently followed Choi back inside.

'Sam!' Anderson shouted. 'How long you been out?'

'This morning. Sir.'

'Goddamn, the boy puts a spade through a Yemeni's skull for calling him a donkey, the bloody Saudis stick him in jail for two years, and whizzo, he's back in six months.' Anderson put an affectionate arm around the diminutive Indian's shoulder. 'Say, it's good to see ya, ya little shit!'

'Yes, sir. Thank you, sir,' was Sam's only humble reply.

Sam was a good lad, thought Anderson. Nice to have him back. The little shit could be bought. Not like these bloody Filipinos, who could be bought but then they spilled the beans. Sam, once paid, remained silent. Incoming fax messages would be more secure now. And the little sod had a room on the site, a room about eight foot square. No bathroom, just an outside tap, and he had a key. He could get in here on Fridays when the rest of the world was working. Net result: he could get all the Friday faxes and store them for Mr Anderson, ready for first day back on Saturday, and Mr Anderson paid very well for this service. Mr Anderson, very nice man. Yes, sir.

Sam eyed Ellis and Clitty suspiciously as he went to make sir's coffee. He would not smile nor serve drinks to them until sir had made the necessary recommendations and introductions.

Ellis got on with the serious business of creating the programme for equipping the intensive care unit. Then it would be laboratories, then who knew what, except that Anderson.

Clitty smarted at the task of the X-ray. He remembered Damman and shivered. Strange, really, as the power was still down and the heat of the day was at its zenith.

'Sam!' Anderson shouted in Sam's general direction, and waving somewhere above his head, eyes this way and that. 'Sam, I want ya to meet Mr Ellis and Mr Clutterbunk, or something. They gonna need coffee. Get to it.'

'Yes, sir.'

Sam diffidently approached the two Britishers' tables and took orders, made introductions, shook hands, smiled, repeated yes sir twice, smiled his dark smile that he reserved for strangers, then proceeded to his station to prepare drinks for two new people who may pay him for some services, pay him money to make up his gambling debts. Oh shit. They'd get to know he was out. They'd come looking for their money. And soon. Double shit.

Without warning the power was restored.

The whirring began, the air conditioners working to reduce the heat, the background noise of the rescue of an incinerated Thai corpse drowned by the sounds of electricity in action. The fish in Choi's tank seemed relieved too.

The Egyptian draughtsmen coughed and spat and returned to technical drawings. The Filipinos giggled and did what they had to do at the behest of the Egyptians, who, in turn, did what they were told by the Inglesi. And the British were told what to do by a Korean.

Anderson reflected on that fact with some hatred and some profound professional jealousy. What on earth did those dog-eating fuckers know about hospitals and health care? The first thing ever built in Korea was the fifty-first parallel, and that was put in place by the Americans. And the natives forsook loincloths and jungle feasts, put on suits, and, in a pretence that they were civilised, assumed the mantle of experts in the construction of anything from hydroelectric schemes and supermarket complexes to hospitals and temples. Bastards. But they couldn't know that much, could they? If they did, why were Brits and Yanks in here advising on equipment? Just went to show. The only thing the Koreans could do was mix concrete.

And even then they usually cheated and put in too much sand, which was why when some of their supermarkets collapsed at peak shopping times, when the stresses were greatest. Oh yes. Anderson became excited in his thoughts of victory, thoughts of their limited expertise. The bloody Koreans may be able to build but they built at cut price. They still needed expertise. They needed us.

Anderson lit another smoke, a present from Sam. It tasted like a turd, so he returned to some Marlboros and smoked contentedly. Oh yes.

Ellis and Clitty, as the new boys, kept their heads down and scribbled things aimlessly on pieces of paper, but still watched and listened.

Choi watched the fish, tuned his radio to the World Service, became frustrated at the poor reception, twisted the controls through all positions, altered sensitivity dials, yet still listened for sounds. Sounds of anything that would indicate the progress, or lack of, of his favourite project.

And in spite of all the listening for telephone calls and the fax machine, the noise of all the electrical activity keeping them all cool, the possible sounds of some impending mutiny or Sam hitting someone with a hammer, nobody heard the gentle sounds outside.

Gently, but with little reverence, the body of the Thai digger driver was pulled from the scorched cab of the digger and laid, prostrate, upon the dusty ground. His body, hideously disfigured by fire, lay on the yellow dirt, fingers, hands, face, all of it scorched black, a body unfit to offer to a widow for identification, grey smoke still seeping from his clothing.

And as the project team disgorged from the office for lunch, they simply observed a dead man on the ground. They all of them got in their cars and went off for lunch. But upon the ground lay a man, a breadwinner, smoke still issuing from his clothes. He had a wife awaiting his return home – the babies, something to eat, the separation, sometime he'll come home, he sends us money, sometime we can be together.

Just as the wife gathers something for her babies to eat, she looks at them, wonders whether to love them, protects them whatever, then loves them some. And while she does so, she has no idea that her man, their father, lies dead, incinerated in a dust-filled pit at his place of work, where nobody cares nor really notices.

The men lifted the body into a canvas, wrapped it up, put on a tag, and sent it to the airport to go back to Bangkok in the hold along with all the Thai expatriate workers' Walkmans, televisions, and CD players. That's all there was to it.

Except Ellis stood by his car, keys in hand, but he paused and watched and offered some sort of silent blessing. Nobody else, particularly those motivated by their two-hour lunch break, seemed to notice the passing of a mortal soul.

Chapter 5

In a low building on the same site as the main project, but away from where the expatriates sat and smoked and made money, a young, bearded Saudi sat at an empty table. An ornately carved nameplate on the desktop announced him to be Abdul Rahman al Khatani, the name embossed in bright gold contrasting with the dark pitch of the wood plate. At one end of the desk stood a phone, in the older style of telephone, with a dark Bakelite body, also edged with gold. And there was the ashtray.

Abdul Rahman moved the sculpture to improve its alignment with the top of his desk. He sighed in satisfaction and looked at the brass clock on the wall, painted incongruously in a delicious shade of pink. The hour hand was missing. The carpet throughout was new and unstained. Two empty and fully upholstered armchairs were provided on the visitors' side of his desk, allowing the young Saudi to hold court with his visitors in some comfort. He twisted his beads around his wrist, first this way, then that, then wondered why his telephone had not rung, for he had been in the office for a full fifteen minutes and it was still only eleven twenty in the morning. Or twenty past, according to the clock. Twenty-seven minutes to *sallah*, prayer time, then lunch. Might as well leave things until after lunch.

But then there were still things to do. He had a job. Few Saudis actually volunteered for work, and those who did ended up as bank tellers or hotel receptionists. Anything, it seemed, to avoid getting the hands dirty. Abdul Rahman had been headhunted for this job, via his father, an influence in the Ministry of Health. The son duly declared to the minister that he wanted to contribute to the success of this major healthcare project in any capacity. The minister's adviser suggested he may wish to mix concrete, at which the young Saudi found the whole project less wholesome, but after a long series of meetings in smoky rooms, drinking chai – the standard sugared mint tea – he was appointed the link man between the site engineers and the ministry. He would in effect be the eyes and ears of the ministry power brokers to help track progress and to report back the sounds and sights of irregularities, whether structural, financial, temporal, or all three.

Once started, one of the things Abdul Rahman had heard was of large financial offerings made to the contractors and their advisers – payments made by the manufacturers and suppliers of medical equipment to be installed in the hospital once the building work was complete. That was, provided the financial inducements were of sufficient size and paid at the right time to the right people. The cost and size of 'commissions' was irrelevant.

Abdul Rahman had pointed this out to Mr Walid, an Egyptian structural engineer at the ministry, but Mr Walid feigned indifference, preferring to focus on the successful and timely construction of the nation's premier infrastructure project. Mr Walid simply wanted to be able to hand over the completed project to the minister of health, and he would hand the entire edifice over to the king for his blessing, eternal gratitude, and a brown bag of money.

Abdul Rahman sat at his desk, dreaming of everything and nothing, when there was a soft knock at his door.

'May I come in?' Ellis smiled as he pushed around the door with two mugs of Arabic coffee steaming in both hands.

'Sure.' Abdul Rahman couldn't think of anything else to say. This Ellis had a kind look about him, something he'd not seen in any of these Inglesi or goddamn Americani, so he stood and offered a chair as Ellis put the drinks on the polished tabletop, sighed a bit, and slumped himself into the easy chair.

Ellis realised there was no quiet, nor birdsong, nor peace of mind, nor calm environment in this place. Like all the other sites of his acquaintance, it was a building site, with the dust and the noise and the shaking and the banging and the shouting and the multilingual swearing. The Yemeni diggers waved due menace at the Thai cement pourers with an impenetrable shower of insult and hyperbole.

'So.' Abdul Rahman crossed his hands on the table, remembered his manners, passed a mug of coffee to Ellis, took one for himself, rocked slightly on his seat as he unfolded his hands and searched for cigarettes in the depths of his *thobe* pocket, passed one to Ellis. With the ignition complete, both men sat back, somewhat warily enjoying the first inhalation and then the second, in silence. 'So, you come from London?'

'Kind of,' Ellis replied emptily. 'You?'

'I live in here.' Abdul Rahman swept an arm to include the building, the site, the city, the country.

Born of an ancient Wahhabi bedu family near Al Kharj, a settlement some fifty miles south-east of Riyadh, Abdul Rahman had spent his early years herding the family goats and camels, making money and fruits in deals which involved animals for meat, milk, and sticks. The mouth sticks were a staple tooth scraper for the contemplative bedu. More recently, though, the community had become host to an airbase, the host of the Royal Saudi Air Force, now in another expansion phase. Abdul Rahman had talked himself onto the base, doing various tasks and exchanges that paid far better than selling goats ever would.

The community became used to the presence of the airbase, and a small town grew up around it to serve its more menial requirements. The town of Al Kharj was as unimaginative and as anonymous as all the towns built through the wisdom and foresight of the king and used a means of forcing the bedus from the land to enjoy the comforts, appointments, and luxuries of the late twentieth century. The housing was free. The electricity was free. The schooling was free. The health care was free. But it was free of freedom.

The raison d'être of all bedu was trade and travel through the vastness of sand that was central Saudi Arabia. Their knowledge of the geography, navigation, trails, animals, water sources, and trade was the envy of the city folk, particularly in the West, where their ability to travel miles with no maps or charts could thumb a nose at cartographers. King Faisal began a process in the early nineteen-seventies, when the West danced to his tune played on the oil pipe. The monarch doubled the price of oil and watched the revenue pour in, while the West hunkered down, enduring cold winters, power cuts, spiralling power costs, and rampant inflation.

Armed with unimaginable inbound revenues, the man decided that as bedus were bedus out of necessity, he would build housing that would make the camel caravan a thing of history. In one particularly curious piece of urban planning, Faisal built twenty tower blocks in the centre of Riyadh, the capital.

On the appointed day, the bedus were instructed to discard their traditions and to move into the red-brick constructions. The police in their blue-and-white four-wheel-drive vehicles roamed the desert, rounding up families, goats, and camels, announcing through loudhailers that by royal decree, beduism was to be transferred to and contained in high-rise blocks. The bedu arrived in tranches of ones and twos, families in tow. Much to the dismay of the police and in secret to the amusement of the bedu, it was discovered that the lifts in the tower block were far too small to take a camel. There were stories of heaving and grunting as the camels were persuaded through the lift entrances, the automatic doors trapping gowns, ankles, and fetlocks, while repeatedly the automatic doors attempted to shut, then open, then shut time and again. When one particularly grumpy camel fractured the shin bone of a policeman in a singularly bad-tempered confrontation, the whole issue was referred to police HQ in Malaz.

Before any decision could be given to the police on site, most of the bedus had already begun their retreat back to the desert, walking on the freeways, the camels stopping to tear at the flowering bougainvillea that decorated the central reservations of the busy urban highway. Several high-value Dodges and Cadillacs being randomly driven by local residents had mortally wounded errant camels. A scene of carnage ensued as bedu sat in the centre lanes, attempting to reorientate themselves, while the Saudi car drivers illustrated their total loss of direction by following the white lines and passing by on the other side.

By the time the police at the new high-rise flats had received their instructions, there was nobody left to shepherd. A royal decree was issued cancelling the whole operation and consigning the buildings to perpetual obscurity, to be used only once more some years later, when the Kuwaitis fled their country from the raid by Iraq on the nineteenth province, and settled in the high-rise accommodation for as long as they had to. It was felt by some that the Kuwait invasion was an occasion when normal bedu practices went bizarrely and savagely out of control.

Abdul Rahman knew all about normal bedu practices: a bit of thieving, a bit of bargaining, a lot of travelling, give a bit, take a bit. Make friends. Steal something, then if the friends discover the theft, work out a way to give it back without loss of face. You don't kill unless you need to. You respect what Allah has provided.

He was still too young to know that, while one might wish to covet his neighbour's wife, it was forbidden. Sex was not yet in this domain, although stirrings often suggested this was imminent. Boys would laugh that, although the rules decreed no coveting other women, there was no mention of coveting someone else's camel. It was felt in the desert that a camel could be a fine bedmate: it could be screwed, it didn't answer back, it didn't smell too bad, and one was too far from the mouth to detect halitosis. What was the major challenge to camel lovers was the animal's propensity to fart.

This made coveting neighbour's camels a particularly brave endeavour, but despite all of this, the pursuit of camels endured, reflecting perhaps negatively upon the desirability of the bedu's lifemate.

The young Abdul Rahman, in a mood of reflection, squatted on a patch of dust, small cobbles pressing into the soles of his sandals, tossing stones slowly from one hand to the other, thinking about this place.

Al Kharj, like so many Saudi new towns, was approached by a six-lane highway. An archway spanning the road announced the town along with an extract from the holy Qur'an. Through the archway were single-storey houses painted white, flat roofs with water tanks atop. All the houses were shielded from the gaze behind high walls lying on either side of the roadway: few to begin with, then becoming more numerous towards the town centre. Many towns had filled their centres in, but Al Kharj still had an oasis of sorts. Much as he tried, the king could not shift from the focal point the place where for centuries the people had come and watered and talked and fed and moved on. Now a town surrounded it, and nobody came and fed and watered, and the oasis was now full of rubbish and plastic water bottles, drinks cans and old car tyres.

Now the place had a hospital and the airbase and shops and telephones and televisions and radios. Abdul Rahman took for granted the presence on most street corners of the mosques, the haven for the five-times-a-day prayer. Although it served as a prayer place, a mosque's original intention was as a place where a member of the faithful could seek clarification on points of holy writ from the imam. All townsfolk had been illiterate, and if they had a problem on the rights and wrongs of their lives, they went to the imam, who, having been taught to read and being a scholarly person, could make judgement on the Qur'an and offer a solution. As the country struggled with its access to the modern era and the medium of telecommunications that was difficult to police, the role of the imam should have increased. It was hard to tell. His only task was to call the faithful to prayer by bellowing at a microphone, his message being amplified and unavoidable.

The 15-year-old Abdul Rahman had a problem.

He loved the challenge of the new world, he loved how different life was on this airbase, but at this stage in his life, he preferred the things he knew well. Things his father had taught him, things they both knew and loved: the culture, their background, their habits, their contentment, the apparent predictability of his life, and the certainty of the grace and blessing of Allah.

The market in Al Kharj was traditionally an informal affair. The main road, now reduced from its six-lane opulence to a narrow, potholed street with wind-bedraggled palm trees on its edge. Hoardings offering Pepsi, Vaseline, and the wonders of Sony. The shops were shut on a Thursday. Instead, the market was set up and everybody arrived. Pickup trucks rolled in from somewhere over the horizon. The occupants bought and sold and haggled and got what they needed, and by four o'clock the market had ended with the whole place restored to normal. It was like a car-boot sale selling camels, goats, fruits, vegetables, and not much else.

Abdul Rahman hurled the stones away and stood up, resolving to identify what it was he currently enjoyed about his life, reject all the changes – no, perhaps that was too single-minded, too narrow. There was something that made his mind special. It must be the camel sale because that made the most money for all of them, himself and family.

But was this right? The camel sale? A sale where the baby camels mostly were sold. The mother camels and their babies torn apart, the babies to be sold for slaughter amid a welter of anguished screams from the mothers. Other bedu would load the frightened babies onto the ubiquitous low-loader Toyota trucks and drive off, their screams unheard and unheeded in the vastness of the desert void.

As was expected, Abdul Rahman observed in their entirety the five pillars of Islam. Even as a 15-year-old he could recite many suras of the holy book from memory. He fasted during Ramadan; he had travelled to Mecca, aged 9, to perform the first of what he assumed would be many Hajj visits; he gave regularly to the poor, even if his trading methods were less altruistic; he prayed five times a day; and he acknowledged that there was only one God, Allah, whose messenger was the prophet Mohammed, peace and blessings be upon him. But from over that far, dusty horizon, and occasionally from the airbase where Western people visited, came stories. Stories of untold wealth, of women available at any moment, of going to college, even of leaving this place to go to the USA or UK to study at prestigious universities.

The obligation of the fast and the rigidity of the religion bestowed on Abdul Rahman battled hard within his head as he thought about the West. All those stories – at least some of them might be true. He had asked the imam for advice, and the imam had said to stay put in the pureness of the desert. He had asked his father, but his father wasn't sure where the West actually was, or even if it existed. He asked his friends; they shrugged their shoulders.

Abdul Rahman tossed a stone between his hands, swapping it from the left to the right, deep in thought, thought punctuated by the roar of an engine. It was distant and closing. He could hear the roar, and then he could see it – the black B-52 with its eight engines shrieking their power as it clawed its way into the sky. The aircraft bucked and swayed as it passed over the airfield perimeter fence where the boy sat with his thoughts, its sound now filling the air and the ground with its tawdry menace. Then, as it banked to its left and headed from sight, the young Saudi's hearing returned and he wondered if the plane was going to the West. There were plenty of aircraft leaving the airfield, blowing the dust and sand from the shimmering runways before turning – and then they were gone.

Then one day a year later, after a particularly successful sale of camels, goats, and milk, and when the maternal camels' grief had no longer been audible, Abdul Rahman squatted to count the grubby roll of riyals in his hand. He was sitting alone, just watching, just listening and just counting. He failed to notice the arrival of a smartly dressed Saudi, in full ceremonial clothing, his gold-edged *guttrah* emphasising the pure whiteness of his clothes. The man stopped, his height bathing the boy in his shadow.

'*Salam aleikum.*' He smiled. 'You have done well today.'

Abdul Rahman squinted into the sun. Impossible to see the man's face, so he continued counting his money.

'A boy of your experience is not be condemned to a life of goats and camels.' The man paused for effect. 'Unless you wish it so.'

'What do you mean, sir?' Abdul Rahman wondered why he should speak to him so, then wondered if this might be about the West and all the stories. Maybe the man was a businessman.

The man lowered himself to the ground, to the squat position he could still achieve with ageing knees, much to his own surprise. His eyeline was a little above the boy, but at least the problem of looking into the sun was negated. Abdul Rahman looked at his new companion, admiring his white *thobe*, the cufflinks, the gold pen in his breast pocket, and most of all, the clean toenails. A smell of an expensive perfume drifted through the dust. The midsummer heat would neither produce nor support such aromas.

'That goat you sold …' the Saudi man began gently.

'What about it?' Then he quickly added, 'Sir?'

'That goat and the camels, the lot together, a very good price if I may say. I was watching.'

'I could have made less. The nice thing was the *kaffir* thought the camel would have lots of babies. I couldn't tell him otherwise.'

'Oh?'

'No. That camel hasn't had any babies for at least five years. We filled her full of stuff, put her out with lots of males, still nothing. So we sell her as a going concern. Then if the kaffir comes back and complains, enough time has gone by to blame the failure to have children on something he's done. Easy really.'

The Saudi man smiled and adjusted his cuffs. 'What is your name, boy?'

'Abdul Rahman al Khatani. Sir.' He began to count the proceeds for a second time, for it really had been a very good day.

'Are you related to Samir?'

'Yes, sir. I think he is my grandfather's brother.'

'Your great-uncle then?'

'Yes, I suppose so.' Abdul Rahman paused. 'Do you know him?'

'He works in my bank.'

'Where?'

'In Riyadh.'

The boy counted again, left index and mid-finger holding the wads of notes as his left thumb and right index finger did all the counting.

'Oh.'

To the boy the conversation seemed to be going nowhere. The Saudi man readjusted the hem of his *thobe* over his pedicured feet, the movement releasing more of that perfume.

'Would you come to my bank?'

The question was as powerful as it had been unexpected. What about the West?

'Sir, I'm only 15, too young to leave here.' He didn't really want to leave here and the goats and the market, trading this all in to work in Riyadh, the capital.

'I guessed that. Do you speak any English, *kalam inglesi*?'

'*La*.'

'Perhaps I could put that straight. I need sharp lads like you. If you find you are able to speak English, it helps. My bank engages daily with the international banking community. English is important.'

'Sir?'

'Yes?'

'Would you say something in English? I've never heard it before.'

'OK. *Schwei*, wait a moment, let me think. Here goes: Madame, how much is it for to sleep with you?'

'Is that really English?'

'Sort of. But the sort of English you will need in the bank will be something like, "What rate on Brent crude on the spot this week?"'

'Sounds like I shall never understand that.'

'Rubbish, boy. If you agree, and if your father agrees, you come to the bank. And before you do that, you go to England and learn proper English, experience those people, their customs.'

'May I ask one thing, sir?'

'Sure.'

'Is England in the West?'

The Saudi thought for a while, reached down to pick up some stones, which he idly tossed from one hand to the other and back, and reckoned it must be.

'In that case, I'll go.'

And, engaging in improper thoughts about the West, Abdul Rahman rolled up the wad of notes and forced them into his *thobe* pocket. Jumping to his feet, he offered a supportive hand to the older man. Giving him a firm shake of the hand, the boy went back to herding goats, happy in the knowledge he'd make money, lots of it. He would get to visit the West, and, most of all, his appreciation of his life could be objectively compared with what others went through, bearing in mind his own background and recalling how far he had gone with his father's own guidance. Actually, to the adolescent, the alternative was far more attractive.

The boy had not even asked the Saudi man his name, but when Abdul Rahman arrived home, the man had clearly already approached the boy's father for permission to use him in the manner previously discussed. The father had protested that he needed his son to bring home the money for all the children, and for Mama, who had remained out of sight during the visit. The father gave a spirited defence of his family, their background, and their lives in this town. When the Saudi man drew a thick wad of notes from the inner pocket of his *thobe* and dropped them on the table, he counted them, then calculated that this offer represented five years' income from the sale of goats and camels.

Suddenly the fate of his son seemed less important, and he readily gave his blessing to the arrangement. The two men embraced in the love of their God and some irreverent thoughts of unimaginable riches.

The Saudi knew a little of England: the strip clubs in Soho, Marks and Spencer, Mrs Thatcher. Plus he could also remember the names of Oxford and Cambridge, the boat race perhaps. He called friends in England to enrol the boy at a school – Oxford perhaps, or Cambridge. Yes, that was the place. Cambridge.

Perhaps not.

Oxford sounded a lot nicer, and everyone knew Oxford.

Oxford it would be for the lad.

Miss Simpson was an English teacher.

A woman of awesome stature and demeanour, Miss Simpson took care of new pupils, who were often visiting England for the first time and whose command of basic English was, at best, basic.

Miss Simpson was also the head teacher of the English School, in the small village of Wheatley on the London side of Oxford, but near enough to Oxford for foreigners to believe they were actually going to Oxford. The English School was housed in a forbidding, detached, four-storey dwelling, converted to house the residential students who came from Far East and Middle East. Japanese students, students from the banking centres of Singapore and Hong Kong, some Tunisians and the occasional Peruvian. On the ground floor, the main study areas filled what may have once been the drawing rooms and living rooms of a landed family of old. One morning it was some surprise to the class to find a dark, handsome boy sitting at a table in the corner of the room as they assembled for the day's English tutorial.

Your Friday, My Sunday

'Students,' Miss Simpson chortled, 'I have the pleasure to introduce you to Abdul Rahman, arrived today from Saudi Arabia. Please welcome him.'

'Hi,' the class called cheerfully, one or two of them slumped over their files, apparently nursing hangovers.

But most eyes fell on the new boy.

Abdul Rahman wished he had his beads with him to twirl; he had nothing to do with his hands. So he waved a friendly *salam aleikum* and hi, smiled broadly, folded his arms, and waited for the woman at the front, the one with the massive tits, to get on with the lesson.

The process of integration was at times painful, memories of herding his goats more attractive than going to the King and Queen, as most of them did at lunchtime, the eating of pork sausages repulsive. At meals, there was no sign of rice with his lamb, chips seemed a strange way of treating potatoes, the odd English expressions like ad hoc and ad infinitum, the way they read the wrong way across the page. Perhaps it was Miss Simpson's ability to stand by the window and blot out the sun with her vastness while explaining the role of split infinitives. All of it conspired to confuse the 16-year-old.

But confusion was not going to stand in his way. He had a job to do when he went back home, and anyway, he was now starting to pick up the verbs and the pronouns and the adjectives.

And he was in the West.

He made friends with his peers. They loved his smile and they loved his smouldering darkness – dark eyes that could dance and smile, a thin face that could crease, and a laugh that was infectious. So the girls said, 'Let's go to the pub.'

The beer, that tasted different too.

After five pints of the supreme bitter, the poor lad had to be carried home by the daughter of a Brazilian banker and the son of a commodity trader in Kuala Lumpur.

Convinced of his own destiny, Abdul Rahman decided to do what they all did on a Saturday night – walk the fifty yards to the King and Queen, and then drinks on him. Armed with a large wad of twenty-pound notes and his Amex card, Abdul Rahman held court in the public bar. The landlord enjoyed the muddied English of this dark stranger. He liked his laugh, and he enjoyed the banter. He wasn't sure of his age but didn't care.

Abdul Rahman felt good; he could communicate in improving English. He could hear it, he could understand it, and now he could respond.

He could also feel it.

Good old Miss Simpson, he reflected into his beer. Wonder what she's doing tonight. Doing the washing? Having a bath? Early night perhaps? We won't get her in here for a beer.

By the end of the evening, the pub did what it did best on a Saturday night after eleven o'clock.

It degraded.

Sensible conversation ceased. Everyone began to become philosophical or violent or both. They talked in meaningful tones, they started missing their first wives, and didn't that girl over there look good? In the haze between sober reflection and savage drunkenness, all past sins were forgotten or new ones invented.

Then, through all the noise, the subject among the students turned to sex.

More drinks were ordered as the main item on the agenda turned to if, when, and where in Wheatley it was possible to pick up a woman. Even the girl students joined in with urgent enquiry, as nobody in the pub seemed to know what was available. Someone suggested a goat or an old sow over at Jenkinson's farm.

A helpful lad who had hovered close to the group for much of the evening, smiling and agreeing but never really involving himself directly, helpfully suggested he may be able to offer some support. He flicked some ash from the tip of his cigarette, which drifted onto Abdul Rahman's shoulder, but Abdul Rahman didn't notice as he shuffled along the bench to make space for this new helper. The helper assured Abdul Rahman that if he had a credit card, the helper may be able to help. He regaled the group with his knowledge of a telephone number he could use to get a woman, scribbled some numbers on a beer mat, wished them all good luck, shuffled his way from his seat, and was absorbed back into the drinking-up time melee.

At close on midnight, the less hardy drinkers ejected themselves into the fresh air for the short walk or stagger back to their lodgings. One of the Japanese students with a keen sense of fun was holding the beer mat. He asked Abdul Rahman for his credit card – just, you know, to see if it works or not. The Japanese crossed the road to an open-sided telephone kiosk, picked up the receiver, and encountered some problems with reading the graphic display instructions for reason of limited height. He squinted at the board on the kiosk wall, with rudeness crudely scrawled in indelible pen, then dialled some numbers. He looked at the credit card, read the card numbers, talked excitedly, and then hung up. He gave Abdul Rahman back his Amex card and told him to wait by the phone.

The rest of the group were already letting themselves in at the school, taking their uncertain paths to bed. Abdul Rahman wondered what to do next among the swaying and singing of the inebriated as they fell from the various licensed hostelries that lined the high street. After all, the King and Queen was probably the least offensive in terms of vomiting and fighting. But from now until one in the morning, there would be the procession of the infirm and inebriated. Some came past him as he stood confused, and smiled and muttered and spat and fell over. One passer-by with some vomit clinging precariously to a bearded face asked Abdul Rahman where he could get some ale. Abdul Rahman shrugged his shoulders and winced at the odious man's breath

Then the telephone rang.

At close to midnight, the relative tranquillity, even with the drunken groaning and creaking of those going home, was still shattered by the shrill ringing from the open kiosk.

Abdul Rahman let it ring again, then again, and then, reaching three, he lifted the receiver, uncertainly at first. He wished his Japanese friend were here to tell him what to say.

Hell, he was on his own now. He would carry on in his own way.

'Hello?' His voice quivered.

'That you, Abdul Rahman?' a silky woman's voice enquired.

'Yes, but how did you know my name?' He felt alarmed but also excited. Where would he meet her? Could he get her past Miss Simpson's door into the school? What would she look like?

'Never mind, honey. I'm Ellen,' the voice purred, 'and you and me, honey, we can make some real music together.'

Music? Abdul Rahman didn't need any music; he wanted to lose his virginity. And quick, judging by the swelling in his jeans.

A car with an open exhaust drove past. Some voices shouted.

'You got company, honey?' the girl called Ellen asked solicitously.

'No. The window's open a bit wide, that's all.'

'OK, honey, so, tell me about yourself … or do you just want to get on with it?' The silky voice sensed the impatience.

'Yeh. Just let's get on with it.'

'Mmmm,' Ellen purred. 'You know how to knock out a girl. Now tell me, Abdul Rahman, what will you have me do?'

He paused to think but found that words would not come. 'Don't know.'

'No?' the voice enquired sweetly. By means of breaking his embarrassment, she pressed on. 'OK, Abdul Rahman, I'll tell you what I'm going to do.'

Just then a small man clutching a newspaper parcel attempted to walk round one of the trees at the edge of an area of quiet reflection, tripped and cursed, then stumbled into a bench donated by the parish council in 1979. Seeing a person in the telephone booth, he paused, hoping to engage this newfound person in some late-night conversation.

'Wanna frie?' the man enquired, unravelling his package.

Abdul Rahman asked Ellen asked to hold on for a moment. He thought later he may have said *schwei*, Arabic for 'wait a moment', but she would have to wait whatever he had said.

Abdul Rahman put the receiver behind his head, as if to guard his confidentiality, and gazed down into an appetising-smelling package of what he thought were chips swamped in ketchup.

'Are they chips?' he enquired.

'No, mate, they're fries.' The little man in a raincoat and smelling of a mix of beer and urine replied with total certainty.

'In that case I won't have one.'

'Suit yerself, mate.' And the man turned and collided with the bench one more time, swore some, called 'Night!' and then was gone.

Abdul Rahman thought of a message of blessing or goodwill, but remained silent, then turned back to this woman.

'Ellen?'

'Yes,' the woman hissed with the remnant of sweetness.

'You still there?'

'Yes, I am, sweetheart. And let me tell you, Abdul Rahman …' The menace dissolved at once and she returned to the sweet lady with a message of desperate wanting and longing. 'Abdul Rahman, honey, on this call you get to get twenty minutes, unless you come first. Then callers usually hang up. But if you waste time, as you've been doing, your max is the twenty and you've had ten, and the clock's running.'

'OK, tell me what you were going to do.'

Somewhere far away, a woman calling herself Ellen, the one with green eyes and claiming to be wearing open-crotch panties and no bra, the one with large breasts she was busy rubbing and hoping and waiting for his mouth, oh yes, sigh, the same one wanted to be finished with this time waster, so went for the kill.

'Abdul Rahman,' she whispered, 'how would you like me to take your cock in my mouth, run my tongue round your glans? I'm stroking your balls, you wanna come, but you're gonna wait.'

'Am I allowed to rub your tits?'

'Sure.' She squeaked. 'Yeh, you rub my tits, and now I'm rolling over onto my back, I'm pulling off my panties – you remember them, Abdul Rahman, the ones with the hole – well then, you're working on my clitoris with your tongue, mmmmm, oh baby.'

The girl sighed in feigned satisfaction. Abdul Rahman looked around the empty village square for anyone to tell him what a clitoris was, but he felt warmed by her sound and her sentiment and felt a swelling and a longing …

'And now you're on top of me, and ooooh, your dick is so large, oh yes, push it inside me, into my vagina, so moist for you, go on, push, push, put it my mouth again. Let me taste you, let me have you, Abdul Rahman, I need to have you now.'

The woman called Ellen screamed a fake orgasm, but he wasn't to know it was fake. As he rubbed the front of his trousers with a free hand, he looked around for anybody listening or watching. Nobody was there, so he pushed a hand into the top of his trousers. He was liking both what he was feeling and hearing.

The problem was the twenty minutes were now up, and he cursed the man with the fries and all the passing traffic, and before Abdul Rahman could resolve what to do, the woman, his woman had hung up. He was never going to meet her. This was some sort of trick, and he had an erection. He wanted to love this woman who had spoken so lovingly; perhaps she would smell like some of the beautiful ladies who had slapped his face when he had touched their breasts at the bus stop on the first date. Or even when he didn't know them.

But here had been Ellen, who would talk him into and through his excitement, and now, having talked to him so lovingly, even she had left him with a rock-hard erection in the middle of Wheatley and with no prospect of taking her home.

Afraid of going back to his residence with an erection that everyone would laugh at, he decided to drop into the nearby public toilets to relieve himself of his semen and his excitement. There was nobody around, after all. And relieve himself he did. He thought of and remembered all the things Ellen had promised: how she was dressed, how she must have smelled, her perfume, her smooth skin, her long legs, her long hair, her breasts, that vagina, her clitoris (whatever that was). The strokes were becoming even and faster, his heart rate higher, his grasp tighter. He began to call names – Ellen, anybody – his caution gone as he prepared for his first orgasm at the hands of an English girl called Ellen.

The sound of a car approaching did nothing to reduce his ardour or prevent his progress. He was so nearly there.

'Oh yeh?' asked the voice of a policeman. 'What are we up to then?'

PC Roderick Williams of Oxford Traffic Division had arrived for some private micturition, to be greeted by some public masturbation.

This was a public order offence.

'OK, fella, put it away.'

This was difficult, as Abdul Rahman was still struggling with the engorgement of a rock-hard erection in his left hand, with terror in both eyes as the officer surreptitiously pulled out his penis, had his piss, shook the drips, then put it away. Job done.

The erection soon subsided as radios reported messages and he was bundled into a traffic car with demands for his papers and for some explanation of his behaviour at this hour of the night.

The police sat and pondered and laughed and sniggered and giggled, then took Abdul Rahman to the station, anxious to tell this story. An Arab wanking in a toilet in the middle of the night. Except this was an A-rab. Still, he was wanking and there we go.

The days that followed were to forever forge in Abdul Rahman's memory the true nature of the West. Here you had women who could promise, who would promise, and what would they deliver?

Nothing.

Unless you could get at a hooker, you got nothing from a woman. 'No, you can't touch my tits, and you have to say you love me before you come in.' It was all talk, all suggestion and no substance, all 'you have to keep your filthy hands away from my knickers', but then none of this seemed of any importance when a cowed Arabic teenager was brought before the chair at Thame Magistrate's Court at nine the following morning.

The clerk brought the court to order, reminding everyone present of the solemnity of the process. The first case of Regina versus Abdul Rahman al Khatani was enabled.

Abdul Rahman may have misheard the details of the proceedings because 'Regina' sounded very similar to one of the words Ellen had used. Whatever he had done, he had killed nobody, so this process could only end up with him being kicked out of the country.

The magistrate, though, was extremely interested in the callback system and quizzed prosecuting counsel closely about the availability of such services, scribbling vigorously as counsel gave details of how the system worked, the numbers available, how it could be accessed by any landline telephone and, more recently, mobiles. The magistrate asked about mobiles.

Abdul Rahman understood enough of the proceedings to hope and pray that the magistrate might try phoning the number and getting Ellen. He could pretend he was young and frisky, and Ellen would offer the same empty promise from her house with the noise of a dog in the background and the noise of chickens and a microwave oven completing its cycle. That way the old boy would be at home rubbing his crutch and making gasping sounds, and perhaps it might reduce any sentence he was likely to hand down.

In spite of the magistrate's avid interest in all the phone numbers, he was not sufficiently moved to avoid sentencing the poor lad to incarceration at Campsfield Detention Centre, pending deportation. The defence counsel mischievously suggested after sentence that the decision rested on the magistrate hoping the fewer people around using that 0900 number would leave more space for him – considering he would have a wife in tweeds, and she would smell of lavender and be adorned with a rich nineteen-fifties hairstyle. A chance with Ellen might brighten up the official's life even if it was a mirage – an escape from a boring wife, brought to his attention by an Arab! Fancy that.

In passing sentence, the moustachioed magistrate had totally condemned the use of devices to degrade the social fabric of our society but was grateful to prosecuting counsel for drawing to the attention of the court the existence of such mechanisms of depravity.

The sooner the deportation took place, the better, the magistrate was heard to mutter as he nodded to the clerk that the court was now suspended and left the elegantly sculptured wooden bench for the administration of justice. Those attending the proceedings stood in respectful silence as the magistrate relinquished his place and opened the vast oak door at the rear of the bench and disappeared from view.

In the brief silence that followed, the irony of a far-off telephone ringing was lost on nobody.

'Come on, son.' The court sergeant smiled and held out a friendly hand. 'Time to go home.'

So, rather ahead of schedule, Abdul Rahman returned home in disgrace. At least it would have been a disgrace if he had confessed his sins in full to his mentor. The Saudi bank manager was glad to see the boy back to help in the branch and very pleased to hear that his English was declared to be so good that any further time spent in England would be a waste.

Your Friday, My Sunday

The two drank coffee, smoked and planned and schemed, alternating between English and Arabic, and then … Abdul Rahman's eyes fell on a British newspaper left open on the manager's desk. Would they report his story in the *Daily Telegraph*? It was not as though it were a major crime, but he hadn't yet developed the trick of reading English script upside down.

Abdul Rahman's good humour evaporated. The manager noticed the change of demeanour that indicated the boy wanted to get on with the job in hand.

Strange lad, thought the Saudi, coming home from the London shagging parlours six months early. Anyway, he's here now, so give him a job he'll be good at. Which was fixing the exchange rate at which remittances sent home were made by the multinational expatriate community, numbering tens of thousands. His tasks would include fixing the rate of the Saudi riyal against the US dollar, sterling, Canadian dollar, Egyptian pound, Filipino peso, and so forth. He could slow down the wire transfers, raise the transaction charges, and monitor any unusual transactions involving high amounts not commensurate with salary alone.

Within a month, Abdul Rahman had scored with the bank very highly indeed. He had examined the account details of a Filipino sales clerk working for a medical equipment distributorship in Riyadh and had discovered high deposits and equally high wire transfers a day or two later. A telephone call to the Filipino's Saudi boss, the company owner, confirmed that he paid him a monthly salary of one thousand eight hundred riyals, approximately three hundred pounds sterling. Could the Saudi owner offer, Abdul Rahman enquired, any explanation of how this Filipino could possibly be crediting his account with over one hundred thousand riyals in cash each month, and sending the same amount home in Manila?

Another job?

Stealing from the company?

The Saudi owner could not, or perhaps would not, offer any help except to say he would mention the bank's concerns to the staff member involved.

Abdul Rahman would have to wait until the next time.

Later that month, he watched through the teller's screen as the Filipino arrived to make his deposit. From the melee of the waiting area of the bank, where depositors sat and chatted and smoked and drank iced water from the dispensers, the Filipino approached the teller's screen. He pulled a leather briefcase with some effort onto the counter, lifted the lid, and pulled thick sheaves of high-denomination notes to be totalled by the electrical cash-counting machine. Beside him sat a dishevelled man on a plastic chair, his *thobe* lifted above his ankles as he cleared his toenails of dust and dirt with a soiled index finger.

Abdul Rahman watched the gold front tooth of the smiling Filipino. The gold watch. Rolex perhaps? The easy Arabic banter with the Lebanese teller. The boy ate well; he was tall for a Filipino too. The Filipino caught Abdul Rahman's eye as he turned to leave the counter, bidding the teller 'see you in a couple of days'.

'How much this time?' Abdul Rahman almost pushed the teller off his chair in haste to see the amount. The note-counting machine whirred and stopped, announcing a total of seventy-five thousand. Less than usual. Much less.

He thought about the things those Filipinos were getting up to, and was lost in thought and envy of how they pulled together to hate the Saudis, when his attention was drawn by urgent tapping against the security screen at the counter.

Standing just high enough to be seen by the teller, a diminutive policeman dressed in a khaki uniform and a grubby beret was knocking with one hand against the glass. With the other hand, he was holding a person even smaller by the scruff of the neck. It was a Filipino male, and he looked terrified.

Abdul Rahman gestured to the policeman to come round to the visitors' entrance, then through to the interview room, where they could drink coffee and discuss the matter. The Filipino was whimpering as the policeman bundled him through the steel security doors. Following Abdul Rahman's signals, the two small people alighted in the interview room. An Egyptian chai wallah came to dispense Arabic tea or Turkish coffee and handed out glasses of hot tea without a sound. He looked disdainfully at the Filipino who, he thought, may have wet himself, nodded to Abdul Rahman, and pulled the door behind him with a dull, lifeless thud.

The policeman was, to Abdul Rahman's taste, obnoxious even by Saudi policemen's usual standards. He explained his quest, picked his teeth for a moment or two, ran an index finger round the inside of his left ear, then glared at the wreck who had been forced to sit on the mat.

His story seemed to make sense. Filipinos on the take. Bastards.

Abdul Rahman turned with half a smile to the Filipino, who remained on the floor. 'Is this true?' he asked.

The Filipino seemed scared of his own shadow, short though he was, but to talk to the police, the Saudi police, about another Filipino was treachery. A betrayal of the unity of countrymen.

'Yes,' he said.

'Let me get this straight,' Abdul Rahman began. 'You and your mates at work give all your money to Edgardo, who comes into this bank and deposits it. Right?'

'Yessir.'

'What does Edgardo look like?'

'He's tall, black hair, a gold tooth, wears a Rolex.'

'Does he now?'

'Yessir.' Then the silence.

Abdul Rahman encouraged the Filipino to continue with his story. 'After Edgardo comes in and deposits the money, perhaps a day or two later, Martino comes in and arranges a wire transfer of all the money back to his account in Manila.'

Abdul Rahman then took up the story. 'Then Martino's wife goes to the bank in Manila, takes out all the money, and distributes it to the wives at home. Is that it?'

The Filipino nodded his agreement but stared emptily at the floor, anxious to avoid eye contact with these Saudis, either of whom could get him sent to prison.

'So if this works so well, why the police?' Abdul Rahman couldn't quite understand.

The policeman had discovered some deposits in his nostrils and was picking vigorously.

'Two weeks before,' the Filipino said, 'we give our money to Edgardo, same as always, an' we don't hear nothing. That's usual. Then some time goes by and then me and my friends at work, we all get letters from our wives and our families saying, our money, where is our money? We haven't seen Martino's wife in a long time.'

Only the Filipinos could think up a scam like this.

Abdul Rahman sat back in his chair, sighed, and wondered which of the two in front of him were the more revolting: the dirty Filipino or the disgusting policeman with a foot on the table and a finger up his nose.

The cost of a single wire transfer of any size was ninety riyals. Most people paid up just to get their wives off their backs, but the wily Filipinos did one better to avoid paying anything – or at least the very minimum possible, hopefully just a few *halalahs*, by giving their money to Edgardo, who put it in the bank, in cash. Then when Martino came in to wire transfer the whole lot to his account at home, he only paid ninety riyals.

Neat.

And nothing illegal about that either.

Except that Edgardo and Marino made a small charge of thirty riyals each person. A charge of thirty riyals to save ninety. That made Edgardo and Martino against the law, as they were running an unauthorised business. To compound it, Edgardo had picked up the money from his countrymen some weeks earlier but had been stopped by the police for a traffic violation. Being unable to explain the large sum of money in a briefcase on the back seat of his car, he was thrown in jail until he could convince the authorities of his innocence. Martino, discovering that no deposit had been made and expecting the worst, had kept clear of the bank.

By a process of vacillation and shrugging his shoulders Edgardo got released from jail after a reference from his sponsor seemed to confirm he was legal.

Just.

So, bold as brass, he carried on doing his collections and making his deposits at this bank, and presumably Martino had sent the lot back to Manila as normal.

But then this Filipino on the floor had heard from his wife that there was no money and there was nothing to feed the babies. Eight of them. 'So I go to the police by way of my sponsor.'

Your Friday, My Sunday

No wonder that bloody Filipino can afford gold fillings, Abdul Rahman reflected as he thought through the whole wretched project, wondering if he could unleash the power of the police on these sallow yellow-skins whose only sin really was to be born in a part of the world where death and poverty were frequent visitors.

Yes, he could.

He conferred briefly with the policeman, who had a finger in his other ear but stood smartly to attention when Abdul Rahman announced that indeed there probably was enough evidence to incarcerate those two Filipinos known at this stage only as Edgardo and Martino.

With the decision made, he went for the ledgers to see just what those little buggers did with all the proceeds from overcharging their compatriots to send their transfers home. By subtracting all the telex money from the deposits, he was left with zero – a figure consistent with an impecunious Filipino.

Another bank maybe?

Abdul Rahman shouted at a Lebanese teller to give him a cigarette, lit it, then furrowed his brain. How did they do it? What were they up to?

He gazed through the teller's screen to watch the public area, full and heaving with humanity. On the next till along, an old Saudi man was authorising the withdrawal of a large consignment of high-denomination notes by the use of a grubby thumbprint. A young relation, his son perhaps, was holding open a supermarket bag into which he pushed wad after wad of notes, until it was full to bursting. He snorted deeply and would have spat, but he remembered he was inside a building. Taking the old man by the arm, he picked his way through the throng and was gone from view.

Then, he would have spat.

Abdul Rahman took a second cigarette from his Lebanese subordinate, grunted his thanks, and turned back to his thoughts of the Filipinos. The police would pull both men in, of course, but how could he ever prove they were running an illicit business without proof of having taken any commissions, fees, or charges? The police would throw them in jail, and when somebody felt suitably motivated to act, they would tell the judge their tale, he would pass sentence, and they would be deported. Of course they would be deported whatever sentence they received, but could they be prevailed on to talk about where they stored the fees? How did they get the fees home? Could Abdul Rahman organise some sort of plea bargain – some information for a lesser sentence, maybe?

When the police had rounded up both Edgardo and Martino, they brought them into Abdul Rahman's office. Both men were frightened but solid in their silence. The police displayed their usual sullen indifference, which he found repulsive. Even the Oxfordshire police were nicer than these two.

The policemen slurped coffee noisily as Abdul Rahman circled the table. Perching on the edge of his desk, he began asking his questions.

'The fees,' he started.

'Sir?' The one with the gold tooth was a picture of offended innocence.

'The fees you charge your friends to send their money home.'

'Sir?'

'Oh, for Christ's sake, where's the bloody money?' Abdul Rahman exploded in exasperation, forgetting he was forbidden to take the name of the Christian prophet in vain.

Silence. Except a slight snigger from two Filipinos, amused to hear a Muslim swearing in Christ's name.

'And what's so bloody funny?'

'Nothing, sir.'

'Get up.'

The two men stood stiffly upright. The one Abdul Rahman had seen at the counter, the one with the expensive watch, expensive clothes, clean fingers, and a gleaming gold tooth. That one was Edgardo, surely. The other, Martino, had seen action and was less poised and less, yes, less expensive than the other. Martino would do a plea bargain. Sure, he would.

Abdul Rahman told the two policemen to wait outside with Edgardo, then set about Martino with the zeal of a man possessed.

'You must be Martino,' he said gently. 'You would like a cigarette?'

'Thank you, sir.'

Martino waited for a cigarette to appear but none did, so the interview went on nonetheless.

Abdul Rahman explained his understanding of the whole scam, that the pair of them were operating illegally, and that they would both end up with a long period in jail unless they helped the bank. Martino stayed silent.

'Martino, you need tell me nothing, but I would recommend that you did. You see, our jails are not known for their … niceness. All sorts of things could happen to you. Much violence, torture maybe. You'd catch some diseases probably. But your biggest problem would be if it became known you had talked to the police. A Filipino, talking to the police. Serious, eh?'

'Yes, sir.' Martino stood stock-still, almost in tears, focusing his eyes on a gilded picture of the Saudi monarch that hung ceremoniously above Abdul Rahman's opulent desk, trying to think of anything but a long spell in Malaz Jail.

'So.'

'So?'

'What are you going to tell me?'

Abdul Rahman returned to his side of the desk, sat on a thickly padded leather chair, rearranged the *guttrah* about his head, folded his hands, and waited.

Silence.

The sound of the telephone ringing shattered the stillness. Abdul Rahman raised the receiver 'Nam.'

The caller appeared to have a lot to say. He listened in silence, first gazing at the desktop, then tracing his finger around the rim of an old coffee cup, then looking up at the Filipino, then back at the desk. He commanded Martino to pass a pad of paper and a pencil from nearby, and he began to scribble some figures and some numbers. Abdul Rahman sighed, wished the caller peace and blessings, and slammed the phone down.

'You can go.'

'Sir?'

'Don't sir me, I said you can bloody well go. Now get out.'

Martino smiled and turned to leave as the banker shouted for the police to return to his office. Edgardo walked in first, smiling his gold-toothed smile, the surly officers following, gazing in awe at the sumptuous bank decor. All four stood in line, as if for inspection.

'You're lucky. How d'you do it?' Abdul Rahman hissed at Edgardo.

'I'm sure I have the power of the Almighty, your honour.' Edgardo paused. 'Besides which, we were always very careful about where and when we made telephone calls and how we used public telephone boxes. Know what I mean?' And tapped the side of his nose and winked with a very large smile.

Abdul Rahman was poised to punch him in the face, but held back because he realised that Edgardo's sponsor was involved in this scam and there was no way one Saudi would fight another Saudi over the subject of a Filipino.

He would find out somehow.

And he would also find out who else had got to know of his telephone indiscretion in a small village in England.

With those thoughts, Abdul Rahman found himself on site, staring at the wall, listening to the slow and solemn ticking of the one-handed clock on the far side. The distant sound of earth movers, the dust clouds, the mechanical crunch of metal against stone, voices raised in dissent, torment, or warning. Abdul Rahman walked to the window and watched the whole enterprise taking place beyond the grimy windows, his beads swishing around his wrist, absently watching.

This must be better than the bank, he thought sorrowfully, angrily acknowledging he had been hoodwinked by a pair of Filipinos. The bank had been impressed with his skills and his attention to detail, and he had saved them some money.

But.

But.

That word had stuck in his mind as he recalled his transfer from the bank to the ministry site. They wanted somebody sharp. In any case, qualifications didn't seem to matter, as the minister of health and the owner of the bank were brothers, so any aptitude towards building a hospital or anything else – a power station perhaps – was irrelevant.

The sun was pouring through the dust as the digger drew up large volumes of earth and sand, dropping it all into a truck for disposal somewhere in the desert, some twenty miles from the city boundary. The drivers and the digger men were all Koreans, he thought, pale yellow skins just like those bloody Filipinos. All of them in filthy clothes, faces and heads wrapped in red and white *guttrahs* to protect against the grime and dust and the drying heat, but all of them just getting on with their work. They all worked a sixteen-hour shift, six days a week. Friday they slept, then Saturday they did another six days until another week was done. Once every two years they were given a month's holiday, if they were lucky. If the project was on schedule, they went. If it was behind time, they didn't.

Simple really.

With little else to take Abdul Rahman's attention, he made some phone calls, called up his brothers, his friends, talked long and hard about things of little consequence. Then when he became entirely bored with phone calls, he set about his job of finding out what really went on, in that hut across the site and elsewhere, with all those Koreans and Filipinos and British and Americans. All of them on the take, no doubt.

His ire rose as he walked from the hut and picked his way between diggers and trucks, stubbing his toes on the rocks and stones, the dirty yellow dust staining the pure whiteness of his *thobe*. He turned a corner around one of the completed buildings and strode as meaningfully as he dared towards his target.

Wednesday

Chapter 6

Ellis watched with some interest as the young and very smart Saudi left the site office. He wondered what the conversation with Mr Choi was about. What was needed was Sam.

'Sam!' Ellis called politely.

The little Indian came from somewhere close to Mr Choi's fish tank.

'Sir?'

'Sam. What's on over there?'

Sam's dark face became darker as he puzzled what sir might require. He remained quite still and quite silent. His black eyes seemed to be reading anything and everything on Ellis's desk at the same time as looking and listening for anything that could prove useful to Mr Anderson.

Ellis waved his arms across Sam's face to break the trance, 'Sam, is there anybody there?'

Sam snapped back to the most immediate task, shook his head, and smiled. 'Sorry, sir. Sir? What did you ask of me?'

'Sam, that bloody Saudi. You know him?'

'Which Saudi man, sir?'

'For fuck's sake, Sam, that Saudi in with Mr Choi while you were farting around at the back of the fish tank. What were you doing round the back of the tank anyway?'

'Tank developed leak when power down. Sir.' Sam thought quickly, then added, 'He might like coffee. So behind tank is best place to be.'

'So what were they talking about?'

'Cannot say I could hear.'

'Sam?'

'They talk about fish and cigarettes. Mr Abdul Rahman, he says he prefers not to smoke Korean cigarettes. Mr Choi insists, so Mr Abdul Rahman smokes one and he feels sick and says he has to go.'

'Really.' Ellis watched the face of a cultivated liar, the face unmoved by delivering a truth or a lie. Ellis pulled a one-hundred-riyal note from his pocket and offered it to Sam.

'How's the gambling debts, Sam?'

Sam grabbed the offering with a smile and a lightening of his mood. 'It's OK, sir.'

'Did you gamble in prison?'

'Not allowed. Sir.'

'Since when did that stop you?'

Sam smiled an enigmatic smile, offered sir a cup of tea, and went to his station in the kitchen just as Anderson walked in, leaving the outer door swinging, the dust pouring in through the space. He threw his papers down on his desk and began his oration.

'Say guys. D'ya see that Saudi scumbag in here? What's he want?'

Ellis and Clitty ignored the opening, as the following verbiage would be much like usual.

'I bet I know what he's doin'. In here to talk to Mr Bloody Choi, talk to the bloody fish, smoke some cow dung, ask who's on the take, do some checkin' an' a bit of inspectin' and tellin' everybody about how he gets caught showing off his John Thomas in a john in the UK.'

Nobody seemed keen to listen, but Clitty seemed anxious to respond. True to form, he did just that, without moving a muscle and without his eyes leaving the final report for the radiology areas.

'Actually, he came in to check the reports that you'd been found in bed with a Filipino faggot.'

Anderson would have loved to take apart this giant for a comment like that, even if it was true. It could all wait; he would have that bloody man one day. His chance would surely come. He disguised his shudder of rage as an acclimatisation shudder at the efficiency of the air conditioners, sat down without comment, farted loudly, and demanded that Sam should bring him some tea.

Abdul Rahman walked solemnly to his office and was surprised to find he had a visitor. Few came to visit near lunchtime, especially not Saudis. Any time after twelve and before three was always free of ethnic visitors.

This old Saudi visitor was not known to the young Abdul Rahman but had made himself comfortable in one of the visitors' chairs. He had let himself in to the office, there being no welcoming secretariat to guard against unannounced visitors. After customary greetings, Abdul Rahman took his place and offered some Turkish coffee from a desktop pot.

Both drank politely, then settled to the business. The visitor stood awkwardly, even in his fading years still towering above Abdul Rahman, then dug deep into his *thobe* pocket and with great difficulty and struggle pulled out a videocassette tape and laid it on the desk, alongside the coffee and before Abdul Rahman's questioning eyes.

'Watch this, *habibi*,' the man said breathlessly. 'You will see our king, our leader, the leader of our holy religion, the custodian of the two holy places, the places blessed by our blessed prophet Mohammed, may peace and blessings be upon him, and you will see the family of our leaders, you will see all of it upon this … thing.' The Saudi waved with some disdain at the dusty tape on the desk and promised to divine Abdul Rahman's opinion in a week or so. All the younger man had to do was to watch it on a video recorder that he didn't possess.

The old Saudi gave a blessing and left the room without drinking the second cup of the coffee.

Abdul Rahman looked at the video and listened to the clock.

Those bloody British. They would have a video player.

But they would go for lunch soon.

Get over there quickly.

Refastening his sandals, Abdul Rahman leaped to his mission, straightened his clothing, and returned to the nest of the British and the thieves.

'Mr Abdul Rahman,' Mr Choi courteously greeted the return of his earlier visitor, 'our pleasure. What can we do for you?'

The bulge of the video in Abdul Rahman's pocket seemed to shriek its presence to all.

'I would like to talk to your members of your staff who are the British.'

Choi thought this a strange request, but acceded anyway. Strange that. They would normally talk to Anderson first.

Perhaps Abdul Rahman thought Anderson was American.

Whatever, Anderson would be upset to be bypassed by the Saudi, so yes, go ahead.

Abdul Rahman approached Clitty, who stood with a broad smile on his face and a handshake that nearly crushed the Saudi's arm.

'Just call me Clitty.' The Brit smiled as he watched the Saudi trying to work out the Polish surname on the computer-generated nameplate stuck with tape on Clitty's desktop. 'What can I do for you, Mr Abdul Rahman?'

Abdul Rahman felt nervous and showed it too. 'I have a videotape.'

'Oh yeh? Any good birds on it?'

'Excuse me?'

'The video. Any good, is it? Good for home viewing?'

'That I do not know, Mr Clitty. It is a training tape.' He thought quickly. 'Medical things, some equipment, I think.'

'Oh. In that case we have a player across there. Sam! Set up the video!'

'Yes, sir.' Sam appeared from somewhere and made for the player, much to Abdul Rahman's alarm.

'No. No need.' Abdul Rahman's tone was absolute. 'It may be something I need to see on my own.'

Anderson could contain his interest no longer and walked to Clitty's table to offer some sort of solution. 'What's on?' he demanded.

Clitty tried to use some British diplomacy to explain the predicament, but Anderson assumed it was pornography and recommended that Abdul Rahman come round with it at seven o'clock.

'Good time for a bit of the old stuff, a good old video.'

Anderson punched Abdul Rahman's arm playfully, winked, and returned to the crossword in a recent copy of the London *Times*. The day's crossword presented a particular challenge to Anderson as many of the across clues had been obliterated by a black marker pen soaking through from the other side of the page. Glancing impatiently at what the censor had deemed necessary to redact, Anderson discovered that the coverage of the Davis Cup had revealed the upper thighs and arms of Martina Navratilova. In common with any public displays of a woman's body, photographs, even sports photographs, fell within the purview of the censor. And it mattered not to him that most of the crossword was thus rendered a total nonsense.

Morals. Bah!

Anderson lit a cigarette and wondered what was so immoral about this Saudi's video that he felt unable to take it to another Saudi's house. They all had video recorders and, though these were illegal, many of them also had satellite receivers. They were all into the Western films, the Western way of entertainment. Could only be one thing. Or maybe two things.

First, it was pornography, or second, it was a plant.

Abdul Rahman would talk to the police about his suspicions that these Westerners had pornography in their house. He would be going round tonight, and why didn't the police come and round them all up? Abdul Rahman would, of course, have been invited and would be treated as a totally innocent party. Innocent because he was a Saudi, and unblemished because he was a Muslim, and Muslims didn't watch pornography. Well, not in the Kingdom anyway.

Neat.

And then there may have been a third reason for the visit. The booze. Anderson, Ellis, and Clitty really had only one thing in common. They liked to drink. Their store of home-made and -labelled liquor filled the bathroom and staff quarters to bursting. All time off from the site was spent drinking, so a visit from a Saudi would probably need to be a dry night.

Anderson concentrated his mind on the front-page photograph of Princess Diana's legs, the Princess of Wales, legs that defied the censor and legs that a thousand dreams were made of. In Anderson's judgement, they were a dream come true. So he just stared and wondered about that moist area about seven inches above the hemline.

Then, with little useful left to do, he set about some task that would entail abusing the Egyptian draughtsmen, and walked across to find one of them with his little finger firmly wedged inside one nostril and a pencil perched precariously on the top of his ear. Ellis watched the swagger of this pseudo-American, but chose to ignore all of it. For the moment.

'Whatcher tryin' to do, buddy?' Anderson snarled at the draughtsman. 'Tryin' to get yer finger to join up with the bloody pencil?'

The Egyptian offered a disdainful smile and continued the task of clearing his nose with a little finger blessed with a magnificently manicured and very long nail.

'Bloody scumbags,' Anderson cursed as he walked back to try to focus his mind on the piped medical gases section of the project. But he really was not interested. Anderson was only really interested in himself.

Born in Brighton, East Sussex, UK, in the year of the great Lynmouth flood, Anderson was brought up to believe in anything and everything British. As a pram-bound baby he was taken by his father to London to view the coronation, and his father sang for the glory of the Empire, and he sang for his new Queen, and he sang for victory over Hitler, and he sang for a new leg to replace the one lost while on a bombing run over Hamburg in 1943. Dad sang his heart out on the Mall.

Then they all went home to the penury of a damp and condemned terraced house located on high ground near the Brighton Race Course. The walk from anywhere in the town always involved a struggle up an incline. Mothers with babies in prams, they struggled. If the milkman's float was down on electricity, it stopped halfway up the street, to run backwards into the kerbing and be picked up later in the day by the dairy's rescue truck. The milkman carried on by foot, and he struggled.

When it rained, the torrent would roar along the gutters, sweeping away rubbish and discarded cigarette ends. When it shined and when overcast, all the children played on the street. They argued, they fought, they laughed, and they cried. More often, though, in Anderson's street, the play was disrupted by his crying. In an unhappy incident that was witnessed by his mother, a child was singing and dancing and pointing at Anderson. 'Mathew Anderson, blind as a bat, he got eyes what go this way and that.'

'I'm not blind. I can see!' the five-year-old wailed, wondering why objects certainly occasionally appeared in duplicate.

Anderson's mother, unusually home from work early, berated the tormenter into silence and in a fierce frenzy of fake rage slapped him in the face.

The boy stopped momentarily and ran off to find his own mother, who came out rolling the sleeves of her housecoat up her pudgy arms. Both mothers swapped insults and abuse while the children returned to the relative calm of playing cops and robbers. Father would watch all the action from his window, as he had little physical capacity for work; he couldn't drive buses with one leg and one testicle. He didn't feel like singing today. Rain was forecast; that made him less inclined to break into song.

The time of Suez was the last time he had felt stirred into patriotic song. He couldn't fight that bloody Nasser, but at least he reckoned he could sing the dictator to hand back the canal.

'Jerusalem', 'Land of Hope and Glory', 'God Save the Queen', 'I was glad': the old man would sing them all with missionary fervour, particularly when shaving in front of a misty bathroom mirror. Mother had heard it all before and suffered the songs with good humour. He was a good man, after all.

When Mother went out to work to fix sewing machines and run up some clothes, Father would negotiate with Mathew to play safely in the street with his friends while Father went to negotiate some business.

That was his way of explaining a visit to the Legion, the Royal British Legion, its local headquarters housed in a single-storey shed close to the hospital and about a third of a mile from the house. He could walk it if his false leg was securely tied on, and if it wasn't, the discomfort was well counterbalanced by the prospect of a few beers with his chums.

Their chats always reflected the tragedy of Winston's demise in '55 and that bloody Nasser. This Macmillan, he seems all right, and have you got a television yet? No, we haven't neither, and have you heard old so-and-so, he's bought a car. Blimey, must have a lot of money, mind you the number 46 got taken off last week, how are we supposed to get to the open market, go via the Old Steine? I'll say not, blimey no. Yes, mine's a pint of Red Barrel, cheers. As I was saying, my missus had to go to Clock Tower on the number 41, change to the number 12, change at Saint Peter's, then walk a bloody half mile to the open market just to buy a bag of spuds, Jesus, and then she has to do the whole thing in reverse. Not like the old days. No.

Silence while all reminisced about the old days, beer was sipped, and pipes and roll-ups reignited.

Then someone, usually Anderson senior, would begin to sing.

'Pack up your troubles in an old kit bag', 'If you were the only girl in the world', 'The white cliffs of Dover'; then most of them, now well fortified with beer, would join in. The landlord – or the colonel, as he was respectfully called – would call time, and Anderson senior would break into the old favourites, drowning out the clanging of the last orders bell as he invoked Jerusalem and finished with a polished salute to the flag, unsteadily singing the national anthem.

The members of the Legion equally loved Anderson and hated him for all the noise, but he was a character. He sang well, if flat, and they admired him most for calling himself to attention with absolute military precision and no suggestion that one of his legs was false.

After last post, he would limp home and settle into his chair while young Mathew continued to suffer the barks and bounds of those with good eyes in the street outside. Father would hum tunes to himself, thinking of his glory days and of when he would next have the opportunity to sing patriotic songs.

Then one day the singing stopped.

While Father was shaving and singing to the glory of the French in Algeria, the mirror offering clear reflection only in one corner of an otherwise fogged surface, he was gripped by a brief pain in his chest. Before being able to shout out more than 'oh shit', he fell to the floor like a stone.

Dead.

The six-year-old boy playing with a boat on the edge of the bath assumed that Father was rerunning the bombing campaign of North Africa, the dropped razor being another downed Hun.

He ran to his mother, who was boiling the clothes in the tub and listening to the wireless. She too thought the sound symptomatic of another bombing run. Or the false leg giving way and unbalancing the old boy.

She didn't expect to find her man dead on the bathroom floor.

In the weeks that followed, she threw away all his ashtrays and his special matchbook and his cigarette papers and his old baccy tin, still bearing the fading face and crest of King George the Sixth. She kept all the photographs of her man in his uniform – on parade, the one of him shaking the hand of somebody important, the picture of all the squadron throwing their hats in the air – and the one of her and him at their wedding in 1948. All of them had their places on the mantelpiece.

She hadn't done very well at having babies; she only had the one. But the old boy gloried in the thought that the whole baby shortage lay in the fact that one of his testicles was blown off along with his leg over Hamburg. Never, never did he mention it being anybody's fault except the Hun's. They would have loved a big family, but all they got was this boy. The boy was loved, and the old man had sung and Mother had done the washing. And they'd only ever had five legs between the lot of them.

Mother went out to work, hoping to go back as a cleaner at the barracks on the Lewes Road, but there was no work there. So she worked at a sewing machine repair shop in Kemp Town, where, at least, she was able to use her dressmaking talents, simultaneously earning a repair wage and a dressmaking salary.

The boy went to school, suffered the taunts of his peers, struggled to pass the eleven-plus. He received a new bike for it from some of Mother's money, thinking one night as he lay alone in his bed, alone in the house, that she did seem to have a lot of money these days. They had long gone from the damp existence of the house near the racecourse. Long gone were the days when young Anderson would watch coach after coach struggle up the hill that was Elm Grove to disgorge the punters for a day at the races, then take them all away from his town about six hours later. They now had a semi-detached house in Hollingbury – still on high ground, but then Brighton was either at sea level or up in the clouds – and he went to a good local school where nobody thought he could see properly.

If mother worked at a repair shop, how come she had so much money now? She had no money when Dad was alive. Maybe he had money and left it behind. Mathew Anderson thought about it all. What was different about his mother?

Nothing.

She was good fun, she worked hard, and she was often out till late.

Claude Pemberton

And he was as happy as he had ever been. Most of all, the bathroom was always warm. Perhaps it had something to do with that telephone, the envy of his friends. It would often ring just about the time he'd gone to bed. Mother would pop her head round the door to say she'd be out for a while, but if any problem, just call Aunty Margaret next door, 'You know her number, night sweetheart'.

Mrs Edith Anderson would get into a taxi and submerge herself for two hours in Brighton low life. For the woman of respectability was a hooker.

Now in her early forties, she had run the mill of babies, put on weight, stared mortality in the face, lost all the weight, then thought about ways to better herself financially in the absence of a wage-earning husband. She added justification to her decision on the basis that her husband had never been able to work properly, missing limbs and all that entailed, and besides she enjoyed what she did. To reinforce that, she had hidden all the old photographs in some box in the attic.

Her modus operandi was simple. She left business cards, euphemistically announcing her as a hostess, with trustworthy housemaids at the Bedford, the Grand, and the Royal Albion hotels. Should any of their esteemed guests require a little female company for a drink and whatever, then they should call this number.

Innocent stuff, she reasoned.

It paid very well too.

So while the young Mathew lay in bed and fretted and stared at two points on a ceiling illuminated through the gap in the curtains by the pale white light of the street light, his mother was servicing well-heeled clients in Brighton's most exquisite hotels. The boy knew nothing of all this; it seemed quite natural to have no father at all, and quite natural to have no mother as soon as the sun set.

Strange really.

He explored the silhouette of the street lights against the wrinkles of the curtains and imagined shapes: shapes that could be faces, shapes that could be ocean-going ships, shapes that could be ghosts. But before he could resolve any of the shapes, he was fast asleep, and not very much later his mother was safely and silently tucked up back in her own bed, much the richer for her night's work.

Hollingbury would never know.

Hopefully.

Happily for Mathew, nobody ever discovered the secret. There were no denizens of Hollingbury with enough money to go to one of the hotels for a night with a hooker who turned out to be Mrs Anderson. *'Oh hello, Mrs Anderson. I was hoping to talk to you at the parents' meeting last week.' 'Oh hello, headmaster or vicar or worse, so nice to see you here.'* The whole operation was discreet, it was secret, and it remained so for its duration. Which was considerable.

The money allowed Mrs Anderson to consider what to do with her son. He was slow at school, nobody seemed to like him, and he'd become more remote just lately. Maybe a special school, maybe a boarding school. Yes. Get him away from this house. Then the clients could come here. No taxi fees for me to pay. Wait, that wouldn't do. Just think of all those taxis dropping men off at half-hourly intervals and picking them up again half an hour later. Suppose they went to the wrong house and said 'hello darlin'' to Mrs Gavaghan, a holy Roman Catholic, or one of her eleven virgin daughters. Oh hell, no. That would never do. Perhaps Mrs Gavaghan would be interested in some sex without commitment, mused Mathew's mother to herself over a cup of coffee. A smile covered her matured and pretty face. Imagine Mrs Gavaghan in confession: 'Bless me, Father, for I have sinned. I've become a hooker.'

'Jesus, Mary, and Joseph,' the priest would utter, 'where d'you carry on? Would you be givin' me your number now?'

No. She wasn't like that.

Mrs Gavaghan would lie on her back while Mr Gavaghan thrashed around and fumbled with her loins. Then they'd all go to sleep and awake to find all their virgins intact. Except, maybe, their 17-year-old, who could be seen on a Friday night outside the Wilmington pub with her skirt hitched up around her upper thighs and laughing and chatting to the lads, their hands actively probing the deepest recesses of their trouser pockets and her nether regions.

Edith Anderson's thoughts turned from her current career and wondered what to do with the little shit. For her love of the boy was sorely tried. He was so puny. He never really played with the other boys, and when he did, they soon all fell out. Then the teasing would start afresh: 'Hey, Mathew, we're over here and here, both at the same time!' The corrective glasses dispensed on the health service could do little to correct his sight, and even if they could, they could not disguise the misalignment of his eyes.

He always seemed to have a runny nose and he always had an ache somewhere. His mother poured another cup of coffee, wondering how much he might have achieved at school today, then sat down and looked through the local paper for jobs. What sort of job might he get when he grew up? He was 13 now, he could possibly be in the job market in three years' time, so what the hell could he do? There were plenty of jobs advertised: turners, lathe operators, shop assistants, packers, assemblers.

Mother sighed as she snapped the paper shut. Young Mathew was probably incapable of doing anything. Period.

To her surprise, Mathew did knuckle down and work. The only way to receive approbation from his teachers was to work hard, and while he suffered the taunts of his peers, at least the teachers now seemed to like him. He came out of school at age 18 with eight passes at ordinary level and three passes at advanced level. His advanced-level exams were in chemistry, human biology, and physics. He applied to become a doctor but somehow nobody seemed to want him.

At the end of one particularly gruelling interview, and as Mathew left the room, he thought he heard one of the panel commenting that with a face like that, he would frighten people to death rather than heal them. But then he had a chip on his shoulder, and he would think he had heard something derogatory about his eyes.

With the qualifications he had, he decided he would still like to work in a hospital, in the operating theatres as an operating department assistant, or ODA. The money was OK, you got to see all the action, and people respected you. If you can't be a doctor, he reasoned, this must be a good alternative.

Your Friday, My Sunday

His decision made, the gangling youth made his announcement to his mother, who sat in the armchair, filing her fingernails.

'That'll be nice, dear,' she said. 'Will they wash your things for you?'

Working in a hospital had to be better than being in the RAF like his father. But then he had little choice. His eyes. Always his eyes, always a bloody problem. One pointed this way; the other pointed that way. He had gone to an RAF careers officer and had been asked to peer into a make-believe bombing simulator. He was pushed to make any visual sense of it. The stiff upper lip had said, 'Now off you go. Can't have chaps like you flying for Blighty. With eyes like that, you might damn well bomb London instead of Moscow. Out you go then.'

Out he went, applied for, and was appointed to a position as a trainee ODA at Cleveland General Hospital in Newcastle upon Tyne. His early duties included the preparation of the trolleys in the prep room, the room where the patient was initially anaesthetised prior to being taken into the operating theatre for surgery. He also had to check that all the piped gases, the oxygen, and the resuscitation equipment were all functioning correctly. The supervisor thought the young lad was adequate. Although he did wonder whether, with eyes like that, he would be able to read the monitors properly.

Under Anderson's care, the operating department did run smoothly. He attended night school punctiliously to pass his City and Guilds examinations: anatomy and physiology (grade A), anaesthesia and drug delivery (grade A), operating theatre processes and procedures (grade A), with a grade B in respiratory criteria and stress in anaesthesia. That grade B grated with Anderson, who had hoped for a clean sweep of grade As. Nevertheless, the consultant anaesthetist seemed pleased enough with his recruit's newfound qualifications and came in one day to tell him so.

'Heard your results today, Mathew.'

Anderson smiled, busying himself in laying out the requirements for the day's list.

'And it sounds like you've made it.'

'Thank you, Doctor. I was pretty pleased with the results, too.'

Anderson continued to lay out the forceps, scissors, tubes, airways, drugs, adrenaline, and clamps, polishing them fussily, just as a maître de table would polish and polish until every last thing gleamed in sunlight or in candlelight. Everything he touched, Anderson planned, would gleam and shine in those lights.

Everybody would know Mathew Anderson was on duty.

The anaesthetist couldn't make out the direction of the eyes but assumed that, as the lad could read textbooks and write, he must be able to see properly. He also wondered if the newest ODA had sought some help.

'Excuse me for asking,' the doctor began gently, 'but your eyes—'

'Yeh. I know,' Anderson retorted tartly. 'They point in different directions, an astigmatism or something.' Anderson pulled at some sterile drapes to make them and the trolley top absolutely uniform. 'There's nothing to be done. Whatever they could do, they did. So now I'm left looking this way and that.'

The doctor leaned against the side of a work top, holding his glasses in his hand with the earpiece gently resting between his lips, watching Anderson as he prepared for the day.

'Too bad,' the doctor concurred. 'Ever thought about surgery for it?'

'Nah. Just corrective glasses. That's all I've ever had. They say there's nothing to be done, particularly not now as I'm in my twenties. Too late, I suppose.'

The doctor had to agree. It was very late. Should have been fixed when he was six.

That's just what Anderson knew, but he also knew that his mother paid him no attention. She had just thought he was an ugly little bugger when he was six, so had got him some glasses that didn't do anything to improve him. He would, presumably, then be brave and come to terms with the fact that he was ugly.

'Morning, Doctor Sheldon. Morning, Mathew,' sang the staff nurse cheerfully as she came in for the day shift. 'And how's my favourite?' She tapped Mathew's stomach with friendly mock affection as she moved serenely past her ODA and through the anaesthesia room, tying up her plastic apron as she went.

Mathew mistook this affection for real affection and decided that juicy Linda, the staff nurse, had the hots for him. Dr Sheldon noted the lascivious glance and concluded the boy was either stupid or naive or both. Just hope he reads the instruments more accurately, he thought. Exams or no exams, we don't need a turd like him who comes in his pants even before a hand is laid and then kills a patient when he can't tell one set of vital signs from another.

The physician left the room to prepare himself for the day. Mathew prepared himself for the killer line to draw Linda into his bed, or maybe the two student nurses now arrived. Either of them would do. Both had half-decent tits, or at least they seemed to have two tits each. Eyes played funny tricks …. Each girl seemed to have a full bra of two tits, one each side.

Most days played themselves out with similarly sexual undertones: patients wheeled in and wheeled out, the quiver of clothing noted, the hitch of the nurse's hemline when turning the patient, the prospect of an inadvertent sight of thigh. These were the things that drove Mathew, and these were the things that made work worth coming to, day after day.

Then an incident occurred that proved there was more money, lots more money, to be made from this job. Yes, it was possible to lie down with nurses and make lots of money.

During a particularly busy list, one of the student nurses with two medium-sized tits shimmied into the room, clutching a business card, and called for Mathew.

'Mathew,' she called triumphantly, 'someone here to see you.'

Mathew picked up the card and in a businesslike manner strode from the room towards the person who wished to see him.

Anderson left the clean area, removed his face mask, and approached the man in a suit who stood outside the operating theatres, just far enough beyond the red aseptic line.

'Mr Anderson?' the suited figure called correctly. Holding out a hand of apparent friendship, he held the ODA's hand firmly. 'Hello, I'm Mark Berry, from Insta-Med.'

'Oh yeh?' Anderson began suspiciously, 'What d'you make?'

'Never mind what we make, Mr Anderson. Think what we can make for you.' The young Mark Berry seemed certain of something and pressed on in a hurried manner. 'Mr Anderson, how old is the piped gases system in there?' He nodded with eyes beyond the closed theatre doors that could only be activated by someone with the four-figure pass code.

'God knows.'

Anderson really didn't know. Late seventies maybe.

'And the ventilators, and the anaesthesia machines, and the gas pipes, how old are they?'

'God knows that too,' Anderson replied with total honesty and an innocent smile. 'Why?'

'See, Mr Anderson,' the young representative moved closer, his rather fetid breath causing Anderson to wince and move a little away, 'if you would like to make some suggestions on what is wrong with the current system, we could help you to replace it. Know what I mean?'

Anderson looked back towards the source of the malodour. Then Mark Berry noticed the eyes. How the hell did this man read the instruments? How the hell did he tell what he was looking at?

The Insta-Med instruments all had audible alarms; so did most other manufacturers', come to that. But this man would probably turn on all the piped gases, and when the patient started to go anoxic, the alarm would go off and the ODA would run to the rescue and reset all the controls. Trouble was, in his dash to reach the instruments, he would probably not spot the anaesthetist's adjacent stool and would splay himself across the theatre floor. What he needs, Mark Berry concluded, is a helping hand to make some money.

What this man Mark Berry needs, Anderson mused, is a new toothbrush and some industrial toothpaste.

'What do you mean?' Anderson asked.

Mark Berry had met some naive folks in his relatively short sales career, but here was someone special. He had not the first clue on how to make money for himself, save his pitiful salary.

'Tell you what I mean. Fancy a beer?'

Anderson looked at his watch and promised he'd meet this character at a local pub at the end of the shift. That way the smell of the pub, the smoke, the spilled beer, and the cheap perfumes might drown this man's halitosis.

The shift came to an uneventful end. Anderson grabbed some clothing from his locker, donning something he considered vaguely fashionable yet sober – something appropriate to discuss business.

At the end of a session with Mark Berry, more remarkable for the beer than for the honesty, Anderson was fully primed to make representations to Dr Sheldon that the anaesthesia systems were expensive to run, expensive to repair, unpredictable in performance, and liable to failure, and the whole lot needed to be replaced in a phased fashion. After all, Mark Berry only needed the order to get his commission. The phasing lessened the shock to the hospital but did nothing to stop the representative from getting his money in full. Nor did it do anything to stop Anderson getting, immediately the order was signed, his 5 per cent commission: some eleven thousand, seven hundred and eighty-five pounds.

For six months thereafter, Anderson harried and persuaded Dr Sheldon. He finally got his approval, and the whole scam was on. On the periphery, Mark Berry advised, cajoled, threatened, and promised.

Dr Sheldon liked the Insta-Med proposal. He also liked Sister Bennet, the lady without whose approval nothing in the department could or would happen. And Sister Bennet loved Dr Sheldon with as much feeling as she hated the cross-eyed Anderson.

Dr Sheldon discussed the proposal in bed with Sister Bennet. Sister Bennet discussed marriage in bed with Dr Sheldon. Dr Sheldon preferred nuzzling between Sister Bennet's thighs and could really make no comment when orally caressing her nether regions. All in all, nothing of substance was ever discussed except the competence of that cross-eyed git. Dr Sheldon was going to change the entire piped medical gas system and the anaesthesia machines all on the say-so of some ignorant ODA whose qualifications were to medicine what mercy was to the Nazis.

And while Sister Bennet climaxed and writhed under the tongue of the esteemed doctor, she thought about the department gossip that suggested her lover was moving to have her replaced in theatres by someone younger – and prettier, the word was. New blood was needed, he'd said. That bloody Anderson was at the root of all the change, she cursed. Then she shuddered and uttered words of undying love as the physician withdrew his mouth.

He mounted his rancid colleague, probably for the last time, and relieved himself. Masturbation would probably have been more seemly, the doctor concluded as he drove home alone late in the night, watching all the bedroom lights – some on, some dimmed, some already extinguished, shadows flickering across drawn curtains, everybody up to something.

Dr Sheldon did indeed get Sister Bennet dumped for a younger and much prettier theatre sister, while Anderson went about getting the entire system replaced. He picked up his cheque from Mark Berry. Then he got fired.

Sister Bennet had the ear, and the groin, of the anaesthetics number 7, the boss lady. Together they explored the irregularities of the department and the intricacies of their respective labial folds. Sister Bennet reckoned that Anderson was responsible. Besides, he was on the take, and anyway he was incompetent because of those eyes. How the hell could he put one foot in front of the other, let alone dispense life-saving therapies to his patients? In bed one night, the number 7 and the dismissed sister decided to give the ODA the push: no references, just the one month's salary in lieu. The little shit could go to hell. I've lost my man, reasoned Sister Bennet, and all I have is the sweet-tasting number 7, so the little shit can carry my wrath.

And so he did.

Out of work with one month's pay plus a generous commission cheque, already banked, Anderson was well funded for the moment, but what to do next? Another hospital? Unlikely, at least within the National Health Service.

Dismissal without references always implied some profound wrongdoing. With references, one could always talk one's way into a job. Not without one. This meant a different future: if in the UK, it meant being away from the health service; if outside, there was always the possibility of a position in foreign parts.

In the course of his recollection, Anderson had dismissed the nose-picking Egyptian from his mind and had returned to his table. He recalled how he had been recruited to the veteran's hospital in Seattle, Washington, how he had run the OR, as they quaintly called the operating theatre there. He recalled how he had been captivated by the American way of life, the beauty of Puget Sound, the people, their trust, and their language.

Anderson sat down to work once more on the piped medical gases project and realised that he even now spoke like an American, having been recruited by an agency to transfer to Saudi Arabia after an eight-month sabbatical in the Pacific Northwest. Now all he could do was to look up at Choi's fish and see the wretched creature pouting at him as it turned derisively and continued to patrol its territory.

Anderson's sole achievements to date had been to speak like an American and to be annoyed by a tropical fish.

There had to be more to life than this. Anderson lit another cigarette as Sam approached to enquire regarding sir's coffee requirements. Sir was thirsty as ever and welcomed Sam's friendly attention.

Little shit.

The troubled day came to an end as Anderson, Ellis, and Clitty drove home to the same house in three different cars. Ellis arrived first and set to putting all the booze into the third bathroom and locking the door. If that Abdul Rahman really was coming, they would need to be clear of the smell or the suggestion of the presence of something that the prophet Mohammed, peace and blessings be upon him, had forbidden mankind to be associated with. Anderson arrived next and shouted that they could probably get away with a few drinks, provided they all brushed their teeth as soon as the Saudi arrived. Some discussion ensued as soon as Clitty walked in.

None of them needed much convincing that they could really get away with it, so Ellis unlocked the bathroom door and pulled out a bottle of *siddiqi* as Anderson collected the Pepsi from the fridge.

'Cheers,' he called cheerfully as the first slug went down, then the next. 'Wonder what the video is?'

Nobody replied.

Then the telephone rang, the bell breaking the concentration of the three men on the way that this drink could make one quite dizzy quite quickly. The shrill command from the telephone went unheeded.

'That'll be him,' Anderson drawled with total certainty.

Nobody moved except to light more cigarettes, the smoke curling to mask their faces in the low light.

'Shall we answer it?' Ellis enquired openly but with little enthusiasm.

An air conditioner cut in to help neutralise the sound of the phone that kept on ringing.

'I say we leave it,' Clitty suggested.

This was a decision to be made quickly.

'S'pose we could answer it. Might be Mother.' Anderson ventured the thought they all had. The ringing wouldn't go away, could be a call from home: the alimony cheque has bounced, one of the kids has fallen under a bus, father has died, or father has just murdered mother …

Ellis got up slowly from his chair to put paid to the cacophony.

'This is world war three,' he announced cheerfully, then looked pensive as Abdul Rahman on the other end cursed them for not answering earlier. Abdul Rahman explained that he would not need to come round to see the video as he had found a friend with a recorder. He'd seen the video, and goddammit, it showed pictures of his royal family at a wedding in the Emirates, where alcohol was being served and there were women dancing on the tables.

'Still going on, is it? Can we come?' Ellis prodded playfully.

Ellis went quiet as some more words were spoken. Then he hung up.

'Thank God for that.' Ellis sighed as he returned to the sofa.

'What?' Anderson asked impatiently.

'He's not coming. Found somewhere else to see his video.'

The fact that Abdul Rahman had the video, a video, and had the confidence to at least ask to view it at the site was to be congratulated. Ellis wondered at this apparent innocence, an innocence which seemed enshrined in their developing conversations, sometimes heartfelt exchanges, when the Saudi sat on one side of his desk, leaned back in his executive chair, and dispensed coffee, while Ellis sat in a leather-backed, upright chair on the outer edge of the table. Earlier in the day he had been in the Saudi's office to talk – no real agenda, just a need for understanding another person, a person who seemed to have no friends but who came in to work, sat there, and made sound comments.

Abdul Rahman visited the ministry. Those visits, Ellis surmised, would be useful to know about, so on a whim he would drop by. There was an incongruous nature to this office: the leather furniture; that settee; the cheap brass ornaments on the desk and shelf units; the embroidered Arabic rug depicting rich, coloured patterns, predominantly red and beige; the grimy windows; the noise; the dust that seeped into the room, the air thick with microparticles.

Ellis could walk into this office and the dark eyes would watch him. Hoping for a gentle meeting, Abdul Rahman would ask Ellis to stay a while, have a coffee.

Ellis usually stayed.

'So …' Ellis began on this occasion, lowering himself into the leather high-back chair.

'So …' said Abdul Rahman, equally unable to give the conversation much momentum.

'So … thanks for the coffee.' Ellis tipped back the small cup, the sharp Turkish coffee gripping his throat.

Silence. This was going nowhere. It needed something.

Neutral ground.

'What used to be here?' Ellis asked cheerfully.

Abdul Rahman wasn't sure he understood the question. The floor used to be empty; now it had got a table, and he said so.

'No, no,' Ellis replied. 'Before the site, before this site was developing into a hospital, what was here?'

'Desert. Mainly,' Abdul Rahman offered helpfully.

'Mainly?'

'Yeh. You see, the road into Riyadh from Dammam came straight through where you're sitting.'

'So what happened to the Dammam highway?'

'The old road, where we're located, was the old highway. Then they put up the flyover, past Sitteen Street.'

'Oh.'

'You know it?'

'I should do – I drive on it going home every night.'

'OK then. The old road came in from Dammam, went across the top of Sitteen Street, went to the left slightly past the military hospital, went past the Marriott Hotel, then came past here before turning right to go towards Olaya.'

'Where dat?'

'Olaya? You know the Alkhozama Hotel?'

'Yeh.'

'That's Olaya.'

'Oh.'

Silence fell on them as a topic of limited common interest ran out of energy.

The air conditioner thought otherwise and rattled its disdain as Abdul Rahman poured more coffee and watched Ellis light another cigarette.

'What's the purpose of that?' Ellis asked, watching Abdul Rahman idly swing his beads from side to side and wrap them round his fingers. 'Looks like you're saying the rosary.'

Abdul Rahman didn't hear Ellis, or if he did, he chose to ignore the comment.

'Oh nothing ...' Abdul Rahman said, anxious to get some meaningful conversation under way before Ellis abandoned him as a hopeless case. Then he leaned forward in his chair and picked up a sheaf of important-looking papers on his desk and launched himself into a proper chat.

'You know what this is? Mr Walid's latest revision.' Abdul Rahman didn't wait for a reply. 'And he seems to think the intensive care or high dependency unit, what's the difference anyway, is too far away from the OR.' Ellis sat forward in his chair, catching a breath of Abdul Rahman's eau de cologne as he unfolded the first-floor plan and laid it out on the desktop. 'So how far should it be?'

'As near as you can make it,' Ellis confirmed. 'If you have a patient in bad shape and he goes direct from theatres to the intensive care, the two need to be as close as they can. There's no point in them being at opposite ends of the hospital.'

'No man, that's true. But what's this?' Abdul Rahman trailed his finger across the sheet and saw that although they were very close on the plan, the text suggested they were on different floors, and the lift was at the far end of corridor A, which fed patients up from the ER, or the A&E as the Brits liked to call it.

Ellis agreed. There was some discrepancy in the drawing, some differences of technical and engineering expressions, but he couldn't work it out, particularly looking at it upside down from where he was seated.

'OK,' Abdul Rahman said helpfully, 'patient comes out of the OR here,' pointing a manicured index finger at the red-lined chart, 'and goes to the intensive care. But the bloody patient has to go up a flight of stairs or he goes all the way along the corridor when he comes out of the OR, goes to lift A, and then back to intensive care. What's going on? Does Walid know what's happening?'

First floor.

Of course.

Design drawings done by the British had the ground floor, where the British-built OR was going to be. Then patients were taken to the intensive care unit, which was located on the first floor, according to the American design engineers.

'I'll tell you what this is, goddammit. The bloody drawings are done by different design teams. The British team call the first floor the ground floor, and the American team call what the Brits call the ground floor, the first floor.'

Abdul Rahman had fiercely wound his beads around his knuckle, swinging them this way and that, unable to comprehend what he'd just been told.

'So …' he began timidly, 'which floor has the OR, the first floor or the ground floor?'

'Depends. Could be either. Or both.'

'Goddammit.' Abdul Rahman mimicked Ellis's expression, one which would ultimately unite them in laughter, and which now allowed them to smile, shake their heads, and drink more coffee.

'So you see, Abdul Rahman, the patient comes out of the OR on the ground floor. He's still unconscious. He gets wheeled down the hall and upstairs to the first floor, thereby inhibiting his recovery by jarring all his stitches and anyway, the porters had to carry the patient up all them stairs, and the lift's too far …'

'Goddammit.' Abdul Rahman giggled at the thought. 'So what we gonna do? This first floor and ground floor?'

'Just remember who the architects were. Which country do they come from? Which country does Mr Walid at the ministry think they come from?'

'And we ignore the drawings?' Abdul Rahman looked at Ellis with a look of horror.

'Yup. Pretty much.'

'You're kidding.'

'Not quite. You need to refer to the profile view, which gives the names of each floor: ground floor, first floor, second floor. If there are more than three floors in the drawing, you either have the wrong hospital drawing, or there's something Mr Walid hasn't told you.'

'Like what?'

'Well, like he's added a floor or two to the hospital and he hasn't mentioned it to anybody. Hopes you'll pick it up.'

'Oh God,' Abdul Rahman gasped and realised he knew little of weights, measures, volumes metric and Imperial, litres, distances, and cubic feet.

'Don't worry,' Ellis said. 'I don't understand anything about buildings, I only know the medical stuff. That's all you need to know, really, and if you don't know, I'll try to tell you, and if I don't know, I'll refer you to Mr Anderson, who can fill you in.'

Abdul Rahman rolled his eyes in horror at the thought of a meeting with the pseudo-Yank. 'I bet you something,' he said cheerfully.

'What's that?'

'He'll know first floor and ground floor, being a Yank and all.'

Abdul Rahman shook his head, smiling, as he looked again at the drawings. Ellis remained seated nearby, not keen to leave, nor really that committed to spending any further time in the Saudi's office. His thoughts were cut short as Abdul Rahman creased the drawings flat on his desktop and began to speak.

'This stuff here, aitch zed, what's that then?' He pointed a finger at some numbers and labels on a chart showing lines in apparently unruly patterns.

'You mean Hertz.'

'Hurts? That's a sort of pain, isn't it?'

Abdul Rahman became frustrated as the technical drawing kept curling from the edges, so he put his heavily weighted, smoked-glass ashtray on one corner, then half smiled as he pushed it to lie flat and open to view.

Your Friday, My Sunday

'No, dummy.' Ellis plunged forward and, pushing the ashtray across the table, reflattened the chart where he could see it and sighed impatiently. 'Look, it's Hertz, abbreviated to Hz. It's the electrical frequency.'

'I thought that was volts.'

'No. Volts is potential.'

'Oh … potential. Potential for what?'

'Potential for the electricity to flow. It kind of explains the rate at which it could happen,' Ellis offered helpfully.

'So,' Abdul Rahman readjusted the chart, 'we got 220, we got 250, we got 110, we got 415, all volts, yes?' He was on a forensic frolic.

'What's the difference? Why have 220 when you could have 250, or is 110 cheaper cos' there's fewer of them?' Ellis could feel his electrical knowledge ebbing away as the Saudi scowled and searched for more numbers on the drawing. Big ones. He found one, a very big one. 'Look here, goddammit,' he chortled. 'Seven fifty volts.' His finger feverishly stabbed at his discovery. 'What the hell's that, man? Some big motherfucker or what?'

'Seven fifty volts,' Ellis explained, 'that's three phase. Better to have three phase, that way you get more current.'

Abdul Rahman was baffled by this number, even more so when Ellis added, as an afterthought, 'Then you single phase it at 250, and that's what comes out of the wall socket.'

'What about the imaging?'

'What about it?'

'That uses 750 volts, says so here,' Abdul Rahman explained confidently.

'Precisely. The imaging needs lotsa current, so it needs three phase, so it gets 750.'

Abdul Rahman was silent; he couldn't think of another question. Ellis thought he might leave. Then the native adviser thought of another question. 'What about the rest of that suite? That's 220 to 250. Why can't it be one or the other? Or maybe you're going to tell me it's 110, like the path lab.'

'Path lab's fitted with American stuff. One ten it'll be in there,' Ellis confirmed quietly.

Abdul Rahman sat in his chair, rocking backwards and forwards, deep in his thoughts and confusion. 'American stuff, 110, right?'

149

'Right.'

'Can I have one of your cigarettes?'

'I didn't think you smoked.'

'I do now. I don't usually, but when I get fed bad stuff like this … give me a smoke.'

Abdul Rahman drew deeply, inhaled, and just when Ellis thought the man might change colour, the new smoker suddenly exhaled. Just like a seasoned smoker. That is, until something caught at the back of his throat and triggered a bout of coughing. The man's eyes bulged and watered; his face engorged and fattened as he tried to catch some breath that simply wouldn't come. He tried to sit forward, to fold his arms across his chest. Then his head slumped to the table, his arms crossed on the tabletop like a pillow. As the spasm subsided, Abdul Rahman was eventually able to sit with a rheumy eye and look at Ellis gloomily with a shake of his head, a shake of utter incomprehension.

'Thank God that wasn't one of Choi's smokes,' Ellis offered amiably.

'I think I've become an ex-smoker,' Abdul Rahman croaked emptily.

The two men sat in silence, hoping the emergency had passed, while the air con whirred and sighed and rattled at its own rhythm.

The Saudi swept some of the ash from his aborted adventure into alternative substances and made a brave attempt to settle into the remainder of his day. 'OK,' he began ominously, 'we did current and volts. What about amps?'

'Amps is current,' Ellis confided gently.

'You've got one current and so many amps. Is that how it works?'

'No. Current is measured in amps,' Ellis explained slowly, 'and if you multiply volts by amps, you get the power.'

'What's the power?'

'Exactly.'

Abdul Rahman was continuing in his confusion. 'What's the power called?'

'Just that. Watts. Watts is power.'

'So, volts multiplied by amps equals watts, right?'

'Yup.'

'And so …' Abdul Rahman lunged at his calculator, the size of a brick, with a bizarre array of mathematical functions, fit only for some research laboratory. His index finger punched the keyboard in a seemingly random number of assaults. 'So … volts … yes, I see.'

'You see what?'

'Exactly. I don't know, except I think it's lunchtime.'

Abdul Rahman tidied his things away and picked up his briefcase on his way out.

Ellis stood to one side and let him pass. 'Glad about one thing, Abdul Rahman.'

'Oh?'

'I'm glad we didn't do resistance today.'

'Oh my God … Just leave me out of this electricity, will you?'

'Sure will,' Ellis agreed and let the man shuffle towards the door for his lunch, unaware of the use of his expression of "OHM y God' being the best expression of this unspoken element of the Saudi's education, the conjunction of the *Oh* and the *M* to give the unit of electrical resistance.

It was all good-natured enough, and the two men laughed, while an air conditioner sneezed and snorted in the far corner.

'Goddamn,' Ellis said, and with a smile the Saudi melted into the sun and the dust of whichever floor it was they were on.

Ellis was caught in his thoughts about the earlier meeting, but it neither stopped him nor the others as they cheered and jumped from their seats to replenish their glasses, to drink themselves into a coma. And it was still only Monday. There were three working days left to this week. Oh well, to go into work on a Tuesday morning with breath smelling of *siddiqi* was not unheard of, so, on with the drinking. There had been little attempt by anyone to make an evening meal – none in fact. The thoughts of a dry evening had accelerated the early drinking process, and now with so much consumed, the idea of food was no longer relevant.

Anderson went to the fridge and pulled out a half-full pack of pretzels and made that his supper. Ellis ate an apple, while Clitty made do with another glass of *siddiqi*.

Anderson decided on some music, approached the tape player, and put on Led Zeppelin, which none of them really liked when sober, but which seemed quite acceptable at this stage of the night. After all, it was still only seven twenty in the evening. There was plenty of time to select better music; just choose anything for now, at least to get the party going.

Some party.

Three bachelors: at least three current bachelors, two of the three having been married, all of them, however, bearing the hallmarks and the vulnerability of three bachelors out on the piss and in need of something. That something was hard to define, which was why the three men clasped their drinks and their smokes with the apparent belief that the solution to their problems lay within the drinks, within the glasses. The vapours would give some signal, some revelation. Yet when the night was done, the glasses went mute, and all the suggestions inspired by the drink had evaporated, shimmied out of their consciousnesses. They were of last night; now it was morning. Last night's salutations became this morning's reflections, and all of last night's bravado dissolved into today's duties.

Shit.

Another day.

The three men woke themselves up in their own ways, cursing another day arrived too soon, cursing last night's excesses, cursing this place, thanking the fact there were no calls from home. There had been that call from that deranged Saudi; otherwise, there had been silence. Nothing to do but drink.

And drink they did.

Anderson woke first and wondered how to build a general hospital. Clitty woke second and farted. Nothing else. When Ellis awoke, he was full of concern for the state of the project, the delays, Mr Choi, all the explanations, more delays, that bloody fish, the bloody MOH questions, the bloody assessors, those bloody Egyptian assessors, those anaesthetists employed by the Ministry of Health to advise on what was appropriate to a modern Ministry of Health hospital, what would work, what could not work, and how to discard those items against which no bribe had been paid.

Your Friday, My Sunday

Ellis joined the others and began the day with a joyous fart.

That sealed the quality of the day that would contain Mr Choi, his fish, Abdul Rahman, a familiar mixture of anger and high dudgeon, questions from the ministry, and questions from the banks, in no particular order. The whole of next week was likely to be a bitch.

Sometimes it was otherwise. Sometimes there might be a fatal accident on site that would cause some ripples, a little excitement. Sometimes there would be an internecine squabble over a Third World fella's gambling debts. Somebody might get a spade through the skull. That was unusual; the threat of extreme violence was more usual.

The only exception to this particular rule occurred one Friday when Anderson discovered he had left his electronic notebook on his desk on the Thursday. In his haste to escape to the land of the grape at the close of business prior to the weekend, Anderson had left his bloody lifeline on his desk. And the damned thing was still switched on as he retrieved it towards lunchtime on the following day. But when moving through the empty office, all the air conditioners switched to zero status, there was only a dull echo and the sounds of anger from towards Sam's quarters outside.

Anderson had picked his way across the office, past the fish pouting good day, past Choi's vacant table, past the Egyptians' empty tables, sunlight playing tricks through the discarded nose pickings smeared on the edges of their drawing boards, the noises from outside becoming more anguished and more violent: sounds of something sinister. Anderson walked more urgently towards the source of the sounds – the angry shout, the shrouded response, the sounds of a simple breakdown in communication or understanding. There, through the window, Anderson spotted two Sri Lankan lads straddling the top of the wall surrounding Sam's living quarters, one of them waving an axe meaningfully, the other brandishing a dagger with equally destructive intention, its blade flashing in the sun. Both of them slipped easily from their perches and landed close to Sam as he, presumably, called for mercy from his apartment.

Wrong.

Sam answered the accusations that he owed his accusers two thousand riyals on gambling debts by appearing in a loincloth and swirling a three-kilo mallet around his head. By his own vigour, he persuaded his accusers that their cause was worthless. They dropped their implements of death and fled from the scene.

Anderson watched the diminutive Sam smile as he spat on the ground and went back towards his bed, collecting the blade and the axe for his own collection as he did so.

Little shit.

How did he manage that?

The two guys hanging off the wall had each been twice Sam's size. Little bugger. Must have something.

Blowed if Anderson knew what.

Anderson smiled enviously at Sam's confidence as Sam swaggered back to bed for the remainder of the day. All Anderson could look forward to was an encounter with the vine.

Anderson farted once more, then thought there must be better ways.

Clutching his electronic organiser in one hand, he dismissed the workings and the machinations of Third World personnel as irrelevant. He threw a curse at the fish as he locked up the office and left things as they should be and went home to get pissed.

After all, that's what everybody did on Fridays, on weekends.

Didn't they?

Maybe.

Chapter 7

The more curious, however, prior to commencing the drinking, maybe at a poolside barbecue, went to view a public execution. A few beheadings, not usually much more than that. Stonings were theoretically possible – the Qur'an said so – but were rarely practised in the major cities. Too much mess, it was said: all those stones in one of the city's prestigious shopping areas, all of them mixed with the blood of the slain.

Oh yes, too much mess. Clitty was first up this Friday morning, almost eleven twenty, nearly time for lunch. Ellis and Anderson were still making sounds and issuing vapours from their respective quarters. Clitty thought about an execution.

Sipping from a lukewarm can of flat Pepsi left on the sideboard, Clitty gazed idly through the stained net curtains. The sun was out there somewhere. None of them ever really saw the apartment by daylight, except on their one-day weekend, so the shadows and the tricks of the sunlight came as some surprise to anybody who cared to look at the reflections created by a dry desert wind, the waving arc of bougainvillea, and, beyond it and higher, a deep blue sky.

Clitty watched and wondered as he clutched the soft drink in a dry palm, his thoughts disturbed by a small sound of movement and the approaching smell of an unwashed mouth.

Anderson.

'Cancher sleep?' Anderson snorted. 'Or have ya wanked yerself wide awake?' Laughing, he swaggered towards the kitchen in search of something to drink, but only after throwing a glance into Clitty's can to see what he had managed to mix at such an early hour.

Clitty ignored the dig and wondered why Anderson would not consider a shower before he started to berate everyone for their shortcomings. Anderson himself would put a sheep dip out of business with the vapours and curds of his own perspiration and overindulgence. Anderson banged and cursed his way around the kitchen cupboards, upending tins and boxes. Finding a pack of cigarettes in one of the butter cookie tins, he drew one to his mouth, lit up, and immediately coated his teeth with more to make anyone nearby wince. He coughed, spat, and laughed as he walked back towards Clitty. 'Ya look like ya shit yerself, man!'

Clitty wondered how else he could look when faced with this odious creature on a weekend in a world where he neither belonged nor wanted to be. There was only the money. That was the reason. The only reason. Why else would one endure that site, these men, this smelly, halitosed Yank, those bloody Koreans? That bloody fish so beloved of Mr Choi? It was the money.

Suddenly it all seemed less important as the vapours of Anderson's nocturnal emissions seeped from the man's T-shirt and his armpits, swamping Clitty in a swathe of sweat and revulsion. Clitty reasoned that, as he had cleaned his teeth and rolled on some deodorant, he would qualify for an early-day smoke, if only to hide the other odours.

Anderson sang and whistled as he crawled over the upturned furniture to the tape player to replay whatever had been on at three in the morning when the partying had finally ground to a halt. He also remembered to update Clitty on the fact that his piles weren't feeling too good and he'd need to get to the pharmacy after prayers and why didn't they go to see a chop.

Funny that.

Clitty had at least considered the same thing as Anderson, for a change.

Ellis appeared at some point, bade his cohabitees a cheery sort of good-day, went to the bathroom, went into the kitchen, cooked some toast, and then, no doubt, was going back to bed.

'Looks like it's you an' me, Clitoris,' Anderson commanded. 'Given that ma man Mr Ellis is so brain-dead he's just gotta get back ta bed.'

Clitty could not think of a worse way to spend a Friday: with Anderson. This Anglo-American creep with piles and presbyopia and problems with his contact lenses and dry eyes in all this air conditioning. For a second

Your Friday, My Sunday

Clitty dwelled on the day, then, for a shorter instant, snagged a quick recollection. It was just a sound of something: a click, or something being set. No matter, it was a sound from home. Yes, that was it, the sound of a rifle being primed. Who the hell was making that sort of noise here? Oh, it was Ellis with a dinner knife stuck in the electric toaster while attempting to retrieve some more toast.

Anderson shouted some abuse about not blowing any fuses and he was now going for a shower and did any of them really care.

Clitty wondered about the money in the bank and about his day off and about that sound. He wondered about many things and wondered most of all why the bloody hell was he here?

And thinking that Fridays were workdays in the real world, Clitty pulled out the usual expatriate protection mechanism with more attractive thoughts. Thoughts of home always came first.

The noise of Ellis retrieving toast from the toaster sounded like a rifle being cocked. Clitty knew little of that sound other than the descriptions his father gave of the sounds of guns as the Germans rounded up Warsaw families and sent them off to work in other places.

The whole idea seemed odd to a young lad sitting at his father's feet in the warmth and comfort of their terraced home in Hastings. Father had picked up his family – his wife, his mother, his father, his seven children – and he put all of them into a truck and drove for days across Poland in late 1938. Arriving at the German port of Lubeck, they got on a boat and came to England in the nick of time. He flew with the RAF out of Biggin Hill, bombed the hell out of the Kraut, won the Second World War singlehanded, then, in 1945, settled in a house on the west hill in Hastings and had three more children, the last of which was George, thus named in honour of the patron saint of his father's adoptive country.

Father George knew little of industry or of other types of work; he was a miller, and no flour was ever milled in Hastings. Father just loved the place. He went to sea with the shallow water fishing fleet, winkled up with the Cinque Ports sailors, and was generally well regarded as a good, if foreign, crewman. A devout Catholic, Father was regarded with some suspicion for his tendencies to say prayers and to cross himself at times of storm as the sou'westerlies tore up the Channel and bent and battered the diminutive boats. The Royal Sovereign lightship some twenty miles offshore offered a weak night-time flashing reassurance to anyone afloat, either heading to port or just passing through. In a tidal swell, the light would appear for an instant, and as the boat passed into the troughs of the waves, there was just darkness. Only darkness and silence, save the roar of the voracious breakers.

The roar of nature and the silence of the soul, both mixed up in the anxieties of being afloat. Somehow Father always made it home, usually smelling of fish. The diet of the following days was oily mackerel, cod, plaice, halibut – it all depended on the season. The boat limped back to port and was drawn up onto the heavy shingle beach, the catch disgorged and sold to the early-morning bidders, all of them anxious to get the ice-laden catches away to market in time for the new day's trading at some fish market many miles from this place. By the time these markets opened, the young George was already at primary school, learning everything English while his father taught him all that was Polish. George's mother never bothered to learn English. Father did, but he still preferred to use Polish at home. Mother was Polish, she spoke Polish, and that was the end of that.

George often took his chums home for tea after school. They liked to see his mum, wind her up because she couldn't speak English, take the piss a little, eat her tea, thank her for her kindness, and then make faces at her foreignness behind her back. Mother smiled and assumed these visitors were characteristic of English boys. Her thoughts longed for home. When all were out at school and she had time to get away from the clothes and the washing and the ironing and the endless chatter of the neighbours, she might try to think and reflect. If the weather was respectable, she would sit on the west hill to watch the small boats floating and bouncing like toys on the approach to the land, thinking of her man, but thinking more urgently of home.

She had often done this. She looked at the southern horizon and thought of where Warsaw might be. Then she would run home and look at an atlas, only to discover she had been looking directly towards Rimini. Whichever projection she used, it was always in the wrong place. Looking sharp left over Dungeness, then Dover, it always seemed too far to the left, but the atlas never lied: Warsaw was much further north than she had thought. It had to be that far north, she thought on one rainy day as she walked away from her reverie. The way it used to snow, those blasted easterlies that began in late September and blew and blew until April, most of the time snow on snow, only church and home fires to keep warm in; otherwise all was cold.

Which was how it had been as the Tiger tanks rolled into town and froze their families. The icy shield of the tanks' oppression matched the foulness of the weather in all its moods. If only they'd all seen the obvious.

Mother would walk for hours along the Fairlight Hills on bad days: bad days were when she remembered that her own father, mother, sisters, and brothers, the whole lot of them, were rounded up by bored soldiers and shot. Shot because the diesel in the invincible tanks had chilled and waxed at the same time as all Poles were shielding themselves against this season. The Germans felt abandoned, isolated, perhaps bored, so they shot some Poles.

Funny, thought Mother as she walked among the gorse, kicking out at the branches, catching yellow stems with an angry foot. She reckoned that everyone was cold. They were all hungry, Poles and Germans, so why the hell didn't they just talk to one another, eat together, thaw the frozen diesel tanks, help out a bit? Then the Germans and the Poles could get on with what they did best: the Germans could carry on invading friendly countries and the Poles could carry on being Catholic.

Mother found herself smiling at the prospect of any sort of friendliness between the two countries just as she realised she could see Dungeness power station through the early-day sea mist. There was little beyond, just a thick haze, thickened by a milky sun. But she knew. Oh yes, she knew. That about seven hundred miles to the east lay her home. 'Long way, really,' she muttered as she walked back through the streets to the house, smiling at people who returned her smile sycophantically while looking the other way. The seagulls had their own agenda, so swooped and shouted thus. They also crapped on cars and people; they winged their way over town; they cruised menacingly down the Queen's Road shopping area, looking down disdainfully at anyone or anything about sixty feet below.

Bit like a tank commander. He looked and then he hit.

Seagulls and Krauts. Not a lot of difference. Loads of noise and shit.

George came home with his own agenda. Mother's thoughts were subsumed by her son's life. Father came home with the breeze of the sea and the smell of fish close about him. And while Mother grieved for home and parried the pains of nostalgia, her family grew up and away from her. She thudded the clothing at the sink. She did all that all mothers ever did: she sweated, she laboured, and she loved. Nevertheless her grief mostly disabled her family's many and frequent attempts to reassure her of their undying devotion and thanks and prayers but, oh God, Mother, shut up about Poland.

Father did plenty of that too, but at the club. Endless reminiscences, the happy days, days at school and work, endless certainties, the price of beer, the pretty girls at the flour mills, the toil and noise of the dockyard, the elegant and welcoming silence of their cathedrals. All the recollection gathered a speed and a warmth as many of the sounds became as near and as real as when they had first been heard. So all of them recalled their most emotional losses, the things that made them yearn to go home the most. Frankly, though, this place England seemed a land of opportunity, even if you did have to spend a few years in the RAF for the privilege. Didn't seem a bad deal. And the beer was, at least, half good. Pint measures, though, were too small. Litre glasses were more in tune with the dedicated Polish drinker.

The pints were adopted under sufferance. As a light summer evening drifted into a balmy sunset, the talk became more emotional, while still denying the fact that anybody even wanted to go back east. Father drank some more, then wondered why Madame was lying quietly in bed, a Bible left open on the bedside table at some Old Testament page when he stumbled upstairs, kicked the cat, then fell into bed, thinking of home, smiling, oblivious to the silent cries from the broken heart a handhold away to his left.

One fart and he was asleep.

Young George fared little better. The junior school years had passed into senior school, terms spent at the Cardinal Newman School, learning everything that all children had to in order to pass the O-levels. All of it, though, with a British spin, especially the history lessons. Never mind, George thought. This place seems OK. Get up, go to school, go down to the café, and meet friends, some of them older, some of them harbouring parental thoughts of home. But this place was home.

Hastings was home.

That was that.

They all agreed this was home, their parentage part of the process of the development of the human race. What were the old buggers on about? They'd escaped from the tanks, for Christ's sake. They'd escaped from imprisonment. They could still go to church.

Good God.

What a trail of logic parents followed.

Funny though. The young Poles all seemed to meet at the same place and usually at about the same time of day.

Interestingly, thought young George, they discussed their parents' problems about being in a foreign land with as much energy as the boys discussed their own immediate problems of girls and school and the new culture. On one occasion when the sad café was heaving with these young, thoughtful people, the noise of animated conversation suffused with smells of cheap tobacco and coffee, an atmosphere dense with philosophy and chatter, there was sudden silence. The door opened as two substantial black males from the comprehensive walked in. They smiled and sat at their own table.

Silence awaited the tenor of their conversation, for in the late nineteen sixties there could only be one topic on their lips. It would be the same type of subject as the Polish boys. This time, though, the emphasis of the conversation was different. The parents wanted to be here. These children thought of home, which was Kingston, or Bridgetown, Montserrat, Grenville, Bedford Point – all these places eliciting smiles of recollection, thoughts of some adventure or enterprise, and long, thoughtful gazes through the heavy haze towards the creamy café ceiling.

The common factor seemed to all of them that the sun shone out there, while the condensation on the rain-soaked café windows confirmed this was England. Spring and early summer did nothing to confirm the prospect of warm sun and the revival of carefree summer months such as those enjoyed all the year round at home.

Bloody parents.

The café owner had a problem with the toaster. He was shouting at anyone who would listen as he plunged a knife into the toaster. Dark blue smoke billowed and increased, twisting upwards. The more he cursed and heaved, the more the toast burned and the greater the smell and the more focused the clientele became on his predicament. The owner groped with the knife, grunting and grating to release the offending article.

It had been quite a sideshow for the Hastings expats. That rattling, the heaving and cursing, all the noises made by the café owner were the same noises now being made by Ellis as Clitty entered the kitchen to confirm that all toast wedged in toasters generated the same sort of response.

'Damn this shitty bloody Italian toaster!' Ellis yelled at the machine, surprised to see Clitty out of bed so early on a Friday. 'Come on, you big donkey, get out.' Ellis was peering into the smoke while somehow wielding a knife. The ceiling-mounted smoke alarm was now at full action stations, the toast wedged firmly in place, the water in the poacher spilling angrily onto the cooker plate, while constructive cooking gave way to anger and intimidation.

'Try turning the toaster off,' Clitty called helpfully.

'What?' shrieked Ellis.

'I said, why not try turning the toaster off?'

More blazing spots of poacher water hissed their contempt.

Ellis seemed confused. A knife in one hand, dressed in only underpants, a poacher out of control, and a toaster threatening immediate meltdown – what was a man to do?

Clitty reached past Ellis and snapped the power switch to the toaster, removed the poacher from the heat, smiled at Ellis, and walked to the smoke alarm in the centre of the kitchen ceiling. Standing on a kitchen chair, he grasped a copy of *Arab News* from the worktop, folded it, and waved it frantically to generate a draught near the sensor.

Suddenly all was quiet.

Arab News was good for something after all.

Clitty continued to wave the smoke away from the sensor as Ellis looked upwards admiringly, and not a little thankfully either.

'Thanks for that, matey.'

'My pleasure.' Clitty smiled from the heights.

'Damn near burned the bloody kitchen down.' Ellis wanted to fill his embarrassment with sound to hopefully avoid close scrutiny of his other weaknesses.

'Poached eggs,' Clitty muttered as he jumped easily from the chair and restored it to its place by the far wall of the cavernous kitchen. 'Utter bastards. Difficult as hell to get right,' he added.

'I usually have a boiled egg,' Ellis said sadly to nobody in particular. 'Should have stuck to what I know best.'

'Yes. And what hope the laboratories in our project when the procurement engineer, i.e., Mr Ellis, he no know how cook poached egg?' Clitty queried, mimicking the Korean manner of springing the surprise question to an unsuspecting target.

'Let me tell you, Mr Bloody Choi,' Ellis sprang into Choi-bashing mode. 'If the bloody laboratories need a poached egg, they get one from the bloody kitchens, the same as all hospitals. I don't need to be multi-skilled. I don't need to know how to build a hospital and cook a bloody egg. It's just that in my free time, I might wish to learn a new skill.'

'And fuck up your breakfast the same way you messed up the X-ray portfolio on the last project?' Clitty asked mischievously.

'Christ's sake. Don't remind me.'

Ellis shook his head, unsure which of the two events, the poached egg or the X-ray scandal, carried the greater level of opprobrium.

From down the hallway came the sound of Anderson in mid-shower, berating the immersion heater for running out of hot water.

'Sounds like we've abandoned gentle decorum,' Clitty observed at the sound of the Yank in some characteristically bad humour.

'Where do the Poles fit into the family of nations then?' Ellis asked innocently, handing a coffee to his rescuer.

'Thanks.' Clitty sipped the drink. It was actually rather good, a decent cup of instant coffee. Then he thought about the question laid before him, shrugged his shoulders, and responded in a surprised manner. 'The Poles? No problem. They're just normal – all of them Catholic, so that makes them less than normal. Shit, what do I know? We have a culture, just like the Brits and those bloody Yanks. Come to think of it, the bloody Yanks have no culture really. Do they? I mean, they have only been united for about two hundred years. Not time enough, surely, to develop any culture?'

'True,' Ellis responded solicitously, 'but it would be more of an immediate worry if that bloody man,' nodding towards the angry sound of the cold shower, 'was actually American.'

Clitty blew out his cheeks and shook his head. That man, it had to be said, did seem to be a hopeless case. Clitty drank from the mug and thought how incongruous the two of them must appear: Ellis in underpants and yesterday's socks, ample stomach forcing the waistline elastic of his pants into a reluctant roll; Clitty dressed in a short-sleeved shirt, slacks, ready for action.

Ellis, though, wondered about his hair, his forty-a-day smoking habit, and looked at the huge man with whom he was sharing his coffee breakfast.

In his innermost mind, Ellis liked this huge person. It would not do, though, to admit to these thoughts out loud.

So Ellis just smiled.

'So how did you get involved in hospital work, you know, ending up here?' Ellis wanted to know more of this man.

'What's wrong with here?' Clitty asked with a little impatience, the thought of the money lying in the bank less than a mile from here making the place rather more acceptable.

'Everything.' Ellis was quite clear in his opinion. 'The bloody Saudis, the bloody prayer times, their supermarkets that close every time you want to go shopping, all the bloody women dressed up like Guinness bottles so nobody can see their tits or their bumps and their lumps, as if anyone would want to anyway. This whole place sucks, and if you get to meet some bloody woman and you want to take her home in your car and the bloody *muttawas* get you and they discover you're in the same car and you're not married you get slung in jail. That's what's wrong with the bloody place, that's what.' The *muttawa* were the religious police, a branch of the Ministry for the Promulgation of Virtue and the Prevention of Vice, bearded men in white thobes, often worn with the hem mid-leg, armed with a stick and guaranteed to instil fear in the mind of a miscreant and a cold shudder at the thought of an unannounced encounter. It was their primary responsibility to ensure that no immorality took place in any place – particularly hotels and hospitals, but also shopping centres, doctors' surgeries, bookshops, road junctions, or any place where immorality had the potential to show its face.

'Yeh, but you didn't come here to pick up women, did you?' Clitty asked menacingly. 'You can pick up women anywhere. London, New York, Vladivostok, anywhere. So why d'you come to Saudi Arabia to pick up women when you know full well that the bloody *muttawas*'ll get you? You came here for the same reason I did.'

'Oh?'

'Yeh. And don't give me oh? We're here for the dosh. So if you get to shag yer brains out with some bird and don't get caught, that's a bonus.'

It was true. Most did come for the money, but there was always the chance of meeting someone, a woman, running from the past, anxious to put right the damage of past mistakes. Many of them were emotionally limping out the rest of their lives, yet living in the hopes, born of juvenile youthful thoughts and dreams, that the ideal partner might just be here.

Perhaps, mused Ellis, it was the same as being admitted to hospital with some illness or injury in the hope of finding a fellow patient totally free of affliction.

'OK,' Ellis concluded. 'You're here for the money, right?'

'You got it. And lots of the stuff.'

'May one ask how much?'

Clitty bristled at the incisiveness of the question and moved uneasily on his seat. Ellis did likewise, acknowledging that his stomach, when he sat forward, rested on his mid-thigh, rolling his trouser belt forward and downwards.

Something needed to be done about this middle-aged proof of earlier excesses.

'No.' Clitty had spoken.

'Fine. But you seem to have little interest in this Medical City project. You've got the easiest section at the moment. After all, it takes little experience of procurement to do mortuary. All you need is the bloody dimensions of the building and make sure the place will hold at least twenty-five bodies.' Ellis paused before delivering what he considered his coup de grâce. 'And you don't have to be sure the bodies are dead anyway. After all, they're only Saudi bodies, and nobody would miss a few Saudis even if they were admitted to hospital alive and well and if they were referred immediately to the mortuary for treatment. Would they know any different?'

'And would anybody care?' Clitty asked rhetorically when realising that Ellis shared the same view of dead Saudis.

'But in answer to your earlier question about how I got the easy section,' Clitty purred, 'you will know I did a devastating job at the Red Sea Hospital project in Jeddah with both the mortuary and the intensive care area, and the bloody car park. So me, Mr Bloody Klitowski, is the bloody expert.' Clitty lay back in his chair and expansively put both hands behind his head. 'And I remain the expert in the development of secondary health care to the Saudi population.'

'Bollocks.'

'Bollocks what?' Clitty disconnected his hands from behind his head and folded his arms on the breakfast tabletop, his angry eyes a small measure of distance from Ellis's rather rotund face.

Ellis wanted to fart, but declined the opportunity. 'Bollocks nothing,' he surrendered, 'but you did say you were here for the money, and you did say you were the expert in the development of secondary health care, so …' Ellis leaned across the table to look at the giant, eyeball to eyeball. '… what is it you really are good at? Womanising, shagging, and drinking, naturally, are excluded.'

Clitty smiled at the offhanded compliment.

'Mr Ellis, sir,' Clitty smiled in mock respect of his colleague, 'may I tell you of my life?'

'If you have to,' Ellis agreed. 'But keep clear of the oral sex, childhood masturbation, and any mention of the pope.' Ellis sighed, then added, 'If you don't mind.'

'Can do, yer honour, so while I recall my life and filter out reference to my sexual proclivities, including the pope, why don't you make some more bloody coffee?'

'Easy to please, aren't we?' teased Ellis as he proficiently turned on the electric kettle. Clitty watched his fat colleague fiddle with the kitchenware. He really was rather, what was the word, *rotund*. Pity he could not dress for breakfast – pants, sweat, and sebum, all of it nearly as gauche as that bloody Anderson, except that Ellis was, at least, genuinely British and not some arcane mix of screwed-up identity born of mixed parentage or life experience, the type of result embodied in somebody like Anderson.

But Anderson was still in the shower – probably masturbating, Clitty thought unkindly as he began the explanation demanded, quite reasonably, by his fellow traveller.

'Left Hastings, got some A-levels, went to Walsall Manor, District General Hospital actually, took a job as an ODA, similar to what you did, then got approached by somebody from DOH/VSO something like that, went to do the G500 at Dammam, that was abandoned, then went to Jeddah to do the Red Sea Hospital, and that, my dear, was where I made my money.'

'And where is it now?'

'Where is what now?'

'The money. You said earlier you were here for the stuff, lots of it, so you're here for the money, so where is it?'

'Oh, I see.' Clitty laughed with mock innocence. 'You want to know where the money is. Haven't earned it yet; got to please Mr Choi first. Then I get lotsa money, then home.'

'And the Jeddah job?'

'What about it?'

'The Jeddah job. You mentioned the Jeddah job, money from that one.'

'So?'

'So. Where's the money gone from that little foray ?'

'Don't think I need to tell you that.' Clitty was becoming uncomfortable as the inquisition came close to home.

'I bet it's in the bank,' Ellis volunteered helpfully.

'Course it's in the bank.' Clitty confirmed an obvious fact, but then looked a little sheepish; he had something to add. 'Trouble is, I'd expected the money to be in a bank somewhere interesting, somewhere I could walk into the branch and do the business, move the money around without hindrance.' Clitty formed his hands into an arch, his elbows on the table, his fingers close to his face. 'But I must admit …'

'Admit what?'

'I have a problem.'

'Don't we all?' Ellis tried some light humour.

Clitty pressed on. 'The problem is the money is here, here in this bloody place.' He waved an arm around to include the flat, the street, the district, the region, the country, the entire culture. 'That's why I'm here. To get the bloody dosh from the bank.'

'So why not just go to the bank and get it telexed out, like the rest of us do? Why the secrecy; why the difficulty?'

Ellis seemed confused by the sinister nature of all the planning and scheming.

'Oh, I'll do it this week, perhaps next week. Trouble is when you send out an amount way in excess of your declared income, well, people start to ask questions …' Clitty's thoughts drowned out any further words.

'How much is there then?' Ellis asked gently, one hand inside his underpants, scratching at some unseen irritant in his nether regions.

'Quite a bit.'

'What? Fifty thousand, five hundred thousand, pounds, riyals, dollars – how much?'

'Yeh, about that.' Clitty was being singularly unhelpful.

'Enough, then, to make it worth coming back for?'

'Oh yes indeed.' Clitty laughed at the apparent simplicity of the question. 'Quite enough to retire on, oh yes, well worth coming back for …' Clitty carried his laughter well. His conviction of his own certainty was absolute.

As Clitty's laughter subsided into a quiet chuckle, and then descended into uneasy calm, silence intervened.

Except for the distant sound of Anderson making all sorts of bathroom noises.

'So, um,' Ellis began tentatively, 'how worth it? I mean, coming back here, you got the money, so why the bloody hell bother? Why not just bugger off nice and fat and greedy, just as the rest of us would wish to be?'

'The bank buggered up the transfer.'

'Oh.'

Silence.

Clitty ventured an index finger up inside one nostril. The right one.

Ellis thought about home and what he could do with some bloody money, a windfall: buy off the bloody ex-wife, buy some silence, instead of sitting here with a couple of lags, lags who'd somehow come into large enough sums to consider retirement. Nice to have a piece of that action. Buy the kids some things, stop them crying every time he left them, maybe turn the clock back, to when they were all friends, when they all laughed together, and when they could all hug each other.

But now all you do is scowl, Ellis thought, and the kids cry and we briefly touch one another for fear of hurting and then we go our own way.

Shit, is money going to put that right?

'What's up, matey?' Clitty had watched Ellis thinking through some things.

Ellis concentrated on anything on the table to avoid the question, glaring at the shape of the cheap Chinese salt cellar, the smug assurance of the ketchup bottle, some spilled vinegar soaking the corner of the *Herald Tribune* laid folded weeks previously, some crumbs, a finger making shapes in the dust, the light from the netted window casting uneven shards of light on the ceramic tabletop, beside which the two men sat in common purpose.

'Nothing.'

'Oh, shit,' Clitty exploded, 'that's the sort of reply you get with lovers, so what's up?'

'Nothing.'

'Nothing, my arse. You sound like some bloody woman,' Clitty said with undisguised exasperation. 'You sound like I farted while I was coming and you feel I deserve a bloody good kick for spoiling things.'

Clitty smiled at his empirical formula.

Ellis had his face close to the tabletop and cheerfulness to match.

From somewhere, Anderson farted. Again.

Ellis was forced to face the possibility of being female and confronted with her man farting whenever he came.

'No way.' Ellis knocked over the rejected ketchup bottle with one sweep of his arm, then wondered what it would be like to be vaginally shafted by some man who could only fart at the moment of orgasm. And probably squirt his stuff uncontrollably, this way and that.

'I was thinking about home,' Ellis explained honestly. 'The kids, the crying, the desperate hugs and holding every time you leave, those big eyes, full of tears, pleading, the eyes every time you leave for months on end. Jesus God, I can't stand all those big eyes and the tears; I can't stand all those bloody goodbyes. Trying to get into the car to leave, all the bloody brave "I'll see you in three weeks", all of it represents just long goodbyes. Those bloody goodbyes are just a substitute. All of them hurt, and all of them are masked by such bloody false optimism. All of them are just the product of the spin doctors, "This will hurt but it's going to be a major success", all of it a bloody sham.'

Clitty tried to fart but may not have succeeded.

'Maybe it was all a sham, but the kids see it as a total sham and will judge it accordingly, yet wish it otherwise.'

'Maybe they won't,' Clitty added helpfully. 'Maybe they see you as someone who loves them and who sees them as a prop and someone who is always there and someone who may be there when their own lives get screwed up …. Whatever, they'll see you as a real brick.'

'Pardon?'

'I said a real brick.'

Ellis relaxed at this explanation.

'A real brick. Oh yes, a real brick.' Ellis laughed emptily. 'A real brick. May just have thought you'd accused me of being a real prick, which of course, I may be.' He paused. 'But then, prick I may be, but honest shit I certainly am.'

'Big bollocks ya definitely are!' Anderson exploded within an outbreak of bad breath as he stood at the kitchen door, leaning in the doorway, picking up any unguarded comments about his own leadership or about the state of the project or about reasons why the whole bloody thing was late and how Mr Choi was going to set his fish on any malingerers and how the bloody British would be held responsible. Unexpected though his appearance was in the kitchen doorway, he could still snore and fart his way through the project: he was still in charge, and any thoughts, any discussions would always go across his table.

God knew why, but it did.

Just went to prove how simple the Koreans were, Clitty reckoned, that they trusted Anderson to supervise the equipping of a hospital project when all he could do was fart and smell and hate everyone who came close to him. Here he stood in the doorway on a Friday morning, weekend, and all he could do was abuse his compatriots – his friends, after all.

The thing was, considering it was Friday, and it was weekend, Anderson had come to see who wanted to see a chop, who'd want to go to Friday Square to see some poor bugger have his neck severed for some crime, perhaps committed absolutely or by chance. The forensic evidence amounted to nought; all it took was the word of two Muslims, two creatures who could vouch for the guilt of the accused, yet nobody sought anyone to vouch for their innocence. As long as somebody was guilty, that was the determining factor. Innocence was irrelevant. As long as you had two Muslims to confirm guilt, that was all that was needed.

Off would come somebody's head. Over a drain cover: the blood could drain that way. The head would leave the body, the crowd would cheer, the fire brigade would spray down the spilled blood, and that would be that.

A soul expunged and nobody cared. That was their justice. A soul was lost, yet sins were expiated, and therefore justice was done. Blood was spilled over a drain cover, a head was removed, and that was that.

'So what's it to be for the weekend then, motherfuckers?'

Anderson sauntered from the doorway, drawing a pack of cigarettes from his breast pocket, took one and lit it, then tossed the pack onto the tabletop in his inimitable 'let them eat cake' manner. 'Have a smoke while ya consider the options.'

'There's one option, and one only.' Clitty smiled, drew out one of the cigarettes from the discarded pack, went through the entire ritual very slowly indeed, finally settling back on his chair, cigarette hanging from his lip, the taste so good. With the first real inhalation completed, he finished the sentence. 'And that's to get about as far away as I can from you.'

Anderson took the bait. 'Ah, but ya can't, can ya?' Anderson ran to an adjacent chair. 'No, see, ya stay here, an' if I say ya stay, ya fuckin' stay, an' if Mr Goddamn Korean Choi, he asks me if you wanna get away from here, you wanna know what I'm gonna say?'

'Anderson,' Clitty began in his best Hastings English, 'may I suggest you wash your teeth occasionally? Then, when your mouth smells less like a rodent's armpit, I shall look forward to one of your monologues concerning the fact that you're my boss, and that when I want to leave the country, I have to put in a form to you which you pass to Mr Choi, and he makes sure I haven't been a naughty lad by asking you, and you'll say that we're equally unsullied by the depravity of the market. And then I may get to have my exit visa processed by the ministry, and then I may get to get away from you.'

Anderson stubbed out his butt in a saucer, a saucer holding a cold half cup of something toxic from last night's drinking, and just smiled. Anderson had done some work on this man and knew that he was never going to leave the country without a visit to the bank. And when he was going to leave the country, he would need to be very nice to Mr Anderson, oh yes sirree, an' then maybe he'd get clearance to leave the country, upon payment in consideration of Anderson's silence.

Otherwise …

Clitty found himself feeling cold. He was unsure if the enigmatic smile of his loathsome boss was responsible, or the prospect of keeping him sweet when once the money was out of the bank. Or was it just the sweep of the air conditioning fan, put up to top speed following the earlier incident with the toast?

Anderson broke open some gum and lit his smoke just as the oscillation of the A/C directed all its air and Anderson's exhaled smoke straight into Clitty's face.

That bloody man, Clitty thought. One day I'm going to kill him. But not while there are witnesses.

Ellis caught that thought and smiled.

'Sounds like a chop then, fellas?' Anderson asked, apparently impervious to the thickness of the hatred directed at him by his flatmates.

Your Friday, My Sunday

Clitty thought it through. Go to the chop, then go for something to eat, then back to drink until some late hour, then back to the site a few hours later. Sounded culturally stimulating. Why not?

Ellis wanted to call home. If not that, he'd rather go for a run, get rid of some weight. No, no, no, that was too energetic, too hot. OK, a chop would have to do.

But a smoke, then a shower first.

The road to Friday Square was followed by a process of recommendation and dead reckoning. Ellis was appalled to find the upholstery of Anderson's Lexus in quite such bad shape. Most of the horizontal surfaces were covered with a light grey, the grey of ash, the vertical surfaces bleached browner than their original hide. The ash vibrated while the hide glinted as the three men sat silently in the scruffy Lexus.

Anderson executed a swift left turn through a red light, normally a nine hundred riyal fine if witnessed by the traffic cops, and down the two hundred yard straight that met the perimeter road of the old civil airport, now the main military airfield in this central Saudi province, the capital, Riyadh. Then a right turn to follow the perimeter wall, hiding the aircraft but exposing the flattened elliptical domes of the AWACs as they were preened and serviced and prepared for action and interpretation of the merest folly of man carried out on some road somewhere in the middle of somewhere else – and yet, in the fullness of time, in some future conflict, unable to pick out a rocket launcher parked out of the midday sun underneath a motorway bridge parapet.

Clear as day was the appearance of a bedu in a Toyota pickup with four goats in the rear. Such was the sensitivity of the AWAC, it was said that the sex of each creature could be monitored from forty-six thousand feet. Few believed the Yanks then, and few in the Lexus believed Anderson now as he spied the parked AWACs and got lyrical on its capabilities, its ability to see a ten-cent coin in the centre of a freeway and determine which way was up.

A rocket launcher was, however, a problem. Funny that, about when high science meets human ingenuity.

Anderson coughed his way through his military exposé, pausing only to chew at his gum and exhale smoke and wave an arm as he took a left under the Dammam highway. He cursed a Saudi driver in the midst of a manoeuvre that defied understanding or explanation, but which ended with the tattered Toyota more abandoned than parked on the edge of the sidewalk.

'I suppose you mean pavement?' Clitty commented airily from the rear seat.

'Nah, I didn't, yer bloody shithead … Get over, yer shitbaggin' bloody driver … what'dya say, Clitty?'

'I'll leave you to do the driving. You're making a complete mess of it without having to explain all your pretty Americanisms.'

God, this car smells of sweat and feet and smoke and cigarettes, Clitty reflected as he peered through the stained side windows. He pressed the electric window control to let air in, any air, just so long as it diluted the fetid stench of this Lexus.

'Which way you going?' Ellis enquired nonchalantly as Anderson turned the car right, down Al Ahsa Street, past the Pepsi-Cola factory, cars and people few and far between. It was, after all, gone twelve on a Friday afternoon. Everything shut, everybody out to pray or sleep or both. One group of folks with action on their minds were these white faces anxious to go to the chop.

Another group equally anxious to ensure that the executions went ahead were in the cab of a black-and-white truck, escorted by police motorcycle outriders as it roared across the bottom end of Al Ahsa Street, past the Lexus as it paused under the direction of a traffic policeman, towards the Security Forces Hospital and down to Friday Square, more accurately named Ju'uma Square by the locals and in all the maps. Whatever, it served as a car park most of the time.

Except Fridays.

Anderson drove tight-lipped, all three men in silence as they travelled close behind the convoy, turning and dipping. The truck pressed on, no signs of faces at the bars high up at the rear of the truck. How many were up for it today? Suddenly the Lexus itself felt like a trap. Hot and hurried.

Still they pressed on.

Sharp left into Sitteen Street, past the hospital, a Pepsi-Cola advertisement calling on everyone to be refreshed, more hoardings with exotic electronic displays, past the lights. Just as it was possible to see the Malaz stadium lights, another right. The convoy filtered right again, past all the ministry buildings dotted along the wide confines of Old Airport Road. The Ministry of Health building was the only building the men knew by sight; the rest were just ministry buildings. Then fleeting views of the water tower, the convoy building up its speed, apparently in a hurry to get the show started. Across the widest road junction in Riyadh, just like la Place de la Bastille in Paris, except this junction had Arabs. And some huge advertisements attached to the high buildings, old advertisements without electronics, without flashing lights, paint flaking from the wood frames, for this was the approach to the old Riyadh, built upon the arrival of oil, thrown together as soon as soon as labourers could be found to fashion the bricks and mix the mortar. Then some royal person had decided the junction needed the largest analogue clock available at the time, and so up that went. What royalty had not grasped at the time was that the electricity supply was not yet reliable enough to ensure a constant power source to drive the minute hand around on a twenty-four-hour basis.

As the Lexus passed by the clock, sure enough, it said half past.

Still no words spoken, only the rattle of some loosened part of the usually faultless car acting as a reminder of their speed, the convoy dancing across the apparent acres of open space, the park on the right, the water tower, the bougainvillea. Then, just as the effect of the normality of what seemed a normal place with normal features with normal outcomes, the road surface changed abruptly from sharpened cobble to one of cobbled neglect, narrowing on the approach to the Batha Market, as the procession slowed under the first of the many iron pedestrian overbridges.

Anderson kicked the throttle with a threatening growl as the darkening vista closed in. The car slowed and the three men paced themselves for a new experience.

Though the market stalls themselves were closed, there were still many people around, people who perhaps should have been praying or contemplating rather than squatting on the pavements, just looking around, exploring all the sounds and the sirens of this juggernaut of justice.

Busy one this week, they would conclude. Round up some Muslim friends, then run round to the square.

Batha Market was an institution, an area of town renowned for an indigenous immigrant population comprising Yemenis, Bangladeshis, and some Sudanese, all of them running stalls on behalf of Saudi sponsors, and all the stalls selling anything that anyone would need, all of it at an attractively agreed price. The commercial area was built in the nineteen sixties and modelled on the designs of all souks: squares of eight or ten stalls, passages on most sides, labyrinthine connections between one end of the site and the far end, poor lighting, squeaking fans, spices and dust, shouting, sweat, bargaining and cursing, gestures and shrugs, smiles and hugs. Except now they were closed and enjoying some quiet time.

At least it would have been quiet but for the road cutting a swathe through the centre, a road that was busy most of the time, though few noticed but on Fridays, particularly about now. Somebody caught sight of the outriders that meant one thing only. Word went round, and they ran through the lanes and covens into the square behind the black-and-white truck plus all accompanying traffic, now following at a respectful distance.

'Where the fuck do I park?' Anderson broke the sense of wonderment at the size of this occasion with a typically Caucasian outbreak of panic.

The Lexus crept slowly on idle, Anderson's right foot hovering on the brake, the car with the non-Muslims being swept forward in the sea of believers, the three hospital experts variously unsure about where they were, what they were expected to do, why they had even considered getting out of bed on their only day off, and, more to the point, how to get out of this place with some dignity. It was not possible to turn round; the momentum of the crowd would make sure of that. Plus it was now possible to see the towers of the Juma'a mosque. There wasn't much further to go, but they bloody well couldn't just park here.

The swell pushed forward.

The sense of panic in the air-conditioned car was relieved by a tap on the window and the smiling face of a Saudi man, his head adorned by his gold-edged *guttrah*, an ostentatious decoration kept for special occasions.

Like executions.

He wore cufflinks, and he smiled with his gold fillings, his aftershave noticeable even through the open windows and above the smell of this place.

'*Salam aleikum*' – the man smiled, casting a quick eye over the three occupants – 'and hiya, mateys! Come to see the action?'

The three men declined to comment, preferring instead to resort to shrugs of the shoulders and the use of facial expressions denoting the failure to quite understand the question.

'Never mind that,' the Saudi man said in perfect English. 'I suggest you park the car here. You'll get no further. The drain's only another forty metres, unless you're going for the chop yourselves, ha ha.' The man was smiling and then laughing and then beside himself with mirth as he turned to be merged into the other Arabs pushing forward.

Funny that.

You could have been in Oxford with an accent like that.

Anderson cursed at a number of things that troubled him simultaneously as he pulled up his left foot to engage the parking brake. As the car stopped, the surge passed by, people pushing in the frenzy, some pushing against the car and snapping back the door-mounted rear-view mirrors. Shouting was the order of the day; waving the arms vigorously came a close second.

As the three men pushed their way out of the car and locked up, all three lit up; all three got pointed towards the front of the crowd by anxious fellow members of the audience.

Clitty thought about how much taller he was than everyone else.

Ellis felt the heat and wondered about his hair.

Anderson knew his breath smelt. Plus his bowels were ready to do a dump.

And there they were. Pushed forward by an expectant crowd, there they were up front, at the front of this sea of faces, and ahead of them was an empty space, the black-and-white truck off to one side, and, more or less dead centre, the drain. The three men, for all of their experiences, for all of their cosmopolitan existence, for all the things they had seen and done – none had prepared them for the next ten minutes.

Ellis looked around, now satisfied that if his hair did go into free fall, nobody would notice anyway, and was surprised to see this large, open space, the size of a few football pitches, totally covered by these people. The long brown wall of the Juma'a mosque acted as the backdrop to the scene, the loudspeakers locked to the towers at each corner now hectoring and bellowing and shouting and preaching and teaching. Policemen holding heavy gauge armaments stood in the square, their beady eyes on the lookout for whatever. Some had radios, and as they spoke into them, their eyes wandered to target their correspondents up on the tops of the high buildings, dark brown eyes darting and watching, guns ready to use at a moment's notice. The hoardings extolling the benefits of Casio watches and the qualities of Pepsi-Cola, the whole ethos of Mammon there in its electrical elegance, the flashing lights, the clever displays, the corrosive persuasion of their message, sat at odds with the antiquity of the ceremony about to be enacted.

The speakers on the mosque fell silent. The engine of the black-and-white truck spat itself into life and moved a few yards from its parking space in the glare of the sun to a more shaded spot in the shadow of one of the high buildings.

The murmur of the crowd grew in proportion to the anticipation.

If the headcount was to be one, that was a bad day. Executions were always better if there were four or five.

Anderson passed round the cigarettes, and all lit up thankfully and wordlessly.

Ellis inhaled deeply and knew he had parked here on a previous visit to the gold souk, the place where all expatriates shopped to impress the folks back home. The eighteen-carat offerings usually enforced the yielding to temptation.

The passenger door of one of the police cars parked close to the black-and-white truck opened. A diminutive policeman clasping a sheaf of papers got out, caught his trouser pocket on the door handle, gracelessly released himself, walked to the rear of the truck, and banged on one of the panels. A door opened and a white-robed person was pushed out by a hand. The figure, clearly affected by the heat and the oppression of the truck, took a while to stand firmly but was dragged anyway by two officials towards the drain. The figure, no more than five foot five tall, half walked and half stumbled under escort, then stood, still manacled in chains, while he was asked to confirm his name, his nationality, his religion, and the nature of his crime.

None of this was heard, but the crowd knew the score and crowed for his head anyway.

Then the speaker on the mosque went into overdrive. In Arabic, the voice announced the verdict passed by the sharia court. It said who the first victim was, who his sponsor was, and what his crime had been. It invited the family of the victim of the crime to confirm that they wished the ultimate penalty to be carried out.

It was at this point that the crowd looked around to see if they could see the family and then apply a subtle pressure to agree to the execution. If the family felt suitably forgiving, the whole thing would be cancelled. Or they might demand blood money, and if the money was payable within a short while, then the execution would also be cancelled. Generally, the crowd hoped for the thumbs down.

In the case of this first one, there was no hope of forgiveness. Somebody intimately involved had indicated a negative response to the prayer.

Just to Clitty's right, a family had bought some ice creams from a mobile vendor and were hungrily licking chocolate sundaes.

This time Clitty passed the cigarettes.

The mood of the crowd indicated an impatience that justice should be done and be seen to be done. Somebody dug Ellis's ribs and told him to see true justice about to be done. He would have liked to vomit, but smoked away the temptation.

The shackled figure by the drain was persuaded by policemen on either side to step forward and make a statement that would anyway be howled down by the masses. And while the wretched creature said what he could in defence of his crimes, a large man, dressed in Saudi *thobe* and *guttrah*, walked from somewhere, a curved knife in one hand, a copy of the Qur'an in the other. He stood behind the condemned man while his pleas for clemency went unheeded.

The policemen unlocked the shackles, and in keeping a sharp eye on any attempt to escape, they pushed the man forward to stand over the drain.

The crowd loved it.

The anticipation was now bearing fruit.

Another policeman, armed with only a cane, hit the condemned man on the back of the legs, and he fell to a kneeling position.

The crowd cheered.

Above the cheering, Anderson and Ellis and Clitty heard the cocking of the rifles of the guards as they stared malevolently at the crowd, their eyes swivelling across and upwards, side to side, the militia on the rooftops watching closely anything that might disrupt the festivities.

At some unseen signal, the man with the knife stepped forward, handing his Qur'an to an acolyte. Somebody prodded the condemned man with a cane in the small of his back, his body positioned correctly above the drain.

The murmur grew to a cheer and then a bellow as the knife rose. The condemned man bent over; the executioner looked around for encouragement. As the bellow rose to a roar, he brought the knife down with one deft slice and removed this mortal person's head.

The head bounced from the neck and landed on the drain surround. Blood spurted from the severed carotid arteries. As the body fell in its final act, the executioner took a second cut to ensure the tendons holding the head to the neck were fully severed.

The crowd bellowed and shouted Allah Akbar, God is great, God is merciful. Somebody punched Clitty on the arm as if an extra-time goal had just been scored.

The hunt was now on for more sacrifice.

As some Yemenis dressed in black overalls pulled away the body and put the head in a plastic bag, the back of the black-and-white truck was opened to reveal another victim. The same thing happened to him, and then another. There was more blood splashed around the drain. The crowd wanted more, and more was to follow.

Each time another one was brought forward, the crowd drowned out the crime with its shouting and its roar for more justice.

The armed police, sensing the frenzy was getting close to orgasm, double-checked the safety locks of their weapons.

The family near Anderson were enjoying some burgers.
Ellis suddenly felt very sick.
There were two victims left.
They were brought out of the black-and-white together. Apparently they were the collaborators in an armed robbery. There was an argument about which one was to be executed first, and some discussion took place between the police and the executioner, who was by now becoming agitated and tired.
After all, he was about to complete a schedule of six executions.
A good day indeed.
The question was resolved on the basis of hitting the bigger man first. As the executioner did so, the victim fell, his head partially disconnected, among the splattered blood and writhed and twitched. The crowd shouted for death, and when the body refused to stop moving, the executioner moved in with a pistol and shot the body through the heart.
This left one more to go.
He was ready to run. There was no more to lose, and he tried, his shackles slowing him as he bolted towards the crowd in some hope of rescue. A policeman let go a short round of shots that laid him low. Then the executioner approached, pulled up the body, and took off the head of one who would attempt to run from justice.
The crowd loved this and sang about how merciful God was and praise be to Allah and Mohammed, peace and blessings be upon him.
The ice cream vendor turned on his Mr Whippy music as the cheering died down. The fire truck forced its way through the orgiastic crowd to hose down all the blood and ligaments and pieces of brain that adorned the drain cover, as the faithful cheered some more. The police pointed their guns straight at the crowd in an effort to persuade them to go home and make more babies in the name of Islam.
In the knowledge that there were to be no more victims – after all, the black-and-white truck was now moving out of the square – the crowd began their slow and rather regretful journey home. The children sang and

danced about the party they'd just been to. The parents were pleased to be able to load their hatred of sinners on those souls lately departed.

They may also have used the executions as a means of expressing their own hatred of their state-imposed religion, Ellis thought as he offered smokes to his ashen-faced colleagues.

The fire brigade sprayed the area clean, one of the Filipino firemen working assiduously to spray a brain fragment from one of the drain elements.

Within minutes the spraying stopped, the area clean of jurisprudence.

Anderson was silent.
Clitty made little more noise.
Ellis wanted to be sick.

As the three of them walked towards the Lexus, now carelessly parked at a crazy angle in the emptied volume of Friday Square, none of them could think of anything to say. Anderson broke the silence with an empty invitation to go get some Kentucky fries.

'Think I'd rather go home,' Clitty explained weakly.

'Me too,' Ellis concurred.

Clitty said a Hail Mary for the first time in twenty years.

'Please ya damned selves,' Anderson called, pulling his cigarettes from a top pocket and handing them out to anxious hands, 'but I'm famished.'

Anderson unlocked the door. In an effort to ignore the effects of the chops on his colleagues, he started up, put on the air conditioning, and played some of his favourite music.

Loud.

Janis Joplin.

That seemed an odd choice to follow an execution, but at least it would drown out the wittering and muttering of those damned Brits.

As the music boomed out and Anderson turned the car, there were still some local religious zealots chatting among themselves. They watched as the Lexus drove past dismissively, the metals seams shaking with the music.

One of the faithful heard, then spat, then thought how appropriate it would be to pull one of these infidels in on a Friday and remove his head.

Little did he know how prophetic a thought that was.

Thursday

Chapter 8

Mr Choi was thinking about Chis-Wick.

He often did this on Saturday mornings, first day of the working week, and before everyone else came in, with hangovers or holiness determining their moods.

He would sit at his table with his hands clasped neatly on the polished surface. He would look at the reflection of the windows caught in the polished veneer, and when satisfied, he would light a cigarette, his first of the day.

Then he would bid the fish good day.

Then he would think of Chis-Wick.

Mr Choi was a man of routine. His recollections of his temporary London home usually followed the same pattern.

He'd remember the house, the way the red-brick terraced houses had been thrown together at the end of the eighteen hundreds. Every house was identical save for the choice of the decor or the source of the replacement windows.

How there was not normally a parking space just where he'd wanted to park. And if one of the terraced houses had been split into a flat upstairs and one beneath, then there were two cars requiring two spaces when only one was available.

Funny people, these British, Choi had concluded. They have to park outside where they live.

Why?

Do they have to plug the car in to something? Is there something specific, some specific property to that particular length of street?

Choi lit another cigarette and inhaled and thought deeply about parking spaces. And the British.

Then when the British became too much to bear, when they became terribly silly and sang Battle of Britain songs and 'Jerusalem', then they'd waved flags. When all of the silliness became entirely incomprehensible, Choi got to thinking about the route from the house in Chis-Wick to Heathrow, and home.

The excitement of driving down Hounslow High Street with the car full of suitcases as the jets, almost within a handhold away, brought their approach to a close with the grace and elegance of the birds they were designed to imitate.

Choi felt another urge to light another cigarette as he thought of going home, and how these bloody British men would be here in a few minutes, and how they thought of England as home – perhaps not Anderson – but how could they think of that place as home when in Chis-Wick there was only one space per house, or half a space per house if you lived in a flat? Even then it was not possible to say which space was whose if someone else parked in your space and he didn't live in the street.

A living nightmare.

Choi gave in: he lit a cigarette, stood up, and was about to talk to the fish when the door burst open as the Egyptian draughtsmen reported for duty.

The Egyptians were always first to work. As usual they waved happily at Mr Choi and meaningfully called '*salam aleikum*' to the Korean whose first language was … well, Korean.

Mr Choi waved good morning, reciprocating the good mood at least.

Next in were the Filipinos. Their job was to be busy; it was difficult to tell how their exact purpose was defined judging by their interminable telephone calls in Tagalog to their friends and colleagues.

One thing the Filipinos were good at was information. Good, dependable information.

If you needed to know something, find out about somebody, ask the Filipinos. They usually knew. But the question did have to be put in a particular way to cut off the temptation to make up the reply. Inventions were another strength of the Filipinos. Until challenged correctly, the Filipino would say anything to fit the nature of the question. Cross-examination

Your Friday, My Sunday

with a threat of personal violence usually produced valuable and accurate information.

Whatever they were good or bad at, the Filipinos were all invariably happy. They could raise a smile from nowhere; they thrived on the giggle.

Next in were shambles of Indians and Pakistanis, each group loathing the other for their correctness and for their religion, for few Pakistanis were not Muslim. The lot of them did accounting jobs. They were all very good at using calculators and blaming each other for any apparent shortages of materials, money, or both.

Their lot was not happy, and their mutual hatred spurred them on.

Mr Choi thankfully received his first coffee of the day from one of the Egyptians, who slopped the drink around the saucer and carelessly across the polished tabletop. Sam, the Indian tea boy, never did that; he was scrupulously careful. But today he was late: possibly indisposed with some ailment, perhaps connected to an unpaid gambling debt.

As if to mimic a well-applauded theatrical performance when the lesser players enter, wave, and form up stage right, then the key players, and then the star, the various nationalities appeared in ascending order of priorities, Saudi-style. Mr Choi observed a misalignment in appearances when the two Yemenis, who would normally sit outside and in the lee of the site building, walked in cheerful as ever, and after the Indians. Or was it the Pakistanis who came in first?

Damned hard to remember. Mr Choi found racial harmony a difficult tune to play.

He lit another cigarette as he set about enjoying the coffee: trying to forget about the project, trying to forget about all the delays, trying to forget that official-looking letter in the pile of mail, trying to forget about those ghastly advisers the ministry had imposed upon him.

Mr Choi sat back in his chair and watched the smoke from his Korean cigarette play with the incoming light. Then he remembered the fish.

Dammit. The bloody thing had eaten nothing since Thursday evening when the office broke up for its day off, its weekend. Still it pouted and glided and watched and observed and may have made a comment. It watched Mr Choi panic as he pulled open the Tetramin multivitamin supplement feed and poured four days' worth into the hole, oblivious to the fact that two of the guppies were missing. The fish pouted and glided to and fro anyway, preening, watching that Choi. Seemed like the eyes were even more slit when viewed through the convex front of the tank. The fish would also have seen the door burst open for the last of the staff stragglers to enter. Choi stopped the feeding as he was stabbing his short index finger at the guppies. It looked like he had had to assume they were hiding behind the plastic replica rocks at the rear of the aquarium.

'How many been eaten then, Mr Choi?' Anderson shouted as he kicked the door shut behind him and noticed his boss with his face an inch from the glass.

Choi spun on his chair and very nearly overshot the straight-ahead position. By positioning his knees on the underside of the table, he was, with some elegance, able to employ friction to slow his speed of rotation and come to rest facing the front.

'Your humour, Mr Anderson,' Mr Choi chuckled, anxious to restore his dignity and superiority, 'is from which legends are made.'

Anderson threw down a copy of the day's Arabic newspaper on his desk and walked over to Choi's table and began the sacrilege of digging through the day's mail before Choi had had the chance of filtering out anything. Anything sensitive.

'What've got Mr Choi?' Anderson picked through the brown envelopes, not bothering to look at the addressee or the source of the letter. No, Anderson would only be looking for the azure blue of airmail letters, those wafer-thin letters folded this way and that with the alternating red and blue and white bands along their edge.

Those were the letters with the news.

Anderson grunted at all the letters for the others. Those others – the Filipinos, the Indians, the Pakistanis and the Egyptians, the Yemenis and the Koreans – all of them watched while pretending to be busy working; all of them watched that man. If *he* had a letter, he would see it before they could see their letters from home. If there were any.

It was one thing to pretend to be uninterested about the contents of a letter when that letter was securely folded in the recipient's pocket. Quite another thing to be looking at the postbag in the fervent hope that someone at home had thought to alleviate this life somehow. But the disappointment of having nothing from home was always felt by everyone, which was why they looked with guarded optimism towards whoever was sorting the mail. Usually Mr Choi sorted the mail, which he then set about distributing with a gentle paternalism that appealed to the weakened spirits of those who smiled widest yet grieved most for home and some love.

Today, though, Anderson began the sort. Bored when there was nothing for him, he handed it over to Mr Choi.

But not before he noticed a letter for Clitty.

Postmarked East Sussex. England. Must be from Mum.

'Hey, Clitoris,' Anderson yelled triumphantly as he took his seat at his desk, 'there's a letter from ya bloody mother!'

Clitty was doing what he usually did first thing in the day. He was brushing his stubble with thumb and fingers, considering the day, considering the plan for the laboratories. He was thinking about getting down to the bank, mailing out some of the money, another step nearer going home; thinking of avoiding another fight with that odious creep Anderson.

Ellis seemed in good shape today, probably because of the thoughts of a lately arranged party to go ahead tonight somewhere at a downtown expat compound. Clitty walked carefully to Anderson's desk.

'What did you say, birdbrain?'

Anderson had not expected Clitty's anger so early in the day.

'Ah said there's a letter from home.'

Clitty lunged again and grabbed Anderson by his open collar. 'No, you bloody well didn't, you little shitbag.' Clitty wanted to spit into the frightened face an inch or so from his. 'You said there was a letter from my *bloody* mother.' Clitty seemed particularly offended by this affront. 'But let me tell you, you fuck-faced shitbag: there may be a bloody letter for me, but it will not be from my mother, because she's dead, and just about as dead as you'll be in a moment or two unless you repair your bloody drivel.' Clitty pushed Anderson away to fall uneasily from his chair and clasp the table edge. 'So just leave the mail to the bloody Korean and keep your slimy remarks to yourself.'

With typical bravery, Anderson waited until Clitty had walked to Mr Choi's table to pull the letter from the personal letters pile, then called, 'Feisty today, ain't we, Mr Bloody Clitoris?'

Clitty watched the eyes of Anderson as he prepared to run from a good thrashing from the giant. Cocky, arrogant, covering some deficiency.

Clitty ignored the jibe, sat at his table, pushed away the drawings of the laboratories, cleared a space, called for a coffee, lit a cigarette, and looked at the letter. Her writing, oh joy.

'My darling,' the letter began, 'it's been like a lifetime. How are you? I miss you, I love you …' and then the folded letter illustrated the unfolding of the devotion of his loved lady. All the feelings he held inside and in silence dissolved into an immense warmth, into a wet warmth upon his face. He folded the letter quietly for later reading in detail, then pulled the drawings, the ashtray, and the coffee close to and got on with the day's work of building a hospital.

All those lucky enough to have a letter did likewise.

The Filipinos received the most letters, and their receipt of letters created the most disruption.

Indians were next.

Pakistanis got one or two.

Presumably the Egyptians had few fans because they received even fewer letters.

Yemenis got none.

The Indian tea boy, good old Sam, he got lots, but most of them seemed to be threatening letters demanding settlement of some debts. He also got similarly toned telephone calls.

Funny thing, Mr Choi was never credited with receiving any letters, but the common wisdom indicated he put all his letters into his drawer long before anybody reported for work.

When everyone had completed their first sweep of their letters, they reluctantly got on with their various tasks until they could get home to the space of their beds and listen to the loving prayers of the letters. If the spirit allowed, they would give themselves some relief, alone, loving their ladies, hoping, wishing, and praying for some better life where they could be together.

Anything instead of this.

The morning went on until lunchtime, and the afternoon went on until home time – time to read those letters.

Prayer times came and went.

Filipinos laughed at Muslims for praying. The Pakistanis, the Yemenis, the Egyptians, and the Indians hated the Christians for not praying, but forgave the Europeans because of their apparent superior intellect. When prayers were over, the normal hierarchy was reinstated.

Otherwise this was an Islamic project; Islam would prevail.

'Bollocks!' cried the Filipinos.

It was all rather like following the fortunes of a football match, although the Muslims would not recognise the corollary.

Mr Choi watched the chemistry at work. Coming from a Zoroastrian background, he was able to observe freely the roots of the Crusades, the missionary zeal of the Christian, and the Muslims at common purpose, and all he wanted to do was to build a bloody hospital and then go home to Seoul.

If only his life were that simple.

He had to deal with the structural integrity of the building. Apparently there was some subsidence underneath C block. The entire project was behind in the capital equipment areas of X-ray; as a result, the theatres were late, the intensive care areas were late, and worst of all, the trumpeted outpatient areas that were to be opened first of all had not yet even been built.

The king was going to bust a gut.

And there would be no hospital to correct it.

Which was not entirely true: the king and the royal family were known to have direct access to at least thirty hospitals, so that in the event of some unforeseen calamity, all the wards in any hospital could be cleared of the tribal elements, cleaned up, and made respectable for the royal inpatient. It was also generally assumed, however, that some of the more intimate treatments would be carried out offshore, in the United Kingdom, Harley Street, or maybe in the United States. The thinking continued along the lines that if it were discovered that the king had syphilis or other diseases generated by un-Islamic practices, this could impact poorly on a doctor's ability to keep his mouth shut. And while the doctor could be thrown in jail for breaching his patient's secrecy, there was never any certainty that the truth would not leak out.

London was different.

A lot of money was spent in Harley Street to meet this very purpose: no records kept in any recognisable form, with the patient able to return to his follies, perhaps wiser, poorer certainly, but at least safe with his secret.

If the illness prevented or delayed an offshore solution, the royal party would repair to the King Faisal Hospital, which was staffed almost entirely by Americans, so it was much like being in the Big Apple anyway.

Except at visiting time. A time when local culture clashed most impressively with the high technology of CAT scanners, CVPs, and intra-ocular pressures. A time when visitors were entitled to visit those patients with written ministry permission to be treated in the same part of the planet as a member of the royal family now being cosseted in one of the secluded private wings. Yes, the visitors came with gold-plated thermos flasks, a bunch of dates, some *naan* bread, some *manageesh* (one of the few Lebanese culinary items admired by Saudis), and a pack or two of Marlboros. And as the afflicted descended into the depths of cardiomyopathy within a haze of breathlessness and cigarette smoke, the visitors held vigil and blamed all those servants of Satan, those damned Americans, for not saving their forty-a-day man of our time.

So they sat and clasped hands and lit smokes in sympathy and listened to the sighs of the respirator, then drank coffee, not understanding. They spat some date seeds at the syringe driver, hoping it would jam. The patient retained the look of one approaching an ante-mortem state; he dozed off and left the visitors to empty the ashtray when they left with their gold-plated jugs and cutlery, the empty plates, and, oddly, a pack of pink linen serviettes.

The staff nurse watched from the nurses' station as the Saudi ladies, fully blacked out, waddled from the side room, their ill-fitting clogs clattering loosely and noisily along the black lines marked out along the course of the polished corridors. The children – girls dressed in pretty ribbons and frocks, boys just junior versions of the older editions now expiring – were all still capable of dancing and singing their way through a concourse requesting 'Silence Please'.

Nurses smiled indulgently and wished the bedu a pleasant night in the smells of their own excrement, then proceeded to clear the remnants of their bedside picnics into a vomit bowl and out into the sluice.

It was thus at every visiting time, and all nurses attempted to avoid it.

On the private wing where the royals were treated for the diverse complaints associated with consanguineous marriages and convergence with the twentieth century, life was different.

First of all, the princes had money.

Money could be paid for favours, so if a colostomy bag was changed with sufficient artistry and sensitivity, this could generate a gift of some value, a cash equivalent of a Seychelles holiday. A successful pacemaker implant could earn a cardiologist enough money to retire, or go to the Philippines a number of times *and* pay for a long course of anti-AIDS therapy. Plenty of money with which to deny God, for a while, the inevitability of an early capture from this place.

So if a prince came in for some procedure, the rule of thumb was to work out how the line of succession worked. If the prince fell below three hundred and twentieth in line to the throne, he would have little in reserve to offer a mere medic eternal rest in some place of apparent solace, sunshine, and somnolence. The trick, according to those who knew, was to make sure that if the procedure got screwed up, the patient did not have an uncle who was, say, eleventh in line. If that was the case, he would have lots of money and plenty of power to make sure his nephew's assailant got locked up.

So hospital life had its risks.

Fortunately most Saudis regarded death as a risk of living and accepted it accordingly.

The problem was identifying those with the wisdom to recognize that fact.

Most Saudis with any class would never consider any other hospital than the Faisal or the private hospitals here in Riyadh or those more commonly found in the humid heat of Jeddah, some six hundred miles to the west on the Red Sea coast. But most would, if the pulse rate allowed, get on a Saudia flight to London, where their complaints could be treated by medics and their urges assuaged by girls of doubtful origin and upbringing, the sort of folks at the end of a phone line.

Oh yes.

Why have a myocardial infarction in the celibacy of Riyadh when the patient could develop ventricular fibrillation in the embrace of a girl with some disorder that would dispatch him only five years later?

Nothing like shagging yourself to death, Mr Choi concluded as he watched his fellow humans develop this project for the good of those people that most observers rejected as time wasters, beyond salvation, smelly, indolent, idle, scum, Saudis. Yet this thing still provided a tax-free income that could be hoarded and sent home. Who cared if the Saudis knew what a hospital stood for? Who cared if they pissed in the corridors? The bloody project paid the expats' domestic bills: all their alimony, all their bloody tax-free liabilities. How did the Saudis view this exploitation as they sat with their aunties lying in bed with something terminal? How could they reconcile their fifteenth-century thinking with twentieth-century technology when all they possessed was a religion that told them to respect themselves? Here was some outsider with some solution to their health worries that implied admission to some monument dedicated to the king, and who was to say it would all work when the Prophet Mohammed (peace and blessings be upon him) had mentioned little about this sort of proposition and had not said whether it was right to surrender one's health to the care of a non-believer.

The question had been placed before the sharia court for a ruling. The court considered the application with concern and concluded that, as the ministry hospitals were owned by the government and the king was a Muslim, he owned the hospital, so it was in order to be treated by a non-believer.

The fact that the entire health service would collapse in seconds if the ruling had gone the other way had little recognition among the many.

Mr Choi thought about that and decided it was time for a crap.

Not here though.

Good lord, nobody did a dump here.

Choi picked up last month's *Time* magazine, picked up his keys, and headed off to the Marriott for a comfortable crap. If he saw some colleagues, he might take lunch; otherwise it was a quick dump and then back to the site before that Abdul Rahman made an appearance sometime during the midafternoon.

'A sporting injury, no doubt?' Choi asked cheerfully as, on his way out, he bumped into Abdul Rahman: early, yes; bedraggled, certainly; and sporting a blackened and half-closed right eye.

The man seemed filthy and disorientated, but said little, avoiding Choi's eyes and walking off in the direction of his own office some distance away. Choi ran and caught up the young Saudi when he realised the man was also limping. Smoking and coughing, the older Korean and the young, fit Saudi, there was little to tell the two men apart in terms of lung function.

'You like to talk, Mr Abdul Rahman?' Mr Choi put a hand gently on the heaving man's arm.

Silence. Just wheezing.

'Who was it?'

Silence.

The wheeze slowed as Abdul Rahman leaned against the doorway and fumbled in his pocket for the door key for his office.

'Did they take anything?'

Abdul Rahman smiled as friendly a smile of gratitude as he could summon up, made some comment that he'd been mugged or something. They'd stolen his watch, kicked his ribs … whatever. He ached.

And he smelt.

Choi knew this man never even sweated, so why was he now more akin to a Korean alley cat than the sophisticate that Choi had at least a little respect for?

'Bugger it, Choi.' Abdul Rahman turned the key in the lock and looked back and tapped the shoulder of the shorter man and held it briefly. 'If you can, secure your telephones.'

In an instant, the young Saudi limped into the gloom of his office, shut the door, and left Choi to interpret the meaning of this revelation.

Choi opened a pack of cigarettes, fumbling and ripping and cursing and swearing at the difficulty of getting at his fix. He tore away the cellophane; the thin gold band dividing the packaging was now somehow unable to be unpeeled. The act of dismantling was crushing the paper carton, but Choi pressed on. At last he retrieved a bent cigarette, pushed it to his lips, lit, and inhaled.

The relief of his nicotine fix relaxed Choi as he walked back towards his car. He was blissfully unaware that Abdul Rahman was at his own desk, telephone in hand, the words from his mouth going directly onto a tape recorder. Somewhere in a dingy apartment building in Malaz, they were listening.

Abdul Rahman had become another target of the paranoia.

The government paranoia.

The religious persecution.

Abdul Rahman, single man, educated in England, devout Muslim, was everything the Interior Police despised in the young, for they were troublemakers. They came back from outside and wanted everything tightened up so that the country could return to its Islamic roots, or they came back and wanted everything to be like the West.

Abdul Rahman remembered the West and shuddered.

Wheatley High Street.

He looked at the bruises on the soles of his feet, wondering if an innocent remark to a friend, still held in jail, could elicit this level of rage from the authorities. Probably so, but then that was the way many revolutions began.

Frighten the small man, keep his mouth shut, feed misinformation, plant informers, cells of three, build up the temperature then … wham.

Choi hadn't recognised, until he sat in his air-conditioned cubicle at the Marriott with *Time* unfolded on his knobbly knees, cigarettes at the ready, an abdominal tightening now subsiding a little, that this man Abdul Rahman had been rolled by the police.

Choi knew about this sort of thing from home. Abdul Rahman would do one of two things. He would be a good boy and comply, or he would stop work and become relatively untraceable among the heaving masses of controlled, disgruntled, unemployed Saudi youth.

Choi thought through thoughts of home, thoughts of similar conflicts closer to home. Then he thought about Chis-Wick, then he smoked some more, and then he defecated. He had little time to read the magazine. He stood up, cleaned up, opened the door, and was a little surprised, first by the two Filipino cleaners standing directly outside the cubicle door, and second by the looks on their faces, as if they suspected there may be sarin gas somewhere in the air-conditioning system.

Choi relaxed on the low, cushioned areas among the water fountains of the Marriott foyer. The decorative glass lifts clung to the internal pillars, whispering silently with some ethereal qualities, upwards and downward. He ordered coffee and smoked some more. The waters splashed. The Filipinos came out from the toilets with looks of utter disdain at him, wiping their brows with their cuffs and drying their hands with some soiled towels.

Unusually, Choi had nothing to do except drink his coffee. And smoke. So he did both in equal measure, aware that he could see the site through the glass doors at the front of the foyer, tower cranes rotating and heaving, lifting and lowering: dust, enterprise, energy.

Then Choi had a thought, a sort of multicultural sop. He needed to look at some of the other projects in the Kingdom. How did they deal with the delays and frustrations and all the biting and barking of these nationalistic workers? He surmised that Abdul Rahman had little to do: he was a Saudi, he wanted to be liked, and he wanted to be useful. He was having a problem with both. Perhaps a day with that Ellis. Ellis seemed a reasonable man, the nice sort of man of a type Choi had known in Chis-Wick. Ellis could go out with Abdul Rahman, go somewhere useful.

But where? Over a long hospital turnkey operation career in the Kingdom, Choi must have served, he thought, in every major town, except

Tabuk, close to the Jordanian border. In a calm reflection, he tried to remember them in an anti- clockwise pattern, beginning with his first in Jeddah, on the Red Sea coast. Jeddah was more relaxed than here in Riydah, and the project was a 400-bed hospital being constructed for the Ministry of Defence. Jeddah was nice. He could send them there.

Or Khamis Mushayt, up in the hills. All the expats liked Khamis, and the hospital was one of his best successes to date. Then he should have supervised the building of a hospital in Mecca, but because no non-Muslims were permitted to enter the city, the hospital was put together by a smattering of Egyptian, Yemeni, and Pakistani builders. Apparently one corner of the hospital collapsed, but there were only Muslims to go and check on the damage, and the scale of the disaster was never established.

Of course, things may have to change, Choi mused, as more people attended Mecca to perform the hajj, and the international eye focused on the event, particularly stoning the monument at Jumrah and then running seven times between the hills of Al-Safa and Al-Marwah, to commemorate Abraham's wife, Hagar, looking for water for her son. The result apparently was the son, whom she'd left lying on the ground, had moved his feet in the sand and uncovered a spring, which gave rise to the Zamzam Well.

Choi drank some cold water from the flask on his table, and pulled a date from the fruit display, and wondered about the hajj and all the commemorations and indeed why the hospitals needed to be built properly. The imperative lay in the Islamic requirement that a person, if fit and well enough, should perform the hajj at least once in his life. Because so many people left it very late in their lives to perform the first or the fifth or whatever number of hajj visits, they were unlikely to be sufficiently well to be able to run between the hills seven times.

Hence the hospitals. Choi believed that some architects from outside would be recruited, Muslim or not, to ensure the proper construction of a hajj hospital, all at the behest of the king, who insisted on showing the world his desire to care for his visitors.

But Choi never expected to get to Mecca. He'd supervised a 150-bed hospital in Abha, then visited and supervised a poly-clinic in Taif, a place with a climate similar to a lovely year-round English summer. He liked Taif because it reminded him of Chis-Wick. Ahhhhh, Chis-Wick.

He started another cigarette, remembering he had added extensions at the Security Forces Hospital at Al Kharj, then from that empty part of the world spent four years on the G500 in Al Khobar on the east coast, overlooking Iran. Nearly all of the Kingdom's oil came from fields in the eastern province. As a result, the infrastructure reflected its strategic importance, although Dammam, the regional capital, wasn't to Choi's taste.

Choi lit another cigarette as the cleaner fretted and swept around him, a hoover ready to clear the accumulating ash on the rich Afghanistan floor rug. Then he decided.

It would be Jeddah. A short flight, about one hour and a half, to visit the nearly completed National Hospital in Aziziyah, a downtown part of Jeddah; explore how the process had been managed; and learn and report back. Of course Choi knew he could just pick up the phone and ask, but he was becoming worried about the lack of pace of his current project. He needed some answers direct from a site like the National, and quickly.

Jeddah it would be, he told the two men the following day. Abdul Rahman couldn't understand why he was being selected to go when he could refuse and report Choi to the ministry. He really didn't want to go with Ellis, and again could have refused and reported Ellis to the *muttawa* for drinking alcohol.

He decided to go, but not by plane. He could not and would not fly. Something to do with wings being supplied if he'd been meant to fly.

The decision was made. They would drive, or rather Abdul Rahman would drive. He would take his car and there would be no argument. But as Ellis was a guest in this country, he was gracious and let the Saudi hold sway.

Abdul Rahman's car drove to their agreed meeting place, the Marriott Hotel on Maather Street, at the agreed time of 4.27 a.m. With Fajr prayer completed, Abdul Rahman had calculated he could get from his home in Sulaiymaniah to the Marriott as precisely as that because prayer was finished at 4.23 a.m. He could be in the hotel parking lot by 4.27 a.m.

And so he was.

'*Marhaba*,' Ellis greeted his driver for the day, rather like 'hi'.

Claude Pemberton

'*Marhaba* to you too. How you doin'?' The Saudi had some sort of smile on his face as he invited his guest into his car.

Within seconds Abdul Rahman had engaged gear and was pulling out onto the freeway opposite the site. Neither of them was sure about the point of the journey, and so far too, a journey that should have them back in their beds by midnight. *Inshallah.*

In silence to begin with, they crossed innumerable red traffic signals, stopping for nobody and for no reason. Then, as the lights diminished, they drove to the edge of the city, the western edge where pylons and dunes replaced habitation: houses, shopping malls, tape shops, stores selling plastic laundry baskets and household sundries.

The sun, still low in the sky, was beginning to throw off the last of the night's cloak, and gently took the sand from a darker to a lighter shade of beige. The slight morning chill warmed, shards of light seeping in through the back window.

'Beautiful day.' The two men concurred.

'We are truly blessed,' Abdul Rahman reflected as he drove onward. The sun played on the remaining patchwork of blue and yellow flowers by the roadside, the results of springtime rains now a receding memory.

Ellis wondered at what point the car would go beyond eighty kilometres per hour. And said so.

'You can go quicker than this, you know. One-twenty, in fact.'

'I know you do seventy in the UK, and in some places you do thirty, so I wanna make sure you feel comfortable at eighty, if even if I'm speeding.'

'Yeh. But that seventy in the UK is mph.'

'Mph?'

'Yeh, miles per hour.'

'Oh.' Abdul Rahman realised his error. 'Better speed up then.'

And he did, the Chevy accelerating effortlessly until a metallic pinging penetrated the silence. All the while the driver kept the speed above one-twenty, the pinging went on and on.

The signs said 'Jeddah, 870 km'.

Only eighty done so far. God. Time for a sleep?

Not with all the pinging. And anyway, as the road stretched onwards and downwards off the edge of the escarpment that took the traveller from the heights of Riyadh to the heat of the shimmering plain below, where robbers occasionally struck, there was nothing to do or say or think. The sun was beginning its upward path, reducing the shadows and bleaching the earlier beauty of the day.

The pinging came and went according to the Saudi's right foot. They cruised in their own thoughts. From the distance came a sign announcing a turn-off to the right to Qalya, then a small, squat building and a filling station, where they stopped for water and a pack of dry custard cream biscuits. A Yemeni came out from behind a dusty glass counter to wipe the car windows, fill the car with petrol, and hold out a hand for a tip, which was not forthcoming from the driver.

Abdul Rahman declined Ellis's offer to drive and both men took up their former positions. He engaged Drive. The car purred its way across the forecourt, past two men walking along the path in contractors' overalls, holding hands, and returned back onto the main highway.

'Just good friends, are they?' Ellis asked with a smile in his voice.

'No worse than those army guys I saw in Riyadh, holding hands like those two.'

Ellis assumed he meant Saudi army guys. He would expect that.

'No. They were two of your guys, army guys or navy or something, holding hands. I thought all you Brits did was go after girls.'

'We do, generally,' Ellis stated blandly.

'So you guys, or these army guys – what were they doin'?'

'I've no idea who those army people are.'

'Brits.'

'What sort of uniform did they have on?'

Abdul Rahman shook his head, uncertain of any sort of uniform. 'Dunno, man. Just uniforms. Tall guys, saw them on Al Ahsa Street.' Abdul Rahman started to laugh.

Ellis could feel the heat beginning to get to him, his patience beginning to wear thin. 'So, you've seen two guys in uniform on Al Ahsa Street, and they were holding hands?'

'Yeh. Army guys.'

'And what about all the Saudi guys and the Egyptians and the Yemenis and the Indians? You see them all walking about holding hands; I've seen them myself.'

'No, you haven't.'

'Well actually, you're right. I haven't seen *all* of them holding hands, just that it's not that unusual. And, anyway, so what the hell are they doing if they're not holding hands? Helping each other across the road?'

What had begun as a reasonable day seemed set to unravel.

'They can do that,' Abdul Rahman stated coldly.

'Do what, hold hands?'

Abdul Rahman wouldn't answer.

They sat in silence. Glowering. Ellis had touched a nerve.

The pinging cut back in to drive away the silence.

'So what you're saying,' Ellis ventured, 'or seem to be saying, is that if the Muslim people are holding hands, that's OK, but if the Brits do it …'

'That's it,' Abdul Rahman agreed. 'They're queers.'

'Where d'you get your ideas from, for God's sake?'

'It's true, man; I've seen it.'

'I'll tell you what I've seen, Abdul Rahman, and then see how we compare. Let's try a cultural question.'

'OK.'

The pinging subsided.

'Right then,' Ellis said. 'Are you lot allowed sex with a woman before marrying her?'

'No!' Abdul Rahman exploded. 'Absolutely not!'

'So what do you guys do about having any form of sex?'

'That's none of your business.'

'It is my business if I see them holding hands in public places, like the shopping malls, and I am allowed to wonder. Anyway, I saw them in the shopping malls.'

'That's different.'

'What's different about it? They can't have sex with a woman, so they walk round holding hands with another man and do what they want because it's not forbidden. That includes sex.'

'They wouldn't do that,' Abdul Rahman stated with dubious confidence.

The pinging came back.

'And,' Abdul Rahman seemed to be developing a theme, 'what makes you so sure those army guys weren't having sex?'

'I have no idea.' Ellis tried to steer the conversation away. 'But you say they were army guys. How d'you know they were Brits and not Iraqis or Tunisians or Jordanians or whatever?'

'They looked like Brits, one of you lot.'

You lot – that was nice.

Terrific, Ellis thought, but he just couldn't get himself to say the unsayable in the confines of a Saudi's car with a Saudi driver and all the pinging. The angrier Abdul Rahman became, the faster he drove and the louder was the pinging.

Ellis wanted to try to bridge the misunderstanding, the developing gulf of ideals and beliefs between them. This one was becoming unbridgeable. The bloody man wouldn't admit to anything going wrong in his country, or own up to the fact of being in a country where men were legally forbidden to be in the company of a woman in public, and even in private it was forbidden because the woman was expected to be chaperoned by another woman. The father of the girl would object to another man's presence in the house on the grounds that the suitor might try to have sex with the chaperone.

Which might explain why the culture of first cousin, or closer, relationships endured. If the couple were all part of the same family, then no chaperone was required, and so the couple could enjoy each other without the male having to walk the streets holding hands with another man.

In the more extreme family structures, particularly in rural settings, and as confirmed to Ellis by some of the more straightforward physicians, siblings married and had children whose specific defects emanated from these consanguineous unions, specifically structural heart defects and insanity – sometimes both.

The defects were often passed from one generation to the next, remaining undetected for many years. But as modern health care invaded the privacy of wild desert villages the reporting of these exotic conditions became more commonplace. The commonest seemed to be dextrocardia, a condition wherein the heart was pointing downwards and to the right, rather than in the normal position pitched downwards and to the left. Many other conditions existed, of course, mostly as a consequence of living in the heat and connected with kidney disease and eyes. As maternity services became more sophisticated, the mother-to-be would be dumped in the back of a Toyota pickup by her husband and taken to the clinic, to be greeted by science, which was eyed suspiciously by a patient who had conditions that would have killed a Caucasian. With defects like these, the doctors concurred, the patient simply ought not to be alive, let alone pregnant. But family was required, and the family *was* treasured in the Kingdom, and children were welcomed and well regarded.

This was all very well for the married person, but for young males there was no possibility of going out to meet girls. There were no cinemas, no libraries, no theatres. There were no cafés – well, yes, there were cafés, but even assuming the girls had been allowed out, they were forced to sit in the women's section, a discreetly curtained area for the eyes of females only. The men would sit on the plastic seats just inside the door of the café, where they could be monitored by the owner and by any passing *muttawa*.

Ellis noted the pinging must have been going on for a while. It just kept pinging, and now Jeddah was only 180 kilometres. Abdul Rahman was doing well – and he was still awake. Ellis felt like dreaming and closed his eyes and wondered how the young might rebel against all this. There were occasional outbursts by the young, the sort of teen rebellion you might expect in any society, and these often took place in the shopping malls, where the religious police watched and waited and sometimes pounced. The latest craze, though, seemed to take place at traffic lights.

This is how it worked, according to the expat community. The young men would drive their expensive cars aimlessly around Riyadh, spinning their tyres, smoking, picking their noses, and playing music loud on the in-car system. When reaching the red traffic light, they would try to look into the tinted glass of a car alongside.

Perhaps there was a girl inside – she certainly wasn't driving; that was illegal.

But if, like the boys, she was looking for action and saw a boy staring at the rear side window, and she liked the look of him, she would wind the window down and they would exchange a cassette tape. Then the light would turn green, the girl would wind up her window, the boy would do likewise, and both cars would go on their way.

As soon as she could, the girl would feed the cassette into a player, usually one in the back of the luxuriously padded passenger compartment.

She would listen to him introduce himself and give contact details, musical preferences, and a gentle invitation to make contact.

The handover of cassettes didn't always go according to plan. The boy or the girl would fail to make the transfer, and the tape would fall to the ground, as evidenced by the sight of crushed cassettes with tape trailing found across the road and woven around the traffic signal bollard. Ellis explored the outcome of a parent or the *muttawa* picking up the tape and taking it home to listen to … then didn't. It was too awful to contemplate.

The three hours in Jeddah had been sufficient to obtain some information for Mr Choi and the return journey began much as the day had begun. Abdul Rahman performed his Asr prayers at 3.28 p.m., in the car park of the National Hospital in Jeddah. Ellis felt it a moving occasion as Abdul Rahman connected with his soul. He felt disinclined to watch, so simply looked towards the corniche and coastline, watching the waves and the offshore wind and the beauty of this place.

Abdul Rahman prayed and Ellis watched some natural beauty. Difficult to acknowledge their differences when so much united them.

The roadside hoardings announced goodbye and farewell and why not try this particular brand of washing powder when you get home. In the graphic a not-unattractive woman was showing it was possible to have a pretty face and clean laundry.

Ellis said so, and wished he hadn't as soon as the words left his lips. He could not unsay them.

'Pretty face.'

'You can't say that about a woman. She belongs to somebody. You can't say that!'

'So according to you, I can't make any comment about any woman, even if her face is on a hoarding on some dusty highway out of Jeddah, and her face is only there to sell washing powder?'

'You can't say that. That's a woman.'

'I know. I saw. But why're you getting so wound up about it? I simply said she had a pretty face, not that I wanted to shag her.'

'But that's what you want, I bet.'

'Oh, for Christ's sake.'

'See? You start swearing. Just like those others. Bet you wanna fuck that woman!'

The pinging started again.

'Actually, no. May I withdraw my first comment about the pretty face? Please?'

Abdul Rahman paused to reset something in the air conditioning system on the dashboard.

'No, you bloody well can't. I know you want to spend your time shagging and fuckin' and doing everything. You see a woman on a hoarding and you want to shag her as well. I hear you and that bloody American Anderson and that guy Klitowski always talking about shagging and getting women and drinking alcohol and having parties and – and – and—'

'Want to know what I think, Abdul Rahman?'

'Not really.'

'Well, I'm going to tell you anyway, cos' I'm just about up to here with all this stuff about sex and how we are all so immoral. I like to think that even with all our faults, we – that is, you and me and all the rest of the crew – are a troublesome lot, but we need to work together and get along. After all, life will be over before we've had any fun.'

'Goddamn, Ellis, what's the matter with you? That's all your life, so it is – fun and booze and shagging and smoking and screwing.'

'You ever been to the UK, Abdul Rahman?'

The Saudi's stomach tightened in a knot. A small one to begin with.

'Yeh. I went to London.'

'Where in London?'

'Oxford.'

'That's a fuckin' long way from London.'

Abdul Rahman said nothing, just pretended to check the temperature gauge and how much fuel was left for the remainder of the day.

'OK, so you went to Oxford. To learn English or what?'

'Yeh. English.'

'They did a good job. Your English is brilliant.'

'Thank you.'

'What else?'

'What else? What d'you mean, what else?'

'I mean you must have done something else when you were in Oxford, apart from studying English.'

'No.'

'Christ. I know you wouldn't have visited any cathedrals or stuff. Come on, man, what did you get up to?'

The Saudi grasped the steering wheel tightly and held his silence and drove on, the sun lowering through the back window, glaring in the rear-view mirrors.

'When I was in the UK, I saw all these pictures and these advertisements. Is that the right word, advertisements?'

'Yup.'

'And they show these women, and they got short skirts and knickers and brassieres, and you see their tits and you see them looking and waiting for it and they all deserve to be fucked. Raped.'

'What?' Ellis exploded. 'Why should they be fucked and raped?'

'They're asking for it. That's how.'

'Why are they asking for it? It needs the man to do the fuckin' and the raping.'

'She deserves all she gets if she dresses like that.'

'Why shouldn't she dress like that?'

'Because she'll get raped.'

'Who by?'

'A man who shouldn't have to see these things.'

'So you reckon if the man can't control himself, it's the girl's fault?'

Abdul Rahman suddenly remembered Wheatley, the phone box, the public toilets, and the traffic policeman. Would Ellis know? Surely, surely not, please God.

'You know what, Abdul Rahman? This whole thing sucks.'

'Sucks?'

'Yeh. Let's put it this way. The way you see it is that a woman should not be on display because a man might react in the wrong way. That is, he would rape her, which essentially means he can't control himself. Am I right?'

'No!'

'OK, so what makes you blame the woman for appearing in her delights and you not take a bit of responsibility for yourself?'

'She shouldn't be like that.'

'Like what?'

'In a condition like that.'

'I think you are so uptight about women and young boys and goats and sisters and chaperones and girlfriends and traffic lights and London and the West and sexually transmitted diseases and all the things you can't get here, you want to blame the women, simply because you can't control yourself.'

Wheatley.

Abdul Rahman braked harshly and pulled the car onto the hard shoulder, darkened by nightfall. 'Get out,' he snarled.

'OK.'

The Arab smelt angry as he tipped his Christian guest out onto a highway somewhere far from Riyadh and drove off at full speed, full of his own virtue and angry with his own hypocrisy.

And Choi wondered at how Ellis had hitched a ride on a chicken truck at past midnight and still arrived at the office on time the following morning, with a smile for his colleagues and a look of disdain towards the young Saudi.

Dear, oh dear.

There was still some coffee left in the jug, so Choi with a yawning gesture sat back, anxious to stay away from those bloody British for as long as was possible. He made himself a little more comfortable and settled deeper into the green upholstered cushions, sighed, and probably dozed off.

He awoke to hear screaming. A woman screaming.

A fully veiled woman was being escorted by security from the building, clearly against her will. She had a perfect vocabulary in Arabic gutter slang, and was wrestling with the guards who bundled her along. The identity of all guests in Saudi hotels was routinely given to the *muttawa* to check out who was staying in which room and with whom, single or double booking. Judging by the intensity of this argument and some of the expressions used, it seemed that the Saudi lady, a married woman, had come to visit her brother, who had come to stay in Riyadh for a while. The *muttawa* assumed that anybody coming to visit family in Riyadh would stay at the family house.

Her explanation sounded like the brother had come to Riyadh to do some business after being abroad for some time. He had called her and asked her to come to see him at the hotel. Notwithstanding he could have been having a sexual relationship with his own sister, there was nothing to suggest this. All she had asked at reception was that the concierge should call his room and tell him she had come for coffee and to come back home for a prodigal brother's feast. Anxious to score some points with his sponsor, the Egyptian maître d' had called the *muttawa*, who turned up in force with their long beards, wild eyes, and long sticks to arrest the Jezebel.

How, they argued, could she be doing other than sleeping with this man if she arrived, impeccably dressed and smelling, well, alluring, and asked for the man in room 276? Her surname was different from his, so she must be of loose nature.

'Oh, so you say you're married?' the *muttawa* pressed on. 'So in that case, why are you travelling like a harlot in the foyer of a hotel where men will see you? You should be at home, where women should be.'

The woman replied in colloquial Arabic which probably equated roughly to, 'Listen, you bunch of wankers, this is my bloody brother. Just because the only sex you get is with a goat or some syphilitic camel, don't take it out on me. If you put one finger on me, I shall scream, and then I shall say that you are attempting to rape me.'

The scrawny *muttawa*, the six of them, clearly could not cope with the thought of raping an elegant, if veiled, young woman, so shouted some sura from the Qur'an and fled the building.

As the woman regained her composure and waited for her brother to come down from the second floor, Choi thought he may have heard her refer to the violent removal of testicles.

Then he wondered how much the fish knew.
That bloody fish heard and saw everything.
How much money was changing hands, how behind the whole project had become, how Choi hated the whole bloody place, how he hated these British, how he wished something would happen to them.

When I get back, I'll murder it, Choi reflected cheerfully as he threw back the last of the coffee and went back to work.

As Choi parked up and walked to his desk, he found Anderson was waiting for him in the doorway.

'Bitchova day, eh, Mr Choi?' Anderson smiled sarcastically.

That bloody man's eyes, couldn't tell if he was talking to you or the bloody birds. The import of what he had to say was about right for the latter. Choi pressed on, agreed with Anderson's summary, and pushed past towards the fish tank.

'Heard about the bloody Saudi?'

'What?' Choi hissed, offended by the callous indifference.

'Yeh.' Anderson chuckled, throwing a cigarette at Choi. Choi fumbled the catch, dropped it, and left it on the floor, preferring one of his own. 'Yeh, the little shit got rolled.'

Choi was obviously not back from a meeting. He had no files, no drawings, no briefcase, no calculator, no brown envelope, just his cigarettes and a small leather purse for money, *igama*, and some family photos. Anderson noticed this, so reckoned it was safe to press on with a non-work piece of baiting.

'Yeh, the little bugger got rolled and turned up all bruised and weeping and crying and wailing cuz the bloody police got him, an' he's all dirty an' covered in bruises an' smelly as a racoon's ass! Bloody great if ya askin' me.'

'I'm not.'

'Pardon me?' Anderson was incredulous.

'I said, Mr Anderson, I have no wish to ask you anything of Abdul Rahman.'

'Oh, yer bloody well will when I tell yer, you do want me to tell yer, cuz I'm gonna fuckin' tell ya anyway, Mr Bloody Choi—'

Choi snapped.

Looking at the odious Yank in the left eye, Mr Choi began to dismantle the ego of his principal detractor.

'Everybody!' Mr Choi barked loudly and effectively.

Everything and everyone stopped; only the whirring of the air conditioners remaining as they were.

'Gather round, please.'

Anderson wondered what was to follow, his verbal arrogance diffused momentarily. The draughtsmen put down their pencils. Ellis and Clitty looked at Choi hopefully. The Filipinos, the Indians, the Pakistanis, even the two Yemenis, all of them drew around Choi's table. Anderson was marooned among the other workers on the visitors' side. A general air of expectation fell, perhaps just like a Friday chop: somebody was to be done down in front of an unfriendly crowd.

Even the fish seemed to have a taste for it and pouted and preened. Choi caught the sight of a fin in the corner of his eye as he surveyed the width and the anticipation of his audience. Dammit, I'll have to kill it later, he thought.

Anderson stood in the centre of the crescent formed around Choi's table as silence settled and Choi stood to speak.

'Gentlemen,' he began with a smile, 'Mr Anderson is about to offer an explanation as to how the project is now eight months behind schedule. We rely on his expertise to have the whole thing built in timely fashion, so we can be sure he will offer some good reasons for his failure to make an effective contribution to the success of our project.'

Choi sat down and lit up. The draughtsmen muttered approval as Anderson realised he had nothing prepared. He had nothing to say in his defence. The crowd wanted words; they wanted to know from which eye the truth would come. Clitty began a distant laugh that went undisguised and was noticed by all.

Sam offered Anderson some coffee, but all Anderson wanted was somebody to pass his cigarettes from the desk. Ellis heard and threw them through the air, the lighter following, all of it falling untidily and spilling across the floor in front of Mr Choi's desk. Anderson fell to his knees and scrabbled around the floor, siphoning the spilled cigarettes back into the pack. Muffled laughs came from somewhere. If this had been a lynching party, it would have been the moment that first blood would have been drawn, yet they held back, let him speak. Then they would have him.

Ellis and Clitty sat back in their chairs, not bothering to join the mob. They too lit up and waited.

Anderson shakily lit up, fingers trembling.

The fish seemed keen to perform, as it had never before experienced such a crowd to the right and to the left of Mr Choi.

So while Anderson smoked and summoned up his excuses, the fish executed a number of exotic passes in and out of Choi's ears and ate something floating carelessly in the light. Then it too waited.

Anderson decided to chew gum and smoke for maximum effect.

'Gentlemen,' he began weakly, 'Mr Choi has correctly indicated that the original timetable laid out has now slipped, and the schedule is now drawing unfavourable observation from the ministry. As ya know, the subsidence of what will be C block has created enormous delays, particularly as C block houses the theatres, the ICU, the CCU, recovery, and the ER. Without the resolution of the underpinning of C block, the hospital as a viable entity remains on the stocks.'

Anderson looked around for some sympathy but all he got was blank looks. There was no sympathy for his cause nor understanding of his dilemma.

It was true the foundations of C block had been a problem. The advisers had been in; they had sorted out the shifting subsoil around the site, underpinned and all, and the problem had ceased to influence progress. But somehow Anderson had continued to use it as an excuse for his own deficiencies.

Choi thought this presentation, so far, had been made in a remarkably English accent, coming as it did from a pseudo-American.

In the same way, he reflected that his brother, a pilot with Korean Air, was required to speak English. The language of international flight was English. So when, say, a Korean pilot, whose first language was Korean, hit some catastrophic event in flight, he would initially talk to air traffic control in English in order to describe his location and the nature of the developing failure of his plane.

Then, when all of the engines finally failed, his English would also fail him, and all he could do was to return to his mother tongue and shout at another foreign air traffic controller in Korean, though the only other language that person could speak was something entirely foreign.

In the same way and when faced with this critical dilemma, all Anderson could do was to abandon his Americanisms and resort to English, a type of Tyneside English mixed up with some Brighton dialect that both Ellis and Clitty found pathetic and very funny. They began laughing.

All those without English as a mother tongue turned to see Sam as the source of all the hilarity. Clitty began to mimic Anderson's pseudo-accent. 'Gee, the underpin got unfixed, the ER, the OR, the stateside, the sidewalk got bollocked, we got upside, downside, slam dunk, goddamn, nitro, credit card, Amex, Bloomingdales …. Aw, come on, motherfucker.' Clitty dissolved into laughter and slapped his knee, to the bemusement and not a little relief from the crowd.

Choi stood angrily to attention, 'Mr Klitowski, please! Mr Anderson is updating us on project progress. Please do not belittle his attempts by your cheap thoughts and reflections on the American dream.'

'Aye aye, sir.' Clitty mockingly saluted, laughed, coughed, and then in desperation laughed some more and lit up, throwing a lighted cigarette at Anderson that a Filipino caught midflight and took for himself.

'Mr Anderson,' Choi said sternly as the crowd began to drift away, 'you're fired.'

'Pardon me?'

'You're fired. Professional incompetence.'

'Oh yeh? So you're a real professional then? All ya ever done is to spend some time in Chis-Wick, fuck about building supermarkets that collapse, sweet-talking the fuckin' Saudis about doing the bloody business, s'pose ya got some nice bloody gratuity comin', oh yeh you're about as safe as a nun's crutch with Missis Bloody Choi banged up in some Korean bloody whorehouse, you make me fuckin' puke.'

Anderson was done. In more ways than he expected.

'Thank you for sharing your thoughts with us all, Mr Anderson I particularly enjoyed your dislike of me …' Choi lit a cigarette without offering Anderson anything but a gilded glare, '… but this project will probably be much the faster, and the better, now that you are leaving.'

Choi let the words hang in the air as Anderson made off to clear his desk, to get out of this place, and to await the inevitable entry into his passport of an exit-only visa (with disgrace), now with no hope of any return.

Anderson left the site and nobody said farewell. He threw his car keys at Mr Choi, who said nothing. He had turned to the tank, balancing the top in one hand, a pot of something in the other. He seemed to be feeding the fish with undue diligence, a hand in the water – a stranglehold?

The taxi eventually arrived and took Anderson off home, his instructions to the driver shouted impatiently: left here; no, not that way, you bloody motherfucker; drop me here, you shit; fuck you; and keep the bloody change.

Anderson pushed open the apartment door, shut out the world, had a shower, masturbated furiously, had a drink, then another, then lay down on his bed and waited for his erstwhile colleagues to return from that goddamn place.

Thank God to be away from here.

Thank God to be going home.

The exit visa should be through in two days.

Two days in which to get absolutely arseholed, sleep till midday, take a cab to the site, pick up the passport, two fingers to the whole place and all its works. Then airport. Then home.

Then what?

Another tranche of drinks kept Anderson quiet until Ellis and Clitty ventured in nervously soon after six thirty. They crept in and found the man naked, laid asleep across his unmade bed, a fallen glass in one hand, flaccid penis in the other.

'What the hell d'we do with him?' Ellis asked kindly.

'Party time?' Clitty suggested.

Ellis thought about tonight's invitation.

'Yup,' Clitty agreed. 'Let's get him pissed – well, at least more pissed than he is now. I hate the creep; the least we can do is to send him off with a headache.'

Ellis said, 'Let's get the bastard as drunk as he could ever be.'

Ellis called up the party giver, confirmed there were three thirsty, tired, rather disenchanted Brits coming to liven things up, what about girls, OK,

OK, marvellous, sorry we asked, see you about eleven, bye. He hung up and looked in the mirror and was disappointed at his rate of wear. Clitty thought about his letter and made some excuses and went off to read it in the relative privacy of his room.

Ellis went for a shower and, loving the coolness, remembered the way Abdul Rahman had reacted earlier in the week on that very hot day. He seemed to become really peculiar, almost hostile on those days. True, he'd been rolled, but this seemed normal for the youngish males in this city of unfulfilled dreams. He'd seemed tense sitting at his desk, looking very hot, and Ellis thought he looked like he was cooking. Unusually, the Saudi had nothing on his head, his *guttrah* and *agal* removed as he mopped his head with a clutch of tissues torn from the gold-embossed desktop box, his moustache grazing pieces of material which flecked his top lip and the shadow of his beard.

'Hot or what?' Ellis volunteered.

'You bet.' Abdul Rahman kept patting his forehead, dabbing at his brow, and noticing that Ellis seemed as hot. He wondered how hot it was. If they had a thermometer, they could at least confirm it; perhaps feeling hot would be justified if they knew.

'I don't think we have a thermometer anywhere.' The two men looked around the walls, beyond the faded pictures of the king, the Custodian of the Two Holy Mosques, the torn town map of the Kingdom with red, yellow, blue, and white pins strategically inserted at centres of population for no particular reason.

'I'll ask Sam; he'll know.' Ellis walked from Abdul Rahman's room to the main office area, where the designers, architects and specialists sat.

'Sam!' Ellis bellowed.

Silence.

Except for the ambient mechanical sounds.

'SAM!'

'He not here,' called one of the fearful Yemeni cleaners from beyond a darkened bucket of unchanged, murky, and stagnant water.

Ellis strode over. 'He not here,' Ellis mimicked. 'Where he then? Wot you dun with him?'

'Nothing, sir.' The Yemeni thought about sluicing the dusty floor again, then changed his mind. 'I'll go his quarters, sir.'

'No, you won't. Anyway all you want is a chance to have a lie-down, which is probably what Sam's doing right now, and he's supposed to be at work,' Ellis insisted.

'I am at work.'

Sam.

It was Sam's voice from the furthest point from his on-site quarters.

'Where you been, Sam?'

'Working, sir. As you see.'

Ellis ignored the slight. 'How hot is it, Sam?'

'Hot, sir.'

'I know that, Sam. But how hot? Do we have a thermometer? There should be one around here.'

Sam diffidently picked his way around the desks, opening a drawer in a desk close to the centre of Choi's empire. With an envious sleight of hand, Sam produced a thermometer and handed it to Ellis.

'But it's empty,' Ellis scolded. 'There's nothing in it.'

'Yes, sir.'

'So how the hell're we going to tell the temperature if the bloody thing's empty? Uh?'

Indeed it should have been on the wall – any wall, some sort of wall, internal or external. Common sense suggested an internal wall. The regulations had a host of recommendations and diktats regarding the duties and responsibilities of employers (very few) and rights and privileges of workers (none), but they were dressed in the words of blessing that a benign entity was allowing the workers to be there in the first place.

Given the Kingdom's tendency to endure a very high noontime temperature, beyond and above blood heat, the regulations covering working temperatures were the most specific and mandatory, yet unenforceable. They were created to follow a typical Arabic logic which, by royal decree, stated that if the external noontime temperature as recorded at the Ministry of Interior building in Takhasussi Road, and published in both Arabic and English editions of the *Arab News*, exceeded 50⁰ C, then everybody could go home for the remainder of that day. This wonderful edict enshrined its own paradox – first, the maximum temperature ever recorded by this means was 49⁰ C, and, more endearingly, the reading in the *Arab News* was, of course, yesterday's reading – and therefore out of date and unenforceable.

But the place still needed a working thermometer.

Sam seemed devoid of an answer as he tried to outstare an imagined object on the floor, his hands folded across his waist, his body swaying slowly this way and that way, in the hope perhaps of salvation. Sam muttered a sound.

Ellis looked angrily at the empty tube, no wider than a pipette, its shattered end torn off.

Silence.

'OK, Sam. I'll ask this only once. You know we have to have a thermometer on display, on the wall, Kingdom's rules, so why and for how long have you been hiding the damned thermometer in one of Choi's desks when it should be over there on the wall?'

Ellis waved the splintered tube like a lecturer's pointer towards a nail banged off-line and carelessly into the plasterboard partition wall. Sam continued his slow oscillations.

'Sam?'

'Yes, sir.'

'Sam, who broke it?'

'It's not that easy to explain. Sir.'

'Try me.' Ellis tried to contain his exasperation.

'Pardon, sir?'

'Try me, Sam. Tell me all you know, which I know won't be much, but try.'

'Yes, sir.'

Ellis sat perched on the edge of somebody's desk and listened to an explanation that just couldn't be true. Sam's story was simple enough to begin with: that while he was cleaning the office – dusting, wiping down, emptying the bins, wiping the dried spit out of the Egyptians' waste bins – he had knocked the thermometer off the nail on the wall.

It was either that or the nail had simply come out of the wall. Sam was ducking and weaving, as he considered the company was most likely to dock his wages for the cost of a replacement. But he thought help might be at hand.

Ellis was baffled but let Sam continue. 'So you see, sir, my brother, he works at Al-Juraa, the laboratory people, and he says he can get me another one, and then I'll put it up and nobody'll know the difference. Sir.'

'So which thermometer am I holding here, Sam? The original one you knocked out of the wall or the replacement?' Ellis was just about holding on to the plot.

'That's the original one, sir, that one you're holding, that came out of the wall.'

'Right … and what happened to the replacement, the one your brother was going to bring in from Al-Juraa? Did you brother stand you up?'

'No. Sir.' Sam returned to monosyllables.

'Sam,' Ellis raised his voice, 'if you're fibbing, I'm going to give you a slap!'

'Fibbing, sir?'

'Yes, Sam, fibbing, another word for telling lies.'

'No, sir, thank you, sir, I mean yes, sir.'

'Right. Sam, last chance. The replacement. What happened to the replacement?'

Sam tentatively restarted his narrative and told how his brother arrived on the site with the new thermometer tucked down his trousers (Sam explained he would have slid it into his socks but he wore flip-flops), and arrived the evening before the loss of the first thermometer had been spotted by anyone. The Pakistani security men at the site gate had given him a hard time but not to the extent of discovering what he had hidden in his underpants – there were some places even these security men wouldn't go. Seeing he was visiting Sam, who lived in the on-site accommodation block, the security staff let him in and told him he had five minutes.

Which was all Sam and his brother needed. They took the bright new thermometer out of its hiding place, wiped it on some nearby tissues, and put it on the nail where it belonged. Sam realigned the nail, and all seemed well.

Sam broke into a dark panic as he recounted what happened next. Most people came into work as normal and pondered drawings, drank tea, smoked, spat, cleared a nostril or two, took phone calls, and called the ministry. So everything was normal and Abdul Rahman was late, as normal. Choi and the British men and the American Anderson were not in, but they were out on site or at the embassy or something.

Abdul Rahman had walked towards the peace of his office, his leather briefcase with its golden burnishes catching the sun through the dust, muttered *salamu alaykum* at anybody who might be listening, and then turned towards the wall and stared.

'Hey, Sam, there's something different here,' Abdul Rahman had called accusingly.

Sam wasn't sure what to expect, so he made sure he was nearby as the key players arrived for their day. He simply replied, 'Yes, sir,' pretending not to have recognised any differences at all.

Abdul Rahman looked across the entire width of the wall left to right, paused, realigned his *agal* around his head, then looked left to right.

Then he saw it.

'Sam. Get that off the wall for me, please.'

'Yes, sir. What, sir?'

Abdul Rahman had pointed at the nail and the thermometer and the smeary hand marks nearby. Sam wondered how the Saudi would have, could have, spotted it.

Sam lifted a chair into place, grasped the nail and the thermometer, and handed both to Abdul Rahman, who glowered in his anger.

'You know what this is, Sam?'

'Thermometer. Sir.'

'I know. But what's in it?'

'Don't know, sir.'

Sam continued his story. The Egyptians were watching, the Yemenis were sniggering that Sam was in trouble again, and the Saudi was tipping the thermometer upwards and downward, as if to watch the bubbles go in opposite directions, captivated by it. Like a child with a toy.

Abdul Rahman then walked around Choi's desk, opened the top of the fish tank, smashed the thermometer end against the metal frame of the tank, and shook the entire content into the water.

'Alcohol!' shrieked the devout Muslim. 'You must never use alcohol.'

Abdul Rahman continued to bellow his fury as the offending liquid diluted within the tank, then threw the debris at Sam and told him that

Claude Pemberton

since the alcohol was now killing all the fish, he'd better replace them as well – before Choi got back.

'You're kidding.' Ellis was aghast. He thought Abdul Rahman was a bit more reasonable than that.

'No, sir. Then the water is making a slight red colour, and I see Mr Choi's car arriving, and the fish are starting to roll about and floating, and some of them sinking, and Mr Abdul Rahman has gone into his office, and he's ordered his coffee – this time he's shouting at Toots for service – and he's making telephone calls to some friends, and he's talking Arabic, and he's laughing …'

Ellis felt rather sorry for the little fella.

'… so then I turn up the heater on the tank, and Mr Choi is almost at his desk when somebody outside calls him away, so he doesn't have to watch all the fish dying, but by the time he gets back, he doesn't see the lights in the tank are turned off and all the fish are now floating to the top. So I tell Mr Choi that the tank was like this when I came in this morning, all the fish floating an' all. So Mr Choi looks about for the fighter fish. He can't see it among all the other dead fish, so he lights a cigarette, and sir?'

'Go on, Sam.'

'Sir, I was already stirring the water and looking to be busy at this point, and Mr Choi is coughing from his smoke and the coffee that Toots bought in, and anyway that's my job – the coffee and the chai – not Toots, so Mr Choi says to go down to the Kuwaiti souk and get replacements and he says he'll give me a good tip.'

There. Sam was done. His mood lifted as it seemed nobody was about to hit him. Ellis didn't appear ready to give him a slap. So Sam carried his good mood into the journey of replacement that Mr Choi had ordered.

He'd called up a friend who had a motorbike, a Honda 50 with a flat rear tyre and bent front forks, and asked for a lift to the Kuwaiti souk. No, of course he didn't usually go up to that souk, but this was for Mr Choi, and he wanted Sam to go to a fish shop.

'Why a fish shop?' a distant voice asked. 'We thought the Korean would be eating something more … canine.'

'No,' Sam had insisted, 'Mr Choi needs fish, fresh fish, still alive, to put them in his tank.'

Then the voice was saying something and Sam was shaking his head as he shouted back a dark blend of menace and mendacity.

'So you see, sir, we rode the bike up to the Kuwaiti souk, I'm sittin' on the back and the tyres are whining and clicking and a police car stops and asks us for documents, which we don't have, and says it's against the law to ride a bike without rear footrests. So we got put into the police station, and then they found our papers were OK, and we rode back to the fish shop, but it was closed because it was too late, cos' we'd spent a lot of the day in the police station.'

'Did you get any fish after all that?'

Finally, yes, Sam did, he explained. They went back after work the following day, again on the motorbike, still clanking and whirring and without rear footrests, and they got a good deal for a discount bag including guppies, fighter fish, tiger fish, and something else he couldn't remember the name of. The shopkeeper, who was an Indian friend, filled a large plastic bag full of tainted and discoloured tank water, put in the discounted fish, and added some strands of foliage which would hopefully sustain the fish on the journey back to Mr Choi's now-clean tank, even if the journey was rougher than the fish liked. They rocked and banged and pouted and carried on pulling faces as Sam arrived on the site, and the security man wouldn't let him in because this time he didn't have a livestock pass for the fish, and anyway the motorbike was making a lot of noise and smoke. In the end, the security man informed Sam he was only joking, then levered up the security gate, and the two men, the bike, and the bag of fish rode towards the offices.

Sam had earlier lovingly prepared the tank – washing the stones in the toilet bowl, wiping the inside of the tank with some tissues from the Egyptians' waste bins, replenishing the water level, turning on the aerator (as shown by Mr Choi), turning on the tank lights – and then set off on his journey to the Kuwaiti souk. On arrival back to the office, it was dark, but Sam picked his way through the desks, lifted the tank lid, poured the fish, the water, and the foliage with a resounding splash, restored the lid, poured an industrial handful of Tetramin into the water, turned the tank lights off, smiled at the stupidity of it all, and went out for a few hands of poker with friends.

'It looks like they're all still alive, Sam. Did you lose any?'

'No, sir.'

'Sam?

'I stood on one as it fell out of the bag, but it's all right now.'

'Well done, Sam. Nice work.'

'Thank you, sir.'

Just then Abdul Rahman, armed with his briefcase, walked past the gathered group. He looked and would have smiled if he hadn't seen Ellis holding the thermometer carcass, just mumbling a reluctant weekend greeting and leaving the building.

'Sir?'

'Yes, Sam,' Ellis replied.

'I hope you won't mind, sir, but we still haven't got a thermometer.'

The shower washed away Ellis's day; perhaps he could enjoy a civilised party tonight. He had to work and live with these people. Pity that included socialising. He towelled himself down and freed up the shower room for the next client.

Anderson lay in his bed and grunted, farted, remembered reality, and slept some more.

At around ten thirty, they were all ready. Spick and span, smelling good, breath freshener at maximum effect, crutches washed, aftershave on, foreskins cleaved, shirts ironed with a cold iron, the three musketeers set off in the car, Clitty driving, in the general direction of the nurses' quarters beside the King Khaled Eye Hospital and not a stone's throw from the British Embassy in the diplomatic quarter. It seemed such a safe place to hold a party when one was so close to all those diplomats, who could whine and weasel their way through official Saudi protocol if anyone got into trouble.

Anyway, the eye hospital employed entirely British staff, just as the King Faisal Hospital employed Americans.

There was nothing to fear.

The party was already in full swing as the three men arrived. An apartment designed for three girls held about eighty people, all of them drinking, all intensely interested in the life story of the person with whom they had engaged. The interest in her life was somewhat encouraged by whatever cleavage was in view. The girls' lives were interesting; what lay beneath their dresses was of more immediate interest and determined the drive to find out more.

The music became louder and people became less careful. There was always the thought they could get a taxi home if the drinking became too much. Anderson was berating anybody who would listen that he'd just been fired, and people did listen. Immediate dismissal was a common occurrence for Third World expatriate workers here, but for an event suffered by a First World manager, Anderson was treated with more than normal sympathy.

To an extent, being slung out had a certain cachet. It could provide a focus for some sort of jealousy. This meant it was time to go home, and everybody yearned for home, wherever that was.

Anderson got stuck into a coloured girl from Slough. Ellis did something similar with a ginger-haired girl originally from Bootle, but she'd done five years' VSO in Sierra Leone.

Now she was here.

Interestingly, nobody seemed interested in Clitty.

The gentle giant stood and smiled and drank and smoked and laughed and was very polite and changed the music. He had the odd dance with some of the unattached girls, but they soon went elsewhere. He seemed somewhere else.

Maybe it was the letter.

As the party began to subside, and all the clinching and holding had transferred to giving each other phone numbers so that they could meet at the next weekend, shifts permitting, it was about then that Anderson announced he was going home, so Ellis and Clitty had better get themselves together.

By about three thirty in the morning, the last dance had been done, the commitments made to undying love. There were only about three hours before some of the nurses had to be on duty on the early shift. Then somebody put on the lights, switched off the stereo, and shouted through the smoke and fumes, 'Piss off, the lot of you!'

Anderson by now felt he knew the hostess well enough to plant a careless kiss on the hallway light switch that operated the outside light. She stood firmly, arms folded, an admirer draped longingly across the top of her cleavage, watching her try to look at this madman as his eyes focused on her tits, his boots, and the light switch. All at the same time.

Ellis picked up his cigarettes and bum-bag from the centre of the carpeted dance floor, kicked over an ashtray, apologised profusely, apologised again as he tripped over the feet of the head nurse of intensive care at the Military Hospital as she lay beneath a coffee table, sleeping the sleep of the overindulged while groaning expletives with appropriate volume and venom.

Ellis staggered past the front door lights, along the garden path, and past the rubbish and the overflowing bins casting a stench along the way. A stench of fish, possibly some chips. Some flying things took off in the thin light, wittering towards the gate. The hosts promptly and simultaneously, in a gesture of absolute good riddance, slammed the door shut and put the light out.

Ellis felt his way carefully towards the grumbling sound of the car's idling engine. Anderson was already muttering and bringing down eternal damnation upon most creatures and most things not of his genetic structure, so Clitty in the driving seat came in for some special attention.

But every time he shouted something, no matter how loud, no matter how offensive – no matter how much he waved his arm by way of explanation – all of it seemed to freeze in the space immediately in front of his face. The air was hot, so *freeze* was not the way it appeared. Anderson fell about and fell over and cursed and shouted at Clitty that he would never be able to build a hospital as long as he had a hole in his ass, then broke into the worst chant.

'Remember Jeddah, cocksucker?' he began, cruelly. Anderson did not wait for a reply because some sense of dizziness had once again driven him to the road surface. The dust, close up, seemed rather yellow. Oh shit, let's have a cigarette.

On all fours beside the car, Anderson fumbled into his pockets and passed round cigarettes to some imaginary companions, lit one for himself, and cursed the imaginary others. Then he drew in, coughed, shuffled to the sill of the door, coughed, spat, swore some more, and passed out.

Ellis, already in the car, considered that putting a rear wheel over the man's head would do very nicely. But that may have been the drink putting an unintended spin on his normal thought patterns, so instead he leaned across and pulled the drunken body towards the unoccupied part of the rear seat. Ellis, preferring the space of that area, resented he had to accommodate this person.

Clitty preferred to drive. He sat majestically, twiddling controls, smoking, looking in the mirrors, waiting for a signal to leave. When the grunting and heaving in the rear had subsided, he would shout 'here goes', engage Drive, then blast home.

The clock on the dash said 3:44. In the p.m.

Must fix that, Clitty thought as he negotiated the changing traffic signals past Euromarché supermarket.

Piece of cake.

Drift home, some Roxy Music on while those shits in the back sleep, groan, snore, and fart. I'll have a smoke, oh, it's nice to relax sometime.

He inhaled deeply. The sound of the road was a dull, repetitive *drub drub*, worn engine, worn tyres, shagged-out driver and load. Everything seemed to be under control on this six-lane carriageway through a residential area, fed by service roads, that made about eight lanes for traffic just to serve a thin ribbon of houses on either side of the thoroughfare.

Oh shit.

Clitty approached the next lights over the brow of the hill and saw all of them set at red. There was usually one of them set at green.

Not this time.

Everything was at red.

And the police were there.

Four cars.

All coping with traffic approaching with suicidal intent.

It needed four cars to sort out a lights-on failure when everything was set at all red. Except when everything failed in the all-green state, in which case police cars were substituted by ambulances.

Lots of them.

As Clitty engaged a lower gear and turned down the stereo, he judged his overindulgence to have been an error, popped some fresh gum into his mouth, and watched the police. As he approached the road junction, he noticed one of them was smoking and one was waving cars off to the right, traffic cones placed across the straight-ahead route. Thank God for that; it wasn't a spot check.

Clitty turned up the stereo as all the flashing lights receded and all the street lights faded out to leave him in a darkened and unfamiliar part of town, his companions asleep, no map, no direction, he as drunk as a skunk, and a main beam light out on the off side.

None of which would have mattered if he had been able to see a Saudi man squatted in the centre of a side road, talking to his goats as they grazed on the late-night grasses on the roadside, wrapping his beads this way and that around his left wrist, his right hand holding the shredded ash, the twig sufficiently threaded to act as a dental floss, to clear the excesses of a lamb supper and other debris from his teeth.

The Saudi man heard the car closing, and realising his left upper teeth were unclean, he swapped the ash from that side to this, swapping his beads from that hand to the crumpled pocket of his yellowed *thobe*.

Still the car came on.

Mafi muskilar. No problem.

It will pass me by. *Inshallah.*

It often happened like this.

A previous driver had seen the man in the road, seen some goats, smiled. Perhaps he had called a greeting. He drove around the human obstruction, then went on his way.

This time Clitty was not sure what he saw in the centre of the road.

Certainly he had reached a good part of the Roxy Music tape and was now in an inspired mood, volume up high, window open, another cigarette lit. Some spirited driving, some late braking: all of it seemed in order, warm air floating along the car's smooth edges.

The man in the road watched his goats, his ears only for the gentle chomping of grass and the whisper of the breeze.

'Thanks be to God,' he may have murmured. 'Allah Akbhar, God is great.'

Then, with a sickening thud, the shock-absorbing bumper of the Lexus ripped crushed his abdomen before he had a moment to protest, or raise a cry, or warn his young son snoozing nearby.

The boy heard the sound and saw his father tilt and fall in a welter of blood and the sound of brakes rapidly applied, the sound of some music playing loudly, the sound then suddenly quiet.

He later told the police that when all three men got out of the car, they variously offered him money, cigarettes, gum, anything, but fuck off, you little shit.

With no knowledge of any foreign tongue, he shouted for his mother, threatening to report these attackers with breaths smelling close to that of a goat's stable, one of them with funny eyes. He'd watched as they attempted to bundle the man away from the direct sight of the road. Then the green-and-white had appeared.

Salvation for him. Salvation for the boy.

He waved and cried unutterable wails, calling upon Allah for help as the policemen turned on the red rotating lights on the roof of the Volvo. It switched to a fend-off position ahead of the dead Saudi lying in a bloody heap some yards ahead of this car driven by infidel visitors.

Oh dear, oh dear.

Dead Saudis were one thing.

When killed by somebody, that was something else.

When killed by a foreigner, that was big.

And to reflect this, the traffic police unceremoniously bundled all three drunks into the rear of the car, where a young Saudi already sat, awaiting incarceration for some irrelevant traffic violation, even he watched in some disgust and winced at the smell.

He had thought only the Yemenis smelt like this.

The police had checked who was driver, who were accomplices; this would be stitched up by lunch tomorrow.

Back to the station on Takhassousi Road, jail for the three, then the background to the case for the presiding imam in the morning.

Paperwork.

Check *igama*. For all three of them.

Check driver's licence. Check all three anyway.

The driver didn't have his licence on him. The investigating officer scribbled in the vacant corner of a yellowed pad that had been used for innumerable previous cases, notes made about the outcomes all now erased by this biro-laden arm of authority.

He shuffled the sheets to find another area of the book to file the details of what must surely become a case for him to remember and relish until his dying day.

Good. '*Qwais*,' muttered the investigating officer. We seem to have enough reason to do a raid. Corroborative evidence is required, you understand.

While the three languish in our jail, we can investigate and confirm they certainly have alcohol in their home; we can find out how come they were drunk so far from home. Who supplied the drink? Oh no, not more parties here in Riyadh; we have surely put all the foreigners on compounds where they can't distribute to our people.

With luck they also do drugs.

That way we have all three.

For the moment though, we have the one. The driver. And he will do very nicely.

He's drunk, he's killed, and we have a witness.

From where they sat, the investigating officers could hear grunts and groans. And from where they sat the investigating officers could hear the imam's sounds calling the faithful to al-Fajr prayer, the morning prayer, both called Al Hamda'llillah. Praise be, it would be off-duty time in an hour.

Within that hour, the dark night offered itself in sacrifice to the dawn as redness streaked across the sky. Clouds cleared, vision was restored, and shadows shrank as the welcome cool of the night surrendered to the power and the light of the day.

Meanwhile, the prime suspect lay curled in a fetal position amid the filth and darkness and heat of the floor of some putrid cell in Malaz Jail, Filipino minders smiling hungrily, stroking his head, his legs, his groin, hoping.

Must have been a serious misdemeanour, they agreed. Once in Malaz Jail, once inside, there was no escape.

No justice, no appeal, no nothing.

Chapter 9

'So ya made the impact required to get deported, then!'

Anderson smiled at Ellis while really gloating at Lizzie, who hummed and preened at the periphery of Ellis's vision.

'As did you.'

'Yup. Sure did. Sonofabitch.'

Anderson waved a careless arm across the coffee table, knocking the can and spilling some interesting-smelling liquid across the dusty surface. Then he couldn't remember whether he was supposed to impress Lizzie with his wit or impress Ellis with the love of his life to date. Neither could he recall the exact circumstances of the deportation.

Lizzie jumped from the bed at Anderson's command, hurriedly cleared the spilled liquid with a soiled towel, smiled at Ellis as he watched her gown sigh and droop a little at the front to show the merest tremor of a breast, then replenished his glass.

And while she watched their eyes, she realised at least with this visitor it would possible to look into both his eyes at the same time. But both those eyes seemed more focused on her breasts or her legs, and she smiled and wondered why they engaged her eyes for the briefest moment, then preferred to feast at a lower level.

'Ya know, Ellis?' Anderson began, seeing that Ellis's eyes liked what they saw. 'Sometimes she smiles so wide to get ya dick a movin'. Well, sometimes I have to think of her lifting that gown and farting just to slow me down.'

Ellis sipped quietly from the can, lit up, threw a cigarette at Anderson, thought about Lizzie farting, reckoned that was impossible, shook his head, then settled back in the grimy settee to try to remember being deported.

It had been many years since he had felt the cold fear of Malaz Jail, since the jarring ride in the yellow bus to the airport, the journey taking them past the upmarket Hussam stores where expats shopped. He'd been there countless times, Indian limo drivers parked outside awaiting their charges, sometimes awaiting Madame. While parked in the heat, they could pick their noses and spit.

The road to the airport peeled off from the Dammam highway, and from then on the buildings became less obvious: more villas set back from the main highway; a service road ensuring a protective gap; high, white, painted walls with bougainvillea draped easily to hide electric meters; plants waving in the cool morning air.

The yellow deportation coach trundled in the slow lane at what Ellis estimated to be forty miles per hour, two police cars at the front, two alongside, two at the rear, all lights blazing, red roof lights rotating. Ellis looked down at one of the police cars to see it had many marks of contact with immovable or unstoppable objects, the blue stripes twisted and bent, bare metal gleaming. No signs of rust. No rain. Too dry. The policeman in the front passenger seat was fiddling with a cigar lighter. Laughing and looking around, he pulled three cigarettes from his breast pocket, then lit one, handing it to the waiting hand of an unseen face. The policeman handed another into the rear, where a young male sat, *thobe* pushed down between his legs, hands manacled. Clearly the car was taking the long route to the police station.

Ellis too thought about a smoke, especially as he was similarly chained, the metal straps tight around his ankles, though the wrist straps offered sufficient freedom of movement for a smoke.

Not surprisingly, the atmosphere on the coach was subdued. What had begun life as a bright yellow school bus was now a seventy-seat coach full with rejects from the Saudi expatriate labour market, all of them having won the displeasure of their hosts through some misdemeanour. Most were guilty of petty fraud, or fiddling accounts, or drunkenness, or distribution of alcohol, or some other transgression against Islam – guilty of anything for which judicial amputations, execution, or long terms of imprisonment were not appropriate. But for many of them, a caning had gone witnessed but unreported.

Everyone on the coach had a good reason to feel relaxed, yet they were in this country for the money, for the family, and that revenue source had now been cancelled. This seemed to matter little to the Filipinos as they all sat in the first ten rows of the coach, each chained to the next man, all perfectly relaxed and smoking freely.

There were also Koreans, Thais, Indians, Pakistanis, and a couple of Yemenis. None of them were about to make any sudden moves. After all, they were being kicked out; they might as well stay put and undergo the due process. They sat and chattered to anybody who would listen, or they just waited until the forty-five-minute journey to the airport was completed.

Ellis sat at the rear of the coach, chained to Anderson. Neither spoke; neither moved. Last night's jail beating had left sore limbs, especially the backs of their thighs, rendering them incapable of movement. Neither wished to speak in any case, preferring to take turn and turn about with the cigarettes. Thankfully the police had given them enough cigarettes to keep them subdued until they reached the aircraft en route to London. Then – and this depended on whether the police at Malaz had packed the men's wallets and passports – they could buy whatever was required as soon as the British Airways flight had lifted its undercarriage clear of Saudi soil. If, however, the police had stuffed all their possessions into a black plastic bin liner and thrown it into a roadside skip, then there would be nothing to smoke for at least the next ten hours.

The Filipinos raised the loudest cheer as the coach pulled into the departures parking area at the King Khaled International Airport. They giggled and called excitedly in Tagalog, and they pulled faces at the policeman who sat in the escort seat beside the coach driver, disconsolately clutching a large pack of varying-coloured passports, each of them with papers giving reasons for exit folded carelessly in between the pages. The policeman stood from his seat. Realising that the escort cars had now peeled off and returned to the city centre, he felt for the keys in his jacket pocket. They were still deep in the well of his trouser pocket. The one with the hole. God, how he hated this. He checked his list.

He had responsibility to deport felons from eight countries: Korea, Yemen, Thailand, India, Pakistan, Egypt, Philippines, and, most unusually, the United Kingdom. Didn't often get them. British guys. He wondered what they did.

The police man was required to clear the coach and synchronise the processing of exit papers in order that the subjects of all this attention would be ready to leave the country as soon as the aircraft was ready.

All the Koreans, they went to Seoul. That was easy.

Yemenis, they went to Sana'a.

Thais went to Bangkok.

Easy trip so far.

Indians could go to Mumbai or Madras or New Delhi.

They always used to send them to multiple airports, but now so many were being thrown out of the country that the decision had been made by a bureaucrat to send them on the one flight to Mumbai. Then they could negotiate their way home – at least they were on their own sovereign territory, so to hell with them.

Same thing with the Pakistanis. They could go to Islamabad or Karachi. On some flights they would say they were on the wrong flight, and the police would become more than a little agitated; henceforth Pakistanis would be put on the Islamabad flight.

The Filipinos went to Manila, the Egyptians Cairo. Both these groups were troublesome, but at least they were simple enough to bundle onto one aircraft.

The British. Unusual. Still, a piece of cake. LHR: London Heathrow.

But no matter how the policeman worked things out, there was always a problem with the logistics. Suppose the incoming flight from Manila or wherever was late or had crashed. Would that prevent him getting home for lunch?

However much he worried, he was left short of information on arrivals and whether he could complete his task in the time necessary.

There was nothing for it.

He stood up and looked sternly from the front of the coach into this sea of anxious faces. The moment of seriousness was breached by one passport becoming loose in the pile. Then all of them slipped from his arms and crashed to the floor in a welter of curses from the policeman and lusty laughs from the Filipinos, who began to sing songs and chatter.

The policeman felt inclined to shoot the lot of them.

Instead, he found a Sarawat carrier bag beneath the seat and pushed all the passports in there – he could sort them in the police office once inside the departures lounge. By that stage, and following some violent steering manoeuvres, the coach was parked partly on the pavement, and a front wheel was pressing on an anti-terrorist block. To an outsider, the coach looked like it had been abandoned.

He barked his command for everyone to leave in single file, waving his instructions inelegantly for the benefit of the non-Arabic speakers. The bag held tightly under his arm, he called for the door to be opened and for all the deportees to line up behind him.

Blinded by his purpose, the policeman led the foray towards the rotating entry doors of the departures lounge, preferring to ignore the perfectly straightforward swing doors to his far right.

Everybody was chattering and looking around and tripping over their manacles and their ankle clasps and bumping into each other and wondering if they could see their planes. Some of the more thoughtful wondered if the police would dish out another beating before being done with them.

As the last of the chain of felons was exiting the coach, the first link began to negotiate the rotating door, which comprised six segments, bordered by highly polished glass panels, and each segment sufficient for two passengers plus luggage. The door itself, like so many official buildings in this country, was electrically operated. It whirred quietly around and around, ushering the expectant traveller into the air-conditioned luxury of the terminal building.

The coolness of the place surprised the policeman. As the segment of the door he'd had to himself spun round, he'd hesitated, and it pushed him to the floor. Suspecting an ambush, he checked his waist holster for his gun. The Sarawat carrier bag was still there, but what was being slowed down was the progress through the entry doors.

The first of the Filipinos, two of them, walked and shuffled readily enough into their segment, overlooking the fact that their joint chains inside the segment were still connected to their compatriots who were poised to enter the next segment a moment later.

As they tried to get into the segment, the connecting chains snagged in the door runner, the door ground to a halt, the circuit breakers cut in, and the door attempted no further activity. For a few moments anyway.

The policeman, recognising his dilemma, shouted some urgent commands at nobody in particular, waving his gun in the air as the Filipinos inside the segment attempted to push the door backwards, the way they had come in. They pushed and they swore as those outside pushed and swore with more noise and even more energy, since there were lots of them with energy to spare.

Then the circuit breaker cut back in. The sudden surge sent a shiver of current around the security circuits, overloading the main fuses and plunging the entire building into silence and darkness. The sun of the early morning did what it could to keep the place illuminated but was in competition with the light-sensitive, darkened glass which shielded the building from the glare and dust of its desert neighbourhood.

Some of the Yemeni airport workers, realising there were prisoners stuck in the rotating doors, shouted words of encouragement and advice to the policeman, who was now showing many signs of a total loss of control of the situation. His brow was hot, the sweat running into his eyes and disfiguring still further his unpleasant demeanour.

He had to decide: ah yes.

Those doors over to the far side, how stupid not to have seen them before. Let's get the infidels through there, check them in, dump the passports, then go off home.

The policeman shouted commands to pull back and instructed those nearest the bus to walk to the swing doors, by which stood one of the Yemeni porters, waving happily and laughing at the fact that seventy men were being deported backwards. The chains allowed nobody the choice but to turn round and walk backwards as soon as the tension from the next man caught the slack of the chain.

Next problem.

The policeman would have liked to process the passports of those nationalities whose planes had arrived, but with the power failure, there was no sign of any arrivals. The carousels, the escalators, the water fountains in the marble gardens had ceased to twinkle and entertain. The entire place had shut down.

And it was becoming unbearably hot. The policeman, understanding little of electricity, waved his gun some more, issued threats, and manhandled a Pakistani baggage handler into telling him where the fuse boxes were.

No amount of gun waving would change the man's story that there was a problem at the airport substation about three miles away. The curls of smoke he could see in the distance were from a fire brought on by some incident or failure, but anyway as a direct result of lousy installation and poor earth connections.

'Bloody foreigners!' the policemen yelled to nobody at all, apparently now blessed with an evolving vocabulary. He lit a cigarette, taking one drag, inhaling angrily, putting the cigarette down in a nearby ashtray, taking out another from his breast pocket, and lighting that too. 'They bring these bloody people in here, and those that don't get deported end up building airports and factories that don't work, and if they do work they burst into flames!' He shook his head at his philosophical analysis.

Ellis found himself smiling at the absurdity and took out the last smoke for himself.

Anderson couldn't be bothered to smoke. He must be feeling poorly.

The policeman, still the focus of everyone's attention, now strode to the check-in desk to demand that these people be allowed to be booked onto a plane. Then they could be treated with a little humanity instead of being clanked around the departures lounge for all to see.

It was gently pointed out to him that there was no power, no way the computers could work; they had all shut down. There was no way any tickets could be processed. There was no way anything was going to happen until the power came back on so why didn't he go and lie down somewhere, padlock all seventy of them to one of the building's vast pink marble pillars, then sleep until the power was restored?

This was the best suggestion he had heard, and he followed it implicitly.

'Ya know, Ellis, that damn cop, he musta been sleepin' at least two hours.' Anderson was yearning at Lizzie as she settled back into purring mode on the bed. 'An' then what's he do?' Anderson didn't wait for a reply. 'He stays asleep, and then the power comes back on, and all the cons, they start to process their own tickets, and then their own visas. They pick up their passports – or maybe someone else's, it didn't seem to matter. Trouble is, the motherfucker cop got the key, so there ain't no way the guy goin' to Bombay, well, he ain't gonna get the same plane as the guy goin' to Manila. Leastways not when the two are hitched together with a bitta chain like a suspension bridge.'

'I'm sure you're right,' Ellis concurred dreamily. This wine, or was it the smokes. seemed to be making Ellis sleepy.

Must be the excitement of the day or the boredom of being in Anderson's company after a long absence.

'So when we goin' back then, bumhead?' Anderson pressed on.

There was nothing to do at home. There was nobody either cared about. There was money to be made on this venture. They owed it to Clitty to do something. They could go back and get him. Would it really work?'

Perhaps the Foreign Office could intercede.

Unlikely. They'd be uncertain where Saudi Arabia was on a map.

'That's not fair,' Ellis criticised Anderson. 'They must know where the place is, not like you bloody pretend Yanks.'

'Yeh, whatever.'

Anderson smiled at Lizzie and she smiled back longingly, the pair of them bored with their plump visitor. He was getting tired. His loins were wanting Lizzie. 'OK, so let's finish off. We're agreed we're going back. We'll try to get the old boy out before they do him. We'll get some money, whatever; we'll be all right. But we can't arrange it here.'

Anderson lunged inside Lizzie's gown. 'Now here's some stuff I can arrange.' He grasped her chest, and she squealed and protested and smiled.

'Where d'ya stay, Ellis?'

'Lincoln.'

'Fuck me.'

'Why?'

'Lincoln. That's a no-hope place. What you doin' there?'

'Housing's cheap, beer's cheap. Hookers're cheap. Any other justification required?'

'Yeh. But … Lincoln!' Anderson shook his head, puzzled, and was forced to spit out the words.

Ellis ignored the question. Instead he laid out a brief plan, including that they were both, even though Anderson disliked being reminded, British passport holders. They'd both need to be back in the UK to put the fine details on any plan, get the passports and visas organised, and try to work out some ground rules for a pair of men whose mutual loathing was barely concealed.

'So let's meet in London,' Anderson confirmed logically.

'Where do you live at the moment?' Ellis was perfectly polite.

'Chiswick.'

'What! You don't live in the same place as Choi?' Ellis was thinking of all sorts of accusations to throw at the man, but had to admit a frisson of excitement to think about Chis-Wick, and the fact he'd heard no mention of the place since getting back home.

But then in Lincoln, you wouldn't hear of smaller London boroughs. Not in the news or in common parlance.

'Nope,' Anderson replied dismissively. 'Just Chiswick.'

Anderson leaned forward and scribbled a number and handed the note across to Ellis.

Ellis did likewise.

Whoever blinked first would call the other.

Ellis left Lizzie and Anderson in some sort of embrace and picked his way from the house, past the garbage and the smell and the nearby squawk of alley cats, the thickness of the darkness more pronounced than earlier. He felt tainted by the night, by meeting that blasted man. Bloody hair gel, bloody special offers. This was supposed to be a holiday, not a jaunt down a very uncomfortable memory lane. He smelt of smoke; he was sweating; his hair was limp with exertion, tobacco, and alcoholic indulgence. He knew he wouldn't get a taxi from here, so he patted down his hair, adopted a press-on posture, and made for the lights on the main road that should, perhaps, get him back to his hotel.

As he penetrated the night air at some speed, he began to whistle. Deliriously at first, but then realising he was enjoying the song he and Cheryl had once ended loving evenings with.

Dammit.

Why think of that bloody woman here?

Why here? Why should those feelings flood back here on a darkened, desolate highway in the heart of a West African nation in the middle of the night?

But he whistled anyway, thought about anything to avoid the prospect of a six-mile walk to the hotel. It was now three thirty in the morning; he was tired, drunk, and dishevelled; and there wouldn't be a taxi nowhere, no place. His thoughts had lapsed into the pseudospeak so favoured by Anderson.

Ellis was deep in thought, thinking of Cheryl – was she moist right now like she used to be; don't think of her with that bloke. He was following the wavy line along the black tar of the pavement, gently lit by the lights approaching the Albert Hospital. Christ, there were still miles to go; press on. So deep in thought, he failed to register the sound of an idling engine emerging from the hospital grounds and closing gently from behind – a taxi offering sir a lift. Where would he like to go?

Ellis paid the man off with all the *dallaras* in his possession. The driver seemed swamped with gratitude. Ellis fell from the cab, negotiated the hotel locked-door policy, and picked up the key and a nightcap from the night porter, who winced at Ellis's breath.

With a sense of relief, Ellis made for his room, to sleep until he could reach that night when this holiday could come to an end, back to business, back to the gloom of the English winter.

Lincoln in winter.

Anderson blinked first.

There he was, in London. He'd been there for weeks. It was now March, so why didn't they meet in London, shithead?

Ellis reflected on the whole project and could not really be bothered to get involved with Anderson again. If he had not given Anderson his number, the entire experience could have been expunged forever from his memory.

That wouldn't help Clitty, would it?

At least Anderson had been flushed out. He'd phoned; he needed Ellis.

'Where do we meet, bumhead?' Anderson shrilled. Vacuous twit.

'Wigmore Restaurant, under the Wigmore Hall, Wigmore Street.'

'That's a bit fuckin' smart for an asshole like you, ain't it?'

'Not in the least,' Ellis said. 'It may introduce you to culture. God knows you need it.'

Anderson ignored the jibe, scribbled down something, and sounded agreement. 'When?'

'A week. The twenty-second.'

Anderson made a note. 'Time?'

'Eleven. Morning.'

'Ya ain't gonna get pissed at that time a day in a Wigmore Street brasserie, yer pillock.'

Ellis didn't want to get pissed at eleven in the morning and said so.

'Please yerself. See yer then.'

Ellis grunted.

Anderson hung up.

Ellis hung up.

Neither really wanted anything to do with any of this, except the money and the life of a colleague maybe, but the money mostly.

At ten thirty on the appointed day, Ellis found a seat at a corner table in a subdued area of the Wigmore Restaurant. The white tablecloths, in contrast with the dark green decor of the walls, reminded him of the inside of an operating theatre, where bright lights and contrasts made a hideous arrangement of colours. But this was a restaurant, so hopefully the outcome would be better, even if the colours were not.

He checked his hair in the tinted mirror forming part of a floral display, seemed satisfied with the positioning and the concentration of hair gel.

At last he had it right. It looked good. At last he had a chance. He could pull birds now his hair was all right. Couldn't he?

Not really.

After all … He looked again into the mirror to see a pathetic, fat face, laden with years of excessive indulgence. He could see the reflection of his paunch heaving heavily on his trouser belt, rolling it outwards. He pulled a hand through his hair; he could see that this was probably his only plus point. He could also see he was getting older when he looked in the mirror and his mother was looking back at him.

He could see Anderson in the mirror, standing behind him, mocking.

The bastard was standing there with one coffee for himself, an unlit cigarette hanging precariously from his lower lip, like a cheap gangster. He was sneering, and yes, that bastard had kept his shape reasonably well, the eyes still pointing in different directions.

'I think ya looks pretty,' Anderson mocked, stroking Ellis's hair. 'Even though you's as fat as a porker,' Ellis wanted lash out, 'and 'bout as greasy.'

At that, Ellis planted a punch into Anderson's right eye – the one that looked forward, not sideways. Then Ellis poured Anderson's coffee over him as he pulled himself from the floor, grasping the table for support, flinching and wriggling from Ellis's assault.

Anderson gasped as he pulled himself upright, surprised that Ellis could punch that hard, that he could be so angry.

Gingerly Anderson slumped into a seat by the table while Ellis rearranged the cloth and the elegant lace drapes which adorned the table cover, brushing away some specks of dirt, and ordered two more coffees in advance of lunch. Anderson wiped his hair dry with his jacket sleeve. With some understanding secured, they sat still, wondering what they would do next.

Anderson pulled a hip flask from a jacket pocket.

Hard as he tried, he still couldn't think without booze. So he emptied it down his throat, belched, and upset some Japanese tourists who were still confused by the recent violence as they neatly poked at an oriental special dish of the house with silver forks.

Anderson wiped a grimy hand across his mouth, burped again, then lit up. Having incurred a stare from the maître d', he plunged the blazing cigarette end into the water of a vase of tulips set neatly on the table, which had surprisingly defied the fall to the floor of the glasses and cutlery when Ellis had his hump.

Feeling suitably fortified, they set about making their plan.

Visas.

Always an international traveller's dread, and problematic for these two in that they needed to develop a valid reason for a return visit to the Kingdom. Researching job opportunities in Saudi, then getting new passports, then booking flights, then doing this, then doing that, then worrying about Clitty, and then worrying if he'd already been executed. They wondered why they hated each other so, and then they made a little peace. A truce. Then they broke it.

'Fuck it,' Anderson announced finally, jumping to his feet and knocking a cup from the edge of the table to crash to the floor with a resounding coarseness. 'Let's get rat-bagged. I've had enough of all this bloody coffee an' all the bloody no-smokin' rules!'

As the two men turned to leave, the waitresses nervously hovered and only set about removing the debris and resetting the tables once the aggressive visitors had left space for the proper luncheon visitors to arrive with their own pleasant aura.

The crowds of Oxford Street pushed and threaded along the pavements, avoiding the drop onto the road wherever they could, using body twists and contortions only ever applied on the edge of pavements in busy city streets. Carrier bags, lots of them, held in tightly clenched hands and under arms, were dexterously poised, used as counterbalances to avoid the drop.

Everyone seemed in a hurry to achieve something and nothing.

Ellis and Anderson shared an equal anxiety, so they went to the pub, the Phoenix on the edge of Cavendish Square. They went to be anxious, to get drunk, and possibly to explore how much of their plans they had achieved.

Before today and after the Gambia holiday, Ellis had returned to Lincoln to mull over how to get a visa to get back into Saudi. They would only need a four-week visitor visa.

Claude Pemberton

Anderson had done likewise.

They both had the same problem in common.

Having been deported in total disgrace, their names were forever on the Saudi Foreign Ministry blacklist. Any attempt to be readmitted would be rejected out of hand.

They could change their names.

They could apply for another short-term ministry job, just to get back in.

They could adopt names, get false papers, false personae, and false qualifications.

That idea was rejected as being too long-winded, too complex, and too easily probed by a sensible Saudi, if such a creature existed. And even if they did get back in under existing identities, would they not come under some overbearing scrutiny when once they made their enquiries after Mr Klitowski in the Malaz Jail?

Did either of them have any friends?

Not really – not enough, anyway, to allow them to adopt others' identities for a short period. Not for free anyhow.

What price? How much would anybody charge for such a small favour?

Ellis had gone drinking with Brian Lister, and now Brian Lister was trawling through the intricacies of a peculiar proposal. The two of them, regular drinking companions, had convened in Lincoln to discuss Ellis's request whereby Ellis could borrow Lister's identity if Lister wanted to use Ellis's apartment. The duration of the agreement was not set in stone but was understood to be when Ellis got back from wherever it was he was going.

For Brian Lister this was ideal. He had been conducting an uncomfortable extramarital affair on the rear seat of his rusty Morris Marina for the last three months, and for him to take his newly found beloved in the horizontal plane in Ellis's apartment suited him just fine. Hopefully Ellis may never come back.

Later that week, Lister handed over his passport, birth certificate, and some recently taken passport photos that seemed quite similar to the portly

Ellis. The pair of them were a similar age, similar habits, and similarly worn. It was as close a match to Ellis as he was going to get.

At the handover, Ellis provided Lister with two sets of keys and explained how the deadlock worked. Then each of them smiled at each other, enthralled by their ability to crack a problem that neither of them wanted to own up to, and retired again to the pub to drink to duplicity.

Drink to anything at all.

Just drink.

Anderson was doing something not dissimilar.

Having long ago realised that few people wanted anything to do with him, Anderson could only call upon some extreme measures to achieve the same level of success, passport-wise anyway, as Ellis had. He thought and fretted and smoked and drank and wondered and drank more, visited pubs and chatted and begged and smoked. Usually as soon as he approached the denouement, that is to say achieving agreement with a third party to hand over a passport, that person would cough or splutter or excuse himself from the building with the excuse he had to get home, the entire conversation expensive and aborted.

The passport problem remained unresolved.

Then, unusually, Anderson had a brain wave.

A stroll past the unwashed claimants in the queue outside the benefit agency the following Thursday revealed three men who had British passports. All three of them were happy to hand their passports over for one hundred and fifty pounds.

Cash.

Anderson arranged a rendezvous in a Chis-Wick pub with the man who most resembled himself, particularly the wonky eyes. They drank beyond closing time, and he came out one hundred and fifty pounds lighter, plus drink.

But he had the cast-iron promise of the passport, so now he and Ellis could cut the bacon. Though cutting bacon in the Middle East might prove problematic.

Claude Pemberton

February and March were usually quiet times for the passport office, which was why Richard Bartholomew Ellis could quickly acquire Brian Lister's name with an Ellis face. All he had to do was own up to the bureaucrats that he'd lost his passport, and he needed a new one. Here were two passport photographs taken in a kiosk in Woolworths in Lincoln; here was the cheque. Lo and behold, in two weeks Ellis was fixed up.

Anderson, though, enjoyed a lesser level of success, his supplier becoming less compliant as another evening's drinking got under way.

The conversation soon descended to the detail of the surrender of one passport. The victim from the benefits office had decided to change the rules of engagement, so demanded another one hundred and fifty.

Anderson said fuck off and the man said no passport.

A period of tense silence followed, drinks glasses clasped as tightly as their top lips.

'You gotta bird?' Anderson began, somewhat accusingly.

'Nah.'

'Wife?'

'Yeh.'

'Love her?'

'Nope.'

'So why you ain't gotta bird?'

'Don't need one.'

'Ya shags ya missus?'

'Yup.'

Anderson fell silent at the man's apparent virtue and even more, his lack of … passion, was it?

He recalled an anguished telephone conversation the previous evening with Ellis, who had announced proudly he was one Brian Lister and what was going to happen with you, you bloody Anderson? Were you going to get some bloody woman's passport, some old hag with crossed eyes, a blue rinse, and bad teeth?

Anderson absorbed the bile and had to admit he was a little uneasy with progress. He actually felt pushed to ask Ellis for some advice.

Ellis suggested a copycat approach to this Chis-Wick passport holder.

'So why not take a mistress?' Anderson pressed on with the man as he asked for yet another high-strength lager.

'Don't need one.' The man sipped noisily with no emotion or interest in cooperating.

'Cuz I gotta condo ya may want to use.' Anderson floated the idea against the background noise and against a top lip clasped by a white ring.

'Tell you what,' Anderson leaned forward in a sense of comradely interest, 'you got the first one hundred and fifty. Now you get a second lot of one hundred and fifty – when I get back, that is. Plus you got the use of the condo, whenever …'

'Where did you say you come from?' The man turned and hated the strange eyes of the man making all these promises, with all these prices and proposals and benefits in exchange for a nearly expired passport.

'Darlington,' Anderson replied coldly.

'Darlington my bollocks,' the man chided. 'You sound like some bloody American creep to me!' He poured the remainder of another pint into his throat, then held the glass out hopefully for a refill.

The man explored the inside of his nose, lit a cigarette, avoided Anderson's gaze as the drinks were ordered, then settled back as the drinks arrived. He also let go a burp of generous volume.

'What d'you want with my bloody passport anyway?' he demanded at Anderson as he gulped greedily and awaited a reply, leaving more white froth on his thin moustache, which he swept away with a long and yellowed tongue.

'I wanna wipe my ass with it.' Anderson required little effort to employ the full drawl.

The man threw a cigarette at Anderson, lit the thing hanging from his own bottom lip, and ignored Anderson's pocket search for a lighter.

The man inhaled deeply. 'Sounds like you need me, Mr Anderson, sir.'

Anderson fumbled through his thoughts.

This little bastard was having no more money. Goddammit, the bloody man was unemployed, probably unemployable. He had a passport, he had a wife, he probably had nine children. Maybe he didn't need a flat, but he needed to get his teeth fixed. They were brown and ugly and chipped and misaligned. Better not to mention that. Time to reinforce the offer.

'OK, here's the juice …'

Claude Pemberton

The man ordered another beer on Anderson's tab. Finding the pseudotalk nauseating, he pulled a grimace, lit a new cigarette from the glow of the old, then waited for what was coming.

'One more time,' Anderson said. 'There's a total of three hundred available, plus you get the unfettered use of my apartment till I get back.'

'Unfettered. Whassat?'

'Free to do as ya wish.'

'Anything?'

'Yup.'

'Where you goin'?'

'I ain't sayin' an' you don't need to know an' I ain't sayin'.'

The man shrugged his shoulders and leaned over, tearing open a packet of peanuts that had appeared. He tipped a generous palmful into his hand and threw them at his face, chewing hungrily.

'OK.' He turned and smiled at Anderson. A nut slipped from his mouth, bounced once on his chest, and disappeared onto the floor.

Anderson reciprocated, smiled, ordered more beers, shook the man's hand, then asked his name.

'Clarence Breakspeare.'

'Oh fuck off!'

'Sure is.'

'Not on your fuckin' passport surely?'

'Not exactly. You see, it depends which passport …'

'Fuck me, Mr Bloody Breakspeare, which passport ya givin' me and what bloody name am I goin' to use?'

'It'll be another two hundred if I tell you the real name.'

'No, it fuckin' well won't, cuz all you have to tell me is the name on the passport and then that name becomes mine at three hundred quid. As agreed.'

Anderson looked around the smoke-filled room with a look of victory, but nobody seemed to know or see or care.

The man known initially as Breakspeare continued drinking beer, demanding refills, then slumped over the table and wondered how long he could shield this awful man from the truth of the name on the passport.

'OK, I'll tell you.'

Anderson almost kicked over his chair in his hurry to pick up the words above the noise of the jukebox.

'Go ahead!' Anderson shouted.

'It's ... Theophilus Andropolis.'

Even the jukebox sounded silent as Anderson worked through the eight syllables of the drunk's name.

'Is that what's on the fuckin' passport?' Anderson demanded over the sounds of ABBA bemoaning 'Knowing Me, Knowing You' and reminding Anderson that he once had a wife with whom he'd shared this song. Then here was this bloody bloke with the Greek-sounding name, picking up benefits when he had a British-sounding passport.

The man smiled, perhaps he even sneered. 'Nah, mate, the bloody name on the bloody passport you're getting' is ...' The man hesitated and thought a little, almost like there was no passport at all. Perhaps he didn't have a passport; perhaps he had five passports and couldn't remember which name appeared on which. 'Here goes. The name is, oh shit, give me more fuckin' beer ...' The man slumped over the ashtray and appeared to pass out.

Anderson had to offer the man his flat. If he didn't have a girlfriend, then Anderson would have to get him one.

Whatever he needed, he would have, but Anderson needed a name and the bloody passport.

Anderson made some discreet enquiries among his fellow drinkers about the name of the man who was being so difficult.

The barman offered information at a price, selected a multiple something from the optics, and put it on Anderson's tab.

'The name, yer see, sir ...' said the Irish landlord, leaning forward in a gesture of conspiracy, swirling an acquired quadruple brandy around and around the glass, 'is ... Oh Jairsus, surely I've not forgotten already.'

Anderson watched and hated the ginger hair and the jovial Irishness of the bloody man, and he said so. 'Listen, ya fuckin' dogs' brains!'

'Yes?' the ginger enquired cheerfully. 'Then what if I do get a bit addled around the brain? Sure enough it happens around about drinkin' time, which hereabouts is anytime on anyone's clock.' The man shrugged, shook his head and continued, 'Anytime is anyone's time for a drink.'

Anderson had to give up the aggressive approach, bought yet another pack of cigarettes, handed them out to anyone in need, and hated Ellis for living in Lincoln. There, surely, people were nice.

At least nicer than here in West London. Chis-Wick.

Choi.

Shit.

Anderson shuddered as he remembered all of it and why he needed a new passport, or at least why he needed a new name anyway and why he had to put a new face into an old passport.

The man slumped at the bar stool decided it was time to go home. He asked for another beer and declared he could not remember what his name was. He would go home tonight or maybe tomorrow night, whenever. He would pick up the passport from home, get back here same time, maybe tomorrow or the next day, get shit-faced courtesy of this odd-looking creep with the peculiar eyes, pick up the money, hand over the passport if he had to, then haggle over the birth certificates and all that stuff. Anderson could pretend to be the person on the passport, and he could go to St Katherine's House and get copies of this, that, and whatever else was needed.

The dark-haired man who might have a name pulled himself up straight from the surface of the bar and attempted a wan smile, gilded by beer. He slipped uneasily from the stool, promised the passport same time tomorrow, smiled and farted simultaneously, and left the bar in a series of exotic and quite clumsily executed manoeuvres, only the squeaky doors closing slowly behind leaving any suggestion that he may ever have been there at all, Mr Bloody Theophilus or whoever he was.

He'd be back tomorrow, Anderson reflected hopefully as he examined all the part-empty glasses abandoned along the bar top and emptied them all, one by one. Wine, beer, sherry, shorts: it didn't seem to matter which drink was what. It was alcohol and it was wet. When he reached the end of the row, he passed round cigarettes in the hope of gratitude. Then, glowing in the transient thanks of grateful anybodys sitting vacantly at tables near the door with the squeaky hinge, he stumbled into the night air and went home in the hope of a shower and some good sleep.

Sleep brought little relief to his tensions.

The tensions of Mr Theophilus, the thoughts that he was just a drunken git with a perfectly English name, instead of whatever he was pretending to be, the Greek name, the whole damn thing.

Did they really want to go back?

Who really needed to go back?

Any mortal soul on a return trip to Saudi Arabia asked himself the same question as the day of travel drew near, even when he did have his own identity sorted out.

For Anderson, this problem was more urgent, more acute. Lying flat on his back on the unmade bed, sheets and discarded clothing contributing to his misery, Anderson stretched his arms into the air, playing shadows across the far bedroom wall, now brightly illuminated by the orange glare of the street lamp and the slow rhythm of the traffic lights.

Twiddling and twisting his fingers, he played a variety of shapes of all sizes and complexity in the light.

It took him back to his childhood in Brighton. Those nights when his mother went out to work and he lay obediently in his bed, watching the shapes of the light filtering around the ruff of the curtain. How he had imagined shapes: shapes of trees, maps, buildings, faces, heads, all of them inscribed on the far wall.

For once Anderson felt something approaching nostalgia for his mother, a feeling that soon fled as he remembered the current predicament.

Ellis might get back in before him.

After all, Ellis had the passport of Brian Lister. In two weeks he could be fixed up to go through the hoops and hurdles of obtaining a visitor's visa from a scowling Egyptian in the consular section, deposited in the dark bowels of the Saudi Embassy in Belgrave Square.

The shit could get out there in two weeks. That was all it took. *Inshallah*.

Then he could ... Anderson lit a cigarette in the darkness and noted the thin smoke curling upwards and across the wall ... no. Ellis was in no position to look after Clitty, not with what they had planned, the bank and the rescue and all. Yet … the bugger could get back in, pull the money, and leave Clitty to his fate. After all, the two of them had been close on occasion. Perhaps they had an arrangement, some sort of agreement, some plan that would cut in when the shit hit the fan. Ellis had a new identity; he could go now. Perhaps he did have a plan.

Anderson dropped the lighted cigarette into the bedding, cursed, and swore at all the sparks he'd created. He beat the sheets and eiderdown erratically, venting his fury on the glowing embers with one hand while the other sought out other seats of fire.

There were none. Only the fire inside.

Anderson lay back down among the ruins of his bedding. Tomorrow could be better, he reflected hopefully, but it could also be much worse.

And before he could say Theophilus, the ceiling spun a few times, and Anderson was fast asleep. His sleep was as dream-laden as it was long. There were people and faces, sounds and smells, aircraft carriers on the horizons launching trouble. There were fishing trips, there were girlfriends, there was his mother uttering silent but angry sounds when his bedroom was a mess. There was his optician with the upturned, concave mirror offering solace as he explained why the astigmatism was as it was, and every time the man turned, he had blood in his eyes, a faint smile curdling the corner of his face.

Anderson would wake, turn, mutter to somebody, pull the smoke-logged bedding this way and that, think about somebody nice he'd dreamt of, then, hoping the dream would continue, fall back to sleep and dream of bleeding the brakes on his motorcycle, falling off it after he had failed to tension the spokes correctly.

The night wore on and the dreams repeated, often in the same sequence, always with the same clarity, and always a turn among the blankets at what felt to be half hourly intervals.

Cars drove by. Lights flickered across the ceiling, merging with the orange of the street lights; other lights wrinkled to throw shapes across the Artex ceiling, a dried tabletop plant still alive enough to cast its own mark of respect on the snoring man's ceiling.

And he snored. A good smoker's snore, combined with the throat paralysis of the beer, or rather the effects of having to buy lots for the man and having to drink half of the stuff himself. The outcome, whatever, was a devastating testament to the effects of an obstructed airway.

None of it, though, seemed to disturb Anderson, who continued to make sufficient noise that would surely wake most of West London. But as day broke and the alarm clicked and grunted a welcome to the day, the sounds subsided, to be substituted by the smell of the newly awakened, along with the bad breath and bodily smells that required urgent and remedial attention.

Anderson awoke, yawned, gasped, reached for his cigarettes, lit one, and farted, all in one action. He was like that.

A rub of his eyes prefaced a perfunctory sampling of his axillary odours. Then Anderson arose with an effort worthy of a fanfare.

The act of rising from his mattress strained all his sinews – the bed located on the floor, safety first if he fell out drunk. The bedclothes slid away. Some burned edges stuck to his arms, brown pieces of his eiderdown sticking to the floorboards. His wind and effluent found voice among the outdoor sounds of the early day traffic.

'Theophilus!' Anderson bellowed at the mirror as he tried applying shaving gel to his face. 'Goddammit, you bloody bastard, you kept me awake all bloody night!'

Only the bath tap dripped its response, trailing water down and across a browning lime tideline running from the hot tap to the waste in some triangular formation. The stain was narrow at the top, widening until it became all-enveloping where the water swirled and disappeared from you with its constant bubbling and a final burble.

Anderson persevered nevertheless and was rewarded with a smooth face and fresh breath. Quite a feat for such a king-sized hangover and king-sized halitosis.

He sat by the window and began his fourth cigarette of the day while watching the shops opposite, their canopies left unrolled to hide the frontages from prying eyes. He watched as people began coming to the newsagent, buying papers, smokes, and lottery tickets.

A passing lorry shook the window, the sash worrying itself at the depth of the sound, the pane apparently ready to shatter.

Still Anderson smoked on in silence, only the awakening day bringing in its own noises. He drank his coffee from a chipped mug. More people picked up their papers, their smokes, their forgotten birthday cards. People in work clothes, people who had quickly switched from bed clothes to work clothes, people still wearing their bed clothes, all perhaps buying some sort of present for some lover or someone who just happened to matter for today. Today was their day.

The shoppers often arrived by car, left the engine running, then ran out clutching their shopping. If they'd arrived on foot, they left on foot, tearing open a new packet of cigarettes for their first relief of the day as they went off. If driving, there were always additional motions to complete, and it took them longer, what with all the seat belts and the rear-view mirror and the clutch and the gear shift and the lights and the watching out for pedestrians.

Anderson stubbed out the latest smoke, drained his mug, and wondered about today.

He worried about Ellis and Mr Lister and his own pitiful attempts to obtain a passport. Turning from the window, Anderson was suddenly startled by the rough sound of the telephone shrilling, its volume competing unsuccessfully with a passing ambulance.

'Hi,' Anderson intoned without an apparent care in the world.

It was Ellis.

While Ellis spoke, Anderson explored the current state of his manicure, rubbing the inside of his thumb along each fingernail in turn. Then, swapping the telephone underside his chin, he examined the nails on the other hand. He grimaced at some of the message, nodding quietly. Strangely, he heard Ellis out without interruption.

'Yeh, I'm gettin' mahself fixed, quick as I can,' Anderson said impatiently, frustrated at his own delay in getting a passport and experiencing a large measure of jealousy that Ellis had for once done something quicker and better than he. 'So there ain't no point comin' the smart-ass, gottit?'

Ellis presumably said something, for Anderson lit up again and shouted, 'Listen, you shitface, I just about had it here with all ya snivellin' and croakin'. Just cuz ya got yaself a bloody passport don't give ya no bloody licence to put about ya bloody insults!'

Ellis smiled to himself as he hung up, smiled at the victory. Anderson was no longer his boss, and now he could tell the wretch, with impunity, that the man needed a new face.

And it had taken just one telephone call to Riyadh to get agreement from a Saudi colleague from the past to raise two visit visas, one each for the two men. The Saudi, who owned and ran a medical equipment distributorship called ECA, owed Ellis for his slick footwork in getting the expensive part of the scanners package approved by Choi and Mr Walid long before the problems set in. Unusually, the Saudi had paid nothing but promised that if ever in the future he Ellis needed any help …

Ellis had to prompt the man a few times as to who he was, how they had worked together for a short time on the project, and how he now came to be asking a favour. Just for the two of them, yes, that's right, we only need to be in for a couple of weeks. No, we won't have the same names. No, nobody should recognise us; it's been over ten years. No, I can't tell you why we need to be back in Riyadh. How are your sons? Good, good.

Fax number still the same? OK then, what is it now?

I'll send all the information on the fax. No, I've not been to the embassy here yet; we're waiting for one or two formalities to be cleared up.

OK, *salamu alaykum*, see you soon.

Ellis hung up cheerfully and not a little thankfully.

The process of procuring a visa to Saudi Arabia had not simplified.

With a depressing sense of déjà vu, Ellis walked from London Victoria Station, turning this way and that through the side streets, avoiding walking into passing traffic, then entering Belgrave Square. On one edge of the square lay the Saudi Embassy, flag draped proudly and furling in the breeze. The highly burnished gold plate, in which Ellis could see his reflection, announced the building to be the Embassy of the Kingdom of Saudi Arabia. To the left, at the top of the basement stairs, was a handwritten board indicating the consular section, and a roughly drawn arrow pointing downward.

The man known usually as Robert Bartholomew Ellis, but holding the new passport of Brian Lister and the birth certificate suitably endorsed by the British passport office, pushed open the wrought-iron gate and negotiated the steep staircase plunging downwards on the well-trodden, damp slabs that led the eye from the drab cream frontage towards the green door of the consular section. One push and the door with its highly polished gold fittings heaved open. Some other nationals were leaving, smiles abounding, mission successful. They squinted into the bright London sun as Ellis plunged himself into almost total darkness. The heavy door closed behind him.

He screwed up his face to see where he should walk. The place smelt – not of anything in particular, just stale air, perspiration, and the smell from the drains. He walked towards the sounds of voices, chatter, Saudi men in their *thobes* and *guttrahs* sitting imperiously behind a glass screen, processing men's passports. Women didn't come here. Their passports were examined more discreetly in some other place.

To one side of the room, a very large, white-complexioned man, dressed in a suit, manoeuvred himself slowly with hands clasped behind his back, bidding people good day but challenging them to start a fight or let off a bomb or pull out a pornographic magazine or even drink from a hip flask.

He didn't need to be there really. After all, nobody went to Saudi Arabia out of choice. They needed to have visas because they needed to be in Saudi Arabia either for financial or family reasons.

There were no other reasons. Who would willingly go to a world where there were no cinemas, theatres, libraries, parks, pubs, discos, clubs, or women?

But the money was good. So everyone sold their souls and got visas.

Ellis watched the smart man out of the corner of his eye as he filled out the complex form with questions asked once and then asked in a different way, just to make sure. He was aware the man was rocking gently on his heels and watching him making a mess of the first page at the first attempt.

And then the second attempt.

Your Friday, My Sunday

He'd forgotten what his real name was – first name, family name, any middle names – and in trying to avoid reading Brian Lister's passport, he relied on a faltering memory.

The smart man watched with some interest, the toecaps of his highly polished shoes seeming to gleam more emphatically today – the guardsman's shine perhaps? He watched Ellis tearing up the first form and reaching for another from the wall dispenser, clearly struggling with the layout of the document.

The man sauntered slowly to offer some help to a fellow countryman. Ellis watched him closing and felt a spasm, a tight knot in his stomach.

'Problems, have we?' the man asked, puzzled, from his full head of height advantage over Ellis.

'Nah,' Ellis observed nonchalantly, 'bloody pen keeps running out.'

'I see,' he observed coldly. He patted his hands together behind his back, looked into the bin with the discarded forms, watched other hopeful applicants, nodded, and returned to his position beside the door.

In what felt like an eternity, Ellis finally completed the form, collected together the false birth certificate and three passport photographs – suitably attested by a lawyer, an MP, a banker, but strangely not a minister of the church – and joined the queue leading to the murky, silver-framed counter behind which sat a bespectacled, overweight, and sweating Egyptian, who clearly struggled with the complexity of each application. An equally challenged Saudi sat behind him and to one side, on a settee close to a television tuned to a Turkish channel. He was doing no work, like most Saudis. They did no work even in London, except to twirl their beads in their indolence.

The Egyptian sat among a sea of papers, stacked high to the right, to the left, along the shelf above the television, now tuned to CNN. Only a small space immediately in front on the desk offered him the facility to examine all these new visa applications.

The next applicant, a thin man of fifty, had done everything right. Except for one thing. He'd expected to get the visa here and now. Even his cheque was written for fifty pounds and dated today. He had all his papers certified by many impressive-sounding organisations. The Egyptian was having fun reading and holding up the papers to show the Saudi, who was fiddling with the TV. He glanced and laughed, then carried on fiddling and shouted at an unseen servant to bring him chai.

The Egyptian turned back to the thin man of fifty, his laughter subsiding.

'Your chit.' The Egyptian held out a hand in impatient anticipation.

'Chit?' the man asked with a totally vacant sense of understanding.

'Yes,' the Egyptian agreed, 'the chit. Where is it?'

'What chit?' the man asked, his loudening impatience beginning to come to the attention of the smart man.

'You go Aitch. Ess. Bee. See,' the Egyptian said.

'HSBC?'

The Egyptian explained helpfully, leaning across to direct the visitor to the bank in Grosvenor Place, as if he'd told countless visitors the same thing. He told him where he should pay his four hundred riyals, and upon receipt the bank cashier would then issue a chit. 'Then bring the chit back here, and, *halas*, it is finished, you have a Saudi visa.' The Egyptian rubbed his hands together as if clearing his palms of dust, dismissed the man, then invited Ellis to step forward for the first phase of his visa application to be activated.

Ellis tried not to look nervous.

As the Egyptian shuffled through pieces of paper, rubber-stamping this one, pausing as he looked at the newly creased birth certificate. He looked up at Ellis's face, then turned the paper to examine the rear, swung round on his rotating chair, and engaged in animated conversation with the Saudi, who was now tuned to the children's channel. The Saudi was paying little attention to visa issues but waved a manicured hand in a gesture of disinterest.

The Egyptian agreed, nodded, and twisted himself back so quickly on his chair, he almost overshot the central position. He completed the manoeuvre clumsily and with a sweaty grimace turned to face Ellis. Ellis thought he may have felt a stomach spasm take hold. In that second, he wondered: if he were to be discovered at this early stage of the process of getting Clitty away from the executioner, what would happen?

The smart man would presumably pick up Ellis by the scruff of the neck and throw him up the stairs and out into the sunlight of Belgrave Square. Then back on the train with you, Mr Bloody Lister. And if he got ejected, what would happen if he got back early to Lincoln to find the real Mr Lister hard at it with some lady of easy desires?

'Please, sir?' the Egyptian called him gently, snapping Ellis's mind away from the thoughts of a liaison with a girl. Any girl.

The Egyptian handed Ellis a paper to carry to the Aitch Ess Bee See, as instructed, where he would pay his dues.

'What about the passport?' Ellis enquired anxiously, thinking that while he was at the bank, they would check with St Katherine's House, to discover that Mr Lister was actually an entirely different person, bearing no resemblance to the man whose concern was obvious to any who knew about impostors.

'We keep it.' The Egyptian smiled as he slipped all Lister's papers into a plastic sleeve to await his return from the bank, then waved at him to be gone. 'Next.'

Ellis's walk to the bank took the same amount of time as he remembered. Three minutes. Two in the queues, a rustle of money, one minute while the bank deposit slip was stamped, and three minutes back to the embassy, complete with his chit.

The Egyptian was ready.

Ellis, smiling wanly, handed the paper to the Egyptian. In a bewildering display of hand movements, the Egyptian sorted all the papers, took a second look at them, frowned, and checked them again as if the action of stamping the visa into this brand-new passport was tantamount to jumping from a cliff. He glanced at Ellis. He glanced at the strip of booth photographs. Then, when he seemed satisfied, he did the deed. With hand held high, the Egyptian plunged the official stamp of the Kingdom of Saudi Arabia onto page twenty seven of Lister's passport. It was a new passport, Ellis mused. Why not page one?

Ellis grasped the document, nodded to the smart man who looked down on him, and then was gone.

That act triggered his thoughts about working with people who were essentially still bedu. Would they ask at Riyadh passport control why his visa was on page eighty-four and not page one?

That's because the bloody man at your London embassy put it there.

We'd prefer page one because it's at the beginning. But then you'd prefer it to be at the back, because you start all your books at the end, or the beginning, depending on your culture, practice, and language.

It would always be thus, Ellis thought as he walked along Wilton Street in the general direction of Victoria Tube, thinking about getting a few beers before beginning the return journey to Lincoln, taking a bit of time to think about what they were to do.

Good old Mohammed at ECA. Ellis toasted his old Saudi friend, raised a beer in fond memory, lit a cigarette, the first for about two hours, then thought he had to use this visa within three months. He hoped Anderson would be ready by then. He also hoped Clitty would still be alive in three months' time.

The flat was unused. No sign of Lister.

Ellis pushed open the door, displacing the freepost and free papers in his push to get in. It was dark, it was late, it had been raining, and the phone was ringing.

Anderson. It had to be.

Only Anderson knew Ellis had been away for the week and would come back tonight, with or without a visitor's visa in his passport.

'Shithead,' Anderson crowed as Ellis picked up the phone, 'what keptya?'

'Nothing did, you lazy bollocks. Anyway, you got your new passport yet?'

Anderson could be heard lighting up and talking to a person who was both female and nearby.

'Get me a fuckin' drink, goddammit,' he shouted at one of his mindless girls. Then, 'No, I ain't got my fuckin' passport; no, I bloody well ain't.'

'So. Do I go on my own?' Ellis enquired sarcastically.

'No. Ya hold on, just ya hold on there,' Anderson spluttered angrily. 'Ya ain't goin' no place alone.'

'Why not?' Ellis asked. 'I got a passport and I got a visa. I never did need you.'

'Ya need me now, shithead!' Anderson pleaded emptily.

'I only need you to change my colostomy bag, you sack of shit.'

Ellis felt bullish and said so. He didn't need this pseudo-Yank. He didn't need all the posturing and piles and problems with the contact lenses, or the squash wrist or the tennis elbow, or the man's bad breath and pointless utterances.

Yet.

He might still need him.

Ellis might just need Anderson. Unlikely as that might seem. Though the two men shared little, both knew the way of life in Riyadh. They knew what happened when – the prayer times, the shops' opening and closing times – the locations of the limousine stops, where the Marriott was, where their site was, where they both used to work. And where the bank was. For one more go between them, this seemed worthwhile. There was plenty of money in it if the scam went right, very little if it went wrong. Life was like that.

'You ain't gotta bag, do you?' Anderson enquired with what sounded like some heartfelt concern.

'Yup.'

'Oh shit.' Anderson exhaled noisily.

'Quite.'

Anderson slurped something noisily, belched, and challenged Ellis. 'Listen, shithead, or may that should be shitbags, I gotta see old matey boy Mr Theophilus in a few days.'

'Oh?' Ellis could easily contain his interest.

'Yeh, an' I gotta offer about three months' salary, use of the flat, the addresses of all my ol' girlies, *and* their bloody phone numbers, plus I gotta leave him enough booze for the time we're away …' Anderson's voice tailed off in frustration.

'Negotiate. Dammit, Anderson, you bloody ratbag, negotiate!'

'Don't ya tell me ta negotiate. There ain't a negotiator better'n me.' Anderson belched in his excitement.

'If that's the case,' said Ellis, 'how come you've not told Theophilus that you'll tell the dole people about his window-cleaning business? And the office-cleaning business, and the home repairs business? Of course we could, I suppose, Mr Theophilus, keep all this quiet, but something could slip out. Unintended of course.'

For once Anderson was silent.

'What's the matter, Anderson? You want me to come down to Chis-Wick to sort out your little short-term deception?'

Anderson drew a deeper than usual breath. Perhaps he's on something, Ellis thought as he watched the reflections of cars' lights travel across the hall ceiling.

Anderson told him to call him in three days. He'd have an answer by then.

It was shit or bust.

Whatever or whoever he ended up being called, Anderson would be in a position, he assured Ellis, to book tickets to Riyadh within ten days. This allowed for actually getting the passport from Theophilus – assuming that piece of deception went according to his plan – getting all the documents attested by somebody except a minister of the church, then taking it all to London, to Belgrave Square, to the bank, and then back to Belgrave Square for the official addition to his new passport. Yes, it should take only ten days.

Which was just as well as, unusually, the Ministry of Interior of Saudi Arabia had announced that following the reconstruction of the holy mosque in the colloquially known Friday Square, the site for public executions was to be specially reactivated with a display of Qur'anic solidarity on the first Friday of Shaban, the eighth month of the Islamic calendar, the month before Ramadan, the month when the savagery of public executions peaked and when the removal of the head of a murdering infidel became particularly attractive to the faithful. That meant Clitty could be coming up for despatch in four weeks. And there were reports of civil disturbances, mostly in Riyadh, some in Dammam, and many in smaller communities throughout the Kingdom. The place could be in turmoil.

Ah well, both men reflected at separate times, book the tickets, get on the plane, and see what happens.

Your Friday, My Sunday

Chapter 10

'We got seen, goddammit,' Anderson muttered as he sidled up to Ellis, now sitting quiet and relaxed, beer in one hand, cigarette in the other, at the airside bar of terminal three.

'Oh?' Ellis queried emptily, enjoying one of his last proper beers for a while and looking up at the newly bearded face of the man Anderson – or Theophilus.

Ellis felt a very small tinge of gladness to see him again.

Funny that.

Nobody ever wanted to see Anderson. If the occasion could be avoided, it nearly always was.

Yet here were the two men, united by mutual loathing and a sense of purpose in getting Clitty out of Saudi Arabia before the whole place collapsed. Perhaps it was the common purpose that allowed a thaw to grace the two men's paths.

''Nother beer?' Anderson asked quietly, mounting the bar stool next to Ellis and calling for the barman's attention.

'Cheers,' Anderson thanked the barman as he placed two perspiring glasses of lager onto two place mats, each equidistant from the tray of salted peanuts. 'Like I said, bumhead,' Anderson sipped and lit up, 'I got spotted.'

'By whom?'

Anderson shrugged his shoulders. 'Dunno. But there was, when ya came through to airside, a guy in a uniform close to the passport bloke, watching anyone with tickets for Riyadh, an' watchin' 'em real good.'

Ellis laughed and drank some beer. 'Probably suspicious that a pair of scumbags like us are up to no good. Perhaps he didn't like your perfume.' He scooped some peanuts into his hand. 'No, I didn't see anyone, other than the usual spooks you find hanging around airport terminal buildings. Nothing particular. 'Cept maybe they need to keep an eye out for trouble, the sort of trouble that tends to upset the equilibrium and the tranquillity of the Kingdom.' Ellis talked into a vacuum as nobody listened nor cared about the destination. All eyes, though, watched an attractive girl saunter past the bar area: long legs, dark stockings, elegant ankles, short skirt, long, flowing auburn hair, dark glasses nested on the top of her head. She held a magazine folded under one arm, a leather bag slung from the other shoulder, a gentle smile.

A permanently lovely face.

The girl looked around, seemingly looking for somewhere to sit, slowed, then perched on the edge of a chair by the edge of the cafeteria area. She pulled her handbag onto her lap and extracted a pack of something, pulled out cigarette, lit up, glanced quickly at Ellis, smiled, looked around as if looking for someone, realised she was in a non-smoking area, and pressed on smoking nevertheless.

God, she was lovely.

And a bit of a rebel.

Ellis remembered the Gambia and decided he was now in love with this girl, and the girl he'd seen on the ill-fated river voyage and had fallen in love with was not much cop after all.

Then Ellis remembered, even as he stared at his new love, that the reason anybody would stare at Anderson at an airport, a Chinese takeaway, or anywhere else for that matter, was that he was an extraordinarily ugly creature, with irritating habits and wonky eyes.

It was probably the eyes that did it.

Or perhaps it was due to the fact that the uniform next to the passport officer had wished Mr Anderson a pleasant flight.

'Oh shit.' Anderson now realised the magnitude of his blunder. 'An' I went an'' said thank you, oh God, shit, and bollocks.'

Mr Theophilus or whoever, Anderson put his head on the edge of the bar and rubbed his hair, much to the anxiety of the bar man, who fussed and polished as closely as protocol would allow.

The girl crossed, then uncrossed her legs, became tired of waiting for an ashtray to materialise, so crushed out her cigarette beneath an elegant foot, looked round one more time, then walked out of Ellis's life forever.

God, thought Ellis, wonder if she's going to Riyadh? No chance.

Nobody that lovely ever went to Riyadh.

Not ever.

Ellis sighed and wished, then came back to the present and to the prospect of filling the next few hours – days, weeks maybe – with Anderson. Anderson no doubt thought the same and offered to buy emergency beers.

This, at eight forty in the morning.

The bar was open; that was their only criterion.

The decision was made.

Beer and more beer.

Last call to gate 15 came at about ten thirty, close to two hours into the drink session, the two men having outdone each other with tales of their derring-do while back in Blighty.

Anderson was regaling Ellis with a suitably embossed story of an event with Mr Choi, a story often told when alcohol outweighed any sense of reality or truth. Exaggeration becoming de rigueur. It sounded to Ellis on this occasion like Anderson had shot the Korean with a bacon slicer.

What had happened was that Choi had had a fire in his flat. Anderson had suggested turning off the pilot light on the cooker before changing the propane gas bottle.

Easy enough. Except Choi thought he was back in Korea, where it was common practice to change gas bottles while burning cigarette in mouth, with little attention to safety.

Choi had arrived a little hairless around the eyebrows, nothing else.

Except now Anderson wanted to retell it in all its extended glory and at greater volume just to impress those other travellers who were taking quiet drinks before periods of separation – thoughts of home, thoughts of those unmeant, angry words, words to regret, kids calling 'goodbye, Daddy' and hugging tight – all of them sitting around the bar area, drinking and smoking in equal measure, reading copies of this paper or that magazine; anything to stop the thinking.

Those not normally acquainted with departure lounges spent most of their waiting time in the airside book shops and the duty-free jewellers and the duty-free spirits and cigarettes shops.

The next type of traveller was the one who wanted to appear nonchalant but who nevertheless sat within close view of the arrivals and departures screens to see what was boarding at what gate and when, and which flights from where were now disembarking wherever. He also sat on the edge of the leather-effect, relaxing terminal benches, clutching his hand baggage on his lap, seeing if he could work out some sort of flight itinerary for all those flights now showing: Johannesburg, Basle, Frankfurt, Moscow, Paris, Berlin, Riyadh, and Kinshasa.

Kinshasa.

That's a new one, thinks the man as he plugs into his pocket travel atlas. Oh look, now we have the arrivals screen: Washington, Toulouse, Ontario, Brussels, Glasgow. Blimey, he thinks, that's only up the M6. Vladivostok, Peking, Dublin.

The man is satisfied he cannot work out any reason why so much variety is displayed on the arrivals screen, so he marvels at the whole thought and waits for the departures screen to show somewhere different in the bottom of the picture. He waits for that curious line to witter its way down the screen from top to bottom. Then there it is, the new entry at the bottom.

Still it's Dublin.

Too bad.

The man decides to pull out a crumpled magazine and read something, just to avoid having to appear nonchalant.

Then he engages Anderson's eyes and wonders if he's seeing things quite right. He looks at the screen, at the bottom of the screen: lo, he sees that Rejkyavik is now there. Then he looks back at the man with the odd eyes. He seems to be drinking beer with someone; bet they don't know what time they're supposed to be going.

For some fifteen minutes the tannoy had been desperately appealing for Mr Lister and Mr Theophilus to go to gate 15 as this was the last, the final, the most final, the absolutely last call for flight SV634 to Riyadh.

Suddenly the penny dropped.

With Ellis anyway.

'Jesus, mate!' Ellis shouted, throwing the remainder of his beer into his mouth. 'Just remembered, this Lister and Theophilus nonsense, that's us, for Christ's sake.'

Your Friday, My Sunday

Anderson did likewise, fell off the stool and somehow landed upright, then followed Ellis at half a canter, the other half a type of drunken limp, laden as he was with hand baggage slung over his shoulder, full of booze for use on the dry six and a half hour flight to the centre of the Islamic world.

Those six hours were long and lonely, particularly as the flight left familiar airways and went down Yugoslavia, then Greece, then swung miles east to avoid Israel, across Syria, then down to Jordan, entering Saudi airspace some fifty miles north of Tabuk, then southeast for two more hours, then …

And while all this navigating was taking place, there were people in the economy section of the plane, all of them with conflicting emotions. Many were just sitting there thinking, staring at the ground some five miles below; others were staring vacantly along the lines of the wings; others were looking, just looking, at the air intakes. Air intakes were not usually interesting. Anything to dilute the wondering about what was to happen. They'd said goodbye to their loved ones; they were even wearing the same clothes. The menfolk, particularly the menfolk, held up an arm to search for the last flickering remains of her perfume among the cabin smells. This shirt had held her, these arms had loved her. Then the tears came. They poured some more drink and probably smoked and cried in equal measure.

Unless they called for the hostess or the steward, nobody came. They were all alone. Most of them preferred it thus: to drink and to reflect; to put on the Walkman, searching out their tracks, the records they'd both once loved and laughed to; just to remember. But now there was only the roar of the engines drowning out the memory of all that love, laughter, and betrayal.

The music stayed to haunt the thoughts, the drink would skew the memories, but those smells, those sounds, those hopes, those broken dreams, those cries, the children's cries to Daddy.

For the first time in years, Ellis realised he was crying proper tears, tears like he really felt he'd screwed everything up.

The trouble was, with the amount he'd drunk, he could only roll all his memories into one soufflé of melancholia and cry at the fact that he was a total failure.

Then, in his thoughts, there she was: Cheryl, holding him, protecting him against his self-doubt, soothing his furrowed brow, reassuring him, cuddling, loving. The engine changed its pitch as Ellis thought he wanted to be sick. He'd drunk enough; he'd heard enough music. The aircraft swayed a little. The setting sun threw longer shadows onto the seat backs as the aircraft meandered and manoeuvred back north-east for the final approach to Riyadh.

Ellis struggled to his feet. Pulling at the headrest of the seat ahead, he raised himself high enough to look along the cavernous interior of the aircraft. He stood, picked his feet across his hand baggage that lay abandoned on the floor where his feet had been, and half fell, half stumbled into the gangway.

Suddenly he caught a waft of air that may have been from his mouth or from his armpits. Either way, it resembled the drains, so he made for the toilet to freshen up. Being at the rear of the economy section, the nearest toilets were only a few feet from where Ellis had spent the journey.

The problem was they were out of action. Overuse, the cabin steward had smiled, agreeing that even though the Arabs may have money enough to fly, they were still bedu and had no idea of what to do in a toilet, aircraft or otherwise.

So sir may wish to use the bathroom just to the rear of the first class. Ellis bade the steward thanks and slowly twisted his way towards the front of the plane, avoiding a foot here, an elbow there, small children dancing on snoozing parents, a piece of luggage falling from a seat. Ellis picked it up and passed it to a dark hand that muttered thanks.

Ellis reached the first-class bathroom, designated for the use of all passengers as the Arabs had sequestered and destroyed all other lavatories throughout this large aircraft, then slammed the door behind him. The noise, the artificial light, that mirror showing all the blemishes and spots and dirty teeth, all conspired to make Ellis want to be sick. Running some hot water, he made the best of a splash wash, emptied the remains of the cologne over his head, face, and underarms. At that point he began to feel humanity reappear.

On the return journey to his seat, Ellis was jolted by the realisation that there were far more Saudis on the plane now than had been at Heathrow.

Lots more veiled ladies too.

Must be some sort of cultural event that only flying on a Saudia journey can accomplish, Ellis concluded as he got back to his seat and poured the last measure of decent Scotch for a while. Anderson, slumped in the seat behind, had woken up and was in the middle of an explanation to a similarly confused fellow traveller for this metamorphosis.

'See,' he said to a young man who anxiously clutched a Biarritz guide to Tunisia, 'when these folks wanna go ta London, they arrive at the King Khaled Airport in a limo, all togged up in *guttrah* and *thobe*, the girlies all wearing veils, being good girls for the *muttawas*. Then they get on the airplane,' the young man leaned forward anxiously to catch the end point of this story, 'an' you know what?'

The man didn't know what, so Anderson pressed on. 'They got hand baggage full of jeans and bras and pants, an' no sooner than the wheels get off the ground outta Riyadh an' up inta the wings, the lot of them, up they get and waddle to the john. Then Jeeeeesus, out they come, and ain't they just the prettiest things you ever did see? An' they sway themselves this way and that, smelling cute. The cut of their tops, the shapes o' their asses, jeez, makes a man wanna jerk off. An' she gets back to the seat where old matey boy, Mister Linchpin of the entire world, he's bin and pulled all the stuff off – all the headgear, all the sheep-shaggin' riggin', oh yes, all of it stuffed into the hand baggage along with those items of Madame's that need to be removed from her body to enter the mores of the West. Then he's looking like a secondhand car dealer with his moustache and his wristwatch and his pair of jeans an' some poncey shirt that makes him look like some fairy. Jeesus …' Anderson's voice trailed off as he shook his head, wondering how he could date one of 'em as she sat veiled, calm. Her husband, with *guttrah*, gently fingering the beads, sat alongside, chattering to another in the same uniform but two rows in front.

That's it, Ellis concluded. They are coming home. Could they really be content to be going home?

The dressing up to look like Westerners was their way of immersing themselves in their target country.

Generally, no Saudi could or would volunteer the truth about his or her metamorphosis.

It happened. Was that not good enough for the infidel?

Anderson poured the remaining drops of Scotch, held the bottle up to the light to check it really was empty, belched in derision, and stashed the bottle between the in-flight Saudia magazine and the vomit bag folded into the rear pocket of the seat ahead.

Ellis found himself doing the same, lighting up once or twice more before the wheels of the plane skimmed the perimeter lines of the grand King Khaled International Airport before gliding across the desert, lower and lower. Then, with a final turn-down of the engine, the entire machine flew, wondered whether to fly some more, and put down with a screech to the tarmac, the engine reverse thrust throwing dust and vibration across the senses.

'Jesus, man!' Anderson shouted to Ellis in the row ahead. 'That you smelling like a dog?'

Ellis caught the drift if not the text of the words shouted over the welcome to the airport and what passengers with onward tickets should do and which terminal they should report to.

Ellis looked from his window to see, in the developing gloom, an Air India 747 just arriving at terminal two, the giant wheels slowly rotating as the aircraft drew to a halt at the flexible gangway held out in a menacing sense of welcome.

To follow an Air India 747 into immigration and the customs hall was never good news, not to bona fide travellers anyway.

A 747 could carry around three hundred and fifty passengers. If its point of origin had been Mumbai or New Delhi, there were, according to Saudi immigration protocols, three hundred and fifty drug smugglers aboard, all of them on false passports, requiring the greatest of attention when presenting themselves for the immigration procedures.

It took ages.

For European travellers like Ellis and Anderson, who were generally bona fide, this would normally be a real nuisance, an obvious delay to getting to a decent bed for a decent sleep. How could three hundred and fifty Indians be more important than that?

But for Mr Lister and Mr Theophilus, the delays could be used to their advantage. After the best part of three hours of interrogating Indians who were all suspected of being liars and smugglers, the sight of Western faces with British passports would prove to be a tonic for hassled passport officers.

True to form, they got stamped in without question.

Same with customs.

A cursory glimpse through their baggage, only a slightly raised eyebrows at the smell of both men's breaths and the incongruity of Ellis's overdose of cologne down the front of his shirt.

Halas.

All done.

Ellis and Anderson, Lister and Theophilus were back.

Picking up their luggage and mounting their bags and effects onto an airport trolley, Ellis led Anderson to the smoked doors through which all travellers passed, to be met by a sea of faces – faces holding signs and placards, and smiles and waves, but nothing for these two.

Somebody in a suit fell in line behind Anderson's shoulder as he stopped to light up.

Anderson had a lighter problem.

The suit offered a light. Anderson grunted thanks, nodded his head, handed back the lighter, then gazed into a familiar face.

'Welcome back, Mr Anderson.'

Anderson felt his bowels tighten.

How could this embassy nerd know anything? For it had to be embassy. He couldn't remember if he knew this face, but the embassy man certainly knew Anderson.

He paid scant attention to Ellis.

But then Ellis had straight eyes that looked straight ahead.

Anybody seeing Anderson's eyes pointing this way and that would remember Anderson.

They would remember his eyes first and his name second. Either way, both made an impression.

The embassy man walked a little behind Anderson as he smoked and tried to keep his temper at being recognised. The trio walked the wide, tiled concourse on their approach to the taxi waiting area, past the kiosks selling drinks and dried sandwiches to travellers too tired to care about eating, or too anxious about the immediate prospect of being here to be the slightest bit interested in anything other than getting the worst bit over – the getting into Riyadh and the unpacking.

Yet the suit was still there, warning against any misdemeanours, warning that things were different. Things had changed. The West and

Western culture had fallen out of favour. Because the royal family was still more keen on the western than the eastern gulf, that made the situation here unstable: first, because few now expected the House of Fahd to stand for much longer; second, they may go for people from the West.

'And I know why you have returned, gentlemen.' The suit smiled superciliously, pulling a cigarette from an ornate case and lighting up.

'Mr Klitowski. The man you know as Mr Clitty.'

The tannoy announced a flight out to Mecca and Medinah.

Otherwise all was silence.

Anderson went for broke.

'OK, shitbag.' Anderson stopped dead in his tracks. The suit nearly bumped into the trolley wheels. 'Clitty, has he been done?'

'Good lord, no,' said the suit happily. 'Not for another two weeks, apparently. Seems like he should have been chopped about five years ago, but the son who was due to give the necessary approval to the execution on attaining age 16, the little sod got leukaemia sometime soon after his fifteenth birthday. Then he went and died. Seems as if the next son gets to be 16 in a little while. At which time, of course, he may wish to dispense family justice. *Inshallah*.'

'Or he may not,' Ellis added.

'Or he may not. But would you be prepared to take that risk?' enquired the suit menacingly.

'As a matter of fact, that's why we're here,' Anderson explained.

'Why the change of name then?'

Obviously the bloody man knew little of the Saudi way: the way you got deported and forever banished from returning under the same name.

The trio had reached the main terminal door. Pushing the doors open, they were struck by the warm evening air, a gentle breeze, the dark night sky now closed in.

A ministry car beeped and flashed, a brief welcome-back speech and a warning. Then the suit was gone. With no more ado, the two men waved at a limo that drew up obediently. The driver jumped out, negotiated swiftly for a rate to the Marriott Hotel, loaded the luggage in the boot, wondered what toothpaste these men used or didn't use, told them to get in, and drove vigorously along the magnificent dual carriageway from the airport to the city.

Your Friday, My Sunday

It was difficult to work out in the long shadows of the last of the twilight whether the bougainvillea and all the flowering shrubs laid on the banks and the escarpments were there to offer the visitor a floral goodbye or a flourish of welcome.

Either way, it was a testament to the power of watering an arid tract of land. Things did grow and they did flower, and if you had water and didn't put it everywhere, all this ostentation would count for nothing. Those who passed by on the outward journey cared not for flowers, just for an accurate exit visa, and for those on the way in, there was just the expectation of seeing the flowers one last time on the way out.

The flowers seemed to serve no more useful purpose than to remind one of the futility of being here.

Few argued with that.

The Marriott Hotel had changed not one jot.

The car park, the chained-off areas for VIP guests, they were still there. The place was still painted the insipid cream of all modern Arabian buildings; still the tiled foyer remained tiled with the same tiles, the same eight-sided star sculptures on the ceiling that confused the *muttawa*, believing them to be the sign of Zion. Even the same polish they used to keep the place clean suggested no change. The lifts in the open atrium still whirred silently upwards and downward, much to the amusement of some Arabic children who played while Father dallied below, and later some European children who chattered and laughed at the enjoyment of a lift that had glass sides and from which the entire place could be viewed.

The men ignored all of it, checked in, realised it was late, cursed the kids at the lift, bid themselves a welcome back, then slept a long and agitated sleep.

Ellis went out for an early morning smoke around seven o'clock, about the same time as he would have been clocking in for work with Mr Choi at the site that had been seven hundred yards from where he stood, but where now the proud King Fahd Hospital graced the skyline. The site had been cleared of the progenitors of the whole project. Now there were car parks and operating theatres, palm trees and red lines painted on the floor from outpatients to X-ray. No signs of any cabins or huts or spots where people drove diggers through service mains, just tarmac areas and white lines and sterility, in both biological and spiritual senses.

Ellis walked along the white lines of the Marriott parking lot to his left and walked up a slope that created the roof of the underground car park. Only the brave parked on the roof in high summer, but at this time of year anyone parked anywhere; the heat was not too oppressive to mention.

Ellis walked up the slope, avoided a departing Lexus driven in haste by somebody Saudi, leaned on the castellations atop the car park wall, and watched the remains of the site as he had known it.

There was nothing to see. Nothing: no objects, no lumps or bumps or anything to remind him of where the site office may once have stood.

Nothing left.

All he had was a civilised-looking hospital, the grey cement walls now bleached by the harsh sunshine. Signboards told people to go this way and that, an entry arm swinging upwards and downwards as patients and relatives came to enjoy the provisions of this free health service and its staff.

It had a car park and anything one would expect to see in a civilised hospital.

Ellis felt the need for a smoke as he was joined by Anderson, who also needed a smoke.

The pair of them looked at what they had helped to build and wished for better. Then they smoked and felt a kindred spirit, for it was not as they had expected.

There was no sign of Choi.

That was a relief. Somehow they had thought there would be something, somewhere to remind them of their time there, but time had moved on.

The hospital was now complete. Why should there be any sign of the contractors? No sign of that hut; no sign of that parking area; no sign of that Saudi's office – what was his name? No sign of anything to suggest that the place had done more than merely arise from the dust.

Wonder what happened to Choi and his fish tank?

To Mr Huh, old Choi's boss, the Korean whose only contribution to humour was a thin, dry smile of goodbye to a guest when once a trade concession had been extracted.

Ellis lit another one, a small bead of sweat tracking down the back of his neck into his shirt, raising the slightest shiver.

The Buicks, the Lexuses, the Cadillacs, the Toyota pickups swished this way and that along the carriageways between the hotel and the hospital, some of them turning late into the entrance, without indication, into the security lane manned by indifferent security guards who waved them through. They put the barrier up or they put it down; whatever, it made them feel important, and they did a job.

Ellis watched a small bump in the tarmac. It became more pronounced in the enveloping sunshine. Was it there they last had their office?

Jesus H. Christ.

'Does it matter where the goddamn office was, for Christ's sake?' Anderson appeared at full bore with voice to match. He must have been asking himself the same question, for his eyes fell beyond the far entrance. As far as memory could tell, that was the last place they had both sat in execution on this exotic project.

Ellis grimaced as Anderson pulled up alongside, smelling of smoke and cheap aftershave, though by his appearance no hairs had been cut from his chin or his nostrils.

Still a grey face, grey misaligned eyes, and a stubbly chin.

'What d'yer say, chief?' Ellis asked deferentially, aching to be able to get on with this man. 'Good to be back or what?'

Anderson was silent for a while.

He put out one smoke and started another.

Then he shook his head.

'I really don't know where I'd rather be. Here's as good as anywhere s'pose …' Anderson's voice trailed off as an ambulance roared past with sirens blaring upwards and downward, the tenor being modulated by the increasing distance as it sped off toward, then past the Minhal roundabout.

'Goin' ta rescue some fuckin' bloody Saudi from having his hands stuck up his ass.' Anderson lounged against the car park wall, smoked, and summarised.

Cigarette smoke drifted as the two men waited and wished they need not go to carry out their mission.

Why didn't somebody from the Malaz Jail come and say, 'Sorry, gents, but Mr Bloody Klitowski has just died of something and he won't be going for the chop. And in any case there is no money in his bank, so you might as well use the return portion of your tickets without delay.' And no more would be said.

Anderson turned and tossed another butt into an enlarging pile of smouldering ruins, some from the previous smoke, some from the one before that. Smoking was still Anderson's thing.

Both Ellis and Anderson had their arms folded as they leaned on the edge of the car park wall, looking towards the pile – perhaps in the hope of some inspiration, perhaps because there was little more interesting to see thereabouts.

'How much did we reckon?' Anderson broke the sound of the cars and the squeals of brakes, the kaleidoscopic sound of Riyadh traffic, the sound of the motorised camel at work, the driver at the helm steering as precisely as his genes would allow.

'Reckon? What do you mean?'

'The loot. How much did we reckon that old Clitoris got stashed away? Did we ever do a calculation?'

Ellis smiled at the irony of the question. Here they were on the parapet of the elevated car park at the Marriott Hotel in Riyadh, a place they felt they had excised from their lives. All those meetings with all sorts of loathsome suppliers representatives. Trouble was you had to see them all just in case you missed the boy with the baloobas. He was often difficult to spot, so you had the initial meeting at the Marriott or the Al Khozamar in Olaya or the Hyatt Regency. But if he invited you to the Intercon, then you may assume he had a sack of dosh.

But the initial meetings were invariably identical.

First name terms were mandatory.

Lots of smoking took place, except in one project, where the two consultants treated smoking as a disease to be avoided. And as a power thing they decided when first-name terms could be used.

On the Britishmen's project, lots of smoking took place.

Then the consultant was praised to the hills, lots of obsequious laughter, gosh did you *really* study there, do have a smoke, may I order more coffee, gosh, how interesting, and no, I studied biochemistry at Chelmsford Poly.

Then the consultant made the odd glance into the rep's briefcase as he struggled to retrieve some interesting product information for use in this, the most exotic health-care project on the face of the planet since the discovery of mitosis. Then, when no brown envelope became apparent, or a banker's draft or some verbal discussion indicating what level of remuneration may be applied for inclusion of that equipment, at that point the consultant got bored and cut the meeting short.

Unless he thought the money might appear at the second meeting.

So he cheerfully stood up and said, 'See you next time you're in town. Oh, you live here? Well, give us a shout when you've run through the specifications with head office. Bye.'

'I think we assumed he must have had about sixty-five thousand. God knows why we reckoned that,' Ellis replied easily. 'But we did some calculations based on Clitty having already sent home all the money from his Jeddah scam, and probably the Dammam G500 before that.'

'Dammit. Thought as much.' Anderson swore, regretting his loss of memory, memory of lots of figures he and Ellis had thrashed out during that meeting in Banjul.

Must be the drink.

'But till we get a bank statement, we won't know,' Ellis said as if he had lived his entire existence in Batley.

'Know what, Ellis?'

'What?'

Anderson lit another. 'Just before we got out here, I did a calculation on how many calories I needed to get through in a day and what I needed to get through to lose all my weight.' Anderson fondly patted a swollen girth. 'And in one of my busiest days, I use two thousand and eight hundred calories in twenty-one hours and twenty minutes.'

'What do you do in the other two hours and a bit?'

'Wank.'

'How many calories does that take?'

'Depends on the level of turn-on.'

'OK. A typical wank. How many?'

'Eleven.'

Ellis pushed himself upright and laughed. 'Ha ha. A premature ejaculator!'

Anderson sniggered, smoothed himself on the car park wall, and was not to be drawn.

'OK then. To have a good wank, you need at least …' Ellis looked at the sky and, remembering some of his best ones, reflected, 'I'd say about three hundred calories.'

Anderson seemed worried.

'Ya say a wank could actually last around two hours and forty minutes?'

'Yup.'

'And that would take around three hundred calories?'

'Yup.'

'Goddamn.' Anderson drew a sharp breath and wondered whether to smoke or pick his nose. He picked the former. 'Howsat then?'

'Depends,' Ellis replied helpfully.

'What on, for fuck's sake?' Anderson asked impatiently.

'Depends on whether you're going to put on ladies' gear and strut round in front of the mirror, stockings on, suspenders done up tight, and the old pulse going at the same rate as a fast rate cycle ride, which is about one hundred and ten calories in an hour. Then you start rubbing your old chap and splashing on some aftershave in the hope of something better. Not a lot more happens.'

Anderson seemed interested. 'So what does happen?'

'As I said, not a lot more happens, so you end up burning up all those calories on a load of burned-out old memories of girls whose tits you've rubbed, girls you've smelled, girls you've touched, and you remember the way they touched you, the things they said, the undying love, and all those who farted or faked orgasms. And the real ones. Then, in a tableau of accumulated memory, you get on the vinegar strokes and bingo!'

'Bingo? What dat?'

'Yup, you've come in your hand, and you've lost two hundred and sixty-four calories.'

'Disgusting.' Anderson shook his head slowly, lit two cigarettes, and ignoring the fact that Ellis was already smoking, handed him one.

Ellis picked up the smoke and threw it at a bougainvillea. 'I reckon we should be in for around sixty.'

'Riyals?'

'Course not, you silly bugger. Pounds sterling, OK?'

'Worth staying for then,' Anderson concluded slowly.

Ellis turned a little to mimic a doctor's examination. 'Do you really remember why we are here? We came back for the dosh and for Mr Clitoris. In that order.' Ellis waved his hands in front of Anderson, who seemed engaged by the flower bed. 'And if you can't remember that, you need a kick in the arse.'

'I need a wank.'

'You haven't eaten breakfast yet. Get a balanced diet, then lose those two hundred and sixty-four. First …'

'First what?' Anderson did seem confused.

Ellis put an arm round the slumped would-be American. 'First, we contact Mr Bloody Mohammed at ECA to pay him a courtesy visit in order that we pay homage to him for giving us the bloody visa in the first place. Then, having done the needful with him, we see what we can do about old Clitty.'

'Oh shit, it sounds like business,' Anderson realised emptily.

'Sure is,' Ellis announced with a finality that Anderson envied and against which there was no argument. 'Let's go.'

'Gentlemen!' the huge Saudi bellowed happily, negotiating the contours of the massive office table and running towards his two visitors as they were ushered into the room. '*Marhaba*, gentlemen, hello.' His white teeth shone and he lost count of how many times he had kissed each of them on the cheek and gripped their hands. 'How was your flight?'

Anxious to make them at home, he pointed at the two leather-bound armchairs with capacity for a few people each. 'Please be seated.' The man sat himself back in his chair and folded his huge hands on the tabletop behind the desktop carving identifying him as Abdullah Kassim Al Jumail. He smiled once more at his visitors, who were puzzled to see no sign of an ashtray. Abdullah followed their eyes across the flawless, polished surface. Even the trembling leaves on the palm trees in the street outside were accurately portrayed on it.

He pushed a crude white-topped button switch, the twin core cable taking the shortest route from the hand of the man out of sight to some unseen room. It had to have been the tea room, for no more than a second later the door swept open.

'Yessir?' enquired an Indian or perhaps Pakistani face, his face contorted a little by concern.

'Iqbal,' Abdullah opened his hands in invitation to his visitors to take some refreshment, 'tea or coffee for my old friends?'

'Yessir.' Looking first at Ellis, then at Anderson, then at Abdullah, Iqbal checked he'd got it just about right, ignored Anderson's request for whisky and soda, and glided quietly from the room. All three settled back in their seats.

'So,' Abdullah said again, folding his hands as before, 'how was your flight?'

The two visitors had no complaints about the flight; at least they could smoke.

Abdullah's smile was now less warm than on their arrival. 'Your flight was OK? Good.' He didn't wait for a reply. 'You mentioned on the telephone from London that you have some business in Riyadh.'

'Sure do,' Anderson replied because Abdullah just happened to be looking him in an eye as the question fell.

'May I ask what sort of business?'

Both visitors thought, oh shit, does he know, how can he know?

Neither answered, the silence only being broken by Iqbal delivering two teas and one Turkish coffee for Abdullah.

'You must be tired from your flight.' Abdullah decided another way to find out.

Say that again, matey boy, thought Ellis.

'But let me tell you about the project after you went and what is going on now, and then you may want to tell me if there is any business we may be able to do for one more time.'

Abdullah sipped a little Turkish coffee, catching a small ground on his upper lip, a ground that was to remain in place for the remainder of the conversation.

'So after your departure, the X-ray was adopted, and your work here, Mr Anderson, was well appreciated by the Ministry of Health.'

Some mistake that, Anderson thought, because to have been in the good books of the Ministry of Health was a rare occurrence. Any such favourable status was usually triggered through some trickery against the local distributor, in this case Al Jumail Trading Company. This had obviously not happened in the case of the X-ray package; otherwise Abdullah would not have wanted them within a million miles of the place.

The two men discussed how the package had been finally approved to the satisfaction of all parties, while Ellis looked out of the window and wondered about Clitty.

The scam of the package that pleased Abdullah so had revolved around the lack of clarity regarding which configuration the X-ray system should be. Abdullah had assured the ministry that it was top of the range. The Egyptian anaesthetists at the Shimaisi Hospital, who were used by the ministry as advisers, threw up their hands and said we know nothing about X-ray. So the ministry concluded that, on the grounds of all probabilities, if the manufacturer said it was so, the Koreans said it was so, and the British advisers said it was so, then it must be so.

And it looked top of the range: the top of the range price was paid, and top of the range commissions were paid to Anderson, to Abdullah, and to the Egyptian anaesthetists for feigning total ignorance of radiography. When the fourth-generation system dressed up as top of the range was installed, nobody was any the wiser as to whether it was top, middle, bottom, or utterly obsolete. But it looked top of the range.

To the ministry, that was all that mattered.

'For the rest of the ministry projects, ah …' Abdullah sighed, folding his hands behind his head, longing for the old days. 'Very little now my friends.'

There was silence as Iqbal came in, apologetically holding an ashtray for the visitors. The room was just as silent as he shimmied out.

Ellis and Anderson lit up in total haste.

'Some O and M jobs, but the big boys, Witikar and Al Jeel, they've got them.'

'So what keeps you busy now, Abdullah?' Anderson could ask anything now he was full of smoke.

Abdullah thought about it for a moment. 'Dodging all the civil unrest; I'm sure you have read of it. The rest of the time supplying to the big hospitals, the big organisers, but they prefer to go to the manufacturers direct. The big boys now have offices in London and stateside. No more of this dumping second-rate crap on the developing world, eh, Anderson, you old bastard?' Abdullah laughed and Anderson felt a defence of his past dubious practices would be swept aside. So he didn't bother, just laughed with his host instead.

Ellis felt the question was about to close in about what business they could possibly be involved in and the purpose of their visit.

'So why the change of names?'

Ouch.

Neither man had expected the question to come so hard straight at them.

Best thing was to give a straight reply.

Ellis described in detail from the date of their expulsion to the day when Ellis found Anderson slumped over a tray of peanuts on the Banjul River, and the realisation that Clitty had only been in the Kingdom to wire his money home in dribs and drabs to avoid any uncomfortable questions being asked by the banks about these amounts being incompatible with their declared income, and so on.

Now that Clitty was about to get chopped, Ellis pressed on gingerly, they wanted to see if they could get the money out to any surviving next of kin.

Abdullah laughed so loud that Iqbal popped his head round the door to see if the ceiling was still intact.

'You're telling me you want to do charitable work for your colleague's next of kin?' The laughter seemed unquenchable. 'Ha ha ha, so how much do I get?'

The laughter ceased abruptly.

Christ, thought Anderson. I never thought he would want more than just a few expenses paid. We'll pay him that, of course we will, but a share of the loot? Jesus!

On witnessing the conspiratorial silence, Abdullah changed tack. 'How much money do you think is there?'

Ellis pursed his lips and shook his head and shrugged his shoulders. Obviously a pair of liars.

'Gentlemen, forgive me. But you are in great danger the way you have set up this operation. I can live with your decision, but I do not regard your silence as being the end point of your thoughts on how much is in the bank. Do I make myself very clear?'

'About sixty.'

'Sixty what? Groats, dollars, riyals, pounds? How much?'

Ellis went for broke. 'Our best estimate, Abdullah, is that Clitty, our colleague, had about sixty thousand pounds in the bank when he was arrested.'

The two men smoked as Abdullah summoned Iqbal for more drinks.

'OK, then, boys, what's the deal? Thirty per cent?'

Bloody hell, he wants a third of the take.

'Abdullah, now hear this.' Anderson put on the best drawl in his repertoire. 'We ain't come back just to grab the money an' rush off somewheres. We know Clitty's got a mama an' all, at least might have had. The least we can do is take what belongs to the man, take it home.'

'Bollocks. And give it to whom?' Abdullah's mind seemed made up, in an Anglo-Saxon way.

Here in front of him were two chancers, and one-third of their kitty was quite fair. Could, of course, take all of it.

Particularly now they'd asked Abdullah to contact the people at the ministry to do a favour and give written permission for two British passport holders to visit a Mr Klitowski in the Malaz Jail.

Iqbal delivered more drinks, cleared up the soiled cups, and left without a sound.

'No, gentlemen. It's one-third or the whole thing's off.'

'Thank you, Abdullah,' Ellis replied gracefully. 'We seem to have forgotten our skills in negotiating.'

'No, you haven't. You just never learned to tell the truth. But what of it? I'll see how I can deal with this for you.'

Abdullah stood up, signalling the end of their meeting, the black coffee ground still hanging tenaciously to his upper lip. He held out a hand and shook both Ellis's and Anderson's warmly.

'That's another thing we forgot,' Ellis said as they waved down a limousine for an appointment at the British Embassy. 'We nearly screwed that one up. Our only friend in here, and he's a Saudi, and we've pissed him off already.'

'Yeh, but he owes us, an' he knows it.' Anderson lay back in the cool leather of the air-conditioned Lincoln limousine, yawned loudly and assuredly, then slept for the half-hour journey to the diplomatic quarter on the very edge of the city.

The British Embassy in Riyadh, like most other embassies, was based in the diplomatic quarter, close to where the men had gone to the party on that night, and known fondly by all expatriates as the DQ, a type of diplomatic souk. If you needed a new car, you'd go to the car souk; if you needed some sewing done, you go to the sewing souk; and if you needed to see a diplomat, you went to the DQ. Everything neat, everything in its place.

The DQ was guarded on its periphery by some bored armed guards who could make life hard or could make it easy; what triggered a guard's response was always impossible to fathom or predict. The approach roads were a riot of floral colour, the buildings a tasteful blend of typical Arabic architecture, combining modern materials and appointments with local tradition. Each embassy was on its own site, guarded by staff as cheerful as those on the perimeter roads.

The approach to the British Embassy took the two men past the abandoned Iraqi Embassy, closed since August, 1990, when Iraq ran amok among the Kuwaiti oilfields and threatened Saudi sovereignty. Anderson reckoned that in all that time nobody had had the sense to go and check that the Iraqi Embassy cat had been fed.

The limousine drew up outside the imposing embassy building, like all the others a two-storey building in soft beige, the Union flag hanging elegantly from a gold-embossed flagpole, the palm trees holding station throughout the gardens, a gentle reminder of a colonial past and all that represented. The driver asked for 120 riyals, the extra twenty being for putting on a Billy Jo Spears tape for his esteemed American guest. Anderson paid him ninety and told the driver to get stuffed. The driver shouted at the embassy guard for some form of intervention or arbitration, but the guard had his finger up his nose, thereby rendering the semi-automatic he was clutching inoperable through lack of an index finger. He shrugged his shoulders and told the driver to clear off before he was arrested for disturbing the celestial peace of the environment.

Maxwell Schofield had a busy day today. Saturdays were always busy: first day of the week, letters from London, faxes in, diplomatic messages and other communications sent out from London on a Friday, the Saudi

Your Friday, My Sunday

weekend. That meant the third secretary had all that plus an annoying appointment in ten minutes. Maxwell, a florid man in his mid-forties, had been tipped for high office in the civil service – until he'd been caught in a Budapest public lavatory committing what the ambassador enviously referred to as an act of gross indecency incompatible with the status of a servant of the Crown. What's more, nobody ever really could find out what kind of indecency was compatible with the status of a servant of the Crown. People asked questions, people wrote to their members of Parliament, but nobody seemed to know. So it was concluded generally that indecent acts should only be carried out in someone else's embassy.

Maxwell fussed and filed his papers just as the telephone rang to announce the presence of his two visitors. The door opened, and a whispering female voice offered their identity.

Straight away, even Maxwell was able to see that this was a pair of villainous-looking creatures he'd surely come upon some years ago in Riyadh. One didn't forget eyes like that man who now said he was Theophilus, or the smell of cigarette smoke that seemed to seep from his pores and fill the room.

That other man, rather rotund, sweating – was that gel holding that thinning layer of hair to the surface of his scalp, or was it just the sweat? Had to be gel. There was some greenish-looking material just over his right ear, like he'd smeared it onto his hair and forgot to rub it away.

Maxwell found the prospect of showing him properly quite exciting.

He pulled himself together for the main purpose of the meeting.

'Gentlemen, good morning. I'm Maxwell Schofield, third secretary and deputy head of the consular section.'

'Is that so?' Anderson asked drily.

Those bloody eyes – that had to be him, but what was his name?

Maxwell ignored the slight and pressed on. 'I understand you have some questions regarding a British national. Let me see.' He shuffled around the papers on his desk to find the name of the only Brit on death row in the entire Arabic peninsula. The Arabs knew his name, so how come Maxwell, the pivotal man in all this, had to scratch around among the seating plans for the embassy dinner, the garden fête, and the Christmas Fayre arrangements? He shuffled some more, then remembered he'd left the information in the out tray without so much as a glance on its way past the in tray.

Maxwell leaped to the out tray. 'Ah yes, here he is, Mr Klit-Off-Skee. Is that he?' Maxwell clutched the beige file, some few centimetres thick, flicking the papers this way and that: a headed Ministry of Interior sheet, sheets of typed and handwritten correspondence. The sheet at the top of the entire file was Ministry of Interior. A translation sheet was attached. After all, the ministry did not translate its missives into a language that anyone could understand, so the embassy hired the services of an Egyptian translator to put a translation alongside the original text.

Maxwell snapped the file shut, sat, and faced down the two glowering antagonists.

'May I ask what relationship you enjoyed with this man Klitowski?' Maxwell was hoping for the salacious inside track.

'None, exactly,' Ellis snarled. 'We represent next of kin.'

'By whose diktat?'

'We know that all embassy efforts to save Mr Klitowski have failed to effect his release, and that his execution should take place within the next few weeks at the most.'

Maxwell opened the file to read the translation. 'Correct. Friday this week, as a matter of fact – a week yesterday.'

He snapped the file shut once more.

'And you're going to sit on ya ass and let him be chopped?' Anderson waded in.

'He killed a man. Justice is to be done.' Maxwell attempted some sort of justification, a type of cultural alignment with local conditions, gone bush perhaps.

Anderson hated this man Schofield, hated him for the inevitability of the man's inaction on Clitty's behalf. So he jumped from his chair and pulled him across the table. 'Listen, asshole. Ya sit here on your cosy little chair, shuffling bits of paper, organizing goddamn whist drives, while one of our citizens goes down the tube thanks to sharia law.'

Maxwell held his cool as Anderson released his grip, the third secretary falling back into the comfort of his chair. 'Yes, sir, but with an accent like yours, are you sure you're in the right embassy? I mean the American and the Canadian embassies are but a stone's throw from here.'

Just then the door opened, and there stood the suit they'd met at the airport. He looked at them briefly.

'Anderson and Ellis, good Lord. You still here?'

The two visitors sat silent, their presence a simple answer to the suit's question.

'He's going down Friday. Did you know?'

The two visitors nodded.

'Maxwell, pass me that file.' Maxwell did as he was told. The suit looked at the translation. 'Here we are. Sentence is confirmed and will take place on Friday, eleventh Sha'ban, after prayers.'

Everybody knew that meant the noontime prayers.

'I suppose it's too much to ask that you may lodge some sort of appeal?' Ellis felt genuine concern.

'Oh, that's all been done long ago,' the suit recalled dismissively.

'Yes, but did you – have you considered the possibility that the son may want to offer some pardon, some sort of forgiveness? Have you spoken to him?'

Maxwell and the suit exchanged conspiratorial glances and agreed that it had not been a successful approach.

'You know the older son died of leukaemia?'

'You are well informed,' the suit noted drily. 'It doesn't make any odds; the younger son and the twenty behind him said take off the bugger's head.'

'Yes, but did you *ask* the next son? Did you ask him specifically?'

'Not quite sure that we did.' The suit glided his way through a panoply of standard excuses for non-action, picking up the file for some sort of prop. 'But it was a long time ago.'

'The offence was, but the boy has just turned 16. This week, perhaps the week before. So at what point may we expect you to get off your arse and ask such an obvious question?'

'We'll do it today,' the suit promised finally, 'and we'll call you. Where are you staying, Marriott? Thought so.' And leaving Maxwell to obtain all the information, the suit fled the consular interview room.

'By the way, Mr Schofield, we understand you hold Klitowski's personal effects. We'd like to take them.'

Maxwell disliked Ellis's approach but thought that to hand the effects over would get these two wretched man from his office and he could wrap things up for the day, get out for a swim, G and T, all that sort of thing.

And Anderson wanted to get out so he could have a smoke.

'OK,' Maxwell offered without a murmur, 'I'll get them, but please be sure to give them to him when we, and if … we have secured Klitowski's release.'

'Suck my dick,' Anderson intoned with a characteristic dismissal.

Maxwell considered it a kind invitation, but he had things to do, so bothered from the room to reappear within seconds with two thin, transparent plastic carrier bags of things.

Ellis and Anderson had the same thought at the same time. Yes, but were the bank book and the card in there?

'Is this all you have?' Ellis asked by way of confirming the bank book was not in another bag outside somewhere.

'Yes. That's it.' Maxwell wound up the meeting, tired and looking forward to a swim. The release of the prisoner could wait, up and until the last possible moment on Friday.

Anything was possible.

In the limousine on the return journey to the hotel, the two men ruffled through the belongings: a watch, a crucifix on a chain, a prayer book, an address book, a wallet. 'Yeh!' Anderson shouted excitedly. 'A bloody wallet!' He ripped open the leather case. Lots of pieces of paper fell out – a card here, a Barclaycard, blimey, then a Saudi British Bank teller card, the ETC.

Anderson ordered the driver to go to the branch of Saudi British Bank in Olaya, where he knew there was a hole in the wall. He'd pulled a few numbers from the wallet, but written in faded in blue ink on the rear of the card were the numbers 5-1-0-7.

The limousine pulled up outside the bank. Ellis told the man to stay put, play some Beatles or something; they'd be back in a minute. The machine in the wall was in an air-conditioned annex to the main bank building, and anybody going into the bank proper would not use this area. Bank staff could observe what was happening in the annex, but few did.

Abdul Rahman al Khatani had had a boring day and was thinking about the fact that this was nearly the fifth anniversary of his giving up smoking. By way of celebration, he would go home and make a baby with Madame.

Then the teller warning system in the corner of his office threw up activity in a long-inactive account. Account number correct, PIN right the first time. Turn on the camera.

Abdul Rahman wondered about the two men who had pulled out five hundred riyals from this account, counted the money, then left the view of the camera. Another camera allowed a view of two men he thought he knew as they got into a limousine and headed off into the traffic.

Mark that account, just in case. Then it's home and who knows?

Ellis and Anderson wondered about the five one-hundred notes and where they should go to buy some alcohol.

'Used to get the best sid at the Ballast Needam compound, but I doubt any of the old fellas are still in business,' Ellis concluded sadly. He really did not know where to go for some illicit booze and cursed himself for not asking at the embassy. As if they would have told them anyway.

Abdul Rahman, meanwhile, was tidying his desk. He put a temporary electronic bar on the account of somebody called Klitowski, smiled at his powers of observation, and wondered where or whether he had seen one of those faces before.

Tomorrow, or perhaps sometime soon, would tell. *Inshallah*.

Chapter 11

First of all, they had managed to find some *siddiqi* to drink - the oblivion of overconsumption of the white friend still alive in both their minds.

Ellis and Anderson both thought of the same supplier. The surprise was that he was still living in the same bachelor apartment in Sulaymania, not more than a couple of streets away from their last place of abode. He was still brewing sid, and the blasted man was still alive. He hadn't been jailed for distribution; he hadn't been shopped by anybody, even though the smell of alcohol fumes could be detected from the moment they opened the door of the limousine as they pulled up in his parking lot. The two men wondered if it could be true that in all these years he hadn't moved on. If nothing else, he must surely have gone mad.

Anderson instructed the limousine driver to remain there; after all, there was no point in attracting attention when carrying illegal substances and attempting to hail a limousine.

The two men approached the three-storey building. Decay and dirt, food tins and drinks cans lay on the narrow pathway from the road to the front door. Anderson pressed a bell push that gave no indication of whether anything had triggered inside. He pressed again.

A scrawny cat mounted the wall and cursed.

'Piss off yerself, fleabag.' Anderson glowered in return.

Still no reply.

Ellis held up a finger. 'Listen,' he commanded.

From inside came the faint sound of some hysterical giggling and whining, a man's voice in trouble and in a state of some excitement.

Anderson banged on the door loudly, 'Bumhead, come on, open the fuckin' door!'

'That's subtle if nothing else,' Ellis offered.

'Yeh, I gotta fuckin' thirst an' I need some booze. Real bad.'

The sound of giggling subsided, then a sound of some shuffling feet as they approached the door, then the fumbling around of various types of keys the man used on a myriad of front door locks.

The two men listened to the wittering as one key was tried, then a murmur, then another key, then silence. Then more rattling as the door was pulled against the stop, then again. Then, much to the surprise of the occupant, the door flew open and flooded the darkened hallway with bright midday sun. The cat gave thanks, squawked, and ran in beyond the malevolent glances of the visitors.

'Yes?' the man asked weakly, screwing his face against the light to ensure his visitors were not police.

'We need sid,' Anderson stated unambiguously.

'Can do, of course.' The little man was about five foot and a bit, skin as pale as cream, a ginger goatee beard somehow attached to the small chin, wizened hands rubbing nervously together, the type of rubbing employed to warm up the extremities, but not in a house with ineffectual air conditioning, where the temperature was already in the eighties and it was still only midmorning. 'But you would need to have made an appointment for collection, you see.' The man rubbed his hands more quickly. 'It's procedure these days …'

Anderson needed to drink alcohol within the next hour and so cut out any negotiation. 'Say, bumhead, how much you charge for a bottle these days? Hundred and twenty?'

'You're not local boys, are you?' whimpered the old distiller. 'Otherwise you would know that the price is fixed at two hundred and fifty.'

'It bloody well isn't, you thieving old ratbag. I'll give you two hundred.' Anderson peeled off two new one-hundred-riyal notes and held them out for the myopic distiller to inspect. He rubbed his hands, calculated the level of his loss, and agreed two hundred and fifty on the spot.

'I said two hundred, Shylock,' Anderson pressed on.

'Do you have any cigarettes, any Marlboro Lights, Lights particularly?'

'Nope. When ya smoke lights, all ya get is fresh air. No, we ain't got Lights. All we got is Marlboro regular, a proper smoke.' Anderson paused, then made his final offer to the little man. 'So here we go: we do a bottle for two hundred and fifty, plus we throw in two hundred Marlboro.'

Anderson passed over an additional fifty-riyal note.

'Where's the smokes?' demanded the weasel.

'Go get the smokes Ellis, they're in the trunk.' Ellis translated the location in his head and furtively negotiated with the limousine driver who sat, indifferently, smiling at nothing in particular, letting the air con click in and out, while Ellis rummaged in the rear for the smokes.

Ellis handed the 200 pack to the little man, his eyes still darting at the near closure of the deal.

'Where's the sid?' Anderson reciprocated the menace.

The little man had left the door open all the time, open to the view from the road. He had become careless.

Most distillers did what most suppliers of illicit materials did: customers had a ringing code for the front door; they repeated it; the supplier opened the door after checking through the peephole; and then, sufficiently confident to open the door, the supplier would push his head around his visitors to look this way and that to ensure they had not been followed by the police.

Not this guy.

'Someday soon they'll have him,' Anderson suggested while cradling to his chest a one and a half litre bottle of alcohol close to ninety-five proof, the bottle a simple plastic bottle appearing to contain plain water. Even the label said so.

Opening the cap, it smelt like rocket fuel.

Mixed with Pepsi, it was marvellous.

The distiller ripped the wrapper from the cigarettes and bade goodbye to his guests. His shaking hands were unable to free the cigarettes, and he cursed and swore at his incapacity and his advancing years.

'Ahmed, or whatever your name is!'

'Yessir?' The limousine driver smiled and was impressed that Anderson knew his name. 'You know my name, sir? How it comes?'

'I just know these things, Ahmed. Now get us down to the Panda Supermarket. We need some Pepsi.'

'Yessir.' Ahmed smiled. He eased the limousine from the service road into the supermarket parking area. As had always been usual, parking here was a breeze.

'You goin' in?' Anderson turned to speak to Ellis in the back seat. Anderson was clutching the bottle of sid between his feet, out of sight. 'Cuz I don't really want anything to happen to this bottla stuff.'

'As if it would,' Ellis retorted. 'But if it makes you feel better, fine; I'll get the bloody Pepsi.' And heaving open the Cressida door, Ellis levered himself onto the parking area and away to get the Pepsi. Anderson offered Ahmed a smoke, which he declined.

'Muslim, sir. Smoking forbidden by Muslim.'

'Since when, for God's sake?'

'Two years, something like that.'

'Nothing like a bit of freedom.' Anderson inhaled extra deeply for the two of them and stared straight ahead.

Few people were shopping here today. A few cars were coming and going; otherwise it was much as it always was.

Including the queue for the telephone.

Calling home was a ritual often performed by the Indians and Pakistanis and others, whose jobs did not put them near to an office telephone that they were authorised to use. Besides which they were simply not trusted not to spend all day on the telephone.

Their employers were not impressed by the staff's occasional assertions that they could not afford a telephone at home, so how on earth could they be accused of using the telephone? Yes, said the employers, but you would do what they all do: you would call your auntie in Uttar Pradesh. She's got a telephone. She would send one of her grandchildren to run across the village to tell your mother that there is a call from Riyadh.

Simple really.

And the person who explained to the employer how the telephone scam worked was usually one of their own countrymen, one of the Indian's own colleagues, keen to curry favours with the boss.

So they queued outside the Panda Supermarket in a long line, hands full of *halalahs*, kicking stones around on the ground with their dirtied sandals, some of them talking and laughing with another hopeful three places further forward in the queue, others standing in quiet contemplation, while all around them the traffic on the Dammam highway roared relentlessly. Cars came and went, the shouting from the one currently using the wall-mounted telephone modulating according to the ambient sound.

Being located just a quarter of a mile from the perimeter fence of the military airfield, there was regular overflying of the phone by military aircraft of all sorts, shape, size, and nationality. The risk for those using the telephone was that their call could be totally disrupted by the flypast of something noisy, particularly the tankers, the reject American KC-135s, Anderson remembered. Were those bloody things still flying?

While the man on the telephone was approaching a critical point in his call –raising his voice, speeding his delivery, and waving his hands in impatient frustration at some family problem somewhere on the Indian subcontinent – there came a familiar sound.

The approach of a fully laden aircraft.

Within a second or two, the sound of approach was swamped by the awesome shriek, the body-trembling decibels of a silvery-grey KC-135 grasping at the sky, its two wing-mounted engines pouring blackness into the air and darkness into the soul. The man sharing a problem with his wife shouted louder and louder until – because he had run of money, there had been a tornado at home, or the sound of the aircraft had stifled conversation – he abruptly hung up, picked at his nose, spat derisively, and climbed on a black bicycle leaned against the supermarket wall, pedalling away with body language suggesting a heavy and angry heart.

Without warning, a blue-and-white pulled slowly into the parking area.

Anderson felt his guts tighten. What perverse luck was operating that the civil police would turn up just as he had a bottle of *siddiqi* on the floor? Christ, the penalty for being caught with this was something of which nightmares were made.

The police driver thought he liked the look of the Cressida limousine with its driver sitting in the front with some other foreigner, also in the front. So he simply parked the blue-and-white across the front of the limousine. Blocked in.

Anderson wondered about all this and thought about whether he could blame Ahmed, tell the copper the bloody bottle was on the floor when he got in, and anyway how was he to know what was in the bottle? The label said it was Nissah water; it certainly looked as if it were ordinary mineral water.

Oh God. Oh Jesus, please help.

The policeman approached the driver's side and addressed Ahmed in Arabic, while reserving a special attention for Anderson, who shook as he lit a cigarette and was scolded by Ahmed that smoking was not allowed in his limousine. Anderson cursed and threw the cigarette out of the window.

He thought he heard the mention in Arabic of the Marriott Hotel and that these guests were just visiting Saudi Arabia.

The policeman looked again at Anderson, wondered about the eyes, tapped the roof of the limousine, and said, 'OK, go.'

Just as Ellis came out of the supermarket clutching a tray of twenty-four Pepsi cans, he saw the police car hemming their limousine in, with the policeman in conversation with the driver.

What to do?

Should he run back inside?

Should he brazen it out with the copper?

Should he join the queue for the telephones?

Before his indecision became too obvious, the policeman returned to his car, made some sort of report on his radio, started up the engine, and departed as quietly as he had arrived.

Back to the Marriott, quick, before anything else goes wrong.

Carefully stashing the bottle away from chance discovery by anyone, the two kept the drunken feast going for two days.

The sid was tolerable at a dilution of two to one. That meant they had three litres of fifty-proof liquor to mix with Pepsi. Half of that went in the first night.

Enough to kill an elephant.

At the start of the third day, Abdullah called.

He spoke to Anderson and promised the passes had been approved. They should be picked up at the gate of the Malaz Jail in two days, or if they chose, they could go straight to the Ministry of Health, who had sponsored Clitty in the first place, and run the risk of being recognized.

'And, oh, Mr Theophilus, or whoever …'

'Yes, Abdullah.'

'One-third. OK?'

'You got it.' Anderson hung up the phone and announced with a beam on his face that they'd got the necessary permission to visit Clitty.

Ellis watched the dregs at the bottom of his glass and wondered why he could not really think why he should want to see Clitty again.

Bit like the kids. When it all got too hard to take, he would run away, when Cheryl came on strong about money or about the children missing him. What was he going to do about it? Well, could he not get home earlier? And what did Ellis the hero do? He picked his things up and moved on.

So now he faced the situation of seeing his erstwhile friend only a few days away from a barbaric execution – the friend who just happened to be driving while all of them were drunk, at the time when some old fool was sitting in the middle of the road.

And what did Ellis do? Refill the glass.

Ellis sat cross-legged on the single bed in Anderson's room, tracing his index finger around and around the rim of the glass taken from the bathroom.

And he was thinking.

He was thinking about his waistline and whether or not the gel was working, and Clitty and Cheryl and the kids, and he just wished he had some of his music with him – all the music he'd packed up in Lincoln, in the hope that when he got to Riyadh, things would be different.

They were different, though they were the same in their sterility. Only the intensity was more focused, more oppressive.

Nothing was different. He could have been sat in the Woolsack, his favourite pub in Lincoln, doing the same thing: smoking, worrying, reflecting, pondering a fading physique, thinking of the kids, wondering if the phone might ring with one of them brightly announcing a happy piece of news.

But here he was in Riyadh, doing all the things he did in Lincoln. Drinking, smoking, reflecting.

Nothing actually was different.

Anderson watched his mucker worrying and fretting about things and passed it off as the thoughts and ramblings of somebody with acute alcohol poisoning, just before they passed out for about twelve hours.

Room service disturbed all the thoughts. Would sirs mind retiring to the lobby so their room could be cleaned, as nothing had been done for two days and surely the ashtrays may need to be renewed? The way the floor manager was holding his nose was suggestive that the room probably did need to be refreshed. The bottle of sid should be hidden somewhere or even taken down to the reception area while the room servants de-fugged their accommodation.

They preferred the latter idea, taking some Pepsi and the plastic bottle and a couple of packs of smokes. 'Take ya time, fellas!' Anderson called cheerfully, slamming the door as one of the cleaners pulled a soiled sock from beneath the bed, made a face, and hinted an expression of come back tomorrow, or preferably never at all.

The following two days were spent lying in wait for the permission documents to visit Clitty. And in more drinking.

Some eating, some chat, and lots of smoking that caused an emergency trip to the Panda Supermarket, this time at three in the morning. But what had become clear was that Ellis wanted to be home. Anderson wanted something, but he was still working out what.

And on the third day they arose.

They didn't recognise him at first. But as the two prison guards dragged Clitty, half stumbling, half mumbling, the three of them abreast, squashing through the narrow entrance of the interview room, Ellis and Anderson realised with horror that they had stupidly assumed Clitty would be just like they had always known him.

The guards pushed Clitty onto a bare plastic upright chair and told him to keep his hands on the table.

Ellis didn't know whether to be sick, say hello, or run from the room.

Anderson took out his cigarettes and was immediately put right with a swish of the cane the guard held behind him.

Clitty's head was shaved bare. He was dressed in a ragged *thobe* with threadbare cuffs and collar and wore open-toed sandals. He slouched in the chair with no sign of recognition of his visitors nor any real sign that there was anybody here to see him.

Ellis put his hand across Clitty's trembling hand., 'Clitty, old man,' he began softly, 'it's me, Ellis.'

At that the guard rustled and reread the permission papers. He didn't understand anything about the West or anything other than the goodness of his religion and the righteousness of what they were to do with the white sinner. The visitors would be out of here in five minutes, and in any case the ministry had approved the visit. Perhaps that name Ellis was a nickname or something.

Clitty raised his head slowly, the firm face now older and lined. He smiled a quiet hello and said heavily, his massive shoulders heaving with the effort, 'I know why you're here. Perhaps if you can get this one right, we might one day get to have a beer in London. If not …'

Anderson said to Ellis, 'I wonder if he's sick or something?'

Ellis stood to attention. 'Bloody intuitive you are, you prick. Being in here for over ten years is enough to send you mad. Why else do you think he looks so frail?'

All five people fell into silence.

Echoing along the long, dark corridors was the sound of Filipino boys screaming as the guards had their way. Elsewhere came maniacal laughter, and screeches, the stench of incarceration, sweat, and raw terror oozing from the walls.

'OK, *halas*.' The bigger of the two guards, the one with the stick, brutally signalled an end to the interview by hitting Clitty in the small of the back, getting him ready for Friday, no doubt. 'You go now, *imshee*.'

The guards pulled Clitty from his chair. He didn't even look at his old colleagues as he was dragged back to the open area holding a hundred or so prisoners in one pen, an area kept for those offenders the guards did not like or perhaps for those they fancied. Get the prisoners to scream: that was the policy, and then they would beg for mercy, and then the guards had a powerful lever on whatever was to happen to them.

Your Friday, My Sunday

Ellis and Anderson listened intently as the shuffling of feet became softer and quieter, until the sounds and sobs of bedlam drowned out any other sounds.

The two men were unceremoniously bundled from the building into the glare of the sun and the unwelcoming heat of another Riyadh day.

'Gotta smoke!' Anderson ripped the pack from his shirt pocket and lit up with no apparent thought for Ellis, who had, for once, beaten Anderson to lighting up.

They smoked once and then twice. They shook heads in the realisation that barbarism lay within fifty feet from where they stood smoking. Yet their old mucker lay without hope, the only expectation being the enthusiasm of a partisan crowd regarding how much they should cheer when his head was ripped from his neck in a single, callous blow of judicial retribution.

Any sort of head would do, but the head of a European Christian was a much better one to savour. Not only was it unusual; it would guarantee that there was a maximum crowd. The downside was that the murdering of foreigners in public had to be judged by the victim's nationality and what level of business his own country conducted with the Saudi administration.

Clitty was British, the Brits supplied much of the Saudi military infrastructure, and the beheading of a British citizen would weigh poorly with the folks back home. So would they or wouldn't they? There were no sounds of clemency from any quarter, particularly now the country was rumoured to be in the throes of painful dissolution and civil unrest.

'You guys wanna stand there all day, please?' the limo driver called eventually. 'Or you wanna go home Marriott, OK?'

The call stung the two men from their introspection, the realisation that they were actually powerless to stop the train of events about to unfold. And they'd really only come back for the money.

The return journey to the Marriott would have been quiet and uneventful but for the fact that a roaming gang, a regular feature of Riyadh streets these days, had unearthed some unsavoury videotapes in a shop run by a Pakistani but owned and sponsored by a sleeping Saudi partner.

'Allah Akbar!' they shouted, beating their chests in excitement. 'God is great!' They threw videos from the shop into the carriageway. The cassettes landed ahead of the limousine, forcing it to slow, then to stop, to allow the occupants to be berated for the contents of the video shop. A window at the front of the shop shattered as a brick was launched from close range by an excited bystander. A blue-and-white arrived and, seeing the cause of the outbreak, turned and left the participants to sort it out for themselves.

Then, from a point just outside the vision of the limo, a glass bottle was thrown, some flames issuing from the top. The whole lot went through the opened door. A bright flash, some smoke, and then flames billowed from the doorway and through the holes in the plate-glass window. Within seconds the entire shop was burning.

Ellis drew on a cigarette for comfort, not comprehending the changed nature of these shifting sands. He looked around to watch an angry crowd protesting with increasing venom and hatred and saw strewn on the ground some of the videocassettes that had drawn the opprobrium of the religious correctors.

In a careless pile dumped on the pavement were some copies of *Mary Poppins* and *The Jungle Book*, and perhaps a little out of vision, a copy of *Mutiny on the Bounty*. Serious subversive material, Anderson and Ellis concluded as the rioters decided to pick upon anything else that may be responsible for this filth. Like white faces.

The crowd massed angrily and began shouting the chorus of the religiously insane. A few of them felt the fenders to try to tip the car over, rocking a little. The driver shouted out that he was Muslim, so don't take it out on him that he's carrying a couple of non-believers, and in any case we watch *Mary Poppins* in Pakistan so what's wrong with that?

'Allah Akbar!' they yelled, completely beyond the pale.

The driver pushed his hand on the horn, engaged gear, and, regardless of who was in the way, drove off in a squeal of rubber, just to get rid of this fare, get them to the Marriott, try to avoid white faces for the future. Just in case.

'That was the biggest fucked-up ride I ever took in here, Iqbal ma man, or whoever you are, so I ain't gonna give you nothin' for a mighty dangerous ride. Ya hear what I say?'

'Yes, sir.' The driver held out a hand in hope. These bloody troubles were screwing his business. 'But like you, sir, you must have a family, like me, I have a family. These problems are not of my doing. They Saudi guys, the lot of them, they've gone crazy.'

'OK, Iqbal, take a fifty. That's all we owe you.'

The driver had only expected a flea in the ear, so was pleased that the American had given him the full fifty – ten more than the fare would normally be. Perhaps he rated the riot at ten riyals extra. True, it was not a particularly original outbreak of civil disobedience, but there had been a fire, a shop burned out – that counted for a few extra riyals to send home to Mother in Islamabad.

The driver waved a cheery goodbye as the two white faces got out and left the doors open, so he had to get out of the car and do something for the extra fare.

Ellis and Anderson repaired this time to Ellis's room for some drinks and to work things out. Tomorrow would be Friday. They had to get themselves together to be ready for the celebrations in Friday Square.

After a day of witness to the Saudi system of justice and the vengeance of a religious mob, the sidiqqi tasted good.

Friday.

The day the two of them had come back for.

The type of day the three of them had once witnessed, though in quieter, perhaps even safer days. On that day the black-and-white van arrived in Friday Square, it disgorged its contents one by one. The charges were read, nobody objected, the families of the victims acquiesced, and then the heads came off. One by one.

Lots of them on a good day.

Neither Ellis nor Anderson could provide any useful thought about what it was they were about to do. They knew they were here; they knew there was some money to be had; they knew their friend was to be executed in a few hours; they knew they were passengers on this train; they knew they had no idea how to predict what it was they would do when Clitty was wheeled out to have his head removed. They had no idea, and would therefore respond to events.

That was all they could be expected to achieve.

First of all Anderson left his room, in quite a sober state for a Friday morning, asked for the check from reception, and then wandered to the road running along the front of the hotel.

He was looking for a limo. A long-term lease, perhaps.

He waved down the first one he saw, but the man did not wish to be involved in anything too complicated today, it's Friday, sir. He wanted to get back to bed and sleep.

The next one was the same.

Double the price.

'Mister, how ya wanna have five hundred riyals?' Anderson opened to the next driver with gusto a price that was beyond dispute.

'Where you wanna go at that price, mister?' The Filipino driver beamed. 'The moon?'

'Don't be so fuckin' clever. Drive in to the bloody hotel and wait.' Passing the driver three hundred by way of an advance, Anderson walked briskly back into the building to pay his bill, pick up his mate, and get down to the main business.

Ellis commanded the limousine driver to stay parked in a backstreet away from Friday Square and keep clear of the crowds. Nice to have a clean run, out and away.

The driver promised he would not move – or at least if he had a further hundred riyals it could make a substantial difference.

Anderson and Ellis walked from the car and turned the corner at the edge of Friday Square, to be confronted by a crowd, an expectant crowd, all of them looking around, craning their necks to see if the black-and-white truck, the purveyor of the condemned, was to be seen.

Anderson lit up. So did Ellis.

Although prayers were meant to precede the public executions, it looked as if everyone remained at their places. They did not at this time go to the mosque. Instead they prayed alongside their lunchboxes and their male acquaintances, and they hoped that today would be graced with a multitude of sinners.

The prayers were begun by the imam calling from the minaret. The faithful all fell to their knees in supplication and hope. The two foreigners stayed in view but out of sight.

The prayers and the responses flowed with the usual level of monotony associated with the repeated recital of the same words.

Just then one of the faithful leaped to his feet and began to shout. A short man with wild eyes, he shouted and he yearned and he achieved broad agreement from his peers. He pointed at the mosque and the minaret that had now fallen peculiarly silent. There was no way that Ellis or Anderson could hear what was being said, but body language suggested that the words from the minaret were no longer to be believed, and what was required was a devotion to the true God, Allah.

'Allah Akbar!' the crowd roared. Then they began to beat their chests. Some of the younger Saudi men removed their *guttrahs* from their heads and wrapped them around their foreheads, just like a scarf. They began to run on the spot, as if in a catatonic trance. They jumped on the spot and they hit their heads and their chests and they called to God and they called for anything. The shouting welled to a roar. The crowd knew what they had come to see, they knew what they wanted to see, but there was no sign of the truck.

They wanted the truck.

They wanted to see the Pakistani who had been found guilty of smuggling heroin in a plastic bottle that had been inserted into his anus.

It had been reported that while walking through customs, the officers were worried that the man was unwell, so odd was his gait. They invited him for an inspection of all his goods and his person. Drugs. That's what they found. And the new Islamic fervour wanted to kill drug runners, so the crowd grew restless and called Allah Akbar, and they shouted and sucked themselves, the lot of them, into a vortex of frenzy that only a blood spill would assuage.

Above the din, the sound of an engine, the misuse of a gearbox, the roaring as a driver negotiated the tight entrance to the square. All at once, there it was.

The black-and-white truck.

Clitty.

Anderson and Ellis exchanged worried glances.

There was no way they could effect a rescue of any sort. The place was packed with armed police who faced inwards at the crowd. They watched the impromptu demonstration, wondering whether it constituted a political meeting, in which case they could arrest the ringleaders.

Whatever, the police stood and watched the crowd. All of it.

The truck manoeuvred closer to the edge of the crowd, the driver, one hand held firmly on the horn, blasting at the faithful not to impede the course of justice. The crowd did move a little to allow access to the drain cover in the centre, but not enough to get it beyond being totally surrounded and utterly at the mercy of the zealot, now beating his chest and signalling that the jurisdiction of the fate of the convicts was theirs. After all, they were good Muslims, and this was their right.

'Allah Akbar!' The crowd was on its feet and began to rock the black-and-white van. The driver could be seen hurling obscenities or prayers as the van rocked a little this way and then that. The crowd took a while to build any sense of rhythm. They chanted and they pushed. Sometimes the truck remained still, but then the rhythm rocked it until it could resist no more and fell to its side with a crash. The crowd roared its approval and went for the kill. The rear doors.

'Please God, help him,' Anderson muttered under his breath.

Ellis nodded agreement.

The crowd ripped the rear doors away from their frame to expose the contents of the van. It was difficult for either man to see clearly whether Clitty was in there. Was this van a decoy? Was the real one somewhere else? Questions, questions. To which there were no answers from where they stood.

Ellis took the cue, threw down his cigarette and started to run into the melee. The crowd was now pulling a cloaked figure from the truck. Oh, not Clitty, please.

They ordered the clearing of a way from the back of the truck to a tree at the edge of the square. Ellis came near to the rear of the truck and saw that the cloaked figure was of coloured skin. If the figure could have blanched, he would have done. He was pulled from the truck and held head high above the crowd. 'Death to drugs, death to the peddlers of drugs, death, death, death.' The chant built as the crowd carried the struggling shape towards the tree, one of the advance party draping a rope around one of the longer horizontal branches, a loop in the centre awaiting. The crowd arrived at the tree and with little ceremony slipped the loop of rope around the neck of the terrified victim.

Then the crowd let go.

The body dropped, but not far enough to break the neck. Only far enough to allow suffocation to be the cause of death.

A long and slow death.

The crowd yelled at the body. They yelled at the bulging eyes and they yelled at its evil and they yelled at the tongue that gagged for air and they yelled at the way the body swayed as the man attempted to release himself from his state. Yelling was not enough for one of the crowd, who ran forward, called for everlasting life, drew a dagger from his pocket, and plunged it into the face, dislodging an eye.

Even the police took a dislike to this. An officer with a gun ordered his way through and dispatched the drug runner with a single shot through his chest.

This did nothing to slow down the blood lust. One down, a few more to go.

Just as well, then, that Ellis and Anderson had watched the rear of the truck as the drug runner was taken away for summary justice.

Clitty was in the truck. He was in there among a couple of Filipinos, a couple of some others – it was difficult to say from where – and a Saudi gunman who had been caught performing highway robbery on the Qatif road. Whatever, there were seven for the chop today. This was to be a good day.

No wonder the crowd was pleased, if in a very angry way.

'For fuck's sake, run!' Ellis shouted at Clitty as he pulled him from the truck, though being on its side it was hard to say which way was up. 'And just keep running.' Ellis had thought ahead and brought a *guttrah* to throw over Clitty's head to help avoid detection.

Anderson coughed and cluttered behind them, but he did a good job to knock people out of the way, people who thought they should slow down these white faces. Generally, though, all eyes were on the state of the drug runner, hanged and not beheaded. Now it seemed that he had stopped moving, they could move on to beheading whoever else was left in the back of the truck.

The man with the sword stood ready as the case of the next victim was read out over the loudspeakers. The imam had to call for silence a number of times in order to let himself read the charges and to question the next of kin as to whether he would prefer the beheading or perhaps some blood money.

As Ellis and Anderson bundled Clitty into the back of the limousine, the imam was reading out the case of Mr Klitowski, British citizen, guilty of murder. Was he to be decapitated or would the boy like to ask for the money instead?

Although the answer was never officially lodged, the boy had asked for the money. But as Clitty was supposed to be standing by the drain when the adjudication was made and his absence had been noted, technically, he was reprieved. And all the money in the bank belonged to this 16-year-old.

Not Anderson.

Not Ellis.

Not even Clitty, nor a third to Abdullah.

The limousine sped out of the backstreet onto Old Airport Road and away as Clitty realised he was free of the chop, at least for the moment.

'Where we goin', sir?' the driver asked.

Anderson paused. He had to get these bloody chains off Clitty's wrists. Where did one go to do this? The embassy? Hardly. That would be a real giveaway. Where else? That's it!

The car souk, the repair place, down at Al Mansoorah – one of those little shits should have a hacksaw.

'Al Mansoorah, the bloody car place,' Anderson commanded.

'What the hell for?' asked the Filipino. 'I don't have a problem with my car.'

'You'll have a problem with ya fuckin' head in a moment.'

Then Anderson remembered the fraternity. The Filipino fraternity.

'You know anybody with a good saw for cutting iron?'

The driver knew he would know somebody and smiled acknowledgement.

The driver set about the twenty-minute drive to Al Mansoorah while Clitty fretted about his irons and confirmed what he had heard: they wanted all his money and the account was impounded and there was no point in hoping to get anything.

'What's more,' Clitty added slowly, 'you don't get much for walking out on your own execution. We need to make a run for it. Otherwise all three of us get the chop.'

The lanes of Al Mansoorah were deserted. After all, it was one o'clock, lunchtime, on a Friday.

'Driver!'

'Yessir?'

Your Friday, My Sunday

'One of your guys must be in here. Get to it!'

'Yessir.' The driver really wanted none of it, but he drove anyway to a car repair shop run by his cousin on behalf of a Saudi. The deal was done, the shackles were uncut, and Clitty was a free man for the first time in over ten years.

'Driver!' Anderson demanded.

'Yessir?'

'Jeddah!'

'What?'

'You heard. I said Jeddah.'

'But sir, I only have a licence for Riyadh. I can only take fares in Riyadh,' the driver explained weakly.

'I give yer two thousand.'

The Filipino shook his head, thinking of family back in Manila.

'OK then. Five thousand.'

Still the Filipino held out.

'Right, you little oriental shitbag, we are taking over this limousine for the foreseeable future.'

'Yessir.' The Filipino knew lots of friends in Jeddah; he'd be all right.

'OK then, for fuck's sake get us to Jeddah.' Anderson paused. 'Here, have another five hundred for sawing the chains.'

'Yessir, thank you, sir.' The Filipino had never had quite such an eventful Friday and eagerly pocketed the money.

Only Ellis and Anderson had legal paperwork to get to Jeddah, but it was Friday, the weekend, and even if the car did have an escaped convict on board, so what? If they wanted to be legal, what were they to do? Go to the embassy? Ask for new papers for Mr Clitty?

Of course not. The plan now had to be a fast ride to Jeddah. The next bit, the important bit about how to escape from Saudi Arabia, that bit they could worry about when they got there.

In a straight line, Riyadh to Jeddah was about six hundred miles. A three-lane highway carried the traffic, unburdened by worries of congestion. Occasional petrol stops adorned the desert land; otherwise the traveller could put his foot down and listen to the obligatory speed alarm.

One hour led to another. Clitty said nothing; perhaps he was too scared. He even declined any cigarettes offered to him.

Prison was not intended as a healthy place, but perhaps if smoking was not allowed, it may do some good.

Even if the prisoner was about to be beheaded.

'Yer know what, Ellis?' Anderson asked excitedly.

'No.'

'In our hurry to get sid, we didn't do the needful with old Abdullah. He got us the fuckin' passes, and we never had the good grace to give him due recognition or thanks. Oh shit.'

'It's only oh shit if we needed to use him again,' Ellis replied coldly.

'We may yet need him,' Anderson suggested.

'Why?'

'Just s'pose we get to Jeddah and something goes down an' we need some help. Perhaps we need him?'

'A bloody Saudi would leave us to the sharks. Forget Abdullah. He got us the bloody visas to get the bloody money that the bloody boy gets. What do we get? Clitty.'

Clitty smiled an apology.

'Must make sure then,' Ellis added, 'that if we get pulled in, our old mate Abdullah doesn't demand his third of the money. Cos' he ain't gettin' nothin'.'

'Press on, driver,' Anderson demanded.

'Yessir.'

Throughout the night they drove. Nobody really slept, yet nobody really stayed awake. The engine whirred and the driver stopped a couple of times for petrol, and all of them fell out, bought some water, relieved themselves, then got back in. Still he pressed on.

Just before dawn prayer, their car entered the outskirts of Jeddah. Jeddah, the jewel on the Red Sea coast, the former capital of Saudi Arabia until the royal family decided to move it somewhere more central where the bedu could be contained and controlled. Even as a Saudi city, Jeddah was generally loved by expatriate workers for its relative freedom and its allowing men and women to sit in the cafés. The abaya was not required here.

It was such a change.

And the men all felt it as they drew along the Corniche with little idea of what they would do next. The Red Sea spread in a warm blue sheet from one side to the other, the early morning sun making little distinction between the blue of the sky and the blue of the sea. The brightness magnified the white of the sand, and each of them screwed up their eyes, preferring to look at the horizon.

The Filipino driver held out his hand to Anderson.

'Some money, please.' And he snapped his fingers impatiently.

'Fuck off, ya little cunt,' Anderson exploded. 'You've had enough from me. Now fuck off back to Riyadh.'

The three men disembarked as the Filipino wondered about his luck and how he might get level in the next few seconds.

Perhaps he'd go to the police and report the presence of the convict. No, that wouldn't work; they would throw him in jail for being absent from Riyadh without his sponsor's permission.

Oh shit.

Anderson handed the driver another one hundred. 'Get lost,' he commanded.

And with that the Filipino performed a U-turn among the plants and the Mediterranean beauty of the Corniche and began the long haul back to the dust of Riyadh. No sleep, no rest, and no gratitude. Was it ever thus?

The team of three, now reunited, stood among the plastic benches and the children's play areas of the Jeddah seashore and wondered what to do next.

Here they were, two fakes with valid visas and one felon with not one paper to his name. If the police were to pay a visit …

'Let's nick a boat,' Ellis suggested helpfully.

'And then what?' Anderson sneered.

'Well … we do about twenty miles, we're out of Saudi waters, and then …'

'Then what?' Anderson really did have a headache.

'Then we pick up a fishing boat or something. A fuckin' aircraft carrier would be nice. That way we're free.'

With no dissenting voices, the three men walked along the beach as the sea splashed around lazily under a light breeze.

They were looking for a boat to steal.

Most of the boats were covered in protective tarpaulins, except a good-sized one that Clitty noticed out of the corner of his eye. His liberty played havoc with his systems and he felt close to crying, though he would wait a little for that.

The engine started at the first turn. Even though the boat was mounted on a trailer and had not been used for some time, the engine fired first time. God is with us! Allah Akbar!

With grim energy, the three men pulled and heaved and dragged and then offered the boat to the shallows of the Jeddah foreshore.

Goddammit, it floated!

Clitty got in first, then Ellis. Anderson, acting as pilot, sat at the rear, closest to the controls.

He fired the thing up. It coughed a little. Anderson cursed and hit something. Then, in a seamless sequence of manoeuvres, the boat picked up speed and headed away from the Saudi coastline.

At a point that Ellis estimated to be well outside Saudi territorial waters, the engine died.

'Fuck and shit and bollocks,' Anderson screamed at the outboard engine, hitting it with his hands, repeatedly screaming curses on the thing. 'Ya bastarding bloody engine, here we are in mortal danger an' ya gotta go an' shit yerself.'

Anderson sat down and shook his head in frustration. 'Bastard fuckin' motherfucker,' he muttered to nobody in particular.

Ellis was oddly enjoying a smoke in the prow. The morning breeze was a change from the last few days. The freedom of the seas and the memory of that awesome Friday in Riyadh made Ellis feel good about this smoke.

Clitty was watching Anderson, behaving like he remembered.

Anderson was smacking the engine and threatening it with all sorts of penalties if it refused to start.

'Fuckin' thing's out of fuel,' Clitty suggested.

'Fuckin' ain't,' Anderson retorted.

'Listen,' Clitty continued, 'we have little idea how much petrol we had when we started, and we've done about twenty miles since then. Fair bet we're out of gas?'

Anderson had no idea where to find the fuel tank and even less idea about how to detect some sort of ignition failure. He felt humiliated and degraded by the smile of the man he had come to bloody well rescue.

'OK, shitface, you're so fuckin' clever, ya come over here and do ya own diagnosis.'

Anderson shifted across the boards as the boat pitched and weaved in the roughening swell, allowing Clitty to pick his way into a position to effect some sort of repair. First hitting the engine with a judicious slap, then turning the rudder control from one extreme of movement to the other, Clitty nearly caught himself in the leg. He shook his head.

Anderson tried to pull a cigarette from a pack and light it, but a spume of water driven by the wind wetted the end and drenched the lighter.

'Damn and shit,' Anderson muttered, throwing the soggy offering over the side.

Clitty shook his head again in frustration and could think of nothing about how to fix a failed engine. He still felt focused on the sounds and smells of the Malaz Jail, the close scrape of yesterday at Friday Square. The challenge of the engine seemed a trifle, yet he attempted to diagnose all the things that ever went wrong with engines: out of fuel, plugs glued up, God knows.

Anderson crouched as far down in the boat as he could and cheered as another attempt to light a cigarette yielded results. But on the way up, his smile and his cheering stopped dead as he realised the cause of the engine failure was probably Clitty's knee. Clitty had pulled the cover from the engine and peered unknowingly at the plates and wires and pipes. Anderson noticed a red button, the sort of button fitted to motorcycles, one that could be tuned ninety degrees to the left or the right in the event the engine lost control. If the red button was turned, the kill button activated and the ignition died. Well, it was that control that was close to Clitty's knee as he sighed some more. Anderson held out a hand, clicking the kill button back to the on position.

'Ya stupid sod!' Anderson exploded. 'We're here stuck in the middle of the Red Sea with no bloody engine, no bloody hope, just drifting and all feeling sick, and all ya can do is kill the bloody engine!'

'Sorry.' Clitty shrugged as if it might have been anybody, even Anderson, who could have knocked it off in these conditions.

'That was always the trouble with ya, Clitoris,' Anderson said, feeling the old venom returning. 'Never could get yerself bloody organised, could yer? First time in Saudi, ya leave the bloody money in the bank, and then ya have to come back for it. And even when ya do get back, ya manage to drink-drive and kill an' old fella' an' then …'

Within a few seconds of each other, the storm and Clitty erupted.

Clitty was first.

Clitty snapped the engine cover back down, levered the throttle control away from his leg, and threw himself across the boat at Anderson, pulling him face-to-face by his shirt.

'Yeh? An' then? What were you about to say?'

Anderson swallowed heavily as the man's breath beat into his eyes. What could he reply?

'I was goin' to say, Mr Clitoris, that ya had to rely on me and Ellis here to get ya away from ya own bloody execution, ya know what …' Anderson struggled to be able to express himself with his arms, at least move his hands, but Clitty had a tight hold. 'If we hadn't turned up about the time we did, those bloody A-rabs would have had ya head off, and ya body would now be packed in a box ready to ship home. Think about it, Clitoris. Ya owe us.'

Clitty wrenched the wretched Anderson to the side of the boat and held his head just over the side. 'I think, Mr Anderson, right now you owe me.' Then Clitty jolted Anderson's neck.

'Clitty, Clitty, don't do it!' Anderson screamed.

Ellis sat at the front of the boat, on a sort of watch. At least he kept out of the way as the relationship between the two opponents now approached its denouement.

'Gimme a good reason not to kill you here and now!' Clitty shouted over the wind, his body heaving with the exertion. Spray sprinkled all of them as the spindrift from the growing waves caught more targets than would be expected in this part of the Red Sea. Anderson lashed out with a free leg and caught Clitty on his shin. Clitty, with the speed of a man recovering from a great injury, did nothing but grimace and rub his leg fussily. 'I gotta say you got me there, Anderson,' Clitty confirmed, 'but next time …'

Clitty's voice trailed off. Anderson salivated in his victory while Ellis watched as the main peril of the storm whipped across the tops of the waves at a frightening speed. Oh God, he wondered, regretting ignoring the content of geography lessons at school, what was the name of that bloody wind that went offshore as soon as the noonday sun cooked the land?

In the last few seconds before the winds struck, Ellis reckoned that if hot air rose on land, it would suck cooler air in from the sea; the wind would be onshore. But this was wrong. It came offshore just as it should have been the other way round. The boat swayed a little. It began to rotate as Anderson considered getting the engine started again.

Then the wave hit.

The wave Ellis had watched for some seconds had now arrived. It was as tall as any Saudi building but as dark green and full of menace as anything to be seen at sea. The wind had driven the sea into a frenzy of tide versus time and heat versus cool, the boat bobbing like a cork in the maelstrom, the wind shrieking. The three men whirled this way, then round like a fairground ride, though without the relative guarantee of a safe landing. The coastline in the distance beckoned, and Anderson began to move.

'Goddammit. I'm gonna start the bloody engine. Let's get outta here!' he shrieked to nobody but his soul as he clambered along the heaving deck, grasping anything to hand and with it offering prayers for the first time in many years. He picked his way around the legs of the giant, ignoring Ellis at the far end as Ellis vomited manfully over the side into the leeward aspect. Anderson pulled the cord once as the wind roared and shouted judgement at the sinners. The boat rocked while the engine did nothing. Still the wind screeched and the boat trembled. Anderson pulled one time just as the boat got hit from behind by a freak third wave, the sort of wave that followed the previous two but was thought not to exist. The first and the second were meant to disperse all the immediate energy of the waves until the next pair. When a third arrived to follow the pair, it had all the energy of a sharp punch.

Which was what pitched Anderson over the side.

The wave caught the boat along its side while Anderson, standing heroically at action station, was hurled soundlessly through the air to land in the trough of the wave, now spent of its vitriol.

'Can the bloody man swim?' Clitty yelled at Ellis at the far end.

'Do we care?' Ellis asked weakly from his perspective, his face wet and weakened by vomit and salt water.

Anderson yelled for help, the wind roaring like an endless express train stopping for no one at any station. The train would run and run on.

The boat pitched around as Clitty pulled the cord and got the engine started and inched towards Anderson. Anderson begged forgiveness and offered eternal penance for all his temporal shortcomings. 'Clitty! Clitty! For God's sake, help me, man!' He held out a hand as his head briefly bobbed beneath the surface, then resurfaced not quite looking the same way. His look of terror remained as fresh and undiluted. 'I dun nothin' we can't see—' His head disappeared and then came up again. He spat and shook his head. 'We can't see about anyhow. We can do some sort of deal?'

'Suck my dick, Anderson,' Clitty confirmed clearly above the roar of the wind and the faltering sound of the engine. 'What's more, if you wanna deal, why not swim to the shore and we talk there?'

Anderson swallowed and kicked his legs more and more, but somehow the effort was telling on his lungs – the breathing, the effort of staying afloat. His legs ached and his arms ached from the effort of staying, looking this way or that way, depending on the wind and the tide or which way which eye was facing.

Clitty sat back in the boat, painfully aware of his own discomfort as he watched Ellis being sick in the front and Anderson choking to one side.

'For …' Anderson spluttered, face submerging and then resurfacing a while later. 'Please help me …'

Clitty thought about it, then leaned the Judas hand of friendship.

'OK,' Clitty called, 'we'll drift the boat a bit nearer …'

'Thank you,' Anderson shouted gratefully. He watched the silhouette of the giant as he brought the boat to stand by not more than a few inches from his head. Anderson watched as Clitty put a rescuing hand out to him. He put his hand out to grab at his rescuer, who only placed his giant hand on the centre of the man Anderson's scalp and pushed his head under the surf.

And held it there.

While the boat swayed and Ellis vomited and Clitty held the head in his hand, Anderson called for help. He remembered his mother, and he remembered all the sounds and the lights on his bedroom ceiling when he was a boy. He remembered his father singing and how he had dropped his razor to the floor. He remembered how he had wondered at that very moment whether his father had thought these thoughts as his life ebbed away on the floor of a Brighton terraced house. He coughed and tried to lever away the hand holding him unto his deliverance, but still the submergence continued. While Ellis watched the wild-eyed satisfaction from Clitty as he pushed and pushed to make sure, the grip of the hand loosened a little.

Then the boat bucked as another third wave got it. As violently as it had started, the confrontation quietened as Clitty's grip finally gave way to a detachment that was marked only by a sudden absence of the wind. To be replaced a second later by a greater roaring. Ellis wondered if the pause in the environmental assault was a freak or an acknowledgement of the passing of another soul.

Whatever, now there were only two of them left in the boat.

Ellis and Clitty. Alone.

And Clitty the bigger man.

Ellis was wondering about negotiating when another third wave came along and swamped the engine.

It coughed daintily and died again.

'Oh God!' Clitty began hitting and slapping all the engine casings. 'What now?'

Ellis shivered at the state of his clothing, swamped and drenched, just like Clitty's – less so than that sick sod Anderson who now drifted over there somewhere, but they were all wet somehow.

More than five hours from their start from Jeddah, the weather changed. The wind stayed the same, the vicious wind, but it went round to due north and brought with it the cloud and the bad temper of the April weather systems thrown up angrily from the Red Sea and the deserts beyond.

The first wave affected them a little.

Clitty held on and prayed.

Ellis thought of his mum.

Clitty thought of the sad café in Hastings, of his mother's long walks along towards Fairlight.

Ellis wondered about the kids.

And he brought a prayer to protect her and to take care of her and to forgive him, never mind that Cheryl had long forgotten him and the children only viewed his presence as something to be tolerated until they grew up.

The second, not the third, wave turned the boat turtle and threw both men into the sea.

Ellis puffed and heaved and wondered if he would be able to explain to the children when they came to accuse him of desertion. Then he wondered about his ability to float, and then he felt a little weak. He cursed himself for going to the Gambia and felt a prayer for Cheryl and earnestly wished to see her. He yearned for her – just to see her eyes, just to see her –as another wave drove him downward, drawing his conscious thoughts to an end.

Clitty had been thinking about getting home as another wave broke up the boat in front of his eyes. He couldn't remember where home was, but he had hoped and he had prayed and he had avoided the sword in Friday Square. Then he thought about Cleveland, and he wondered what his mother might have said about all this if she had still been alive. Then he began to feel pleasantly warm, thinking of somewhere to sunbathe and have a beer, somewhere to make up for the recent past. And as Clitty recalled the old past and a newly dawned past, another wave drove him under, and all he could think was a prayer from the priest that said something about going forward, oh Christian soul, and stuff about the cherubim and the seraphim. The remembrance of the sounds of the choir and the smells of incense at High Mass dissolved into the final act of the sea as it pushed Clitty one more time, and finally, beneath the waves and unto his God.

Within minutes the sea wiped out all evidence that the three men had ever existed.

Printed in Great Britain
by Amazon